After peering around, Orielle lifted her hand. Golden magic limned her fingers, both warning and threat. "Come out and play," she offered. She tried to breathe slowly, deeply. A vagrant wind cooled her cheeks.

For several breaths nothing moved. Then a tall figure separated from the tree that had hidden his wide shoulders. Even in the shadows, his blond hair glistened as it fell over his bare shoulders. Slanted eyebrows slashed together over eyes as blue as the sky. His features were sharply boned in a narrow face. A golden pelt covered his broad chest. He wore only leather breeches, with no shirt and no boots on his bare feet.

And he stood on his toes. Yellowed claws extended from his fingers.

Wyre. Partially shifted. Real trouble. Wizardry had little defense against a shifted wyre.

"Good morrow," she told him.

He grinned, a flash of white fangs that were sharp and scary. "Playtime." And he leaped for her.

SPELLS OF AIR

A TRILOGY OF NOVELLAS

TO WIELD THE WIND
TO CHARM THE WIND
TO CURSE THE WYRE

BY REMI BLACK

FAE MARK'D WORLD

WRITERS INK BOOKS

OTHER BOOKS BY REMI BLACK

FAE MARK'D WIZARD

Weave a Wizardry Web
Dream a Deadly Dream
Sing a Graveyard Song
Kindle a Fae's Wrath (coming soon)

FAE MARK'D WORLD

To Wield the Wind
To Charm the Wind
To Curse the Wyre

CONTENTS

To Wield the Wind

On a mission for the Wizard Enclave, Orielle ventures into the Wilding, a strange frontier filled with magical creatures. There she encounters sprites and wraiths, gobbers and wyre.

All view her as prey.

~ 1 ~

Orielle guided the dapple-grey gelding along the narrow trail traversing the steep slope of the mountain.

Lights winked in the trees ahead, like the spectrum glints in her mother's diamond pendant, a gift for the spell she'd worked for the king.

She reined in the horse to watch the dancing lights. On the trek to this height, she'd spotted the rainbow-colored sprites a few times, always too far to see clearly. The old man who had warned her of the Wilding said that she would see strange things, but these strange sprites were beautiful. Like winged jewels, they flitted among the autumn-changed leaves. A cluster darted in and out, winking in unison. When light reflected off sun-glinted water, it moved randomly. The sprites seemed to create a fascinating pattern of light flashes.

Ghost snorted. Orielle patted his neck. At the light tap of palm to horsehide, the sprites flashed white then blinked away. She sighed and hoped they would return.

"Sprites," she told Ghost. "Flower-lights." She remembered reading the description while she studied in the archivist's tower. Old Rombrey wouldn't let students carry the thick tome out of his tower, and her tutors required that she con information from its multiple pages. For hours she'd perched on a stool and shivered in the stony room, far removed from the brazier that the old man kept near his table. Before today's flower-lights, she'd thought that old book contained nothing more than myths. Before she ventured into the Wilding, she should have had another dip into the *Creatures of the Hinterlands*. She hadn't bothered to read the chapter about dragons.

She hoped she didn't encounter dragons.

The sprites were not the first odd things she'd encountered since entering the Wilding that verged the Shifting Lands. She wanted to see them again.

She hoped she did not see another stunted creature like the one that had invaded her campsite last night.

Enclave-raised, with never a toe ventured beyond the settled lands, Orielle had compassed her world with mundane and powered, wizard against sorcerer, Rhoghieri against wyre. Wizard-trained, she came into the border lands to renew the Enclave pact with the Rhoghieri. She expected mountain cats and vipers, bears and hornets, not the stunted creature that tried to drag away her food bag while she slept. Ghost had woken her. When she sprang up, the thing abandoned its prize and scuttled into the darkness.

When her heart stopped racing, she paced her wards, designed to keep her safe from mundane and the evils of Frost Clime.

Her wards weren't damaged.

Where the creature had crossed, the ward spells remained linked, limning golden when she checked their strength.

Orielle spent the rest of the night watching for more trouble.

These glinting sprites were her second encounter with odd creatures. They looked too pretty to be dangerous. Last night's creature had had claws that punctured the thick hide of her food bag. A closer encounter with it would be lethal.

"Maybe I shouldn't have volunteered when Adorée backed out," she told the horse. His ears flicked forward. Safe in Mont Nouris, her wizard trials appointed a year away, Orielle had itched for adventure. Her sister hadn't given a reason for changing her mind about the ArchClan' request to go to Iscleft Haven. Orielle snatched at the opportunity before someone else did.

"Too late to back out now, Ghost. Come on."

When the grey horse refused to move forward, she dug in her heels. Iron-shod hooves remained firmly planted. His ears flicked forward.

Orielle sat back and stared at the trees with their riot of changing leaves, red and orange and bronzy, colors so rich she wished she knew the name of the trees. She hadn't excelled at flora and fauna.

The leaves shivered at a vagrant wind's touch. The sprites had vanished. Nothing moved under the trees' canopy. The well-traveled path she followed maintained an easy route along the slope and into the forest. A Lowland farmer had pointed her to it and in the next breath warned of the Wilding's dangers. Orielle ignored the warning, thinking her trials would be nothing more than a trail that switched back and forth until it reached the rocky escarp that towered above the trees. Yesterday and last night, though, she began to believe that farmer.

And now something lurked in the trees ahead.

Ghost snorted a warning when a mundane creature menaced. He had neighed last night. Whatever lurked ahead was neither mundane nor a stunted creature with stubby talons.

No birds chirped or flitted about. No little mammals scurried along the limbs or scratched at the roots.

She wished she had Fire or Water, to spook whatever lurked. She wielded Air, and that not as well as she wished.

The rocky bulk of the mountain loomed overhead. Once she achieved the crest, she would overlook the Wilding, land untrammeled by civilization, inhabited only by magic users. Far east would glimmer the Shifting Lands. Far north was an off-shoot of Faeron, and farther north the forests and tundra of Ultima Thule.

Orielle wanted to achieve the crest by sunset. Did a creature lurk in the trees? Did it wait to leap upon her and Ghost? Or did it plan to rush them when they started the upward trail? Spook the horse, and she and Ghost would fall hundreds of feet to the valley.

For a solid week she had listened to one Lowland farmer after another tell of ogres lurking in the boulders, hiding in caves, and creeping through trees. Orielle shivered with the children while the wives bustled about and old folk smoked the ubiquitous puff pipe, saying "aye" at dark times in the stories.

Now that she'd seen sprites and that stunted creature, she couldn't dismiss those warnings as stories to keep the little ones from wandering off.

Ogres. Trolls. Wyre? Shape-shifting wyre, sent by the sorcerers of Frost Clime to block the way to Iscleft Haven? Wyre and sorcerers, waiting for Orielle to ride into their trap?

Imagination would doom her one day.

Trained to alert to sorcery, Ghost had warned her of last night's unnatural creature. Loud noises would also affect him, like the soldiers who had drilled in the well square of the last town of the Lowlands.

Outcasts lurked on the fringes. She hadn't kept her mission to the Haven secret. She was a young woman traveling alone. Easy prey, the lawless would think. She had more than enough power for them.

Orielle put her heels into Ghost as she clucked. He snorted but started obediently.

A dark shape slunk from one tree trunk to the next.

She reined in Ghost. Once again she peered at the shadow-draped trail. Once again she spotted nothing and no one.

Stripping off her riding gloves, she tucked them into her saddle bags. Then she started the horse forward.

When they passed close to the first tree, his ears flicked. He snorted at the third tree. He balked when the trees surrounded him.

She could still see nothing and no one. After peering around, Orielle lifted her hand. Golden magic limned her fingers, both warning and threat. "Come out and play," she offered. She tried to breathe slowly, deeply. A vagrant wind cooled her cheeks.

For several breaths nothing moved. Then a tall figure separated from the tree that had hidden his wide shoulders. Even in the shadows, his blond hair glistened as it fell over his bare shoulders. Slanted eyebrows slashed together over eyes as blue as the sky. His features were sharply boned in a narrow face. A golden pelt covered his broad chest. He wore only leather breeches, with no shirt and no boots on his bare feet.

And he stood on his toes. Yellowed claws extended from his fingers.

Wyre. Partially shifted. Real trouble. Wizardry had little defense against a shifted wyre.

"Good morrow," she told him.

He grinned, a flash of white fangs that were sharp and scary. "Playtime." And he leaped for her.

Ghost chose to rear. Orielle lost her seat and slid back. She landed on her feet, sheer luck. The drop jarred her, scared her. She stumbled sideways.

And into something. Something that loomed higher than her.

A tree? A wyre! No. Hands had caught her. They shoved her backward. Panic flashed over her then winked out when she realized the man wasn't a shifted wyre. He wasn't a wyre at all. And he stood between her and the wyre.

Ghost tore the reins free of clawed hands. He bounded away. His white tail flashed as he thundered through the trees.

The wyre didn't look at the lost horse. He ignored Orielle and scanned the man. Brown hair, brown leathers, brown boots, shining sword. Then the wyre grinned. "Rho."

"Wyre," the man retorted. With the steely blade between them, he lifted one hand.

The wyre flew back. He thudded into a tree trunk. Red leaves scattered over him. Claws scratched the ground, then he scrambled up. Those blue eyes flickered to Orielle. He grinned, sick anticipation stretching his lips. "Don't leave, pretty wizard."

The Rhoghieri's hand came up again.

The wyre laughed then dove behind a tree.

And disappeared.

While she gawked, the Rhoghieri grabbed her hand. "This way." He headed back, towing her along.

"But—my horse—."

He didn't stop. He didn't acknowledge her protest. They passed the sunny spot where Ghost had stopped before.

On the switchback to the lower trail, Orielle lost her footing and began sliding. The Rho's strong grip kept her upright. Her free hand scraped over rock and sedgy grass. The stiff riding boots kept her ankles from rolling off the roots and rocks that skittered under her. When she stumbled again, he kept her from tumbling downslope, but he used her momentum to leave the well-worn trail. They rushed downward several feet, then he tugged her along as he climbed higher and higher.

When he stopped, she fetched into him. "Oof." She grabbed his arm to steady herself.

Sun dazzled her eyes, so she looked down and away.

They stood on a thready trail, ribbony compared to the path she had followed. The trail coursed the mountain's flank. Behind him, grass gave way to boulders. Below them, far below them—the wyre stood on the wider path. Clawed hands rested on his hips. The sun gleamed on his sweat-slick skin.

He grinned. "Come out and play," he shouted her words.

Wind whooshed down the slope. It blasted over the wyre. He tumbled backward, down the slope.

She nearly came off her feet when the Rhoghieri jerked her forward. "Don't stop."

He didn't, so she couldn't.

~ 2 ~

The narrow trail climbed through tumbled boulders and skidded over loose scree then found beaten ground with protruding rocks. It entered a grove of white-barked trees, slim and straight, golden leaves shivering in a wind that rushed with them. The sunlight flashed in and out, blinding her then winking behind thickly leaved branches, shining hard and bright only to have the golden veil intervene.

Orielle lost the thready trail. She lost the sun when they plunged into dense evergreens, their needles dense and soft and fragrant. She lost track of time, of distance, of her rasping breaths and her escalating fear. She gripped the hand that gripped hers, doubling her clasp to stay steady and moving. She watched her feet, his feet, the hide boots scuffed with age, scraped by their rapid passage over sharply cleaved rocks. He stepped quickly, firmly, and she tried to step where he had.

He had more weapons than the sword he hadn't used. A boot knife with a smooth wood handle, dark with age. Another knife in his right-side boot had heavy carving that their steady movement kept her from deciphering.

The Rho wore mail under a leather jack and heavy linen shirt, both colored like rich soil. A ring chain cinched a long belt knife, thin as a poniard. The scabbard for his sword had Fae scrolling. She wondered if the sword were Fae steel.

He looked like a man heading for trouble, not just happening upon it.

The wind kept with them, blowing from the back, carrying their scent ahead of them and not back to the wyre that tracked them.

They climbed through the evergreens. A giant slab of granite leaned precariously against a snapped trunk, and a new tree had grown around it, merging wood to rock. Past the granite the Rho stopped.

Orielle plowed into his back. When he didn't start again, she released her clasp, but he didn't free her other hand.

The wind died.

Grit filled her dry mouth and throat. She coughed. Her ankle throbbed. Tugging at her hand got his attention. He glanced around then dropped her hand like it was a snake.

"Thank you."

He grimaced then returned to scanning the trees ahead and downslope.

She scanned him. He had her years, but life had given him more experience. A ridged scar cleaved one brow. An old break had flattened the bridge of his nose. A second scar followed the line of his jaw. Similar white tracery had covered his knuckles. His calloused palm spoke of long hours with weapons or tools. The Fae-scrolled weapons reminded her of the *comeis* and the guards for her great-aunt Letheina, ArchClan over the whole Enclave. Did a Rhoghieri need to bristle with weapons? He hadn't used the sword against the wyre. He'd thrown an Air spell and crashed the shifter into a tree. He'd thrown him downslope with another gust of Air.

The silence had twisted into awkward. "Will I pass as a mountain goat now?"

The joke didn't draw his attention.

She coughed and tried again. "I suppose the grove is a trap for unwary travelers."

"A trap?" His scowl withered her. "Aye, you can call it that. You shouldn't have invited him into a game. The wyre love games. And where there is one wyre, there's a pack."

"I didn't invite him into a game."

Storm-colored eyes rolled. "You said, 'Come out and play'."

"*That's* the reason he grinned at me."

"He would have grinned anyway. Wyres like to eat magic. Gives them a rush."

Her ignorance flashed bright as the sun. She had volunteered for this venture into the Wilding. Two days into the frontier, and she had walked into trouble. Every hour on this trail only pointed out how little she understood of those long lessons about wyre and sorcery.

And her pathetic reading of *Creatures of the Hinterlands* would get her killed.

"I didn't expect wyre this far from Iscleft," she conceded. "Frost Clime concentrates its attacks there."

"Iscleft—."

Avoiding a direct look, his eyes angled toward her. The look askance was like common folk avoiding a wizard's gaze. In the Lowlands, once she explained her mission, few people had looked her in the eye. Protection from being hexed. Her tutors had droned through their explanation about the aversion while she and her friends giggled about superstitions.

"You're far off course for Iscleft," he said.

"I'm not heading to Iscleft, not yet."

"You should be, with wyres on your heels."

"I didn't bring them!"

He snorted. "What the blazes are you doing this deep into the Wilding? Only fools come this far into the Highlands."

"I'm heading for Iscleft Haven."

"The Haven. What kind of fool are you?"

"My name is Orielle. I'm from Clan Galfrons in Mont Nouris."

He nodded, her naming of a wizard clan confirmed his judgment. "Enclave fool."

She punched his arm.

"Weak Enclave fool."

Snatching Air, she thrust it at him.

The sudden gust staggered him. He straightened. When he turned around, his eyes looked grey as sooty smoke, a surprise with his dark hair. "Do that with the wyre next time. Five times the force."

"I thought wizardry didn't work on wyre."

"Wizardry doesn't. Elements do." He offered his hand. "Shall we go on then?"

She sighed but accepted his grasp. When his fingers firmly wrapped around hers, she felt the same safety as when he'd thrown Air at the wyre.

"My horse?"

"If your horse followed the scent I gave him, he's with mine."

"You can do that?"

He didn't answer. He walked fast, but she no longer felt towed behind a juggernaut.

The Rho climbed above the granite slab, across the old scar, filled with long wisps of grass browned for late autumn. The trees thinned as they climbed. He didn't head straight up the mountain's flank, but his steep path was more grueling than the gentler trail. Orielle's legs burned long before he stopped a second time.

Gasping, she sank against a boulder. Her parched throat longed for a drink. Ghost carried her waterskin, though. Tossing back the black cloak, spelled against cold and rain but not against heat and weariness, she leaned into the wind that teased with coolness.

"Here."

She opened her eyes. A scarred hand offered a small flask.

He had frowned at her last gratitude. She took the flask inches from her nose. Before she could lift it, he turned to peer downslope.

Orielle jiggled the flask. She wanted to drain it, but she didn't know when they would find fresh water. Two swallows eased her throat. A third began revival of her energy. She stoppered the flask then balanced it on a knee.

He turned back. She offered the flask. He hefted it. Dark eyebrows rose, and her withered pride revived a little. *Not such a fool*, she wanted to say. Then she watched his throat apple jump twice as he swallowed. He wiped his mouth with the back of his hand. The same hand that had gripped hers so tightly.

A tingle that had nothing to do with magic coursed through her. To hide from those grey eyes, she peered into the trees around them. If he followed a trail, she couldn't see it. Where had the wyre gone? Did they still track them? How had that wolfen known where to set his trap? How long had he waited for her?

How had the Rho found her in time?

"How did—?" Her voice cracked. She coughed. "How did you know—?" Another cough seized her.

He waited until the spasm ended. "Crossed your camp this morning. Smelled the gobber that had been there, too. So I tracked you. Curiosity, mainly, until I sniffed the wyre on your trail. Came on his scent about midday."

Gobber distracted her. "Is that what that was? It tried to steal my food bag."

"You've never seen a gobber."

Orielle treated the slow words like a question. "No. The description I read wasn't really accurate. I saw sprites—if that's what those sparkly lights are—." She paused, expectant, and he nodded. "They were in the trees. They scattered before I saw the wyre. The sprites were not described accurately either. That book needed illustrations."

Those grey eyes lightened although the sun rode the azure sky behind him. "I guess most people who can draw don't live past their encounter with a gobber."

She suspected that he laughed at her, but he hid his amusement. Only that ashy cast in his eyes revealed—something. "You're saying I was lucky."

A smudge darkened the grey. "Lucky with the gobber. Lucky I followed your trail. Lucky you faced only one wyre and not the whole pack of 13."

"Thrice lucky is better than thrice damned."

He tucked the flask inside his jacket and cinched it with a jerk of the laces. Then he held out his hand.

Orielle's legs still burned, and the spurt of energy from the water hadn't reached her feet. "Do you think he's following us still?"

His hand dropped. He scoured the trees below, the flank level with the boulders. The well-traveled path had disappeared. He surveyed the crest still far above them.

She wondered where his horse was. And had Ghost found the horse? Or was he racing back to the last comfortable stable in the civilized Lowlands? Or gutted in some gully, fresh meat for the wyre? Or other predators?

She shivered.

"I've tried to confuse our trail," the Rho said. He offered his hand again. When she accepted it, he lifted her easily. "We're leaving tracks. That can't be helped. The wyre track by scent, though, not sight. That's a boon. But—." His grip shifted, tightened just a fraction before easing off. "I can only mask so much. We need to deaden our scent. You should spell that cloak you're wearing."

"It is spelled, against rain and cold."

"Spell it to mask your scent."

"Do I stink?"

"No." That light returned to his eyes. "The wyre would find you a juicy morsel."

"I don't think that's a compliment."

"Just mask your scent, Orielle of Galfrons."

The Enclave tutors frowned on the tricks that Orielle and her friends had practiced, sparkling their gowns and hair before a party, washing a fabric with magical hues that shimmered, creating auras that brightened and shadowed with their moods. She re-cast one of those spells, replacing brilliants with exotic chypre.

His eyes watered.

"Too much? It's the rage at court." She coughed as she got a mouthful of the scent emanating from her clothes. She exchanged the chypre for rose, the heavy pink blooms that filled her grandmother's garden.

He choked. "Not that either. Something natural, dammit."

"Roses are natural."

"Something from the forest around us. And not all at once. Confuse your scent with other scents. Pick one that's predominant."

She blanked the attar and snatched at the trees, the deep resin, the rich needles, the sturdy bark. Ghost had nosed the trees near the stream. The scent mixed with her aunt's herbary and scythed grass and—.

"Good choice."

"Don't hurt yourself with that praise."

"I didn't know if you knew the spell."

"We aren't supposed to use magic this way," she shared. "It's like casting glitter over my gowns. My tutors would punish me."

"I won't. This should confuse the Wilders, too."

She sniffed her hood. "What is this scent?"

"That's spruce. Add in other scents."

"Spruce," she whispered, naming it so she could remember it. She knew cedar. The wood saved her winter clothes from the moths.

He bent and ripped up wisps of grass as she mixed a whiff of cedar into the spruce. He held the grass so she could catch the odor. She sniffed and crinkled her nose. It lacked any green scent. She smelled mold and something like old root and rot, like decay or age or—. "Ugh."

"You can use the deer scat on the trail over there."

"No!" She quickly peppered the grass into the spruce and cedar.

He chuckled then sniffed and nodded. "Good enough to confuse a Rho."

"And a wyre?"

"Confuse a Rho, confuse a wyre. An old lesson. This is a start. Mix in other scents as we pass them until nothing's left that you started with. It may not stop him, not if he's determined, but it will slow him down. The slower he goes, the better for us."

"And where do we go?"

"To the horses."

"He could just track the horses."

"If he thinks of that. Let's hope he doesn't."

~ 3 ~

Sunset from the mountaintop captured her heart.

Vibrant orange and coral, pinks and lilacs flung themselves across the clouds dotted along the horizon. A golden glow spread upward, turning to rose gold before pinking the edges of the clouds drifting overhead. Here on the crest, the leaves had browned and died, stripped from the limbs by the ever-present wind.

Leaning against an exposed boulder pitted by weather, Orielle drank in the colors while she snatched a rest. The Rho had climbed atop the boulder to gain vantage over the obscuring trees.

She rested in a shallow bowl of soft dirt. With the horizon before her, the breeze cooling her face, and a hawk performing a lazy wheel through the afterglow, she might imagine herself on a picnic.

But the vista was endless forest, more ridges and mountains to climb, no smudged smoke trailing up to mark the Haven's location deep in the Wilding. The forest sheltered wyre and other predators, the ones she had expected and the ones that had surprised her. Gobbers. Ogres. Surely she wouldn't encounter a gryph?

To the east, the next mountain towered. Snow clung to its steep crevasses on its north reaches. Beyond were the jagged spires of snow-capped mountains, nearly impenetrable barriers to the Shifting Lands. "There be dragons," she murmured, quoting another ancient tome. She didn't remember reading much of it. In her schooling, surrounded by powerful students who wielded multiple elements, she had scarcely dreamed her one-element self would venture into the Wilding. Adorée wielded both the Air and Water of the Letheina clan as well as the Earth of Galfrons. She would have made a better emissary to Iscleft Haven. Why had Adorée accepted the appointment then refused it?

The Rho hadn't mentioned camp. He hadn't mentioned where he expected to find his horse and hopefully Ghost. Did he know wards that would keep gobbers out of their camp? Gobbers and other creatures of the Wilding, creatures that her tutors had glossed over.

He leaped down, landing with a muffled thud that barely disturbed the exposed dirt. He straightened then touched her arm. His finger touched her lips. Then he pointed behind him. She peered around his wide shoulders.

The dancing lights wove among dead leaves.

He didn't let her watch as long as she wanted. He stepped away from the boulder, and the sprites darted away.

Orielle sighed. "They charm, don't they? 'Jewel on the wing.' That was printed in the margins of that book, *Creatures of the Hinterlands*. 'Jewel on the wing' and something about a sting."

"Bite. Painful as a hornet's sting. You don't want to anger a nest of them."

"Is that the way of the Wilding? Danger in the glove of beauty. Remove the glove, and sharp talons will claw you?" His head cocked, like a hawk trying to figure out its prey, so she explained, "My training is useless here."

"I wouldn't call it useless. You can punch with Air." He rubbed his arm. Had her earlier thrust with the element left a sore bruise? "I doubt any of your Enclave wizards would do better."

"The little I know won't keep me from being killed."

"That's the first step to learning, admitting you don't know. The second is a willingness to learn."

"Don't get excited," she warned him. "My tutors complained that I fell back two steps for every three forward." But she smiled to diffuse the complaint. "Do we continue off-trail? For I don't think you'll camp up here."

"Too exposed," he agreed. "You're willing to go on?"

"As long as you know where we are."

"I always know where I am."

Was that arrogance or truth? Rather than search those eyes with their silvery cast, Orielle swept an arm toward the changing forest. "I don't even know the trees. Fruit trees I can name, even out of season, but these—I'm limited to red leaves, yellow leaves, orange leaves, and evergreens."

"Don't forget the plum leaves, city lass."

"Oh, aye," she agreed with a country expression, and surprise flickered over his battered face.

"Ready?"

For answer, she pushed off the boulder. Turning, she stumbled over a stack of rocks hidden behind a stunted evergreen. The rocks toppled.

He hissed then dropped to his knees, gathering up the rocks like they shouldn't touch the ground.

"What?"

"Hsst. It's a cairn. You know what a cairn is?" A rock slipped from his cradling hold. He snatched it back with the others.

She knelt beside him. "A way marker."

"Grave marker," he corrected. "We have to re-seal the grave."

She gaped. "Like—a formal ceremony?"

"Yours the deed that disturbed it; yours the hands to restore it. And pray we didn't release more than we disturbed."

He was serious. Energy emanated from him, waves radiating over her, impelling her.

"Now, wizard."

"What could we release upon the world?" she whispered.

"The cairn," he mouthed.

She brushed back the little tree with its prickly needles and saw what it had hidden. Four irregular stones forming a square sunk into the ground—or so old in place that time had built up the soil around them.

Orielle swept off the imbedded rocks. One flat surface looked like frozen ripples. Another had a scuff across it. She didn't know what ceremony he wanted, but the sealing chant of the dead was the same for human and Fae, wizard and mundane, townie or farmer.

She flattened her hand over the plain rock above the one with scuffing. "Earth" then "Air" as she touched the scuffed one. The rippled one was "Water." And the Rho exhaled, slow, long. He clearly had feared she would get it as wrong as her other knowledge was. "Fire" was the fourth rock.

"Earth and Air, Water and Fire," she named and touched them again. He handed her a rock, flatter than others. A base, she reckoned as she carefully placed it. "Blood and breath, flesh and bones." A rock for every word.

The light was fading, more quickly than she'd thought it would. The wind had a cold nip, reminding that autumn was harbinger of winter.

He handed her another rock, uneven of shape, harder to steady in place. "Sun and shadow, soil and stone." The sealing chant was slower as she timed each word to a rock's placement. "Sleep and peace. Sleep and ease. Return you to the path to Neothera."

He gave her the last rock, one extra beyond the sealing chant. Orielle asked with her eyes. His gaze shifted to the cairn.

With a crack, she set it on the top. Both hands wrapping the rock, she repeated the chant. And she poured magic into it, imagining the power sinking through every placed stone and into the ground. Soft sifted dirt, the shallow depression, and the cairn the only evidence of the ancient burial.

She shivered as she finished. The world felt fogged, distant.

Then the Rho gripped her arm and hauled her to her feet. He towed her away from the cairn.

Her hands prickled from the evergreen's sticky needles. The twilight brightened. Had a shadow—? Orielle peeked over her shoulder. No. The ancient grave at the boulder's base would catch the last light of the sun.

But she shivered.

The slope on the mountain's east wasn't as steep as the west, facing the Lowlands. Shading trees clogged the incline. The way remained tricksy, but the Rho kept her moving, faster and faster, faster again as they hit a narrow trail and turned onto it.

The trail crossed another. He took that one, climbing briefly before descending again.

She clung to his hand. Roots snagged her toes. Stiffly-fingered branches snagged her hair. Light faded rapidly. How was he seeing?

She heard water, rushing, drowning the sunset bird calls.

The trail angled sharply down. The Rho stopped. She plowed into him.

Grim—for that was the name she'd dubbed him—steadied her before she pitched over. "You hurt?"

"Tired," she gasped.

"Camp's ahead."

Camp. Pampered by the Enclave's comfort, Orielle would never have imagined that a fire and a seat on the hard ground would inspire her to keep moving past aching muscles and joints. Pampered by the Enclave's safe walls, she had considered the wyre a nebulous threat rather than lethal hunters. The hardships she had expected were the journey to the Haven and the carefully marshalled arguments to convince the Rhoghieri Haven to return to the alliance. When they'd abandoned the pact three generations before, the Enclave's only threat came from a rebel heretic named Saldoran. Frost Clime now threatened. Frost Clime was winning.

"Waterfall ahead," Grim said, an explanation for the drowning noise that she mutely appreciated. "We'll cross above it before we continue down."

She started to ask how Grim intended to make camp in the rapidly-falling darkness, but her ignorance covered so much that she decided to wait and see. She sighed at more walking, though, and hoped the waterfall obscured the soft sound. "Will the horses be at our camp?"

He lifted a shoulder. Orielle expected another explanation. As a teacher, he was more patient than her Enclave tutors. Yet those grey eyes sharpened. He focused on something just off her head. Then he grabbed her shoulder.

His fingers bit into her flesh. She cried out as he jerked her around. He swiped down her back, over and over, long sweeping motions, like he brushed off a clinging web.

"What?" She didn't remember backing against anything. She had leaned against the boulder. She craned to see over her shoulder.

Those viselike fingers kept her from turning. "Hold still."

He flicked his fingers, flinging something off. Again he swiped down her back and again, brushing off whatever clung. He flung away a misty, webby thing. She heard a high-pitched whine, like a summer insect buzzing her ears. Then the sound vanished with his last swipe down her back.

The day brightened. The chill left the air.

He kept brushing her off. His grip eased, but he held her still while he brushed her shoulders, her back, down the length of her cloak.

"Take this off." He tugged the oiled cloth.

A tug removed the brooch, a luck charm from her mother. She held the circle and stick-pin while he gave her cloak a strong shake. A wind kicked it, billowing through the cloak, ensuring no trace of the thing lingered.

When he settled the cloak back in place, he took the brooch from her fumbling fingers and fastened it quickly.

While she searched the ground for what he'd gotten off her.

Shifting fog caught her eyes.

She gasped as the fog lifted from the ground. Misty tendrils rose, a cloudy mass that shaped into a head and thin shoulders, a torso with separating arms, wisps of hands and elongated fingers. The ghostly mist didn't form a lower body as it hovered above the needle-carpeted ground.

In the air between them and the mist, Grim shaped a ward. The sigil glowed amber. The foggy mass retreated. The ward faded as the fog drifted upslope, obscuring tree trunks as it flowed past, following their back trail. Like a man with legs, the ghost climbed, hazier as it left the twilight cloaking the lower slope and mounted the upper reaches.

It had ridden her back.

"Just a ghost," she breathed, reassuring herself. "I'm not afraid of ghosts."

Wispy fingers clung to a tree trunk, digging those elongated claws into the bark to slow its ascent.

"Not a ghost." Grim's hand again swept down her back, ensuring nothing else clung to her. "A wight. Ghosts don't have tangible form. A wight does. Give it enough emotional energy, and it grows claws and teeth that can draw blood. Give it blood, and it becomes bones and flesh with an insatiable need for more blood."

The misty head turned toward them. It watched. It wanted fear. It waited for her fear so it could flow back to her, wrap its arms around her, cover its mouth with her own, and suck in her screams, dig in its claws, piercing her flesh as easily as last night's gobber had punctured the thick hide of her food bag.

How do I know that?

Emotional energy. Orielle groped for Grim's hand. He twined their fingers, reassuring warmth and solidity after the cold that had blanketed her on the mountaintop and ridden her back down that steep slope, when only his sure-footed passage kept her upright. Fear and hate. Feeding like a wraith.

"A wight is a wraith," he said, although she didn't realize she'd spoken aloud. "What exactly do they teach you in that Enclave?"

"Apparently not what I needed to learn. Did my magic draw it?"

"Cairns seal graves for a reason."

"I freed it then. And it wanted my fear. I am very glad there are no wyre here."

"Me, too. Give it terror, and it will take shape. Link it to your power, and it will never leave you, tapping into your emotions by taking the form of your dead bloodkin."

Her heart hammered at her close escape. She retreated to flippancy. "The only dead kin that I would fear would be my cousin Raigeis."

"Hsst. Don't give it name."

"It can hear me?" She peered through the deepening twilight, but the wight's misty form had vanished. She shouldn't have taken her eyes off it.

"It's touched you. Clung to you. The connection will linger until sunrise."

He pulled her after him, toward the rushing water ahead.

But not before she tried one last time to find the wight.

~ **4** ~

Orielle didn't think she fell asleep. This fraught day wearied her with its pre-dawn beginning with the gobber, leading to her encounter with the wyre, and ending with a wight on her back. How could one sleep standing up? But she must dream, for bone-white horses threaded through the straight trees. Snow-white riders, stiffly erect in their saddles, wore cloaks of ice blue and storm purple. The material flowed around them, drifted by a gentle wind.

Only the metal bits of the night-black bridles jingled as the horses circled the camp. No snorts or huffs of ice-fogged breath broke the silence. The hooves were muted thuds. The saddle leather didn't creak.

Nor did the riders speak. In their frozen marble faces, their black eyes spoke for them. *Who? From where? From when? Why?* Deep questions, rolling like distant thunder.

First to cross the camp wards was a woman, her features carved as sharply as ice shards, a smile greeting Orielle while her black eyes lacked any warmth. Silver hair streamed to her waist, like waterfalls over her glacial blue gown. Her arms were long and thin, the joints of wrist and elbow prominent. The gown flowed behind her like wings. She was beautiful and eldritch strange. Orielle knew Fae without their glamour. The Fae had an unfading beauty equal to this woman. They shared the longer limbs, the slow-swift drifting movements, the ever-present golden aura of magic. This woman was not Fae. She was like to them, but stilly silent, frozen life, without the golden warmth of power, as far from Fae as the Fae were from human, even the wizards who wielded the same power.

The woman's dark eyes flickered. Long icy-white lashes swept down then up. Her close-mouthed smile revealed her satisfaction at Orielle's awe. She looked pure as ice—the purity that cleaved coldly sharp decisions that lacked the human inclination toward mercy.

A man followed, then a second. Knights, guarding their queen. Carved of the same frozen ice, similar yet different, harder than the hard woman. One had a drawn sword, the flat blade leaned against his shoulder. The metal glowed with the blue of glacial ice.

The other didn't draw his sword. Icy violet gleamed dully through a scabbard worked from silver and ice filaments. The snow-white fingers of his left hand curved around something. A shadowy tendril left his hand but vanished into the darkness, inches from rider and steed.

Those pale fingers tightened.

Orielle's upward glance snared the knights. She felt the ice of a deep Mont Nourian winter, the frozen wind from the mountain heights whipped to a frenzy by a storm, the shaking chill that only a blazing fire could dispel.

The other riders encircled the camp. Silent, frozen, untouched by drifting wind that lifted the snow-white manes of their horses.

Their camp had no leaping flames to offer warmth, just smoldering coals that held more ash than heat.

She shivered. The second knight smiled. Had he sent the ruthless cold she endured? When his lips parted, she saw his teeth, sharpened to fangs. He stopped his horse beside the woman. He released his reins, the black leather straps sliding against the bone-white horse. He stretched his free hand toward her, and she sensed a cold deeper than winter.

Orielle thought she dreamed until Grim appeared. His hand grazed hers as he bowed deeply. The touch broke her sleepy stupefaction. She curtsied as deeply as she would have to the ArchClan of the Enclave or the king of Mont Nouris. She watched the woman, stranger than all the others, for she had led the men across the camp wards. Orielle's magic hadn't stopped them nor alerted her.

She feared these creatures more than the gobber, more than the wyre.

"Who comes through my Wilding?" The woman's voice had rich tones that rang deep to her bones.

Grim bowed again. "I am Rhoghieri, Lady Bone."

"Havener." The black eyes glittered with a strange inner light. "I know you. We keep the pax. This one, woman who is not-wizard, name her."

At the command, the second knight's smile increased.

Orielle had skipped many lessons, but she knew the power of names. Cringing inside, she lifted her chin, striving to balance bravery and respect. Fear and insolence would feed icy cruelty.

Grim had edged closer. She clasped his hand as she sank into another curtsey. Then she tossed back her hood.

The first knight lifted his sword. Extending his arm high, he brandished the steely blue blade. "Aiwaz Solsken," he shouted.

Orielle fell back from his thunder.

Grim caught her, dragged her against his side. "Steady," he warned, for the sword knight had dismounted without moving, slipping between one blink of her fluttering lashes and the next.

Sword held in both hands, he approached. The eerie blade lit his snow-white skin, giving it the glacial tones of the Lady's gown. Sigils writhed the length of the blade, as tall as she was, with a brightly glowing gem pommel. She crowded into Grim as the knight held the sword aloft. She had to tear her gaze from him to focus on the woman.

The sword knight stopped his advance.

Orielle dared not look at him. Despising her cowardly instinct, she straightened away from Grim and managed a step away.

The knight shifted with her, keeping the blade between her and the Lady.

A third curtsey would seem mockery. Orielle bent her head then dared the Lady's gaze. "I am as you called me, Great One. I am a not-wizard of the Enclave in Mont Nouris."

"That is not a name."

"I have learned to be wary of names, Lady."

"Not so, for this wight knows a name."

The Lady's words were a signal, for the leash knight jerked the black rope he held. His right hand snatched the air. When his hand lifted, a ghostly form appeared. Wispy tendrils coalesced into a thick fog— wearing the face of her dead cousin Raigeis.

Orielle winced. Grim, behind her, grunted.

She forced herself to survey the wight's guise. He had Magister

Raigeis' arrogance, the flared nostrils and lofted chin, the swept-back grey hair, the stiff carriage of a man who understood his importance.

But ghosts didn't walk the earth, not as tangible beings. The wight had taken her cousin's form to terrify. Emotional energy, Grim had said.

She looked at the creature masked as Raigeis, once second in command of all the wizards in the Enclave, dead now and another in his place.

"A foolishness that I regret, Lady." Once again she dared that cold stare. "I wished to impress the Rhoghieri."

"The wight did not frighten you when it tried to attach itself to you?"

"No, Lady," she lied. She looked again at Raigeis. His features were blurring. Did the wight lose energy when it had no emotions to sustain its guise?

"You are arrogant, Lady Aiwaz Solsken."

"The Rhoghieri says that I am foolish. I have never before ventured into the Wilding. I have much to learn. For example, I cannot discover, Great Lady, how you and your knights cross my wards."

The Lady's laugh was a sharp tinkling sound that could have broken glass. The leash knight permitted another smile. Orielle dared not look at the sword knight. He had advanced when their gazes met. Would he advance more if that again happened? She would not peek to see if his grin matched all the others encircling their camp.

Behind her, Grim hissed, displeased with her once again.

"A bargain we will strike, Not-Wizard."

"No," Grim whispered.

Not feeling reckless, Orielle wished to offer his word as her own. How did she refuse this magical queen? Should she even attempt to wiggle out of the proposed bargain? "I have nothing to offer," she tried. Grim's groan told that she'd said the wrong thing.

"We will find an appropriate offer at the appointed time. *Cyning honorel*. Wight, *na strincte*. The name returns to Neothera. Take it. It offends my sight."

The darkness that had cloaked the wight descended over him. Her last look saw Cousin Raigeis dissipating like vapor. A muffled howl rose. The knight jerked the leash, cutting the howl into a whimper. Another jerk stopped that tiny sound.

"What will happen to this wight?"

"You have care for a creature that would suck away your magic?"

"No," she hastened to say. "I would not want another traveler to fall into its trap."

"Have care to yourself, not for the next traveler this wight meets."

"It returns to its place, on the crest at the cairn?"

The Lady's smile widened. Sharp fangs glinted, as sharp as the

Leash Knight and just as deadly.

And the wight whimpered.

"Eventually. It will pay a tithe for its lie." She spoke again, the strange language like Faeron but not, the words harsh yet with an enthralling undertone that could trap the unsuspecting.

The knight shifted the glowing sword to his left hand. Once again he extended it to the sky. The storm-purple cloak fell back. His snow-white forearm had lightning-jagged scars. Muscles bunched at the sword's heft, but he held it aloft, his strength making the steel weightless. Orielle stared at the glittering tip of the sword. She watched for lightning, but nothing struck. His right hand extended. Elongated fingers cupped her face.

They froze her skin. His gaze seized hers.

"Lady—," Grim called.

"She is safe, Rho. For now." Again her tingling laugh jangled the silence.

The knight loomed before her, inches from her, but that snow-cold frame emitted no heat. Black eyes bored into hers as his cold, bony fingers pressed hard into her flesh. A faint pulse beat in his temple, the only sign that blood pulsed within him, pumped by a heart, making him mortal as the long-lived Fae, mortal as Orielle.

Is the Lady mortal?

His fingers moved, and her thoughts scattered, driven away before the blizzard of icy shards penetrating her mind. His black eyes seized hers as he learned the bone structure of her face, his touch as intimate as a lover's first exploration yet colder than deep winter, crueler than quick death.

Her breath fogged the chilling air.

"Do you fear me, Aiwaz Solsken?"

"I fear what you do."

Her breathy words caused a flicker in those black eyes. "It is good that the wight lost its grip before it felt your fear."

She shuddered.

His hand lifted away only for his index finger to return, to trace a symbol in the center of her forehead. She tried to follow the shape. He obliged by redrawing it, three, four, five times.

His teeth weren't fanged. They looked slightly pointed with only the eye teeth sharpened. An odd puzzle to snag her mind rather than the eerie tingling of his finger on her brow, writing a symbol over and over. Then he whispered, imparting the secret, "Once for each tenet."

"Thank you."

"The Lady gives it. I am hers as you are the Rho's." He stepped back. He slowly lowered the sword, steadily sheathed it until only the blue gem above the cross-guard gave its light to the moon-cold night. Without a flicker of his black eyes, he turned, walked back to his horse, and vaulted into the saddle.

With his leaving, devastation whorled through her, scoured with blizzard-sharp ice.

"Would you steal my knight, Not-Wizard? He seems to court you."

The words jarred her frozen mind. "Oh, no, Great Lady. He is yours, none of mine."

That fang-toothed smile returned. "Well answered, though I would send him in your need. Call upon me should you need my aid. I will send one of my knights."

Orielle bowed her head. "I am humbled by the gift, Lady."

The smile vanished. "Kyrgy deal in bargains, my offer matched to yours. Remember that, Aiwaz Solsken. You have *much* to learn of the Wilding. I hope you survive to complete our bargain."

Obedient to an unseen signal, the horses turned as one. The Lady and her two knights rode into the forest, their horses swishing their tails as they crossed the wards. Then the others followed, knights and dames, as stilly silent as before.

As she had not seen their arrival, Orielle watched their leaving, and Grim at her shoulder watched as well. Tall figures on tall horses, their cloaks blending into the darkness. Between one blink and the next, they vanished.

~ 5 ~

Grim gripped her shoulder and whirled her around. "What did the Kyrgy knight give you?"

Orielle tried to shake off his grip. "Did you not see? He wrote it on my forehead." She scrubbed at the numbed skin.

"Whatever he gave you, don't use it. Lady Bone will tally your use of it. Kyrgy gifts are not gifts. Use it, and you fall into her debt."

The Lady had stopped smiling when Orielle called the mark a gift. "A bargain she said. Who is she? What is she?"

"A Lady of the Kyrgy. She rules this Wilding." He began kicking the coals, stirring up the flames.

"Kyrgy?"

"You have no lessons of them?" He tossed dry kindling on the reddening coals. In the flare of light, he looked as grim as the name she called him. "It's an ancient word. They are the Choosers."

The old tome had listed the seven septs of Faeron. She had skimmed the information, for the Fae had renewed their alliance to the Enclave. After generations apart, they began to enter Mont Nouris . Proof of the pact, Fae warriors from the septs were bound to the clan leaders, serving as *comeis*. But she hadn't tried to learn all of it. With her weak power, she knew she would never be chosen for a mission to Faeron. As she hadn't been chosen for this mission. She had volunteered.

Written at the bottom of the page listing the Faeron septs were three brief lines about Dark Fae, those who had abandoned Faeron to course the world. They chased the unwary and criminal. "The Wild Hunt," Orielle whispered. "Their steeds are of bone, their hounds are shadows with eyes of red coal. They answer to their queen and king and to no other." She shivered. "But we saw no hounds. Choosers of the Dead, for those who are caught in the Hunt have a choice. Do you know more?"

"I never heard of any hounds."

"But you know of the Hunt?"

"We take care not to be caught on the nights from Saber Moon to Worm Moon, and especially not at Dragon Moon. The Hunt always rides then."

"We are mid-month. Lady's Moon has just passed."

"So, what we saw tonight was the Lady on a ride and the wight caught in it."

The Lady's image remained as clear as when she'd stood before Orielle. Silver hair falling as straight as a waterfall. Black eyes glittering like obsidian. Narrow face, slanted eyes, sharp chin. Even her smile was a narrowed vee. She was both strange and fear-filling. Nothing like the Fae *comeis* who guarded the Enclave's clan leaders as part of the alliance.

"I would not mistake her for Fae."

"Have you seen Fae without their glamour?" Crouched by the fire, he fed sticks gathered before they had turned in. He built a blaze of flames that would be seen for miles, if anyone remained awake. She hoped no one looked.

"I didn't realize they had a glamour."

"Makes them look more human."

"Then, without the glamour, they would look like the Kyrgy."

"A blend."

"She wanted my name. Do you know hers?"

"Best you only call her Lady Bone."

The name cast shivers over her. "Why did she accuse me of stealing her knight?"

Grim took her arm and towed her to the fire's warmth. How did he know the knight's touch had iced away her warmth? "He gave you a name."

"Aiwaz Solsken."

"Look what he is, Kyrgy rider that he has become, all ice and snow. You glow like the sun, Orielle, your hair and your skin. You are a creature of life. He's not, not any longer."

"Because he's death?"

"Not death. He rides with the Lady. The wight is death, of death, escaped from Neothera. The Kyrgy neither live nor die; they are. They stopped their life by giving up the sun. Because as long as they follow the Lady, they rarely see the sun. Solsken he named you, a relative of the sun. Aiwaz is ... like living. No, not quite that. We humans, we have a life span woven for us. The four sisters weave our lives and set the length of our life. We don't live past that." He rolled her pallet beside his. "The Kyrgy riders, those chosen by the Lady or the Lord, they will outlive their appointed lives. The riders will live for centuries."

"What? Those knights, all those riders, they're human? They can't live that long."

"The riders are human. Not the ladies or the lords. Certainly not the horned king. But the knights, the dames, they were once human. Lady Bone gave them a bargain, and they won, for they ride with her rather than watch their bones bleach on the shores of Neothera. She extends their lives even as she consumes their lifesparks, and they give her utter devotion."

"You're confusing me. This Lady and some other Lord, they are Kyrgy. The knights and the other riders were human but are now riders with the Kyrgy. And they'll all live for centuries."

"For longer than the Fae. The Kyrgy, they're immortal. At least, I've never heard of them dying or being killed. They're not gods, but treat them better than gods." He lay on his pallet and flicked the blanket over him. "Get some sleep. Dawn will come faster than you want."

"Don't we need to stand watch?"

"No creature will venture near when the Lady rides. We're safe."

"Even from that wyre?"

"Even from him."

She sat on her pallet. He'd put her between him and the fire, solicitude she appreciated when she still shivered from the knight's touch. "And a gobber? Are we safe from them? That one crossed my wards last night."

"They all fear Lady Bone, Orielle."

She lay back. The ground was hard, but she was weary. And hungry. Her stomach was no more than an empty cavern, dark, darker than Kyrgy eyes.

The sword knight had once been human. No longer. She could see the human in him, better than in the knight who held the wight's leash. Yet he began to look like his Lady. The other riders she hadn't seen very well. She wished she had, to judge how they differed from the two consort knights. What would be the life of a Kyrgy dame or knight, once human, riding ever with Lady Bone, never seeing the sunlight?

The knight had given her a name to use with Lady Bone. Aiwaz Solsken.

"Grim," she whispered, afraid to ask but desperate to know, "what will she do to the wight? She said it would pay a tithe for its lie."

He didn't answer. She strained to listen. His breaths were regular and deep, the ones she had heard during her drowsy watch.

Remembering the wight's whimper, Orielle shivered. *No creature will venture near when the Lady rides*.

Once more she saw the Lady's black eyes and sharp features, sharper teeth and bone-white skin, that waterfall of silver-white hair. The sword knight's scarred forearm.

She turned onto her side, dragged her cloak's hood over her tousled hair, burrowed under her blanket, and willed sleep to come.

~ 6 ~

In dawn's cold light, Grim's sharply angled chin reminded her too much of the Kyrgy.

Prepared for the day, Orielle considered the Fae within the Enclave. She tried to give their faces the elongated angles and stilly sharpness that the Lady had. She left them their nature's colors of hair and eyes and skin, but she tried to lengthen their bones.

And she was left with the eerie revelation that the Enclave allied with creatures who neither looked nor thought as humans did.

No wonder the ArchClan had opposed the renewed alliance, over-ridden by the other clan leaders and grudgingly accepted only when the sorcerers of Frost Clime started the war.

She cupped water into her hands and drank before she splashed away her uneasy sleep. After last night's encounter, she hadn't expected to sleep, but fatigue cast her into deep slumber. Grim had had a hard time waking her.

The water ran too quickly to offer a pooled mirror. Her element was Air; she could still the water and see if the sword knight had marked her forehead. Wouldn't Grim have remarked on that?

Hood back, hair swept back so he could see any mark, Orielle returned to their camp. She approached him with a tentative smile, but he scarcely looked her way, handing over a tough piece of jerk before tucking the pouch beneath his leather jacket. Then he headed off for his private business. She hurried through the rest of her ablutions.

When he returned and asked if she were ready, she stood with alacrity. "Will we reach the horses soon?"

"Good morrow to you, too, Orielle."

"Good morrow," she hastily returned. "The horses?"

"If we're lucky."

"Luck." She didn't express her philosophy on random chance. She'd learned too many things she didn't know. Then she'd learned too many things she'd rather *not know*. Falling into step beside him, she pondered the Kyrgy. How had they entered and left the camp without triggering her wards? Would Grim know that answer?

He led her along the mountain's flank, up from their camp but not following their path down. She thought they were heading deeper into the Wilding, yet they returned to the stream that fed the waterfall. She balked there, digging her bootheels into the thick mast of moldy moss and tree litter. "Where are we heading?"

"I'm taking you back."

"Back?" That sounded like a stupefied child. "Back where?"

"The Lowlands." He steadied her progress over the rocks.

Orielle batted his hand away and crossed her arms. Her glare was ruined by an insect bugging her eyes. She waved it away. "I'm heading to Iscleft Haven. When I leave there, I'm going to Iscleft itself."

"Iscleft," he repeated flatly. "Where Frost Clime gains ground daily."

"Why do you say *Iscleft* that way? As if—I don't know. I could say you made it 'roll with doom', only that's too fanciful."

"Doom." He watched a wind flutter the leaves. A few released their grip and swirled down, letting the wind guide them. "I just came from Iscleft, Orielle."

"You were a soldier there?"

He grinned and looked pointedly at his sword, flicked fingers on the mail hood draped heavily on his chest.

"I didn't think the Rhoghieri were soldiers," she clarified.

His expression darkened. He turned abruptly and began walking beside the stream. She hastened to stay abreast.

"I'm a mercenary."

"Oh." The syllable carried a wealth of condemnation that she hoped he didn't hear. His shoulders' twitch revealed that he had. She hastened to cover her slip. "You were a mercenary at Iscleft. Why did you leave?"

He paused so long she wondered if he would answer. He helped her over a fallen tree, the barren branches dipping into the sparkling water, the huge root ball exposed up the slope. He steadied her cautious steps over a flat boulder slick as glass with splashed water, then guided her through the rocks that had tumbled down with the giant slab.

Grim pulled her up a steeper slope, but he paused where the ground leveled. "The war's changing," he finally said, just when she thought he was too offended to talk. "Iscleft needs help."

"That's what my cousin Camisse said. She commands Chanerro Pass, you know. And your mission is mine. I want to convince the Haven to help us defeat Frost Clime."

His lowered brow didn't welcome her persuasions added to his. "You said you were Galfrons clan, not Letheina."

"Yes. Why? Oh, because Camisse is my cousin? It's convoluted," she explained, her hand tugging at his, for she talked with her hands. "I can draw it for you, but basically, my grandfather is brother to the ArchClan Letheina. He married Lady Cardray then chose to ally with Galfrons rather than his sister."

"Who is your grandfather?"

"Malboys."

Without a flicker of his eyelashes—and his were long and dark, a thick fan wasted on a man—he resumed walking.

Orielle skipped to catch up. "You know of my grandfather? Do you know my brother Saithe? He's a great wizard. He's serving at Iscleft."

Grim stopped. She ran into his arm. Peering around, she saw nothing ahead. Then he turned, and she saw his bleak expression. "Saithe is dead. He was killed in the last battle that I fought in."

Everything stilled, more frozen than Kyrgy lives. The stream roared in her ears. "How?"

"Wyre." She barely heard him. "They came over the wall onto us. His power was useless against the shifters. The wyre slashed his throat open."

She jerked free. She whirled away. She wanted to hide, to wail her grief—but the steep slope above her, the widening stream below, and thick-trunked trees and bushes behind barred escape. The vivid colors of autumn rioted around them, mixing with summer's lingering green and patches of a crystalline blue sky, but she saw only grey, a fog of grief.

"Orielle." Grim rested a heavy hand on her shoulder, pressing her into the ground. "My sorrow at your loss. He was a good man, a strong ally against Frost Clime."

"But not against wyre," she choked.

He hauled her around. Sooty eyes searched her frozen face. She refused to give him any tears.

"Shall we go on?"

His eyes narrowed, then he gave one nod, turned around, and began walking.

His pace slowed. She didn't complain. He didn't talk. He didn't look around, not even when she stumbled because tears blurred her eyes. She caught herself with a quick grab, and a slender tree offered itself to her hand. Then she couldn't release it. She stared at her fingers wrapped around the silvery bark. She willed them to open. They remained closed tight, fingers not meeting thumb. The tree branches shook, freeing more leaves that drifted down, landing on her cloak, sliding off to join the ages-old forest litter.

Grim's big hand covered hers, pried off her grip and offered support. She didn't lift her gaze from the fallen leaves, thinking of how many leaves fell every autumn with no one to know, no one to grieve.

He touched her face, offering warmth where the sword knight had given ice. She flinched and lifted her eyes to his, smoky grey again. He smeared the wet on her cheeks. His finger scratched her skin, but she only blinked.

His hand dropped. He started to turn.

"You said—." She cleared her salt-clogged throat. "You said his power was useless against the wyre, but yesterday you said I could use power to fight them."

"You can use the elements, not your magic. Your brother knew that. Everyone does. But the attack was unexpected. He fell back to old lessons rather than the new ones that the Fae taught us. Wizardry *is* useless against wyre, no matter how strong it is. Remember that, Orielle."

"The Fae teach lessons about power?"

"Elemental power. They taught me a great deal about Air, even though I can wield it with ease."

"Are Rhoghieri still allied to the Fae?"

"The old alliance holds, though none of us cross into Faeron, not anymore." He looked away, a sign that he hid more information, and that gave her mind additional questions to throw into the abyss opened by her older brother's death.

They hiked on. Eventually, the stream widened to a creek. At a bend a second stream flowed in. Orielle stood on a moss-covered rock and watched the water cascade over earth-stacked boulders. The widening creek spilled on. The water poured around the great rocks and rushed toward another bend, spreading over stones and pebbles smoothed by the incessant rush. Broken timbers piled at the creek's bend, carried by floodwaters swelled by the spring melt and left to bleach over the dry summer and autumn.

After the bend, the water spread out, losing depth to width as it became a river. Stripped of their bark and bleached silvery grey, fallen trees dipped their upper branches into the water. The understory was sparse. The lower trunks were charred by a fire that had burned the forest litter but not the trees. The flames had destroyed tender shoots and bushes, leaving the hardier trunks. Orielle didn't see the doe until she flicked her ears. Silvery brown, she stepped cautiously, picking her way through the trunks, stopping to mouth off a green leaf that other grazing deer had missed.. The doe's head lifted. Her long ears flicked toward Grim, crouched beside the water refilling his flask. Then the doe bounded over a fallen tree and vanished.

They moved lower, closer to the river which opened to the sky, still crystal blue. Without covering clouds, the temperature would drop overnight. She hoped for another campfire although by the chilly dawn she'd scooted so close to the fire that she'd woken beside the coals.

Another deer drank from the river. She froze as they emerged onto the river's wide shoreline. Then she bounded away, splashing through the water to the other bank, covered with laurel.

Grim walked ahead. The beach's sandy grit retained his footsteps until he angled away from the water. Casting westward from its midday height, the sun warmed. Orielle flicked back her hood and lifted her face to the sun. A hawk spiraled, large loops that gradually worked down-river while they walked up-river. She glanced back at the mountain they had crossed then compared the next mountain, higher, steeper. Remembering the burn in her leg muscles, she didn't relish the climb.

She broke the hours-long silence between them. "How far is the Haven?"

"Four, five days if we don't reach the horses."

"So far?"

"Rhoghieri were shunned by Lowlanders when we left the alliance. Too much of the weird. We settled with the mountains between us and the Lowlands."

"Wizards are outlawed in the lands south of Gramina Aurus. That's one reason the Enclave keeps a strong presence in Mont Nouris. You could have maintained the alliance. The Lowlanders wouldn't have troubled you then."

He lifted a shoulder, let it drop. "We keep a border with Faeron. The Wilding's trouble enough, especially for the last six years or so."

"When Frost Clime rose."

"I wouldn't connect the Wildings with Frost Clime. The creatures don't like control; the sorcerers want to control. Like your own life in the Enclave, come when I call and do what I tell you when I tell you to do it."

"The Enclave's not like that," she protested even as she flinched at how many rules bounded her life.

"False freedom."

"The tenets guide us. Sorcerers have no tenets. They don't care that blood-magic corrupts. They seek lesser wielders to enslave and chain their power. They try to control minds. Wizards shun those spells." Her defense drew the line she had almost forgotten. "Those aren't rules. Those are ethical choices. It's not the spells I had trouble with. It's the tenets. Serve. Sacrifice." She listed the two tenets that she and her friends are argued against while they drank coffee under an awning at their favorite café. The smell of jasmine, the droning of bees lazily gathering pollen: the memory blinded like the sun overhead.

"Did you want to rule?" he asked, reducing those many debates to naught.

She hunched a shoulder and remembered the last three tenets, the important ones that her friends had never debated. Freedom. Balance. Energy. With heat, she named them for him. "These are necessary."

"Freedom's not being free, Orielle. It's chaos—only some early wizard didn't want to teach little wizards about chaos. Wise, too, seeing what power can destroy. Binding chaos keeps it under control."

His words reminded her of the symbols that the sword knight had traced on her brow, the loops of the four elements encircling chaos. Binding it, to use Grim's words. Sorcery celebrated the random effects and didn't attempt to control it. Rombrey, her oldest tutor, the one who stayed impatient with her, he claimed that unchanneled chaos was weaker than chaos bounded by the other sigils. She quoted him to Grim.

"That would be the way of it," he agreed then jumped onto a boulder that had fallen ages ago from the steep slope on the river's far side. Trees had grown thick behind it. The boulders that had tumbled with it lay scattered across the riverbed, creating stepping stones for giants. He reached down to help her climb.

Even as their hands joined, she felt a prickling sense. "Grim," she whispered.

His head cocked—then he stilled. He looked away, across the river. "Up." He hauled, and she landed beside him on the boulder.

"You feel it?"

He didn't answer. He stared at the thick laurel covering the opposing mountain. She could see nothing, but she didn't need hawk-eyes. Now that they were still, now that they weren't clomping over the pebbled shore, she realized how silent it was. The birdsong had died. Even the hawk had abandoned its slow spirals.

"What is it?"

"Wyre."

She pressed her palm into his back. "The same one?"

He shifted, and the mail under his jack shifted with him. She didn't know how he stood the weight. "Likely. He's brought a friend."

~ 7 ~

The wyre had brought a friend. "Oh, good. One for each of us."

At her false brightness, the crease deepened between Grim's dark brows. Maybe it had never left. "You do remember that your magic is useless against them?"

"I was never a good student."

"Orielle—."

Her hand patted his back. "I do know. I won't forget Saithe. Magic rolls off the wyre. Cut them down with swords or depend upon the Fae. Or use the elements, that's what you told me."

"Use your strongest elements."

That limited her to Air. Water was good, better with the river close. The others were pretty much useless.

"We need fighting room. Have you fought any battles with elements before?"

"No, I'm a city lass." Her flippancy this time quirked his mouth. "I'm not a novice. I've taken contracts outside the Enclave. I've fought a sorcerer and defeated him. We did," she admitted.

"This will be first time by yourself, then." He jumped down then reached up to catch her. He swung her easily to the ground. "This way."

He headed toward the wide shore between river and trees. In spring flood, the waters would cover the sandy grit. With the dry of autumn before the winter rains and snows began, the upper shore had lost its softness. The moss had browned and crumbled underfoot.

Grim had pegged her green. Her mother had objected when Orielle volunteered to go to Iscleft Haven in her sister's stead. She had personally felt only pride when the ArchClan accepted her petition. Her mother's protest embarrassed her. *Not by herself,* Maman had remonstrated. *Send another wizard with her. At the least, send a guard.*

Fool that she was, Orielle had claimed help wasn't needed. Frost

Clime was days upon days north of the road she must travel to the Haven. Enemy sorcerers and wyre fought the wizards and Fae allies at the Iscleft citadel. The battle wouldn't shift south.

But not all sorcerers and wyre fought at the towers that guarded the Iscleft passage. And Grim had hinted the Haven would be dangerous for wizards.

He stopped and fronted the river. She came to his left side. He hadn't drawn his sword. He didn't take a fighting stance. But his fingers flexed then curled into a fist.

"What do you know of fighting wyre?"

"Not much. If nothing else, I can push them with Wind."

His scowl vanished. He tossed her a grin, and she tumbled past appreciation of a good-looking man straight into attraction. His "clever lass" only deepened toward temptation.

"Clever city lass," she reminded, fighting that strange lure.

He stared at the darkness within the laurel tangle. "The wyre don't attack together. They split up. While I fight one, the other will come for you."

"So, they're clever, too."

"Don't be too—."

"Don't be too what?"

But he refused to finish it. Had he meant *flippant*? Or *stupid*?

She didn't want him to think she was totally useless. "Should I stay at your back?"

"Aye."

"And may I know your name? I think, with two wyre before us, that I should know your name. In my mind I've been calling you Grim."

He didn't just look at her; he turned. "Grim?"

"I do apologize. You're not really such a grim person. But you started off by snapping at me—."

He interrupted with "Grim will do." Then he turned back to face the river.

"But it's not your name."

"Stay behind me, Orielle. Be ready."

Be ready. She supposed that meant keep looking around, especially behind her, and prepare to use Air rather than spells.

She wished she could easily recall the greater spells. The convoluted ones that her tutors claimed reached into the deepness of magic slipped her memory. Her tutors hadn't understood her fumbling, but then they hadn't understood the reason she had to read something over and over to retain it but could recall what was said to her in passing with perfect ease. If Grim ever expected her to draw a magic circle and begin chanting, he would be disappointed. Her two contracts, neither lasting longer than a fortnight, had seemed disappointed that the only formal magic she wielded was ward spells. Those she had no difficulty remembering.

She pressed her shoulder to Grim's back and looked behind them. Nothing but the rocky river and the tree-covered steep slopes and a slaty sky that deepened toward purple. When had clouds moved in?

On the river's other side, birds burst from the waxy green laurel. They arrowed across the water and rushed past, the woosh of their wings loud over the rush of the river. Then two men emerged from the tangle. They stepped onto the boulder fall that pushed the river away from the mountain. The shirtless one looked like the wyre who had set the trap at the rocky escarp. He stood taller than the other, his golden mane bright in the cloud-covered light. But his eyes had an eerie green glow rather than the brilliant blue eyes of that first wyre.

The second wyre had dark hair swept back from a high forehead. He also looked familiar although he shared only the long claws of his comrade and the same toothy grin. His hair looked burnished in the subdued sunlight. His eyes glistened like the sparkling water, a curious greeny lightness, tinged with—something she couldn't discern. Claws extended from his long fingers. His shirt hung loose on his torso, the material cut for a bigger man. Both wyre stood barefoot on the boulder, toes curling over the cleft edge.

They jumped. Even fearing them, Orielle admired their grace. They splashed into the water, knees bending to land lightly. Then they began wading across.

Grim thrust out both hands. Air burst out, a visible wave of energy that surged across the water. The wind-backed wave hit the two wyre. The shirted one staggered and fell into the water. The other braced into the wind. It gusted past him, flowed up the boulder and into the laurel, grabbing at the waxy leaves and stripping many away. It continued upslope, to the evergreens, tearing through the heavy branches before dissipating.

The dunked wyre sputtered in the water before losing his footing and slipping into the current.

Orielle remembered the deer. She hadn't thought the water that deep. But the doe had crossed far from the boulder fall. Perhaps it was deeper where the water spilled over the granite.

The first wyre came on. The water crested at his hips. "That your best?" he taunted.

Grim drew his sword. Even untrained, Orielle knew the blade was shorter than other swords. The chasing, though, looked like Fae steel, like the Kyrgy knight's blade. "Come taste my best," the Rho offered.

The wyre grinned. He ran forward. The water churned at his knees, slicking his hide pants to his thin legs. His speed increased at the waterline.

Grim surged forward. Steel clanged against claws.

Orielle backed away. The shorter sword kept the Rho close to the wyre, parrying the swipe of sharp claws. The wyre tried to get past the steel guard, but Grim defended faster. Claws screeched across the keen edge.

With a snick and a slip, the wyre leaped around, testing for a weakness. He landed an arm's length from Orielle. She cried out and staggered back. He swiped at her. She flung up an arm in defense. His claws snagged her cloak. He jerked. Cloth ripped. She fell away as Grim attacked the wyre with a tossed elemental spell that pushed the shifter away. He followed with a flurry of steel.

Orielle scrambled to her feet.

Movement caught her eye. She whirled to see the dark-haired wyre charging toward her. Sandy grit flew in clods from his feet.

She jerked magic and flung the spell at him. He flung up a hand as the energy flew toward him. It struck, gilded as it flashed, then evaporated into glistening wisps of silver. He didn't slow down.

Thrusting out her hands, she drew power that limned her fingers— then remembered Saithe. *They came over the wall onto us. His power was useless against wyre. The wyre slashed his throat open.*

Her power would be useless.

Unless she kept to the element.

Air.

The wyre sprang.

She crouched and dug her fingers into the sand and grit and pebbles. A wave of water-smoothed pebbles roared up and surged toward him, pelting him.

He landed a foot from her. She added the gritty sand, aiming it at his face.

He fell back, sputtering, wiping his eyes.

Behind him, a fallen branch lifted from the ground and speared toward him.

He saw her eyes focused past him and whirled then ducked with a speed she regretted when the branch flew past him. The sharp end buried in the sand.

With a growl, he leaped toward her. She yanked more pebbles into a shield then whorled them around him in a tightening vortex. He yelped as the pebbles struck as one.

Orielle reached for larger rocks. When she swept her arm toward him, the river stones followed. He dodged the stones that would have felled him like a great tree.

Snarling, he jumped up. He tried again to reach her, but she lifted a vortex of wet sand. He growled then whirled and ran.

And her vortex fell apart instead of following him along the shoreline.

She jerked the branch out of the sand and hurled it after him. It landed far short. He looked over his shoulder then dove into the water. And she regretted that she didn't wield easily Water, for she could have created an eddy that would drown him.

He dragged onto the far bank. She shook the laurel limbs, but the Air had lost its strength. The wyre ducked into the tangle. In a few seconds she saw him climbing into the evergreens.

"Orielle?"

She turned.

Sword painted red, Grim stood over the fallen wyre. A Grim of battle and hate, storm-dark eyes roiling with the energy to destroy. His hands remained locked on the sword hilt. The runes glistened silver through the runnels of red.

"I am not hurt," she managed. "Are you?"

He shifted his shoulders. His head lifted a fraction, his body eased. He lowered the bloody sword. "I saw him leap for you. I couldn't get to you."

"I found a few rocks to throw at him. And a stick."

At her light words, the darkness released its grip. He became Grim again, not a weapon looking for a use. The storm-grey seeped from his eyes. "Clever city lass," he praised. "You didn't hesitate."

She shrugged, refusing to tell him her near-mistake with magic. "Rock throwing is quite fun. I just—have to convince my hands." She held them out. They shook uncontrollably.

He seized one of her hands. He held the bloody sword behind him, hiding it. But the running blood wasn't causing her shakes. "Adrenaline. It will pass."

~ 8 ~

The wyre had lost his claws and fangs. In death, he looked an innocent man, not a shifter who wielded an inner beast as his weapon.

Grim sheathed his river-cleaned sword. "We need to move. We've another hour of light. Dusk won't last long, here between the high mountains."

Still a little shaky, Orielle fell into step beside him. Unspoken was her hope that he had plans for supper. "Will the other wyre follow?"

"Maybe. I don't think he'll attack the both of us." He sniffed. "Spruce again. Good choice."

"If he's with a pack? That's not the one we encountered yesterday."

"Don't know where that one's off to, but the whole pack would have attacked us, not just these two."

She nodded at that sense. Surreptitiously, she fingered the rents in her cloak, torn by the wyre's claws. "The wyre that I fought, I think I've seen him before."

Grim slowed then resumed the steady pace that covered ground. She was proud that she could match it after only a day in his company. But her feet in the riding boots did hurt.

"Where have you seen him?"

"A Lowlands tavern. I think. I'm not certain."

"He tracked you." He nodded, accepting her indefinite words as truth.

"If it's the man I remember. Those light eyes—."

"How would he know to track you?"

She gathered her cloak around her, pretending to shiver in the wind gusting down from the snow-capped heights. Never breaking stride, he looked around, constantly scanning for more trouble. And Orielle regretted bringing this up—it only revealed more of her foolishness. Yet if the wyre had tracked her, Grim needed to know.

Maybe in a week of traveling with the Rho, most of the Enclave foolishness would be knocked out of her.

"He could have heard my conversation with the host when I asked for directions to Iscleft Haven. I know," she added, before he could make her feel worse, "I should have kept my wizardry and my mission secret. I thought I needn't worry about danger. The Lowlands between Mont Nouris and Iscleft are under the Nourian king's rule. Gramina Aurus doesn't contest the king for it."

"A nominal control, not a real one. There's danger in a prairie that's tough to plow and towns that are only waystations for occasional merchant caravans. Haven't you heard of raiders? I thought you said you held contracts outside the Enclave."

"In Gramina. In towns. I know I'm foolish," she quickly added when he snorted, "but I'm learning."

"One good grace. A second is your cleverness, using rocks and the sands as weapons."

She waited for him to continue, but that brief statement was his only praise. He turned off the shore and climbed the gentle flank of the mountain, offering her a hand over fallen trees and outcroppings of granite that looked more like colossal statues carved in antiquity. They had tumbled so long ago that the forest had grown around them.

At the head of one of the statue-like blocks, he leaned on a weathered rim that looked like a figured crown. Lichen obliterated the face. Nestled in the crook of the neck, a small tree tried to grow on the shoulder. Its roots dropped over the squared joint and trailed to the leaf-littered ground.

"If this wyre was in the Lowlands, if he heard you and decided to follow you, he may have conveyed your mission to a sorcerer. That would explain—."

"What?" she prompted when he paused so long she feared he wouldn't finish.

"You saw his eyes?"

"They were silvered green, not blue like the first one."

"Silvered. Under the influence of sorcery. Were his eyes that color when he attacked you?"

"I was staring at fangs and claws."

"Sorcery would explain their partial shift outside a moon phase—although the Lady's Moon nears. I think the one yesterday was the prime."

A sorcerer helping wyre shift whenever they wanted. She shivered then proffered the fear building inside her while they headed down the mountain. "Will we have three wyre attack us next time or four?"

Those grey eyes sharpened on her. "Good question. You wield Air. Anything else?"

"My family wield Air and Water. No Earth, not like the rest of the Galfrons clan."

"You can shape Water, too?"

"Only in drips and drops," which earned a chuckle from him. "You're also Air. Does the whole of Iscleft Haven wield Air?"

"We're all mixed. A little Air, a little Fire, a lot of Earth. A couple of drops of Water."

His use of her words pleased her more than it should have. "Fun. You practiced turning Fire into a flaming storm or smothering it with Earth."

His chin went up in an odd agreement. "Something like that."

. ~ . ~ . ~ .

After sunset, while Grim fished with dangling line and Air-tickled water, Orielle worked downstream until she found a feeder stream. She followed it up to a spill-over which poured out of a tiny pool at the base of rocks. There, she splashed the water. No mud or silt stirred up.

She shed her cloak and boots, rolled down her frivolous blue stockings and washed them out before hanging them to dry in a steady little breeze. Then she kited up her skirts and waded in. She suppressed a squeak at the cold water. Soap was tucked in her saddlebags, off on an adventure with Ghost. She washed as much as she dared. When she finished, her sleeves were soaked to the elbows, but she felt clean. That bit of breeze would quickly dry her clothes.

Her tutors would be furious at a wasteful use of power.

The swift water had cleansed her of the dregs of trouble along with the grime of the wyre attack. Feet numbed, she climbed onto a rock and chafed her toes to warm them. Chill bumps asked if she was certain the quick bath was worth it. She gave a decided nod and increased the breeze to finish drying her cloak. Then she untangled her stockings and garters from an obliging bush, felt the toes and decided they were dry enough. The walking had worn a hole in the heel of one and the toe of the other. She rolled one up her leg then pulled up the ribbon garter decorated with white lace, the wrong choice for this adventure. A winkle of magic removed dingy dirt.

As she tied the first garter, she heard a snort, unmistakably a horse. Ghost? With her soap!

Under the tall oaks the twilight had deepened. Far upslope she saw the granite paler than the upright trunks. Spruces grew closer over the stream pouring down the slope.

Light flashed, like a bird's wing catching the last sunlight, but she saw no bird and heard no trill of alarm. Far distant, an owl hooted, seeking company for its nightly hunt. She didn't hear an answer.

Then the horse's snort came again and a jingle of bridle bits. This time the sounds came strongly enough that she could track them.

Across the stream horses walked, horizontal movement among vertical trees. She lost them in the evergreens. Snatching up her second stocking, she quickly rolled it on and tugged the open toe over to the side. The faint tinkle of metal proved the horses continued their descent. On the verge of calling for Grim, she saw a bone-white steed picking its way out of the spruces. Behind it was a russet hide, then came a dappled grey moving without the stately grace of the first horse.

The horses worked down the trail to the pool. A Kyrgy knight held the reins of the following horses. The bone-white steed emerged from the trees as she jerkily tied the second garter. Tossing down her skirt and petticoat, she scrambled up, looking for her boots. They stood at the rock's base. Toes curling in their blue stockings, Orielle flung her hair back and faced the Kyrgy rider.

Ghost tried to crowd past Grim's chestnut, but the bigger horse shifted over, blocking his advance. She could see their packs and blanket rolls attached to the still-saddled horses. The chestnut had an unstrung bow tucked along the saddle.

The bone-white horse paced steadily forward, stopping a couple of feet from the rock.

With twilight deepening under the trees, Orielle wavered on the rock. A tinny sound whined in her ears. The bird songs had vanished. She felt a strange hollowness, like an emptiness had opened within her.

The sword knight stared, black eyes unblinking in his stony face. Had Lady Bone sent him? Were the horses included as a great temptation? She might break down and bargain for horses.

She curtsied. "Sir Knight."

He inclined his head. "Lady Wizard."

That was a nicer greeting than *Not-Wizard*.

He shifted forward then stood in the stirrups. The tall white horse remained motionless. "Do you now travel alone, Lady?"

"The Rhoghieri is fishing for our supper."

Like a bird, his head turned a little. He listened while she eyed his horse, the nose a bare yard from her face. Unlike other white horses, the Kyrgy steed had no darker coloration around the muzzle or the ears. A perfectly white hide, a long mane of a silver whiter than the moon, and long ears with no relieving pink flesh. And black eyes, as black as the man's, as black as Lady Bone's. Those black eyes reflected her miniature form until the long silvery lashes swept down. When lifted, her image had vanished. Nothing appeared in the blackness until the horse blinked again. And there she was, returned to a reflection in the horse's black eyes.

The knight no longer looked for Grim. He watched her. The absolute silence chilled more than the water had. Orielle shifted. "Those are our horses."

Something flickered in the knight's eyes. His smile came slowly. "I found them."

"Finders, keepers? The child's charm only works for objects, not living beings."

His smile widened, revealing teeth as white as bone but not sharply fanged like the Lady's. Dark, dark eyes glittered black and blacker in his snow-white face, no longer statue-still. His focus wasn't her, though, but something beyond her. "Do they still say that then?"

The words jarred, especially that *still*. They sounded displaced, neither here nor there, now nor then. She didn't ask. She didn't want to engage in his present or past. An abyss waited there. "A wyre scared Ghost."

His gaze re-focused. Whatever had amused him had vanished. "Wyres don't come to the Wilding."

"You'll find the body of one an hour downstream. We buried him then covered the grave with river rocks. The Rho killed him. The one who attacked me escaped. He's still in the Wilding, I would think. Partially-shifted."

"Partial shift is not possible outside of moon phase."

She riposted that with Grim's shared knowledge. "Sorcery makes it possible. The dead one's eyes were silvered green." She nodded at the minute lift of his eyebrows. "Yes, I was close enough to see. The same greeny silver tipped his claws. Sorcery helped him shift. The Lady should know who travels her realm. You should tell her."

The bone-white horse tossed his head. She backed a step. Her fascinated gaze watched the slow lift and fall of the silvery mane, an unnatural slow motion in the still, still air. She heard no birds. She barely heard the water cascading from the little pool. Here, hollowed out, surrounded by evergreens, she warned of sorcery and wondered if the Kyrgy Lady used it on her knights and their horses.

The man's black eyes narrowed. "Do you dare to give orders to a Kyrgy?"

"The Lady gave me a gift. I give her one in return."

The horse advanced a step, close enough that she could touch it. She didn't want to. She could feel its breath, cold as icy winter, cold as snow-bound mountains.

The knight stared until Orielle had to look away. Her breath came rapidly, her heart pounded. She curled her fingers to make fists and pressed them into her thighs, hoping to hide her trembling. When she realized that she could not, she sidestepped the steed's nose and dropped down to slide off the rock. She felt for her boots with her toes. When she stood booted once more, she gathered up her cloak and draped it over her arm. Then she flicked her hair behind her.

And looked up to see him watching.

He leaned forward and stretched a hand toward her, closing the distance she had gained. "Your cloak is torn, Lady Wizard."

Orielle remembered the rents torn by wyre claws. Without taking her gaze from the knight, she searched for the rents. Finding them, she lifted the cloth to display how close the claws had come. "The wyre struck at me. He missed."

His brow contracted minutely. One hand dropped to his sword. As he touched it, the round pommel began to glow the eerie blue of a glacier, when the light shining through the fissures offered false hope. "The Lady will learn of the wyre. I return these horses to you and the Rhoghieri. The bow has his tang."

"I thank the Lady for her gift."

"The gift comes from me to you. Lady Skuld has dipped no claw in this exchange."

"And what will I owe you, Sword Knight?"

His minute smile returned, the briefest sign that he liked her name for him. "Only your good will, Aiwaz Solsken." He nudged his horse forward.

Orielle crowded against the rock as the tall horse loomed. Its first steps shifted to one side and brought the knight's left hand to her. He held out the reins of the dutifully following mundane horses. Yet when she grasped the reins, he didn't release them.

"Where do I find the grave of this wyre?"

"Just past the bend of the river, above the flood line. Look for the rock-covered grave." He'd had three questions to her one. Surely that put him in her debt.

He released the reins but didn't urge his mount forward. "The Kyrgy lady dislikes wyre, and sorcered wyre most of all."

Court life had taught Orielle that lesser people did not mention the debts that their betters owed. "You honor me, Sword Knight."

"You will have need of me, Aiwaz Solsken. Call my name three times into the wind. Your element, yes? It is the Rho's, and you are his. Call for me. For Sangrior. Say it."

"Sangrior."

Thunder rolled across the sky, dotted with the first stars.

His frown was a minuscule crease of his marble-smooth brow. "My ears delight to hear my name from living lips. A living name is often forgotten."

With his true name, he offered a great gift. She wasn't about to return the favor. "The Lady knows, doesn't she? That you gave me your name. Will she punish you?"

"The Lady will not punish for personal gifts freely given."

"You honor me," she repeated. Her curtsy deepened, and the bone-white horse seemed taller as she dipped and straightened. "Fair journey, Sir Sangrior."

"Fair journey, Lady Aiwaz."

He urged the horse forward. It passed her. The tail swished, as silvery colorless as the mane. The black hooves found purchase on the forest-littered slope. Sangrior's path twisted through the trees. She watched the descent—but the ghost-white hide vanished long before the trees would have obscured it, paling like mist then disappearing.

Without the intimidating Kyrgy steed, Ghost pushed back the bigger chestnut. His hooves slipped on the leaves and moss, then he shoved his nose into her hair.

"Don't try to make friends," she warned him. "You abandoned me to that wyre. I was lucky Grim came."

Ghost nudged her shoulder. He wanted his forelock rubbed, a sign that he was forgiven. The chestnut, a hand-span taller than her horse and muscled for war, gave a white roll of his eyes, but he came forward when she chirruped to him.

She led the horses down to the shore then upstream. A trickle of smoke hung over the water, faint, dissipating even as she sniffed it. Orielle scattered more of the scent as she led the horses along the shoreline. The glow ahead leaped with bright flares. The silhouette crouched beside the fire had to be Grim, cooking his catch.

While they worked along the shore, in and out with the curve of the river winding around boulders, Orielle considered the Sword Knight. He gifted the horses to her. He'd given her his name. This man dealt in names, for last night he'd gifted her with Aiwaz Solsken, going beyond his Lady's command. And today, he gave her the Kyrgy Lady's name, Skuld, greatest of all those gifts.

Names.

She had no doubt he would check the grave of the wyre that Grim had killed. She wished she had evidence of the two other wyre.

She wished most of all that she understood more about the Kyrgy. The Sword Knight had acted without the Lady's permission, breaking Orielle's assumption that the companion knights and all the riders were bound to the Lady's will.

Her only certainties were that she hadn't offended the knight or the Lady.

But his backward-looking gaze, that word *still* when he asked about the children's charm, those haunted her.

~ 9 ~

With full night rapidly approaching, Orielle headed for the leaping firelight. The horses, surer-footed in the dark, followed without hesitation. Ghost kept shouldering forward to nuzzle her loosened hair. When she stopped to pick out her next steps, cautious of ankle-turning rocks in the near-dark, he shoved his nose into her neck and blew warm air.

She shoved his head away. "Don't think that's an acceptable apology for running off without me. I know you were scared. So was I."

Ghost snorted and tossed his head.

The chestnut watched from the full length of its reins, keeping well back, a sign of distrust.

"And you—." She pointed a stiff finger. "The both of you, going off with that Kyrgy knight without a nicker of protest, I daresay. You both should know better."

The grey stretched out his nose. She obligingly scratched his chin. His long lashes half-closed when she transferred her scratching to his forelock.

Grim's horse sidestepped. His head came up, then he shied, straining at the reins.

"Whoa, whoa, boy." Then she caught the smell and gagged at the sweet sickness of it. Sparkles of light in a rainbow spectrum danced over the swiftly running river.

Escaping the smell, the big chestnut crowded forward. Orielle jumped in front of Ghost as the big horse plowed past her. Her arm wrenched forward, and she forgot the smell and the flashing lights as Grim's horse towed her behind him. She dropped Ghost's reins, yet the grey followed without urging.

She stumbled over a rock and twisted her ankle. "Whoa! Whoa!"

The horse stopped several feet beyond. Grabbing the stirrup, she staggered into his shoulder. The grey stopped behind them. When she caught her breath, she reached back for Ghost's dropped reins. She peered past him, but whatever the lights and smell meant, she saw nothing.

Getting a better grip on the reins, she maneuvered around the big chestnut. The fire remained ahead, enticing with light and warmth. The river's rush was a muted roar. They had an easy walk to the camp. "And let's make it an easy walk," she warned Grim's horse, which flicked his ears at her.

She puzzled over the sparkling light while she led them along the shore.

The crunch of iron-shod hooves on the pebbly shore alerted Grim. He stood, arms akimbo as they came along the edge of the river.

The flames licked around a skewered fish. He glanced up and down the shore, then bent to turn the fish.

Orielle faltered. *Do I tie the horses to a nearby tree or let them crowd around the camp?* Ghost nudged her, so she led them past Grim and the fire and the fish and to the water.

The horses dipped their muzzles into the water. While they drank, she unhooked the waterskin and refilled it. Then she dug into the food bag and came up with two cakes of bread and pinches of salt for the fish. She turned and held them out to the Rho.

He extended his hand. She poured in the salt then handed over the journey cakes.

"We'll sleep better with full bellies" was his first comment. "I've got trail oats in my off-hand saddlebag. The horses will need it. Give them a handful then tie them under that hickory." He pointed to a tall tree with a curved trunk. Its golden leaves gleamed in the firelight.

She hadn't crossed any wards. "Are we camping here by the water?"

"Farther upstream. I'll take a torch from the fire."

Linking protective wards in the full dark was troublesome, but she said nothing. She slipped Ghost's bit before she fed him the oats. He snuffled her hand, wanting more. She shoved him away, dipped into the oak sack, and went to the chestnut, offering oats with her palm flat. He nosed her hand. Remembering the bit, she reached for it, but the grey nudged her arm. The oats scattered. The big horse backed up, tossing its head. She crowded with him, grabbing the reins at the bit and drawing his head down.

"My fault," she murmured and slipped his bit. "But if you bite my fingers, we'll have more than words." She held the reins tight as she fetched more oats. Smelling them, the chestnut stopped pulling away. She opened her hand. "Good horse," she praised as he lipped carefully over her palm. "Good horse. I haven't forgiven you for back there, you know. You hurt my arm. You'll need to make it up to me."

The horse snorted. Finding no more oats, he pushed for the water. She let him pass, keeping the reins as she bent to wash her horse-nipped hand.

"What happened back there?"

Grim stood by the fire, testing the fish with a knife.

"I think we surprised a nest of sprites on the move. Whatever it was, your horse wanted out of there, and he towed me and Ghost after him."

"Hunh. How did you find the horses?"

The question she had dreaded. "I didn't. The Kyrgy knight, the one who named me, he gave them to me. He said we owed him nothing but our good will."

That slanted Sangrior's actual words, but Grim's scowl, fiercer in the leaping fire-glow and shadows, didn't ease.

"And the Lady?"

Ghost dropped his head to her hand and nuzzled, clearly wanting more oats. Orielle idly rubbed his nose then patted his neck before draping an arm over his shoulders. "Now that was curious. He said that Lady Skuld had dipped no claw in the exchange."

"Skuld? He gave her true name to you?"

"Yes. I was shocked, too. I understand what he meant, but why did he say 'no claw'? She has 'dipped no claw in'."

"If you saw her claws, you would know."

"I thought the Kyrgy were like the Fae."

"Dark Fae, aye. Dark appetites, dark dealings. Less likely to show mercy, more likely to enjoy cruelty. They play games with humans. And not your friend, for all that this knight seems to be courting you."

He used the Lady's word which reminded her of the Lady's displeasure. And that roll of thunder when he shared his name. Did the Lady know that he'd also given her true name? Aligned with that revelation, his return of their horses seemed insignificant. "Me? I doubt that. It's more likely a Kyrgy game with a human, just as you warned me."

"You may make him remember being human."

"Me?" she squeaked again. "No. No." But she remembered Sangrior's comment about 'finders keepers', the children's charm. "We have the horses. Does it matter how?"

"We have them," he agreed, "and whatever bargain you made with the Kyrgy knight, we'll figure a way out."

Orielle liked that *we*. Whenever trouble crashed onto her from pranks with her friends, she had borne the punishment and penance alone. To have someone offer help, to know he stood beside her—a sparkling joy seeded within and grew quickly. Bravely, she confessed more. "He knew the horses were ours. He said the bow has your tang."

A tricksy dance of the flames flickered in his eyes. "Tang—scent, same thing."

"That sounds like a predator tracking a scent."

"I did say the Kyrgy aren't friends."

"But—he returned the horses. He only wants our good will in return, Grim. He said the horses are a gift from him to us."

"Us? Or to you?" He snorted. "I doubt this knight considered me. The Kyrgy ignore the Rho. He's courting you. A wizard of the mighty Enclave. Courting you at the Lady's behest."

Orielle crossed her arms. "She called me Not-Wizard."

"When he named you Aiwaz Solsken, she didn't blast him."

"You said she was displeased. You said the Kyrgy give no gifts. But here are the horses, a gift from a Kyrgy knight. Not a bargain."

"Leave the horses and come eat."

He had the fish divided and the salt sprinkled on the steaming white flesh. Her mouth watered; her stomach rumbled. She started to lead the horses back to the trees.

He snapped up. "Where are you going?"

"To tie the horses."

"Mine will stay ground-tied."

"Unless we're attacked again."

"He'll fight first."

"Ghost will wander."

"He'll stay with his new-made friend. Come on. You can have the rock."

The rock was scarce ten inches high, yet her bum would be out of the damp. And a flat surface capped pebbly sand. "You?"

"I can stand."

Abandoning the argument about the horses, she dropped the reins and entered the fire's sphere of warmth. She kited her skirts so the hem wouldn't soak up the damp shore.

The fish was excellent. Neither spoke as they ate, picking out bones before scarfing up the salty flesh. Orielle flicked the tiny bones into the fire where they vanished with a sparky flare. The oat cake crumbled. She caught each crumb.

"Jam," she sighed and licked her fingers.

"What?"

"I miss jam."

"What kind?"

"Strawberry. Peach. Apple conserve. Blueberry. Grape."

"Not blackberry?"

"Seeds."

He offered a hand up. While she dabbled her fingers in the river, he retrieved a long stick lying behind her rock. In seconds it flamed for a torch. "Come see our camp."

The fire cast a welcome warmth. The broad shoreline gave a good view of any approaching predators. "Are we not camping here?"

"We're farther upstream, well away from the smell of fish. We don't want predators drawn to the smell."

"I've never set camp wards in the dark."

"I have."

Orielle caught the horses. Ghost *had* strayed back to the water. Ears flicked forward, he stared across the stream. Darkness cloaked the world beyond the firelight. The big chestnut drowsed, ignoring even her hold on the reins. Whatever had snared the grey's attention, he came willingly when she tugged the reins.

Damp as the shoreline was, she still asked, "Aren't you going to put out the fire?"

"What's to burn?" he countered. "Rock and sand?"

She wasn't ready to abandon the dispute about the Kyrgy. While she had only the barest knowledge gleaned from tomes written hundreds of years before, Grim had active knowledge. Yet he'd said they were Dark Fae, and Fae lived centuries. The writer of *Creatures of the Hinterland* might have met Lady Skuld. Didn't that make the tome active knowledge of the long-lived Kyrgy?

Trailing behind, a horse at each shoulder, she called up to Grim. "I told the knight that we killed a wyre. I said that was a gift for the Lady Bone."

He swung about. The torchlight cast a golden glow, making him the sun's kin along with her. The world had shrunk to him and the horses and herself in the sphere of light. The pebbly sand crunched at their passage. The river's constant voice, dimmed by the night, seemed muted. "What else?"

He didn't say it on a sigh, waiting for her to dole out all of her mistakes. He asked because he would need the information. It armored him, armored them both, like his mail shirt did.

"I told him about the wyre's partial shift and his glowing eyes and what that meant. He was surprised."

"Is that a guess, Orielle?" He turned back and continued leading.

"The Kyrgy *are* hard to read. They're so still." She remembered the displacement, caught between the hard rock gripped by her toes and an icy frost that emanated from the knight. She saw again the slow rise and fall of the horse's silvery mane. "His horse reacted. It tossed its head. I know that could mean much more than a controlled reaction sensed by his horse. But the knight said the Lady dislikes wyre, especially sorcered wyre. He agreed to tell her of the wyre. He wanted to see the grave. Proof of my words, I suppose." The wight had taught the lesson of never deceiving a Kyrgy.

He stopped again. She gained several steps and caught his grin. "Clever city lass. You've overpaid the debt."

"That's a good thing, isn't it?"

"Lady Bone will decide if it is."

Grim didn't ask the question she expected: *What's the knight's name? Sangrior.* The name rang within her. And she realized that she'd known his name, long before he said it. Had he planted his name in her mind when he named her Aiwaz Solsken?

Or when he gave her Lady Skuld's name.

And she knew Volk, who had leashed the wight. She knew more names.

No names spoken, Lady Aiwaz.

The words rang in her ears, louder than the jingly bridle rings and the iron hooves on pebbles and the river's incessant singing. The words had Sangrior's voice. She shivered in the returned chill. Ghost snorted.

No names, she agreed. If saying a Kyrgy name brought them near, she would stick with Lady Bone, not the name that the sword knight had revealed.

~ 10 ~

`Ware attack!

The words rang her awake. She woke to a horse's terrified neigh and the warning still rolling through her head.

Throwing back her blanket, she sprang up. "Grim!"

"Here." Facing away from her, he stood with the horses on the fire's other side. He held Ghost's reins. Eyes rolling, the dappled grey strained at the reins. He kicked back, throwing dirt into the darkness. The chestnut's jug head arched forward, big teeth bared, like a snarl at something beyond the ever-shifting light.

She scrambled into her boots then rushed to Grim's side. "What is it?"

"Don't know. The horses alerted. That woke me. Then something tested the wards."

Nothing moved in the smothering dark beyond the sphere of firelight. Ghost made too much noise to hear anything. "Grim, did you use the symbol of chaos that Lady Bone reminded us of?"

"Do you want to be in the Lady's debt?"

"If I use it, since she gave it to me through her knight, we would risk that. She did not give it to you. Can you not use it?"

"You've parsed a fine distinction. She, however, would sense any disturbance in the element and interpret it however she wished. There."

Twin shards of glowing green gleamed in the darkness. Then they vanished.

"Wyre?" she whispered. "The whole pack of them?"

"Doesn't smell like that."

She sniffed. An acrid tang pierced her nostrils. The smell reminded her—no, memory eluded her. "You should have called me earlier."

"I didn't call you."

"You didn't shout `Ware attack? Look!" Again she saw the twin gleam, joined by another pair. She flashed light.

In the brief seconds of the bright spell, two stunted creatures stood frozen. Open mouths revealed fangs. One gripped a broken branch like a club. The other twisted a coil of rope. Even in the spell's warm yellow light, their eyes glowed, like the partially-shifted wyre. Sickly green rimmed their eyes, obvious sorcery in use.

Her spell faded. Leaves rustled as the gobbers shifted position.

"How long can you hold that spell?"

Her power might not be great, her hoard of spells might be few, but what she did have, she knew how to use. "As long as you need it." And she re-lit the bright spell.

He thrust Ghost's reins at her and drew his sword. In his left hand, he shaped a sphere, ghostly pale, swirling with the energy of controlled Air. "Be ready."

She remembered the gobber fleeing her camp. "It's only two. They won't attack."

"More than two. Be ready, Orielle." On the word, he whirled and jumped behind her.

She heard a high-pitched squeal, pig-shrill, and saw a trio of the creatures dodging back from the swing of Grim's sword.

A fourth gobber flung dirt on the fire. The flames sputtered. More dirt landed on the fire.

Ghost tried to rear. She jerked his head down. "Not now."

A hard thwack hit her leg. The branch-wielding gobber swung again. She arced the bright spell at it. The creature screeched and dropped the branch to cover its round eyes. It stumbled away, into another, the one with the coil of rope.

Orielle shined the spell toward that one. Scrunching its eyes, it swiped a free hand at her. She dodged the short claws and landed against her horse.

Grim fought a trio of gobbers with the sweep of his sword. Another stood at the fire, dropping dirt on the coals to smother any chance of fire. Two crept behind Grim. She cast a hurried glance for her own safety and saw more gobbers lurking at the verge of the mage light, eyes greeny silver, mouths gaping to reveal triangle-sharp teeth.

The big chestnut stomped a gobber trying to grab his reins. He kicked another behind him. She released Ghost. The horse reared back. A gobber slid off his back. Runnels of blood dripped from his back and rump. With an outraged neigh, the grey fled into the night.

Flicking up more power, Orielle swept away the creatures at Grim's heels. Then she whirled and blasted Air at the waiting gobbers.

Something dragged on her skirt. A gobber, claws dug into the heavy cloth. It reached for her extended hand maintaining the bright spell. She swiped at it. Chittering, it snapped at her hand. A gust of wind only lodged the short claws deeper into her skirt. Remembering scrunched eyes, she directed the mage light at its face.

The silvery glow left the round eyes. It yowled. Then it snatched away, but those claws dug deep into cloth. Jerking around, it flailed and scrabbled. The shifting weight destroyed her balance. She stumbled to her knees.

A silvery coil dropped over her head. Orielle released the wind spell to hook her fingers in the tightening rope. The gobber shrieked in her ear. His strangling grip didn't ease.

The mage light faded. She poured energy into it. With the last air in her lungs, she cried, "Sangrior! Sangrior!" The noose tightened, choking the last naming to a mere breath. "Sangrior."

She toppled and felt fists pummeling her chest, driving out the last breath.

Thunder clapped. Moon-silvered light flooded the campsite. Gobbers screeched. Fists and claws left her body.

She dragged in a blessed breath and jerked the noose choking her.

A lightning-bright flash of power re-ignited the doused fire. Orielle winced and gobbers shrilled anger and fear.

Cold hands lifted her. Cold hands tugged the noose from her neck and over her head.

Her bleary eyes cleared. The sword knight knelt before her. "You came," she croaked.

"In good time, Lady Aiwaz."

Grim knelt beside him. "Are you hurt?" He fingered the rents that the gobber had left in her skirt.

"She does not bleed, not even a scratch. Did you spill gobber blood, Rhoghieri?"

"Not a drop. They're too fast. They stayed back from my sword."

"The gobber cannot bear Fae-wielded steel. It is very well for you that you did not hurt them. They are the Lady's."

"Not with those green eyes rimed with foul silver," she claimed, voice still hoarse as her throat recovered. Talking hurt, but Sangrior needed to know the sorcerer had controlled this attack by the gobbers.

"Green eyes rimed with foul silver? Lady, are you certain?"

"I was eye-to-eye with two of them." She coughed at the remnant of their acrid odour, the fetid breath that flooded her face when she tipped over. She pointed at the rope Sangrior absently coiled. The braided hemp shed sparks of eerie green as it passed through his hands.

He hissed. Those black eyes reflected the flames. "Sorcery. The one who tries to use the gobbers, he will the Lady punish."

Remembering the wight's fear, Orielle shivered. Grim pressed his shoulder against hers

"You are fortunate to have survived, Lady Aiwaz. The sorcerer targeted you."

"We are fortunate that you came when called. Did you warn me, earlier?"

He didn't answer. He coiled the rope tightly, shedding more sparks of sorcery.

"Why do you help us, Sangrior?"

That odd look returned, far from now in time and place. "I remember—." The long fall of his white hair sifted over his shoulders like cocoon-spun threads. "Do not kill the gobbers. The sigil of chaos will protect you."

"We'll not be using that." Grim remained firm. "We do not wish to be in the Lady's debt."

"I may not be able to come when next you call. The sigil offers additional guard."

The Rho started to argue, yet when she touched his hand, he fell silent. She wished their own disputes were so easily ended. "The sigil will limit chaos. It controls the element for our purpose rather than allows its energy to run free."

"The Lady gifts this knowledge," Sangrior added. "In the Wilding, power protects. You wish to avoid debt to the Lady? Be in debt or be in Neothera. The choice is yours."

"As it was yours," Grim gritted out.

Pale lids closed over those black eyes. Sangrior sat still as marble, cold as bone. When his lids lifted, his eyes were flat, without any glimmer of light. "Use the sigil. It will not bind you to the Chooser."

On the words, spoken like a vow, Sangrior backed away from them. He turned edge-side then seemed to fold upon himself. Wind swirled. Leaves and twigs spun about. Then the wind swooped toward him as he folded again and vanished.

The fire lost its lightning ferocity and faded to flames trickling over half-smothered wood.

With a muttered oath, Grim refueled the fire. "See if my horse is injured."

The chestnut rolled its eyes at her. Speaking softly, she shined the mage light with amber-glow to reassure him. Once she caught the reins, she could examine him. No sliding claws and pointy fangs had cut him, but he shivered at her touch. She ran a reassuring glow over him, adding warmth to her soothing magic, for the night had grown chill.

Or their narrow escape had kicked through her body, giving her shudders worse than the horse.

The fire blazed up, adding true warmth to the campsite.

Grim spoke softly as he joined her. The horse flicked his ears and turned his head to look at his rider. Adding his touch to hers, he patted the horse's neck then offered a handful of oats from his stock. The horse snuffled and, in the way of animals, cast off the memory of the attack for present comfort.

Orielle stepped back. "I will renew the wards."

"And use the chaos sigil?"

"We are foolish not to use it."

"Lady Bone will know."

"Then I will pay my debt to her when she comes to collect it. Or do you wish to have another attack from gobbers? Or trolls? Wyre with gobbers, eager to feast on us. Or the sorcerer driving an ogre in?"

"They would feast on me. The sorcerer will want to play with his captured wizard. I'm expendable."

She shuddered. "I shall definitely use chaos now."

"When you finish, we need to talk."

Guessing his interrogation would be worse than anything her tutors pealed over her, she hunched her shoulders. Then she shook off the worry. *Gobbers are worse. Trolls. Ogres. Keep perspective, Orielle.* She tossed her head and blinded him with her smile before walking to the edge of the firelight and carefully drawing the first ward, linking the next with the sigil of chaos.

~ 11 ~

Grim had the big chestnut settled when Orielle linked the last ward to the first and sealed them both.

As she had encircled their camp with magical protection, she considered the best answers to give him. She would not lie. That opened a way for darkness to enter. Whatever she omitted would reveal itself in a few hours, so she should tell it all.

Except—.

She still didn't want to reveal Sangrior's belief that she belonged with Grim. That pushed them into a greater connection when all she had wanted was a guide and a guard to Iscleft Haven.

Sangrior hadn't used Grim's name. He'd said, "You are the Rhoghieri's." Had he meant more generally rather than personally?

Or did he play mind games just as Lady Bone did?

She trudged back to the fire. The flames burned merrily over the new fuel. Remembering the gobber tossing dirt onto the flames, remembering the ones who had crept behind Grim, claws outstretched to pierce his hide trousers and get to the big veins and tendons, she shuddered. The memory of the silvery loop tightening on her neck, the gobbers crawling over her, their fists pounding, knocking the air from her lungs—she would never forget that.

Swallowing, she touched her tender neck.

Grim dropped beside her. Startled, she flashed mage light, then she came back to the present and released the magic to the Air. It dissipated into the curling smoke.

"Throat hurt?" He poked a log. Flames shot up then began consuming the bark he'd shifted into the heat.

"Not so much hurt as remembering."

"Keep that memory. It'll keep you alive. You had enough breath to call for him. How did you learn his name?"

An unspoken plaint ground through the question. Was he angry that she hadn't called for him? He'd had a clutch of gobbers attacking him. "Would you have killed the gobbers? That would have displeased Lady Bone."

"I'll kill anything that's trying to kill me. Don't try to distract me, Orielle. The Kyrgy knight gave you his name. Was that when he returned the horses? What else did he do? What bargain did you make with him?"

"No bargain! I swear. The only thing he asked for was my good will. I *told* you that!"

"Aye, you did, but maybe we need to rethink what a Kyrgy knight calls good will when it comes from an Enclave wizard."

"Not-Wizard," she reminded.

"An insult from Lady Bone, designed to provoke you. And disappointed when you weren't provoked. What's the knight's name? His true name, for he came when you called for him three times, the way that magical beings like Kyrgy and Fae must come."

Grim should have heard it, but she supplied it anyway. And she reminded him of Lady Bone's true name. Then she turned the focus on him. "And Rhoghieri and wizards, do they come when you call for them three times?"

"Rho do. If nothing else binds them in place. And wyre. But wizards and sorcerers are mundane first, magical second. Calling your name won't bring you to me. I can control you with it, with the right spell."

She blanched, remembering her journey through the Lowlands, giving her name blithely to anyone who asked. The Enclave didn't teach guarding the true name—although the wizards followed custom, the birth name and clan name as identity, but the second name, the family name, not given and generally forgotten. "If you had the whole of my true name, you could control me. You don't."

"Best if I never do."

Insight blinded like sunrise. "That's the reason you've never given your true name to me."

"Grim serves."

He didn't trust her. He knew her ignorance about the Wilding. He knew her Enclave-taught arrogance. Ignorance and arrogance equaled death. Luck had graced her so far. How long would it last?

That first night in the Wilding, the gobber that crossed her wards could easily have attacked her rather than fled. Without Grim, the wyre would have killed her. The wight would have haunted her to madness—and created easy prey for the Wilding predators. Even Lady Bone and her knights, they could still catch her with the cruelty Grim had described.

"I am a fool."

"The Enclave teaches fools. Outside the Enclave, you learn. Your knowledge of the Wilding grows. Does the Kyrgy knight know your true name? Even if he cannot use it to call you, your true name would speak to his heart."

"No, not even half my name." She still refused to reveal Sangrior's statement that she was Grim's, but she shared, "He woke me. Before the attack. He called me out of sleep. *'Ware attack*. I thought that was you."

He finished stirring the wood in the fire and tossed in his stick. "He spoke into your mind?"

Orielle shivered and wrapped her arms around herself. "I don't like this, Grim. How did he do that? He doesn't know my name. He knows my element is Air, but I've been careful not to give the Kyrgy a link to me. I didn't use the symbol until tonight. I didn't make any bargains."

"But he's connected to you."

"How?"

"You've answered to the name he gave you, Aiwaz Solsken. It's accurate enough to be the connection. Through Lady Bone he gave you a true name, called you by it, wrote it on your forehead when he gave you the chaos sigil."

She remembered the brief seconds when he wrote the sigil, over and over. "He didn't have time."

"The Kyrgy can collapse time, the way he collapsed space."

Yawning fear opened. "Did we do something, say something, swear an oath or accept a bargain that we don't remember? Lady Bone seemed pleased, there at the end."

"There's a spell to discover if you've lost time and memories. I don't know it. A Haven mentor may know."

"How far to the Haven?"

"Three more days with our single horse. With Ruddy packing double."

She didn't badger him with *I told you so* about Ghost's proclivity to run. "We still have food and our waterskins."

"And a sorcerer and a wyre pack in pursuit. Twelve wyres, for we've killed only one. There's the gobbers as well. That's odds I don't like."

She picked at a claw-torn rent in her skirt. "Sangrior said Lady Bone would not be pleased that the sorcerer used the gobbers. He said they were hers."

"So they are. She rules everything in this Wilding. Even those who come from outside. Turn in, Orielle. I'll keep watch for a couple of hours then switch with you."

"Does so much remain of the night?" With a wide yawn, she stumbled up to do his bidding.

The gobbers had stepped on her blankets. She shook them hard then crawled under the top fold.

Sleep slipped away like water every time she thought she would sink into its blessed blankness. She stared at the flames and denied herself any watching of Grim.

He remained patient with her ignorance and arrogance.

Had the Kyrgy spelled them both to lose time and memory? She tried to track every second, every breath of that meeting with Lady Bone. She saw no place for a spell to be cast, no memory that seemed lengthened or shortened.

Could the spell be in her meeting with Sangrior, up by the little pool, as dusk deepened to dark. That tinny sound, the hollow feeling—were those clues?

Sleep slipped over her while she puzzled over it.

.~.~.~.

Constant alertness exhausted Orielle, much more than the previous day's constant hiking.

Grim scanned for trouble throughout the day. He remained alert while she lost concentration or looked so intently into the tangled laurels that she stumbled. Her head ached before the sun reached its zenith. It pounded as evening approached.

Deeper into the Wilding, the mountains crowded together, allowing passage with steep trails and switchbacks. Any supplies brought to the Haven would have to be packed in, not brought by wagon. An hour's climb barely halved their ascent. They rode double only when the trail didn't sharply incline. In the morning, Grim let her ride while he walked, but by afternoon her sense of fair play demanded she walk in her turn. With the trail clearly marked, he put her in lead. She thought it courtesy to help her avoid horse droppings until she figured out that he didn't expect her to notice if anyone crept up behind them.

They encountered nothing that night.

Nothing the next day.

And still nothing the following night. No wyre. No gobbers. No Kyrgy.

Just a distinct sensation they were watched, a sensation that deepened into a crawling, creeping tension.

"What is it?" she hissed.

He shrugged. He walked with one hand ready to draw his sword, the other with fingers limned with power. "What would you guess?"

She could shrug, too.

Handing back the waterskin, she headed up the trail. Grim walked faster than she did. He'd be on her heels quickly enough.

The day had started with fleecy clouds herded across the sky. Now, slaty clouds heavy with rain obliterated the sun and rode the air currents barely above the trees with their fading colors. Wind gusted from the mountain's crest, lost to the clouds, with snow creeping down the upper slopes.

Her breath fogged in air colder than first waking. She watched the fog dissipate and looked up at the wispy clouds trailing fingers down the upper slopes. The wight's wispy fingers had gripped the trunk.

A wind gust tore out of the clouds and ripped through the trees, tearing off leaves and twigs and pelting them.

Orielle flinched then scrunched her eyes and plowed into the palpable Air. Another gust tugged her cloak, cast off her hood, and streamed through her hair, whipping it around until she was blind. She snatched it out of her eyes. Holding it back with one hand, she looked back.

Grim and his horse didn't follow her.

Her heart jumped into her throat. Thinking she'd taken a wrong turn, fearing something had clawed them off the trail, she headed back.

The wind pushed against her. She stumbled forward. Her out-flung hand was seized—and Grim stood before her, the big chestnut switching its tail at a wind that merely teased.

She clung to his hand. "I lost you!"

His dark brows drew together. "You were only a few feet in front of us."

"You disappeared!"

His scowl became fierce. "We vanished? Where?"

"Until you touched me."

He hauled her behind him. When he drew his sword, the Fae scrolling glistened. Extending it before him, he stepped forward. Nothing happened. He walked past the point she'd reached. She trailed close, expecting him to vanish again. He remained visible.

He stopped and poked forward with the sword. Nothing. "How far on the trail did you get?"

"You're past where I was."

He turned and visibly jerked. He stared at the reins in his hand.

"Orielle." A quiet voice and a slow cadence of the syllables of her name. "Can you see my horse?"

Half-afraid to look, she swept her gaze along the reins as they passed her and never reached the chestnut.

Although something suspended the reins in the air.

"Touch your fingers to the reins and go back for Ruddy."

She took a hesitant step.

"You'll have to let go of me," Grim reminded.

He was the only human warmth on the mountain. She prised her fingers loose and transferred them to the leather reins. Walking forward slowly, she saw the big horse emerge, the air clearing, misting away like a fog. The horse flicked his ears forward. He snorted when her fingers slid up the reins to his bridle. "He's here."

"Say again." Grim's voice was muffled, though he was not more than three steps behind her.

"He's here," she repeated, louder, and turned to look. Yes, three steps back. If she hadn't known him, that scowl would have frightened her. "I still see you."

"Clearly?"

That *was* Grim. His mouth moved when he spoke. His dark hair, those storm-grey eyes—but the sword wasn't in his right hand.

"Come back. Something's wrong."

He took a step.

White fog billowed between them. The temperature dropped to icy.

The chestnut shied back, stretching the reins taut.

She heard a shout, muffled by the fog, dying away. Orielle grabbed the reins and pulled, towing them in like a lifeline thrown to a drowning man. The chestnut backed, taking the slack.

Grim shouted again. The reins stuck, not coming toward her, not receding back into the magical trap. She tugged hard. The icy-fanged wind ripped at her exposed skin. Gritting her teeth, she hauled back with her whole weight. "Let him go," she threw at the fanged wind.

And he stumbled through.

She released the reins and jumped forward, grabbing his leather jack and hauling back, just like the reins. "They nearly had you, they nearly had you."

He dropped his sword on the rocky trail and grabbed her, hauled her against him, and stopped her gabbling with his mouth. A fierce kiss of fear and need and lust, hunger that woke her own need and lust, passion that obliterated anger and fear.

A shriek pierced their ears. It caterwauled up and up, quenching their need for each other. The sound intensified to pain. Then it stopped, as quickly as his sudden appearance. The icy wind died. The horse shook his head and snorted, unaffected by the shriek.

Grim reached for her—then dropped his hands, shook his head.

And Orielle's heart flinched.

He reached again, only this time he took her hands. He turned them over. "You're bleeding."

Thin lines of red oozed on her skin, across her knuckles. "The wind. It cut like ice."

One shake of his head stopped her. "That wasn't wind. We need to get away from here, get your hands cleaned up before infection sets in. We'll find a lower trail around the mountain's flank."

He sheathed his sword, snatched up Ruddy's reins, then braced an to herd her down the trail.

At the first switchback, Grim stacked three rocks, a barrier sign that even she knew. And beyond, as the trail climbed to the switchback, he placed another three plus two more. *Danger. Go back.*

The icy presence watched them far past the trail marking.

~ **12** ~

He used their water to wash the thin marks "from talons." Then he sprinkled a greyish powder that soaked up the blood and started the clotting. "Do you have any healing power?"

"A little."

"Use what you can. This can get infected too easily."

He turned away and built up the fire as she called up the spells she'd learned when she first decided she would join her brother Saithe at Iscleft.

Grim had led her halfway down the mountain before he took an animal track leading along the mountain's flank. As the clouds packed the sky, they had climbed through clearings, crossed slopes with dry grasses bent by the steady wind, and maneuvered through tumbled rocks that the heights flung down when ice cleaved giant slabs from the granite. They re-entered forest and wound through straight-trunked trees losing their golden leaves. Descent took them into evergreens. Her thighs complaining of the climbs and her knees complaining of descents, Orielle trailed behind the Rho.

Then the mountain's slope gentled and widened, a natural bowl with an ancient spillover of earth still gashed and furrowed. Autumn-changing trees grew around the perimeter while wildflowers bloomed in the warmer center.

He stomped down the wildflowers and grasses until he had a circle for a firepit. Ruddy grazed the dry grasses and nipped the last sweet flowers. With no task given her, Orielle watched the clouds sailing overhead, slaty grey becoming deepening purple, while Grim started the fire then fetched a waterskin to wash her oozing cuts.

Talons. A specific word. What magical creature had set a trap, tore at her hands as she towed Grim free, then shrieked its disappointment at their escape? Did he know? He had to, for he had warned her about infection.

He came back and inspected her healing. Then he touched beneath her eyes and studied them. "A little red."

"So are yours. From walking into the wind?"

He started up, off for another camp chore.

She grabbed his shirt sleeve. "What was that?"

"Ice Huldra."

Huldra. She'd scanned that entry in *Creatures of the Hinterland*. A lovely woman who showed herself only when she was ready to kill the man she had lured into her trap. Her tutor had laughed and called the entry proof of a lonely monk's wishful fantasy. The Enclave needed to send its tutors to the Wilding, to have their eyes opened the way hers now were. They might not survive, though. They would need a Rho guide.

"I saw no sign of a trap. No spell markings. I looked!"

"As did I. Nothing but the vanishing. If we had continued, we would have walked into her cave and never known until she cleaved us open to feed on our warm blood."

She shuddered. "She nearly caught you."

"Nearly caught both of us. You walked into her trap with me totally unaware. I'll get more wood for the fire, then you can set the camp wards."

Will he not mention that kiss?

He didn't, not when she came back from setting the last ward wrapped around the chaos sigil, not when he let her finish the tea, not when he told her that he'd take second watch. Yet he stayed close through all that, and he kept touching her, her loosened hair "like spun gold in the firelight" and her hands "to see if any infection has started" and her cheek "to see if your eyes are still red."

.~.~.~.

The Kyrgy came, a marble knight on a bone-white steed, more

knights and dames behind him, slowly riding a circle behind her wards, until they encircled the camp except for the broken earth at the bowl's spill-over.

Awake this time, Orielle stood and turned, keeping the lead rider to her fore. Lady Bone did not lead them, nor did she join them.

Sangrior didn't lead them. This knight had a leaner face, a longer chin and sharper nose, prominent cheekbones that angled his face like Lady Bone's. Orielle had focused on the leashed wight and not the knight that held the leash, consort with Sangrior to Lady Bone.

Although she didn't want to wake Grim, her panic increased when the riders stopped circling and advanced their horses to the rim of the wards. Ruddy turned as she did. The horse bared his long teeth, but he didn't charge. He stood his ground, head tossing, ground-tied reins flipping around.

The riders didn't cross the wards. Only the lead knight did, edging his horse across the magical line. She felt a sharp pang through the magic. And his horse shied, a slow dance sideways curbed by steely spurs.

If he felt that sharp pang, he didn't reveal it.

Once across the wards, he dismounted. He dropped his reins. The horse's head came up, nose lifted, neck arched. Then the silvery tail flicked. The right forehoof stomped the grassy ground.

Ruddy responded, stomping his own held ground. His long jug-head shook, as if driving away biting insects.

When the knight approached, long strides crossing the wind-waved grass, Orielle curtsied, staying dipped until he stopped two ells from her.

She rose smoothly, grateful for that court lesson. "Sir Knight." Into her mouth eased the name *Volk*.

He didn't extend the same courtesy of a courtly bow but loomed, stern and straight, a living steel sword. "Lady Aiwaz Solsken."

She expected him to announce his mission, but he said nothing more. Glancing at the waiting riders, she heard more names echo. *Khristofin. Alledyne. Saircuista. Wythe. Laroise.* She tried to mask her expression, but her lashes flickered at each naming.

How do I know this?

And she recalled Sangrior's `ware attack!

Courtesy had served before. "I welcome you, Sir Knight. I would offer bread and salt, but our supplies will not stretch to include your escort."

The black eyes seemed to glint with firelight. "You will reach the Haven tomorrow by sun's zenith. Will you welcome us there, Lady?"

"I will not refuse a visit from a Kyrgy knight. The Rhoghieri of Iscleft Haven may be surprised and thus refuse your entry."

His humorless smile revealed bone-white teeth, sharply pointed like Lady Bone's. This was indeed the Leash Knight. *Volk.* "The Haven exists at the Lady's will. Should we choose to ride to the heart of their circle and feast on blood and flesh, they have no right to stop us."

That answer sounded like Lady Bone. Blood and flesh sounded evil, but she shifted it to the half-cooked meat her brothers preferred rather than the charred meat that her mother liked. Her lack of disgust caused his eyelids to flicker.

She reckoned this *Volk* was more a mouthpiece for Lady Bone than Sangrior. She wanted to ask about the Sword Knight, but she dared not. "Lady Bone herself may come to my hearth and be welcome."

"Would you feed her, Lady Aiwaz Solsken?"

He laughed, and the riders laughed with him, mockery rather than amusement, and Orielle knew that his word *feed* was not her use of it. She heard the big chestnut snorting, stomping, off to her left, but she didn't look away from Volk. When the laughter ebbed, she aimed a dart, not certain it would strike true. "I thought the Lady intended me to feed the Ice Huldra who waited on the mountaintop."

Mockery vanished. Once more, he became cold marble. "A mistake, not intended by the Lady. The Huldra has learned that only the Lady herself may touch you."

The Lady's touch held danger, life-stilling that it was. Yet her claim would keep other predatory creatures away. Orielle curtsied, accepting the unintended honor. "My thanks to the Lady for her watch-guard."

For a long second his brow constricted. He must want to correct her deliberate misunderstanding, but he did not. Doing so might unveil Lady Skuld's true intent.

And Orielle had her own quandary, wanting to ask about Sangrior but not wanting to give him a question to turn into a debt to him. "The Rho and I—we thank the Lady also, for allowing Sir Sangrior to come to our aid last evening. The ensorcelled gobbers overwhelmed our campsite. His aid—." She stopped, seeing more treacherous debt in gratitude. "We did not wish to harm any gobber, for we know all creatures of the Wilding are under the Lady's shield. Yet sorcery clearly influenced these."

There. She'd drawn a strong line. Lady Skuld could not equivocate now. Sorcery *was* at work in the Wilding. Either she allied to it or drove it out; the Kyrgy lady could not ignore it.

"Do not try to be clever, Not-Wizard. The Lady has great power. She uses it when she chooses."

"She is the Chooser."

A spate of harsh language came from a rider. Volk cut it off with his hand's quick down-thrust. "You offend my fellow knight."

"The Rho claims my education is much at fault. I understood that another name for the great Kyrgy was the Chooser."

"She offers the choice, Lady. You choose."

"As Sangrior chose to help us. But his was the wrong choice. I heard the thunder of the Lady's displeasure."

"Your education may be weak, but your understanding is strong. He did choose, to ride with the Lady. And now to help you when she did not offer that as a choice for him. You may call upon *her*. Only with her permission should he have come to you."

"He said that I reminded him—." She stopped, too late.

"You remind him of a past he should not cling to, not when he rides as Kyrgy knight. His devotion is to the Lady. No one past or present can claim an nth of his loyalty. Now he helps you, twice, and gives you his name, a wedge into the heart of the Lady's riders. He learns his lesson now."

The hardness of those words flogged her shoulders. "I do not deprive the Lady of her knight. His loyalty remains to her."

"Yet the wedge remains. With that wedge, you can ride into the heart of the circle. Knowing this wedge exists, the Lady cannot remove it. My fellow knight cannot remove it. Nor can you. Only one thing removes the danger of the wedge."

Ice shivered over her. "She would have me as a rider. I will not do her much good, Sir Knight."

"The Lady would have a wizard riding with her."

"A trophy."

"Not so. A power different from what she wields. A weapon. Your life will bind with hers. Since you are Aiwaz Solsken, you will ride with her for a long time."

What does a knight who lives for centuries call a long time?

"That choice is not possible."

When Grim spoke, Orielle flinched. She looked around to see him standing just behind her shoulder, like a shield-mate. She wondered how much of this dialogue he'd heard. Volk hadn't acknowledged him at any point. He didn't look at the Rho even now. That obsidian focus, deep yet depthless, remained on her.

The encircling riders remained marble-still, their horses also frozen, while Ruddy continued to snort and toss his head.

"This wizard may have the wedge to the heart of the riders, but Lady Bone allowed a Huldra to set a trap," Grim countered. "Did she intend a feast for her creature? As long as the Lady allows the Wilding creatures to threaten an Enclave wizard, she shows her alliance to Frost Clime."

"The Lady needs no allies," the consort knight snapped.

"Frost Clime will court her. They will flatter her. But they will never devote themselves to her. They would bind her to them."

"No one can bind the Lady. The Rhoghieri knows this."

Grim stepped a little past Orielle. The knight's horse tossed its head. The eyes rolled a little, revealing yellowish-white around the black iris that filled the socket. "We do." He crossed his arms, a weaponless barrier that still stood firm. "We keep the agreement. As for this sorcerer who uses the Lady's gobbers, when he came to the Lady, what promises did he offer? Has he kept them?"

At the accusation, Orielle clutched his arm. He'd warned her about questions, but he threw two at Volk.

"The sorceress did not come to the Lady."

"So, a sorceress comes to the Wilding. She twists the gobbers to her use with foul magic. She brings wyre to prey upon the innocent creatures of the forest. She did not disclose her presence here, and she asks no permission for her deeds. She offers no recompense for her misdeeds."

"This Not-Wizard comes to the Wilding as well."

"This wizard is with me, and I am Rhoghieri, part of the agreement with the Lady, an agreement I keep. This sorceress has no agreement to keep."

"Do not think to command the Lady, Rho."

"I do not. Which of her riders keeps the truth from the Lady? Which rider knew of this sorceress but kept silent?" He aimed the questions like darts and continued firing them. "Which rider reveals their devotion is not to the Lady alone? Which rider creates a second wedge, aimed to Lady Bone's heart?"

"That rider should be punished," Orielle hastened to add, "as Sangrior is punished."

Grim touched her hand, warning her, and she fell silent—.

The riders shifted restlessly. His darts had found homes all around the circle. Grim's big chestnut began a turn then stood still. He kicked back although nothing stood behind him.

The darts angered Volk. "Lady Bone cannot be killed by the likes of you or by any sorceress. Do not think to threaten her."

"I do not. A rider does. Tell her."

"You do not command me."

"If you do not tell Lady Bone, these riders will believe you are a traitor to her. She fears a wedge. She is right to do so. Let her look among her riders for this wedge that opens the heart of the circle to foul sorcery that allows no limits. Let her use her claws and sharp teeth on that wedge. That rider will deserve her attention."

Volk bent his head. "You speak true. Such a rider threatens us all."

A horse snorted then shied sideways, bumping into another one. Ruddy whirled, ready to face the new threat. A woman rider thrust an arm at her fellow, shoving him off-balance. She brandished a silvery sword. *Saircuista* echoed in Orielle's mind. Then the dame dug her spurs into her horse. With a scream of outraged pain, the big horse plunged across the wards, straight at Orielle and Grim.

The chestnut plunged forward as she fell back. The Kyrgy horse brushed past him, seconds faster than Ruddy's rush.

But the horse had slowed the rider the bare seconds needed for Grim to draw his sword and brace to meet the attack. As the horse barreled toward the Rho, Volk flowed into position. The horse veered as the Kyrgy's sword clashed with the rider's weapon. The blades clanged together. Then Saircuista's sword screeched as she wheeled her horse around, retreating before Volk's defense. The steed sat back on its heels, half-reared, turning in the air. It dropped, hooves thudding into the ground, angled away from Orielle and Grim. The rider swung her sword again, cleaving downward.

Volk's blow shattered the woman's sword.

Saircuista cursed and flung the useless hilt at Orielle who danced backward to safety. Then the rider drove her horse forward. The bone-white steed leaped the dying campfire. It crossed the other side of the wards. She collided with another rider. A half-breath more, and Saircuista disappeared into the night-cloaked forest.

Volk swung an arm. Several riders whirled their mounts and followed.

He wasn't finished with them. He advanced on Orielle and only Grim's stepping between kept the Kyrgy knight from reaching her. "You know her name?"

"Saircuista," she repeated. She didn't remember shouting it, but she must have. Volk acted offended by her knowledge.

"How?" he demanded.

"I don't know. I know several of the riders' names. I know yours."

He grimaced. His finger stabbed toward her. "You are a wedge. Sangrior is a fool who deserves his punishment."

Grim barred Volk's further advance with a blocking arm. "This lady does not seek to harm any of you, least of all Lady Bone. She only wants to defeat Frost Clime."

Orielle met those black eyes, bright with firelight, and tried to breathe. Long seconds beat off, then Volk sheathed his sword. The pommel glowed, deeply purple where Sangrior's was a glacier's light. "Lady Bone did not send the Huldra," he allowed. "Your escape pleased her, but she did not care if you were eaten. The sorceress and Saircuista's disloyalty, these will anger my Lady. Be grateful you have not offended her."

"I am"

"We are."

"I am not the fool that Sangrior is," Volk warned. "I am not tempted by a Solsken. Get you to the Haven, Lady Wizard."

"And Sangrior?" The question burst out without her planning.

"For him, Saircuista's defection will be a welcome distraction."

He strode to his waiting horse. As he mounted, the two remaining riders streamed around the camp, outside the wards as they followed the riders hunting Saircuista in the dark forest. Earlier their pace was stately; this ride was swift, thundering.

In the silence after, Grim went to his horse, standing on shaky legs beside the campfire.

~ 13 ~

Grim listened mutely to her recounting of the Kyrgy. "This knight, the one who had kept the wight leashed, his name is Volk."

"Shared that with you, did he?"

Orielle sidestepped that answer. "What do you think that wedge is? Did Sangrior cause it when he gave me his name? Or when he came after I called him to me?"

"Names are powerful. I've never heard of them creating a weakness in a group."

"They are all bound to Lady Bone."

He scanned the trees around them. "I don't like talking about this out here. Too many ears."

She wanted to discuss the wedge created by Saircuista's alliance with the sorcerer. *Sorceress*, she corrected herself.

Grim kept his comments few. Last night he'd told her sharply to get to sleep while he tended to his horse. Ruddy trailed behind them, no longer limping but moving cautiously down the steep trail. The collision with the Kyrgy horse hadn't dealt a physical injury, but Grim had refused to ride the horse, slowing their approach to the Haven.

On waking this morning, she had peppered him with questions. He'd only shrugged and pushed her to get on the trail faster than usual. He remained reticent still.

Maybe he wanted to mull over last night's encounter. The quick logic of his sharply aimed questions had impressed Volk and the other riders. She hoped the Kyrgy knight repeated every word to Lady Bone.

"Saircuista—."

He interrupted. "That knight shared a lot with you, didn't he?" His stride lengthened, and Orielle had to pick up speed to stay ahead of the trailing horse.

"Not really that much."

"More than the Lady intended."

She huffed. "Why would that rider ally with a sorceress? Maybe she tires of her time as a Kyrgy rider. What will happen to her when she breaks the binding to Lady Bone?"

"She will age."

Orielle opened her mouth to ask *Not Death?* and then *How quickly will she age?* Then she choked down the questions, for Grim wasn't interested in a conversation.

Her mind twisted around the problem of a binding to a Kyrgy. The binding prevented death, yet it also stilled life. Then another question popped up and then out before she could stop it. "Is the wedge that Vol—the wedge that the leash knight spoke of, does it work in reverse? I mean, does it open me to Lady Bone? Does it open the sorceress to the Lady?"

Grim stopped and turned on her. "I don't know these answers, Orielle. I doubt the Lady knows. I've never heard of this wedge, but then, I've never heard of a Kyrgy rider not being absolutely loyal to the Lady." His head cocked. "I know what draws me to you. I doubt the knights have the same lure. But something drew him, the sword knight, as you called him. The Lady recognized it, that first night."

"He misses the sunlight. He misses living with people of all ages around him. Lady Bone accused me of luring him into a courtship. Because he named me *Solsken*. That displeased her."

"Aye, when he should have only given you the sign that would forge a link from you to her. Is it a prophecy?" he muttered, turning away with the question. "Come on. We should reach the Haven by mid-afternoon if we don't keep stopping."

"And then we're safe."

His abrupt laugh was like Volk's, without humor. He looked over his shoulder and quirked an eyebrow. "That depends on your definition of safety."

She stretched her stride to gain his side. "What will I find at the Haven?"

"I don't know. I left after my father died. The elder who replaced him, he and I never got along."

The simple statement opened up a wealth of trouble. "Your father was an elder?"

"One elder. A chieftain." He stopped so abruptly that she strode past.

He grabbed her arm and towed her back, and she saw that his left hand rested on his sword hilt, pushing it forward to speed its withdrawal from the Fae-scrolled scabbard. Ruddy braced his iron hooves on either side of the trail, but his head hung down, tired as she was.

She scanned ahead and behind. Like the deer trail they had used to shake the wyre off their heels, this faint trail meandered up and down the slope, steeper as it dropped toward the river. She wished she had a clear road, like the one she had taken from the Lowlands into the Wilding, to that copse at the rocky escarp where the prime wyre had set his trap.

Grim shifted his shoulders and started walking again—although he kept his dual grip on the sword and her arm. "I'm seeing ghosts where there's nothing. Come on. Never good to linger in the Wilding."

Ghosts reminded her of the wraith which reminded her of Sangrior ... which turned her thoughts back to Saircuista and the sorceress and the wyre.

Did something track them? Now she remembered the camp attack and the thin rope tightening around her neck. "Gobbers hiding?" she whispered the suggestion.

The trail dropped sharply. Trees crowded the path. On the switchback below, she saw the tangle of laurel, the trail keeping above the leafy maze. The trail crossed a rocky slab without leaving a trace on the granite, just the thready beaten ground on one side then the other.

"With all we've faced, I keep expecting a troll or an ogre. Or a gryph. Grim, have you ever seen a gryph?"

"Once." His glance held amusement mixed with resignation, for clearly she struggled to stay quiet. "At distance."

"Fighting for Frost Clime?" The only worse thing would be a dragon on the wing. Rumors claimed Frost Clime wanted to free the dragons from the Shifting Lands. "Do ogres and trolls fight at Iscleft? My brother wrote once that he fought more than sorcerers and wyre, but he didn't say more than that brief line. I always wondered. The sorcerers could terrorize the Lowlands if they drove the Wilding creatures into the plains. Do you think they'll do that?"

"That's three questions." He offered her a hand over another rock slab. Ruddy's hooves rang as he picked his way across. "You could let me answer one question before you jump to the next."

"Well?"

"What jumped into you this morning? You haven't chattered like this before."

"That sorceress. Could she want to drive the magical creatures into the Lowlands? That would disrupt all the lives in the Lowlands. Is that the reason she came into the Wilding? Or does she want an alliance with Lady Bone?"

He hadn't given her hand back. She let him steady her progress, for it kept him from striding along at full speed.

Another thought popped out. "Maybe the sorceress thinks she can control the Wilding creatures the way that Frost Clime controls the wyre. And that gryph you saw."

"The wyre are allied to the sorcerers. They're not really controlled. The gryph—I don't know why it helped them. Ogres and trolls would be hard to control; they can't keep a single thought in their pebble-sized brains. Trolls, especially. If you can hide, they'll get distracted. We teased them, as boys."

She waited to hear more, but he didn't continue.

The only people more arrogant than wizards were the sorcerers. They likely thought they could control trolls and ogres. "That sorceress controlled the gobbers who attacked us." She remembered their green-tinged eyes.

"Manipulated them. But she might think she can control them. The sorcerers think they can control dragons. No one controls a dragon."

"The Fae did, once."

"Until the dragons rebelled and nearly destroyed the mundane world during Dragon Dark."

"Could the Kyrgy control dragons?"

He stopped. He looked struck. She'd finally said something his quick reasoning hadn't raced over.

"You did say the Kyrgy are like the Fae even though they have left Faeron."

"A few remained," he countered, the words slow as his mind tracked through her question. "Still as dangerous there as they are here in the Wilding."

"But Lady Bone and the other Kyrgy left Faeron. When?" She teetered on a precipice of knowledge. If she plunged over, she would find an answer—if she didn't die when the knowledge moved up to meet her. "When the dragons rebelled?" she whispered, fearing the words spoken louder.

He didn't answer. He didn't seem to see her, standing before him, the dappled light shifting as a wind blew through the evergreen branches overhead.

"Two questions," he murmured. "Were the Kyrgy part of banishing the dragons to the Shifting Lands? Or did they leave Faeron because they refused to banish the dragons?" He started walking, so quickly that she stumbled and would have fallen without his tight grip. "You'll need to read the records for those answers."

"I studied history. Dragon Dark and the formation of the Enclave and the Riven Peace. Nothing about the Kyrgy and dragons."

"You studied Enclave history. The Fae will have more records."

"I don't like reading. Maybe you should read them."

"Maybe I should. We'd have to go to the Maorketh's court."

Orielle liked that *we*.

She managed to stay silent until they reached the narrow valley between the mountains. The steep slopes with their exposed boulders and rampant laurel funneled the swift river, a broader cousin to the one they had crossed before. Under the trees the moss grew thick on the ground and on the half-rotted fallen trees, downed long ago. Green stained the rocks beside the water, slick near the waterline. Rains in the eastern Wild must have fallen to swell the river. The water looked deep and cold.

After searching for a crossing, Grim turned north. "We'll go upstream to the ford. We cross quickly enough."

What would wait for them at the expected crossing?

But she didn't point out the danger, merely followed him. And the big chestnut trailed them.

The ford had a wide shoreline, just like the one where they'd fought two days before. The mountains tucked in their feet, letting the river broaden. The banks were lower, dropping gently to the shore. In places, the laurel tipped waxy leaves into the swift water.

The expanse from bank to bank allowed a view of the sun-drenched sky. Light glistened on the water. It dried the rocks to a dull grey. Densely growing evergreens crowded the lower slopes. Then the leafy trees began, their riot of colors slowly dying as the mountain climbed. Where the leaves were already gone, snow dusted the ground, softening the harsh lines of the steep incline, undulating along the flanks.

They crossed where the water streamed over the pebbled riverbed. Grim hoisted her onto the horse. Ruddy tossed his head but accepted her in the saddle. He swung up behind her and urged the horse into the cold water.

On the far side the mountain towered, the slope brushing against the single drapery of evergreens.

The opposing shore wasn't as wide as it had appeared. Grim lowered her to the cobble-covered beach then jumped down. Ruddy shook like a dog casting off rainwater.

Since they couldn't climb the steep slope, they followed the curving shore, moving ever upstream.

They rounded one bend after another. The mountain kept rising. Gradually, it stepped back to the river, narrowing the watery expanse, gentling its slope as they rounded its flank. On the far side, the one they had left, the mountain's shoulder plunged to a narrow gully. Muddy water gushed out, pouring into the river, the silty color gradually mixing with the clear. The next mountain climbed just as steeply, an impenetrable wall they couldn't have descended.

Up ahead, the shore narrowed, but a wooded island split the river. Riverside, the water rolled from a bend. Mountain side, it swirled and eddied, catching storm wrack in its undulating banks.

The big chestnut stopped. Grim tugged the reins, but the horse refused to advance. As soon as the Rho released the tension on the reins, Ruddy backed several steps, snorted, and tried to back further.

Orielle ventured ahead. She scanned the looming mountain, wondering if Grim knew of a trail to take them above the river and up the mountain. She saw no switchback trail in the dense forest.

She glanced back. Ruddy refused to advance. Grim gripped the reins beneath the bridle bit and held the horse's head down. Waiting for the debate's winner, she studied the island with its spruces and other evergreens crowded on the leeward end, growing more sparsely where the water constantly gnawed at the shore.

On the island, the headmost tree had recently lost its battle against the encroaching water. It had fallen athwart the river, the treetop swept clean of needles, the bare branches weathered grey by the bleaching sun. The trunk lay across old wrack piled against slabs of rocks. The root ball stretched pitiful fingers that had lost their grip when enough soil swept away. Moss and grass had seeded in the earth clinging to the roots.

Something moved on the other side of that root tangle.

After another glance at Grim and his horse, she continued, keeping her eyes on the island.

The something was a creature, crouching peasant-style. Its back was rounded as it hunched over something on the ground.

Another creature crouched alongside, its back also to her. And another. The fourth knelt opposite. It crammed something in its mouth. Gobber, feeding. They wore tattered clothing, something she didn't remember from the night battle.

She froze. A fifth one was on hands and knees, its face buried in peeled open flesh.

As she watched, a sixth gobber crept from the trees and knelt beside the fourth. It stretched out a claw-tipped hand. The third reached across and knocked that hand away.

The gobber's shift let her see what fed them. Dappled grey flesh.

She backed a step.

And the fourth one looked up from the hunk of meat. Red round eyes narrowed. It jabbered.

The other gobbers turned.

As soon as they saw her, they jumped to their feet and ran to the island's shore.

And the gobbers waiting in the trees crept forward to take their turn, feeding on Ghost.

Backing toward Grim, Orielle watched the gobbers dip feet into the running river only to back away. One of them jabbered and pointed downstream. They ran back into the trees. She didn't see them cross from island to the opposing shore, but they quickly appeared. They flew along the narrow shore, hopping from boulder to boulder, scrabbling over fallen trees, ducking through the laurel, with a speed unexpected from such stunted creatures.

She reached Grim. He was scanning the densely forested slope. Ruddy had splayed his feet. His eyes showed white. He shivered. Did the horse sense what had happened to Ghost?

"Come on." Grim headed for the steepest slope.

The horse followed before she did. She watched the single stream of gobbers running for the ford. The water had swirled above Ruddy's knees. The creatures shouldn't be able to cross—unless they could swim.

Then she saw a taller figure drop down to the shoreline. Two gobbers tumbled to a stop as he straightened. He wore hide trousers but no shirt. Golden hair straggled over his bare shoulders. A golden pelt covered his broad chest. Long claws revealed his partial shift.

The wyre looked across the river. Blue, blue eyes snared hers.

She'd thought Grim killed him. Now she knew the blonde wyre that they'd buried under the rocks had lacked the kiss of the sun that graced this one.

A second wyre landed beside him. She recognized this one, too. She'd fought him before Grim killed the other. He'd retreated then.

A third jumped to the shore. The gobbers squealed and fled.

And the sun-kissed wyre smiled.

She ran.

~ 14 ~

Arms crossed to shield her face, Orielle plowed through the spruces into which Grim and his horse had disappeared. In that labyrinth of evergreens, he had found a single entrance to another thready deer trail that wound up the slope.

She thought of the wyre heading for the ford, and she plunged into the trees.

At a switchback he waited. He silently pointed her along the slope, abandoning the beaten path for the maze of low-limbed spruces. "Hide," he whispered. "Remember your scent."

She swept heavy spruce over her cloak and headed into the trees. She glanced back when he slapped the horse's rump. Tail flicking, Ruddy lunged along the deer trail.

And Grim dropped down, returning to the shore.

She bit her lip, wanting to help fight the wyre. He had experience, though; he had deliberately brought her into the trees and told her to hide.

Maybe she could ambush the wyre who tracked her. For some *would* come after her. Grim had warned her of that, the wyre habit of attacking on two fronts.

She threaded through the trees, easing her way past branches that didn't want to give. The slope dictated when she had to climb up or down. She crossed downed trees. Several ells beyond she came upon a recent slide, tumbled earth with sun-baked clods creating a shallow bowl.

Crossing the slide would expose her to eager wolfish eyes. Kiting her skirts higher, she climbed to cross above the disrupted earth, going hands and toes when the slope angled sharply upward. She remembered Grim's trick of using wind to carry scent ahead. The breeze cooled her. She climbed and climbed then began angling to the mud slip.

Poking her head past a jutting tree branch, she eyed her ascent. The top of the slip was still feet above her. She needed to climb higher, for she wanted undisturbed trees as a shield. She withdrew—then saw movement downslope. She froze, eyes above the branch.

A man jumped onto the slide. Dried dirt slipped and skittered under him. He stepped more cautiously until he reached a slender tree torn out by the slide, its root ball thin and scraggly, its pyramid top pointing downslope. He climbed atop the trunk. Bare toes gripped the bark. Hands on hips, he surveyed the slide's descent. Then he turned and looked upslope. His chin lifted. His nostrils flared.

Orielle hastily mixed wet soil with her disguising scent of spruce.

The wyre continued to scan the upward slope.

She didn't recognize him. His dark hair caught no gleam from the dreary light. His brow was thick, nearly meeting above a flat nose. His shirt was loose, flapping in a breeze contrary to hers. His fingers sprouted no claws, but she was certain he was a wyre.

He turned and spoke. She was too far away to hear, then his gaze returned to sweep the upward slope. He pointed. The angle was near to her.

Cautiously, she turned her head but saw nothing that should have caught his attention. The earth was a mix of dry and moist. A mundane creature had bounded across the dirt during the night. At the top of the slide, the forest litter dripped over the edge, tugged out of place but still clinging. Leafy trees above the released ground leaned precariously, downward roots exposed, yellow leaves shivering in the vagrant breeze.

Her vagrant breeze.

She sent the Wind drifting across the undamaged slope, let it play among the leaves, then released it.

And looked back at the wyre.

A wolf had joined him.

The creature's body came to the man's waist. It stood on the dirt, larger than any wolf she'd seen on trips to the deep north of Mont Nouris. A greyed pelt covered the barrel chest. Silvered eyes shined with greeny power.

A shifted wyre.

The wolf put his paws on the fallen tree, lifted its snout to the air. Ragged ears flicked forward.

Orielle added more dirt to her scent.

The wolf dropped back to the ground and started a cautious venture upslope.

A shout drifted up; a howl followed it. Two wyre.

Behind her, above her, came an answering howl and another shout. Two more. They had to be tracking Grim.

She froze, scarcely daring to breathe.

The grey wolf leaped to return to the trees. The soil it abandoned slid a little, tumbling down, exposing richly dark earth. The fallen tree rolled a little. The unshifted wyre rocked and flung out his arms to maintain his balance.

The wolf didn't look back. With a flick of its hoary tail, it disappeared into the trees.

She listened, heard nothing, tried to snare Wind from behind her to catch whatever happened—and heard another shout. Two more followed it. Something crashed through the branches, snapping the ones that didn't give. A high-pitched yelp broke. Then a howl lifted. The sound shivered down her spine. It sounded nothing like the wolves on that long-ago trip.

Snuffling behind her warned of an approach.

The wolf, on her trail.

She jerked magic—then remembered Grim's brief account of Saithe's death.

She stared at the orb of power, shaped for a spell and useless against a wyre.

But not against land.

The man still balanced on the fallen tree.

She flung the orb at the dislodged soil beneath the trunk. The power blasted over the ground.

The wyre leaped—but the ground had started a gradual slide, taking the breadth of the exposed dirt with it. He landed on slowly shifting earth. Then the slide gained speed. The tree slid past him. The dirt under him tumbled then collapsed, and no outspread arms saved his balance. He flailed then scrabbled at the dirt pouring around him.

And the slope above joined the slide, more dirt and rocks and the yellow-leaved trees crashing down with a glassy roar. He lost his balance and fell. The earth submerged him.

The slide poured downslope, reaching the old end and tumbling past, pushing trees ahead of it, heading for the shore.

Then the earth slowed. Rocks rolled across the top, but the soil piled and packed on itself. And she could see the river, stained with dirt.

The distant shouts came again, one then the next, a single howl, all farther away.

Turning to face the oncoming wolf, Orielle snared Air for her hands. It rushed through the trees, bending the branches around her, snatching her hair into a whirlwind.

The wolf came, nose to ground. He heard the Air. His head lifted; those greeny silver eyes narrowed. His mouth opened, almost like a grin.

The Air thrust him backwards. He reared up, pawing at the palpable force. She twisted her hands, and the Air spiraled, twisting the wolf in a vortex. The grey-fuzzed muzzle lifted. He tried to howl, but the spiraling wind gusts whipped his head around.

Over the wind's rush came the sharp crack of breaking bones.

The wolf stopped flailing. His head lolled.

She pulled the Air back, half afraid the wolf would spring, half afraid she had killed him.

The shifted wyre fell to the ground. He lay limp, a child's discarded toy on the forest litter. As she watched, his form blurred, fuzzed. She blinked. He changed, returning to his man-shape.

Orielle climbed from the protecting spruce branches. When she straightened, the wyre was wholly man—and wholly dead, his head canted severely over.

Wind teased her as she ventured closer. When she stood over the wyre, she saw his eyes rolled back. He lay naked on the needles and leaves discarded by the trees for years. He was old, a grey-haired man still in his prime.

She bent and pushed his shoulders, not quite believing he was dead. He lolled to his back, but his head didn't move.

Bile rose in her throat.

She turned and vomited. When her stomach emptied and her gut stopped heaving, she felt shaky and sweaty.

And he was just as dead.

As Grim would be.

The shouts, the howls no longer came. The wyre had tracked their prey and found him. Two and two. Four against Grim, two of those shifted.

And the gobbers, if they had dared to follow.

Her stomach heaved again as she recalled what the stunted creatures had done to Ghost and would do to the next prey they brought down.

That would not happen to Grim.

Orielle sped downslope, using the Air to push branches out of her way. When the slant became too steep for a safe descent, she angled for the trail. And then she ran.

Four against him. She had the Air, just as Grim did. While the wind teased around her, it lacked the force of what she'd whorled around the dead wyre. She would have to be clever, the way she'd been with the unshifted Wyre. Grim had his sword. He always threw a readied spell before using steel. Did he not wield the Air with ease?

Four against two. They needed better odds.

Sangrior—but Volk claimed the Sword Knight would not come if she called.

She slid the last feet of the trail and burst upon the shore. And saw nothing.

But heard steel.

And growls.

She ran upshore and found the slide.

The dirt had tumbled into the river, partially damming the water even as the water eroded the fresh soil blocking its progress.

She glanced upslope.

The bulk of the slide had crushed the laurel then stopped. Large rocks peppered the richly brown soil, the color of Grim's clothes.

Orielle scrambled over the piled-up mud nearest the water. Clods slipped under her, but momentum carried her up.

And she saw the battle beyond. A knot of fighting, with a center that flashed metal. Two men leaped back from the sweep of steel while a wolf lunged in to attack Grim's back. The wolf went tumbling as the two other wyre sprang in, attacking with claws.

A white-shirted man crawled over the pebbly sand, trying to reach the water.

From the top of the mud slide, she pushed Air at the shifted wolf. It gusted over him. The wolf flattened against the ground. When it swept past, brilliant blue eyes turned her way. He sprang up. And barked.

One of Grim's attackers fell back. Following that barked order, he turned toward her.

She glanced at the shifted Prime, for those blue eyes could only belong to him. Then she jumped from the muddy heap to the shore, pebbles grinding under her boots.

When she straightened, the half-shifted wyre was nearly on her. His eyes were greeny silver, like the wyre she had killed. Eldritch green tipped his claws, giving them a poisonous tint. He snarled. His face blurred, his snout lengthened, then the shift vanished, but she'd glimpsed the wolf he would become.

Thrusting both hands, she threw Air. He staggered then grinned. "Lost hold of Air, little wizard?"

"I killed two of your friends," she retorted. "I'll kill you."

The fighting around Grim became fiercer, the men grunting, the wolf snarling. He half-turned—and she saw the Prime leap for Grim's back.

The wyre missed his leap for the Rho's neck. His teeth snagged his shoulder and clung, worrying at the leather jack and the chain mail that protected flesh and tendons and bone. The other wyre drove past Grim's distracted guard. They fell to the shore, Grim underneath, a tangle of leather, flesh, and fur.

The wyre turned back to her and laughed. "Ready to die, little wizard?"

She flung her one Fire spell, designed to light fuel in a hearth. The flames exploded on his nose. The spell had no force and all wyre knew that wizardry couldn't harm them. But he recoiled from the searing heat. It blasted over him and winked out.

Orielle dove in a bare second behind the spell. She jabbed her belt knife into the side of his neck. The sharp blade of good Fae steel slipped past the ringed esophagus. Blood spurted then gushed as she twisted the blade.

He swiped, claws tangling in her spelled cloak.

She sprang back, her knife embedded in his neck. And the wyre dropped to his knees, the eldritch sorcery in his eyes fading, his claws receding.

She darted in to jerk her blade free. It stuck. She worked it loose while his clawless hands fumbled at her. Once her knife was free, she headed for Grim.

He was on his knees. The Prime wolf circled him, kept at bay by a dagger of gleaming Fae steel. The other wyre lay motionless.

The wounded one had reached the river, but he lay face-down in the swift water.

The wolf darted in. Grim jabbed with the dagger. Then he twisted, screamed, and the dagger dropped from his hand.

But the wyre didn't leap upon him. He turned to Orielle.

And his shape blurred.

~ 15 ~

Grim writhed and fell, thrashing with a pain she didn't understand. His convulsing body ground over the pebbles.

Watching the shifting wyre, Orielle edged around him then halted as the transformation ended. The Prime rose from a crouch. Naked, he blocked her advance to Grim.

"Well, pretty wizard, we meet again." He stretched out a hand. Long as a weapon, yellow claws extended from his man-shaped fingers. His voice held no threat, but those claws did. "You invited me to play. Here I am."

Grim's scream cut her answer. She stared at his writhing body then jerked her gaze back to the Prime.He had closed the distance between them. "Stay back," she warned and flung up a hand. Power ringed it, spinning faster and faster.

He laughed. "Wizardry can't hurt the wyre."

Grim squirmed. Those storm-grey eyes fastened on her, then his face contorted, matching the twisting of his body. Pain ripped from his throat.

"What's wrong with him? You bit him. Is he transforming?"

The amusement vanished. "He's dying. Rho don't transform. A wyre bite poisons them. But you, pretty wizard, you'll transform." When he smiled this time, she saw his elongated canines. His tongue flicked out. "I'll enjoy your taste."

Sangrior was lost to her. She didn't hesitate. "Volk. Volk! Volk, come to me!"

By her third calling of the Kyrgy knight's name, the wyre scowled. When thunder clapped, he flinched. When the light flashed and the knight appeared, he sprang.

Volk thrust him backwards. His sword flashed. Violet ice rimed the blade.

The Prime snarled. "Lady Bone allies to this wizard?"

"The Lady needs no ally. Your sorceress crosses the lines. She tampers with the gobbers, who belong to my Lady. She allowed your hunts, yet you kill for the pleasure of it. She takes one of my Lady's riders without recompense."

"The gobbers accept the rule of the sorceress."

"They cannot make that choice. All the creatures of this Wilding are my Lady's."

"Whether they want her rule or not?"

Volk did not attempt to control his expression. He scowled openly, deeply. "They do not make that choice. They are my Lady's."

"And this wizard?"

"The bargain between my Lady and this wizard supercedes the death your sorceress will give. Only when the pact between them ends may the sorceress have her."

The wyre shook his head. His pelted chest thrust forward. "Not so, slave. We are old enemies, Frost Clime and Enclave. Your Lady must cede to us." He grinned at Orielle and once again extended his hand. "Come to me, pretty wizard. Come and die."

Volk stepped before her. "She has my guard."

"Then face death, knight who cannot live." The Prime crouched. Fangs crowded his unshifted mouth. His claws extended, reaching the length of a short sword.

Laughing, Volk swung his blade, cutting Air with a hiss.

With a growl, the wyre dropped to all fours and shed man-shape. A quick blur, faster than the other wyre, and he became a large wolf. He sprang.

The storm-violet sword slashed upward. The wyre yelped as Volk's blade cut into his front leg. He fell short of the knight. Blood splashed onto the pebbles. He crouched on his haunches then sprang again, using his back legs for power. Volk thrust upward.

The blade pierced the wyre's chest. Momentum thrust the knight back several steps. With the screech of a man, the Prime writhed on the blade, then strength left his body. His weight forced the sword down, to the shore.

The limp body blurred, and a man lay lifeless, the violet blade piercing his chest.

When Volk pressed a foot to the man's chest, Orielle sped past him and fell to her knees beside Grim, curled into a ball and shuddering as the wyre's poison worked into him.

The Kyrgy cleaned his blade in the river. Then he came to stand over her. "I will not ask how you learned my name. The suffering has lasted long enough."

"You killed the Prime."

He had looked to count the other dead wyre. Black eyes swiveled back to her. "Another will take his place and his strength from the pack. Nine remain. They will hunt you, Not-Wizard."

"Six remain. I killed two up on the mountain. And we buried the seventh, remember?"

Lifted eyebrows were the only evidence of his surprise. He had returned to the guise of marble knight with icily controlled emotions. "A good accounting then."

Grim screamed. Pain spiraled through him.

"Can you help him?"

"I have no powers of healing, not for a Rho poisoned by wyre bite."

"Can Lady Skuld help him?"

"You have her name, too?"

"Please."

"What will you give, Lady Aiwaz?"

"I will not let him die. Can she help him?"

"No." Grim growled the word. "No. Let me die." Then the poison screwed through him and tore out a scream.

"Volk!"

"You will create a great debt to the Lady. She will have you."

"So be it. Call her."

He did nothing. But a flash as quick as lightning blinded her. When she blinked, Lady Bone stood beside her knight. Sangrior stood at her shoulder. He didn't stand as straight, his shoulders were not as squared. He carried no sword.

Blood oozed from cuts on his neck, looking black against the marble whiteness of his flesh.

Orielle didn't curtsy. She stood and tossed back her head. She pointed to Grim. "Can you heal him?"

"No greeting?" the Lady asked, but she smiled, for she knew she held the higher hand. Gliding forward, her white gown trailed behind her, like a wraith crossing. The pebbles didn't crunch at her weight.

She stopped at Grim, a rocking ball that twisted on the ground. "No," he ordered, the word grating. Then the Lady stepped over him and reached Orielle.

"I will need his name."

"I do not know it."

White eyelids closed over black eyes then opened slowly. "Truth. He did not trust you enough. For a Rho to trust a wizard, that would be a great thing. The Rhoghieri of the Haven will not so easily fall into alliance with the Enclave."

Politics didn't matter to her. "Can you heal him? Will you?"

The Lady's long claws grazed Orielle's chin then traced over her jaw, lifting to touch her cheek then her temple. She stood still and let the Kyrgy examine her. This close, she saw that the Lady's eyes were not wholly obsidian. The sclera was black rather than white, but the iris was colored a deep blue.

"Do you bargain for him, Not-Wizard?"

She met those midnight velvet eyes without wavering. Grim groaned. She wanted to kneel beside him and take the pain away. *Am I bargaining for him? He would refuse it. So the bargain is for me, to know that he is in this world, not dead, not cold, not lost to Neothera.*

"For me. I bargain his healing for me."

The claws tightened to pinpricks. Lady Bone's smile widened, revealing the sharpness of her fangs. "You surprise me. Wizards do not count Rho lives as important."

"I do. Did you prophesy then, when you called me *Not-Wizard*?"

"You gain wit. What bargain will you make?"

Her gaze swiveled to Sangrior. What tithe had he paid for his help to her? What tithe would Volk pay? How did she create a bargain that did not leave her indebted to Lady Skuld for centuries? "I do not seek to become one of your Kyrgy slaves."

Volk lunged to her side. A knife she hadn't expected pressed to her throat. "Shall I kill her, Lady?"

Sangrior lifted a hand. Red marks, jagged like lightning, had joined the white scars on his arm. "Lady, she does not understand."

Lady Bone released Orielle and touched fingers to Volk's blade. "Stand down, my love. This Not-Wizard is no threat to me."

"Lady, she insults you."

"From ignorance," Sangrior flashed.

"Did I not cleanse the hold this Solsken has on you, my knight?" She returned to his side. Her touch to Sangrior's cheek seemed tender, but three thin lines of red opened.

He didn't flinch. His gaze dropped from Skuld's and fastened on the shore. "Lady, you know all. She has no hold on me, not now."

"You defend her when you should be wholly mine."

"I am wholly yours," he swore, "from my first ride to this day. But the Solsken is ignorant."

"Does anyone go into a bargain knowing the whole of it?" She tapped his chin then gave him her back. "Have you forgotten, Not-Wizard? I am Kyrgy. These knights, all my riders, they are not slaves. They choose to be with me."

"They choose between death and the limited life you offer, for however many years you extend it. Yet they are bound to you until you use them up. They are your slaves."

"Do you see them escaping?" Then Skuld blinked. Her smugness faded. Unspoken was Saircuista, who had broken her bargain with the Lady and allied with a sorceress.

Orielle knelt beside Grim. His skin looked waxy, the veins stark beneath the flesh. Red-rimmed eyes fastened on her. He shuddered when she touched his shoulder. The bleeding had stopped, but the poison wracked him.

"No," he mouthed. Then his head strained to one side as he fought another wave of poison. Veins stark on his temples, pulsing, feeding the wyre venom to every part of his body. "Not this," he gasped.

The Lady scowled. She extended a hand—and Grim froze, locked in that painful ball.

"What have you done?" Orielle ran her hands over his locked muscles. His mouth had opened to scream, but nothing emerged, neither sound nor breath. His body no longer shuddered. "What have you done?"

"Given us a space of time. He will not distract you while we bargain."

She scrambled to her feet, but she could not drag her gaze from him. "Is he still in pain?"

"Whatever pain he felt at the moment I stilled him. He lives. He hears. He feels nothing more than that moment. The wyre venom will advance. That I cannot stop, not unless I stop his heart."

"It is cruel."

"Your bargaining is cruel, for his pain will increase until he dies. Come, end this quibbling over slaves, and tell me what you will."

She knew only one thing that Lady Skuld wanted and only one way to limit it. "You wish a wizard as a rider. Very well, I will ride three times with you, three moons for the Hunt. I will do this, Lady, after I serve my mission for the Enclave. I must serve the Enclave. I offer these three rides. I do not make a bargain."

A predatory smile revealed those sharpened teeth. "Do you think to avoid a choice?"

Hands on hips, she tossed back her hair and tilted her chin. Sangrior's eyes followed the glint of her sun-kissed hair. Volk scowled. He fingered the knife that he still had not sheathed. He would rather she blindly agree to the Lady's terms. She narrowed her eyes at him, letting him know that she had his mark. Then she looked back at Skuld. Facing the Kyrgy, seeing her very alien appearance, something shrank inside her, but she gathered all the arrogance that Enclave wizards wore like a spelled cloak. "Someday, Lady, your choice may loom before me. But that day is not this one."

The Lady pursed her lips, hiding her teeth. Her slitted eyelids hid the blackness of her eyes. "How much of your life will this mission consume?"

"I come to recruit Rhoghieri for the war at Iscleft Citadel. I come to renew the alliance between the Enclave and the Haven."

"You are young for such a mission."

"Nevertheless."

"And your ArchClan gives to you this power? You are highly regarded. Your presence among my riders will impress others."

She didn't correct the Lady. Better that she never learn Orielle had volunteered in her sister's stead. Better that she never learn Orielle was the weak Not-Wizard that the Lady had named her, a Not-Wizard beginning to suspect the ArchClan never intended this mission to succeed. A lie of omission was still a lie. Better to have fewer lies between herself and a Kyrgy. "You called me Not-Wizard. That is a truth greater than you know. I have not passed my wizard trials. Will you accept the offer of a Not-Wizard to ride the Hunt thrice with you in exchange for healing this Rho?"

"Volk."

At his snapped name, the knight sheathed his knife. His cold gaze swept Orielle then dismissed her. Sangrior wanted to speak but dared say nothing. "Lady." Volk bowed. "What have you?"

"Will this Not-Wizard be a worthy rider?"

"She killed two wyre using only elemental power. She may be ignorant, but she learns. She fears, but she fights. She does not run from danger."

"You have impressed another of my knights. No doubt, this is how you won the Rhoghieri to you. No doubt, this is what my Sangrior sensed in you when he gave you a name of power." Her gaze cut to the subdued knight. "A name given without permission. But he learns."

She flicked her fingers. Sangrior flinched then straightened. His gaze fastened beyond Orielle. His jaw tightened. His shoulders squared. He became again the sword knight of that first encounter.

"So, Aiwaz Solsken will not bargain with me, but she proposes an offer in exchange for a healing. A healing this Rho needs. Look you. His veins blacken with the wyre venom."

The jutting veins in Grim's temples writhed black under his waxy flesh. Sweat beaded and dripped, a faint runnel of red.

"Tell me, how much time do you think three rides will consume?"

That was indeed a question. She was wary of naming any specific time in human terms, for the Kyrgy would bend the time to fit her reckoning of it. The Fae did not track time as the mundane world did. How much more different would be a Kyrgy view of days and months and years? She had risked much just in saying *season*.

Time.

Or event.

Ah, that was an idea. "Three Moons or until you partake of evil."

The Lady gave her laugh, that jangling tinkle that grated edged nerves. "You parse words very carefully. Name an evil."

Name anything, and the long-lived Lady would avoid that thing—even if it were her heart's sweetest desire—until Orielle died waiting and watching.

"What do you call evil?" she retorted.

Again the laugh, exposing the tips of her teeth. "Oh, I will enjoy having you as a rider. Volk spoke truth when he said you fear but fight anyway. My friends will think you a peculiar rider. They will envy me."

Lady Skuld had friends? Then Orielle realized only other Kyrgy would be the Lady's friends, not her knights, not her riders.

Peculiar, yes. Jealous? *Yes*. And desperate to have what Lady Skuld had managed to win, a wizard of the Enclave.

"I will ride three times or until you do evil. Your friends may envy you for having a rider who is Enclave-trained."

But the Lady's expression darkened. "Enclave-trained. You abide by the wizard tenets."

"I am bound to them."

Thunder boomed, so loudly it shook Orielle's bones. It drowned the Lady's words. Sangrior recoiled. Even Volk took a step away from the Kyrgy.

"Bound by or abide by?" Lady Skuld demanded. Her eyes glittered.

"Bound."

This time the thunder cracked open the sky for a jagged fork of lightning. A distant tree split in two, the heartwood flaming from the intense heat.

"I cannot accept someone already bound." The Lady's voice crackled like the fire consuming the tree's heart. "Give the Rho to me."

"He is not mine to give. I can only offer you what I can do."

Her eyes slitted. "Perhaps he is not mine to heal. My knights chose to ride with me rather than go with Death, a lady more terrifying than me. Perhaps I cannot heal him, but I can extend his life. Give him to me."

"No. I will not let him live in agony, even the half-life you offer."

"Volk will tell you he lives a whole life."

"Will Sangrior say that? Can either knight live without the sun?"

"They stand now in the sun."

"But how long can they bear it? If you cannot heal the Rho, then be done, Lady. Though it grieves me, I will ease his passage." She looked at his locked body. Sand and grit caked his leathers. Black venom tracked through his veins, rooted through his skin, invading the whole of his body. "What I learned of fighting and courage, I learned from him. He does not deserve this agony." With nothing else to add, her arguments emptied out, she looked back at the Kyrgy.

Lady Skuld studied her, then she dipped her chin. "You are clever, Not-Wizard. You fear and fight, with power and with words. I would relish your riding with my company. In all my years I have never heard of a freely given offer to ride. This alone gives a peculiar distinction." She drew a symbol in the Air. For long seconds it hovered, black lines in a complicated swirl, before it wisped into smoke and drifted away.

The fire in the burning tree died.

A wind kicked up, blowing their cloaks around, black and storm-purple and glacial blue. It caught Orielle's hair and tangled it in the air. It lifted the knights' silvery hair and streamed it behind them.

It did not touch the Lady.

"You are bound by wizard tenets. I am bound by Kyrgy law. I accept your offer, for it is freely given and worth much more than any choice. But I cannot heal him without a bargain. That is Kyrgy law. The bargain demands a risk. What will you risk, Not-Wizard?"

Cold ice cracked through her. Here, in this now, she came closer to death than all the fights with the wyre. Lady Skuld remained expressionless. Her black eyes, those knife-sharp features, the vee'd smile, all revealed that she thought Orielle's choices limited. For Grim's healing, she had nothing to risk but her own life.

She stared at him. Locked against pain, he could offer no help, although his stormy eyes burned into hers, desperate to repeat the *No* that the Lady had silenced with her spell.

She needed common ground with the Lady. What did she want that the Lady also wanted? It must be something that the Lady could not give herself. Skuld had no lack of power, but perhaps more Kyrgy laws prevented her actions.

Had Grim given a clue, when he argued with Volk last night? He'd said the sorceress brought her wyre to prey on the innocent creatures of the Wilding, a condemnation that the Lady should have acted on but had not. He'd said the Rho kept the alliance with the Lady. What had prevented the Lady from wiping out the sorceress, especially when Saircuista defected to the sorceress?

She didn't know. She suspected Skuld would not tell her. But Orielle could still use it.

Common ground. Wyre gone. Sorceress gone.

"I will rid the Wilding of the sorceress and her wyre."

"No, Aiwaz Solsken," Sangrior burst out, proof that Orielle had guessed what the Lady needed but could not herself do or command her riders to do.

Lady Skuld's hand jerked. He turned, folding into himself, then a flashing door opened, and he vanished.

His scream died when the light winked out.

The Lady flicked her hand. Volk came to her side. He watched the Kyrgy. "Tell her," she commanded.

He bowed. He didn't look at Orielle. "The sorceress is greater than you, Not-Wizard. She will kill you."

"If the sorceress has me at the point of death, then Lady Skuld, you can have my life. I will take this risk for you."

Volk reared back. Ice blasted around Skuld. The shards pricked Orielle's exposed flesh and left a rime on Grim's curled-up body.

"I am Kyrgy," she shouted, and the words struck like a blizzard wind, colder than cold, filled with snowy death. "You are mundane. You are *naught* before me. Do you think I cannot rid this sorceress from my Wilding?"

She sparked her only spell of Fire. The tiny flame bent against the cold then grew brighter. "I know you can." She lifted her voice, but the roaring wind died before her last word, and her call sped to the river and beyond. Lowering her voice, she held out the little flame. "But you have not removed her. I know Saircuista's defection drives a wedge into your circle of riders. I can remove this wedge."

Volk started at her revelation. Had he not expected her to share his words with the Kyrgy?

"Only Saircuista's death can remove it." Frost dripped from her words.

"Or the death of the sorceress."

The temperature rose.

"My knights cleave to you, Solsken. Perhaps their loss of the sun gives you an advantage I had not anticipated."

"Humans have frailties. We are not purpose-driven Fae. We are not Kyrgy of the Wilding."

"But you would serve me, for a season?"

"Is this offer acceptable?" Orielle retorted, needing proof.

"I wish more."

"I wish less. We both lose; we both gain."

"So be it." The Lady stepped to Grim's curled body. "I will heal this Rho. You will rid my Wilding of this sorceress and her wolfen. You offered time with me, Not-Wizard. You will ride three hunts at my side. You will see how a Kyrgy keeps the wizard tenets." Then she clapped her hands.

Blue light sparked where her hands had struck together. It shaped into a sliver, like the double-horned crescent moon. Then the center bulged, growing into the Womb Moon, fat with potential, dappled silver like the Moon that would oversee any Hunt through the Wilding.

Lady Skuld spun the gibbous orb. The light floated toward Grim and hovered over his body. She twisted her hand, much as Orielle had, up on the mountain, and the orb dropped onto his locked body. The light increased, blinding them. He screamed, the power unlocking his body, and the light streamed over him, cocooning him.

Then the Lady dropped her hand. The light poured into him and disappeared.

And Grim lay straight and painless on the sandy grit.

He scrambled to his feet. Blading his body, he blocked Orielle's view of the Lady. "What have you done?"

"Aiwaz Solsken saves your life, Rhoghieri." Volk stared at his Lady, she who was all his world.

"At what cost?" Grim demanded.

"Not the cost you think. She bargained neither your life nor her own. Three moons she will ride with me." Lady Bone shook her head, her hair streaming over her shoulders, a thick silver cascade over the clinging white gown. "Will you ride beside her, Rho?"

"I will."

She laughed, the high-pitched tinkle that set nerves on edge. "She said that she learned fighting from you. Will you help her rid my Wilding of this sorceress and her wyre?"

"Is that the bargain?" He fronted Orielle, and she couldn't look away from his intense eyes. As soon as she nodded, he gave his assent to Lady Skuld.

"And when the sorceress defeats you and you are on the point of death, will you give me your life? Just as she swore?"

"If she goes to you, then I go as well."

"Such devotion. May you inspire my own knights, Rho."

Lightning flashed. Thunder rumbled. Rain poured from the sky.

And Lady Skuld and Volk vanished from the beach.

~ 17 ~

"You should not have bargained with Lady Bone."

Orielle brushed a clot of sand from his sleeve as she hid from his searching gaze. "I weighed my choices. I considered what was most important to me." There, she'd dared her own admission, just as he had with Lady Skuld.

Grim didn't respond, turning away, and she deflated. He walked away, kicking stones on the shore. She hurried to catch up.

The big chestnut found them as they scaled the mountain, coming out of the trees. It must have waited in safety while they fought wyre and dealt a hard bargain with Lady Skuld.

The ride to the Haven passed without trouble. On the mountain's other side, they found another creek, clear and twisty. They followed the creek upstream and into a narrow gorge where the water roiled. The mountains stepped back, and the gorge opened to a wide valley, forested at its entrance, but Orielle caught a glimpse of cleared pasture before the trail dropped to run beside the slower waters.

A man leaped down from a tree and landed in their path. Expecting wyre, she jerked Air to her, then Grim's hand touched hers. He gave a shake of his head. So she studied the man who blocked their way.

He had Grim's dark hair and narrow features, but his eyes were muddy brown. He wore leathers and a green shirt but no mail. He carried a stave rather than a bladed weapon.

"Son of Holt," he greeted Grim. "Two years it's been."

"Son of Sourrect." Grim touched his forehead, a brief salute that the other returned. "Two years, three months, odd days."

The man grinned. "There'll be some not happy to see you."

Leaned against Grim's back, she expected he would tense. Instead, he chuckled. Grim, laughing!

"All to the good. Shake them up, change their minds."

The sentinel gave that curious lifted chin of agreement which she'd seen from Grim more than once. "And who is this golden lady?"

"Lady Galfrons, from the Enclave, come to parley with the Elder."

"Enclave." The word wiped away the welcome. The man glanced into the trees. She saw movement. No one revealed themselves, but she knew other sentinels watched, listened, waited, keeping the guard .

"Does Tobit still serve as Elder? I heard of a challenge."

"Four challenges, all defeated. This one's not the first to come from the Enclave," which was news to Orielle. "He'll give her a hearing. She's pretty enough."

"Like that, is it?"

Grim had lost his humor. She had tired of people focusing only on her appearance, including the wyre with his *pretty wizard*. "The Elder should listen to me because I'm from the Enclave and for no other reason."

The sentinel's eyebrows lifted. He gave a whistle. "Got a mind of her own, don't she?"

Disgusted with the assumptions, she dug her nails into Grim's side. The leather prevented damage, but since he'd shed his mail, he felt the prick of her anger. He shifted a little. "We had trouble with a wyre pack.

Killed seven. The six will be on the prowl."

He gave an appreciative whistle. "Precautions?"

"The usual."

The man stepped aside so Ruddy could carry them on. "We'll double our sentries. On you go."

Grim saluted.

The man's gaze bored into her back long after they passed. "What was that about?"

"Not here." The upward tilt of his head warned that others lurked in the trees.

"People can eavesdrop on rooms," she warned him.

"You don't know a Shield spell? I do if you can't."

The Shield, dropped over the conversation, would prevent any spy from reporting—unless the spy could read lips. She'd heard of spies who had that knack. The spell was tricksy but not too difficult, not like the linked wards that guarded a camp. A novice learned it then learned to expand it. She shifted behind him. He wanted her to use magic, then. He wanted others to know. Since she'd already admitted to multiple problems with her training, she confessed, "As long as it's just a few of us and not a big room."

"A Shield for two will work."

She leaned her head against his shoulder blade and wished this day were ended. She felt bone-deep tired, and diplomacy was before her, requiring as much caution as she'd used with the Lady. "I didn't know the Rho could work spells."

"The Rho don't. A Fae taught me."

"Using the elements?"

"Yes. Quiet now."

They emerged from forest into tilled soil. On the right, the harvested fields had thick stubble with turned soil at a distance. Hayricks dotted the opposing fields.

The cleared land revealed the waves and ripples of the surrounding mountains, earth formed like frozen water. Horses ran alongside a pole fence. Workers began to dot the fields, toiling to finish the harvest. A wagon rattled ahead of them on the straight road. Over Grim's shoulder she was smoke pillars, then their chimneys, and then a palisade surrounding the smoke and chimneys. At the corners and on either side of an open gate were towers, manned by archers.

The Haven looked like an armed camp. They trailed the wagon heading for the gate.

"The gate shuts at dusk. It doesn't open, for anyone, until the Elder gives the word. Don't be caught outside."

"Gobbers and the like?"

"Gobbers. The season before I left, a wyre pack besieged us. No danger at the moment."

"How do you know?"

"No flags."

As they rode into the village, she eyed the towers and the men watching from the parapet along the palisade.

People stared. Many lifted a hand in greeting, and Grim returned each one. Children ran behind his horse until a different game distracted them. The men who followed didn't turn aside.

The wagon turned onto a side lane. Grim guided Ruddy on, to an open square with a well. He swung a leg over the horse's neck and jumped down then reached up to help her dismount.

Three men came forward, calling the name *Holtson*, slapping his back, giving pats to Ruddy, and staring at her. Grim unburdened the horse by handing her the saddlebags and blanket rolls.

A tall man parted the encircling crowd. A vagrant wind tugged at his grizzled hair, curling over his square head.

One of the men talking with Grim saw the tall man. He sobered and gestured a warning. "Grim."

And her Grim answered to the name. No wonder he'd been surprised when she used it. If ever a name suited a personality—.

He swung around to meet the tall man who stood a half-head bigger and broader of girth. The man's wide grin didn't make up for his beady eyes, the color of a clear sky. And Grim didn't smile his welcome.

"Grim, son of Holt. You return. Do you come to face justice?"

"Justice? Are you saying I committed a crime? What crime, Tobit?"

"You left without permission, before we cleared the forest of wyre. You endangered the Haven."

The three men had fallen behind Grim, leaving Orielle beside him. She swung the packs off her shoulder and to the ground.

"We killed all thirteen of that pack. Did you suffer more attacks after I left? Brok, did you?"

The man who had first greeted him answered. "No, no more attacks."

"Luck that was." Hands on hip made Tobit looked larger than he was. "You had no right to leave."

"I had permission. My father granted it."

"Your father was dead, with a question of the cause of his death never answered. You did not swear loyalty to the next elder, to me. I gave no permission."

"So, it's a crime now to leave the Haven."

"It's a crime to leave the Haven in danger and a greater crime to refuse to answer questions about a death. You can disobey an Elder, but you will face consequences for it."

"I heard no edict rescinding my permission to leave. My plans were set for six weeks."

"You quibble. Justice still needs serving."

"Forget the crime," someone in the crowd called, and a murmur of agreement rippled around the square.

But the tall man gave a signal and three men came around him and headed for Grim. "You going to give us a battle?"

"Will I get a hearing?"

"We have justice here. I will hear your complaint, then you will hear mine."

Fair enough." Grim turned to Orielle. "Stick with Brok. You should have nothing to fear, but Brok will see you have a meal and a bed for the night."

"But you—."

"Brok will explain." Then he turned and met the three sentries.

She watched Grim led away. When she glared at Tobit, he grinned. "Now, what about you, pretty lady?"

.~.~.~.

The adventures of Orielle and Grim continue in **To Charm the Wind.**

TO CHARM THE WIND

Grim, an outcast from Iscleft Haven, is the keen steel that stands with Orielle against wraiths, wyre, gobbers, and the Dark Fae known as the Kyrgy.

Yet when they reach the Haven, the elder arrests Grim. The Haveners aren't interested in a renewed alliance with the Wizard Enclave.

Is her mission for the Enclave in vain?

Will she ever escape the Wilding?

~ 1 ~

Orielle watched the sentries lead Grim away. Head high, he walked between two burly men with a third leading the way to the gaol the elder had promised that Grim would endure.

The crowd opened as the men approached. No one spoke as Grim and his guards passed through. Then they closed quickly and stared at her, a stranger come to their Haven with Grim.

The pale blue eyes of the elder Tobit gleamed. His broad grin angered her. "Now, what about you, pretty lady?"

The naming implied she was no more than a play toy. Her wizard trials were a year away, but she'd fought wyre and gobbers in the past days. Fought and defeated them.

I am an emissary for the Wizard Enclave. I cannot begin my mission by antagonizing this elder.

Yet she refused to be anyone's play toy.

"The last person who called me *pretty lady* died. I killed his friends, too. They were wyre. Their bodies are at the recent slide by the river's bend—if the gobbers haven't feasted on them."

"Wyre?" the elder questioned as the word rippled through the people. "We have no wyre this far south."

"You have a lair of wyre and a sorceress who spelled them to shift out of Moon-Turn. We left their bodies by the river. You can look where the slide plunges down to the water. The eldritch green of sorcery will have faded. And the gobbers looked particularly hungry."

"We'll not be inspecting their remains in the dark," he blustered. The elder folded his thick arms over his broad belly. His scowl felt weighty, like a stomp from one of his big feet, planted wide. "If the gobbers eat them, we will find nothing but bones in the morning."

"True." Orielle didn't push hard, for she didn't want the elder erecting an impenetrable stubborn wall at her next point. "Can Rho not scan the remains and identify your natural enemy?"

Before the burly man could answer, a woman stepped forward. "I propose a compromise. We can easily check in the morning, Tobit. And our scouts can identify the bones of the wyre."

The elder's scowl pressed on the woman, but she didn't bow beneath it. Silver-haired and bony beside his bulk, she opened a door for his escape from the blind alley that his blustering had driven him into.

"A compromise." Orielle seized it, for she'd seen her own blind alley. "May I ask to attend Grim's hearing?"

"That's only for the people of this Haven. You have no place here."

A stir behind her, then Grim's friend Brok stepped beside her. "She's under my protection, Tobit. You heard Grim."

"He has no voice in our Haven. He abandoned us two years ago."

"Even so. She's under my protection."

"Do you even know her name?"

Orielle winced. Who had had time for introductions? Then she lifted her voice and stirred the Air to carry her words, wanting everyone to hear, not just the people at the fore of the crowd. "Greetings, Elder Tobit of Iscleft Haven, from the Wizard Enclave in Mont Nouris."

The air changed. A feral tang burdened it, those few words waking anger.

She could not tell the source of the anger, so she continued with the formal greeting she had rehearsed every day for the past weeks of her journey from Tres Lucerna, across the border of Mont Nouris, through the Lowlands, and into the Wilding to reach the Haven. "I am Orielle of Clan Galfrons, sent by the ArchClan to renew the alliance between wizards and Rhoghieri. Frost Clime threatens all of us." Her own spurt of anger compelled her to add, "which you will discover when you examine the wyre that Grim and I killed at the river's bend."

Murmurs rose from the crowd. Support or dissent, she couldn't tell. She hoped no one threw a rock.

Tobit's scowl increased. "You're Enclave." Two words, heavy as boulders.

If he'd said *wizard*, she would have had to lie. That was never wise. "Enclave and friend."

"Wizards don't make friends with Rho."

"I am friend with a Rho. I think I offered *you* alliance."

The retort drew laughter and removed that wild tang of hostility. A whiff of it remained, but diffused.

"She's honest," someone called. The crowd's mood shifted more, a palpable lightening of the heavy rancor.

"You going to enslave us to the Wizard Enclave, Tobit?"

The shout drew more laughter.

Tobit chose to laugh, but humor didn't glitter in his close-spaced eyes. "Not tonight," he shouted back.

People trickled away from the crowd, mothers with children on their hips, men with tools still in hand, youths with better interests than an Enclave visitor who didn't want to spark trouble when she came begging for Rhoghieri help.

And Orielle hadn't drawn the crowd. Grim had. His return had drawn the Haveners to him like the compass north drew a thin metal needle.

"Prove it," Tobit demanded. And the people who had slipped away came back, eager for any excitement to break up the monotony of days.

"I beg your pardon?" She hoped she had misheard.

"A polite wizard? I didn't know such a thing existed!" He relished the rippling laughter that time. "Prove it. You say you're Enclave. Wizards are proud of their spells. Show us one."

"Are you certain?" she asked as she scrambled through the spells she relied on.

"Afraid we won't be impressed, wizard?"

"I am a guest. I would not overstep."

Tobit swept his hands expansively. "You wouldn't endanger us. That's against the Wizard Tenets. Unless the uppity Enclave has changed in the last decades. Show us the element you wield. Show my people a reason to ally with the Enclave against the sorcerers and the wyre who threaten the Iscleft Citadel and Mont Nouris."

"And this Haven," she reminded, "for Grim and I killed seven of the pack. Six remain."

The hostility returned, pressing, as if the very Air had stony weight.

Tobit smiled still. His eyes still looked flat and hard. How many did he fool with that guise of humor? "We will wait. This Enclave wizard must need hours to access enough power for a single spell."

Orielle held out her hand, palm up. Power sparkled, a swirling vortex that danced in the heart of her palm before jumping from fingertip to fingertip. A simple spell, her first, learned when her power quickened. Prettiness rather than usefulness.

Tobit guffawed. "Child's play. You fought a wyre with that sweet sparkly spell, pretty lady? You're lying. No wizard spell can fight the wyre, let alone kill them. The least of us know that."

The taunt ran fire through her. Grim had reminded her that wizardry couldn't fight the shape-shifting wyre. Her brother Saithe, a great wizard, had died for that reason. He defended against a wyre attack with magic rather than elemental power. Grief had shaken her when Grim gave her that news. Yet Saithe's death had helped the warning to stick. Without it, she would have died when she made her own mistake with magic as she fought her first wyre.

Anger sizzled through her at Tobit's taunt. She shoved it down then tilted her head. She gave her most charming smile, well practiced in the courts of Tres Lucerna. "Oh. You want to know how I killed the wyre. You should have asked that. I used something like this. With rocks." She spun the vortex into a tight spiral. As it lengthened, it jumped from her hand to the paving stones of the well square, gathering grit and dust into its whirl. She shoved it at the elder.

The spell blasted him with gusty force. Tobit leaned into the wind. The power rippled over his flesh. His grizzled hair and beard streamed behind him. Then the wind rushed past him and leapt into the sky, tugging at pennants and laundry, snagging chimney smoke, and dissipating into the cold blue sky.

Tobit tilted back his head and roared with laughter. Several of the crowd joined him. Lips pursed, the white-haired woman beside him merely drew her hand down her long braid. Her gaze darted around the crowd to judge Tobit's mocking laughter then returned to Orielle.

When he'd laughed enough, the elder pointed at Orielle. "Prepare" was his only warning. He clapped his hands together.

A boom shuddered under her feet. Orielle staggered.

Brok grabbed her arm and hauled her back. The ground where she'd stood had cracked open.

"Is this a battle then?" Brok shouted while she gaped at the cracked ground. "You wanted proof of the lady's wizardry. You've given a taste of your power. I'd say we're done here."

"Far from done," Tobit declared.

"No."

A single word, spoken rather than shouted, but weighted like a boulder. It came from her left.

A gnarled staff leading his way, a man stepped from the crowd. He lacked the bulk that grounded the elder but shared the big man's grizzled hair and beard. "No," he repeated. "The lady wizard is a guest. We'll not have a battle on her first evening with us. She fought wyre to reach us."

"We have only her word—."

"Evidence we can easily check."

"I say she has this evening for rest," the white-haired woman proposed, ever seeking a compromise. "Time enough on the morrow to hear her mission."

"She's told it—." Then Tobit shut his mouth, and Orielle belatedly saw the crowd's agreement with the woman. The elder wisely didn't press his argument. "Is that the word of you all?"

The crowd shuffled then, close to her right, people edged back, a wave that separated one man from the common sea, younger than the other mentors. Brok's tight grip on her arm eased. "Fortis," he murmured. "Grim's friend and therefore yours."

Broad of shoulder but short and stocky, Fortis gave a cheeky grin, one she believed for the humor twinkled in his dark eyes. "Lillias and Surrect have the right of it. Done for now."

Tobit smiled, but his beady eyes narrowed to slits. "Done for now," he agreed. "All go about your business. A night and a day before us. Then we'll hear from Grim and this pretty lady."

"Night and day," the other leaders echoed. Lillias, Surrect, and this third one, Grim's friend, turned into the crowd and were quickly lost in the shuffling sea of bodies.

Tobit watched her. Orielle dared not smile, for she knew he would misinterpret her relief as glee. "My thanks," she called.

"Tomorrow," he said, more threat than promise. "After Grim's hearing. Brok, you offered protection." Then he walked away.

Standing at Tobit's back, a man with a patched eye laughed. The sound had an ugly edge. Three long slashes had scarred him from brow to cheek, above and beneath the patch. Scars from wyre claws. A wyre had taken his eye but not his life. He laughed again then followed the elder.

And Orielle added him to the tally of Haveners actively against her mission.

"Come," Brok snapped.

~ **2** ~

"This way." Brok headed off.

A man led away Grim's horse Ruddy, heading away from the palisade gate, in the same direction that the sentries had taken Grim..

Orielle peered that direction. The patched man had gone that away, trotting behind Tobit's rapidly disappearing bulk. One person lingered like her. A grubby boy, finger in his mouth. Then a woman called, and he hared off.

She hefted her pack and scooted after Brok.

As soon as she gained his side, her ears popped. He'd dropped a Shield over them, to prevent anyone overhearing their conversation. She hadn't known Rho could perform simple spells like that. She would need to revise her view of the Rhoghieri.

"Grim know what you are?"

"Of course."

"And he brought you *here*?"

"He's been fighting at Iscleft Citadel." Used to Grim's stride, she had no difficulty matching Brok's. Surely though, he should have known where Grim had spent the last couple of years? Since Grim had left under the dual shadow of his father's death and Tobit's reluctance to release him, maybe he hadn't sent any word to his friends. "Grim knows that Frost Clime is increasing its forces by using the wyre from the far north."

"And he knows you're a wizard?"

"About that," she started.

"Stay here," he ordered and veered away.

Orielle would have followed, but Brok hailed a man wearing dark leathers. She used the opportunity to look around the lane.

Higgledy-piggledy houses staggered along the lane. At a thick-trunked oak, the lane opened up. The tree had grown with the buildings constricting it, bending its branches upward against the walls. The oak's spreading branches grew against the upper stories. Past the oak, the houses crowded back in. A final house blocked off the lane, two doorways opening onto the lane.

Children played beneath the oak. Baking bread and simmering stew and strong spices scented the air, reminding her of the long days since her last good meal. Leaning out of upper windows, two women talked across the lane. Bright kerchiefs hid their hair. A cloth dangled from one woman's hand. As one, they looked at Orielle. She flashed a smile which they didn't return, choosing to duck inside their dwellings.

Brok's leather-clad friend headed into a side lane. Brok returned with a scowl as fierce as Tobit's.

Orielle didn't ask where they were bound. She waited until the Shield re-settled. "Where did I go wrong?"

"Where didn't you?" Before they reached the oak, he headed into a narrow allée that had hidden its existence from her corner view.

"I know the Rhoghieri are not friends of the Wizard Enclave—."

"Not even when we were allies."

"That man in the crowd, he said *enslaved*. Did the wizards enslave your grandparents and great-grandparents?"

"You get to the heart of problems, don't you?" He took another allée. If he continued deeper into the maze, she would be lost.

"How else am I to learn?"

He didn't answer.

But he kept the Shield in place, so she plowed ahead. "I made several mistakes, didn't I? I expected a council and a formal hearing. I expected a welcome."

He snorted. "In the Wilding?"

"I didn't expect gobbers or wyre or an Ice Huldra or—."

"Ice Huldra? You got lucky."

She remembered the ice-sharded wind, the trail vanished behind them, even Ruddy disappearing. "Both Grim and I did, yes."

Brok apparently took pity on her. His pace slowed, and he bothered to look at her. His muddy green eyes reminded her of someone, yet the memory didn't dredge up. "Look, you can be clever, or you can be smart. Grim doesn't abide fools, no matter how pretty they are."

"I know," she said ruefully. Grim had said something similar. "Have I damaged Grim's standing for that hearing?"

"Not that much. Maybe. You shouldn't have challenged Tobit."

"He called me a liar. I don't tell lies." Then her conscience bit deep and worried its fangs in her flesh. The Rho had called her *wizard*, and she hadn't corrected them, hadn't told them her wizard trials were months away. The Fae hated those who skirted the truth, omitting the words for an exact lie. *Be damned to lies, speak truth, and face any consequences*, one *comeis* had told her. She found it honorable but hard.

Her grandfather Malboys also deplored lies of omission. His sister, the ArchClan for the whole Enclave, used lies as a tactic, carefully selecting her truths and obscuring the facts.

Orielle had volunteered for this mission after her sister had backed out. Had the ArchClan hidden the truth about the mission by omitting necessary facts? Adorée hadn't warned Orielle when she volunteered, but she hadn't explained her reason for withdrawing.

Brok stopped at a door. He jiggled the latch, gave a kick to the bottom panel of the door where it butted against the jamb, then pushed it inward. Then he stepped back and bowed, his hand sweeping toward the opening. "My lady, welcome to my castle," he mocked.

Deep shadows crowded the interior. Orielle reminded herself that Grim trusted his friend Brok. She stepped inside.

Her few seconds of blindness lasted as Brok pushed past her. He found his way without difficulty. He scraped something, a long rasp, over and again. Minded of her lessons, she dropped her pack on the floor and kindled a light sphere.

The light revealed a tiny room and Brok on his knees at the hearth. He scraped his knife on a flint. "Here. Light this," he ordered then chunked sticks onto cold coals and heaped ash. He backed away as she approached.

Lighting a couple of sticks used simple magic. She added more tinder and kindling then rocked back to her heels and looked around the room.

Brok had dropped into a chair at the square table shoved against the angled wall. Above the table was a shuttered window He propped a booted foot on the other chair. That left two more chairs, both against the wall, one crammed into the still-shadowed corner and piled with ... clothes? An old quilt tacked up partially hid the narrow door to the interior. What lurked behind that door? More rooms? Between door and hearth was a tall chest. The hearth served as kitchen, with a lidded iron pot on the slab, a kettle on the out-swung arm of the pot-tinder, and an iron griddle for flatbreads and simple fry-ups. Between the hearth and the interior door was a tall chest.

She spied no candles. The bowl of the lantern on the mantle had a scant amount of oil. A ceramic jar snugged against it. On the table was a half-eaten loaf of bread, but it looked stale and hard. Her empty stomach wanted to make itself known.

For all its lack, the room was neither dusty nor cobwebbed. She saw no dirt, no moldy food, no filth. Its emptiness edged her nerves. Something was ... missing? Or didn't belong? She couldn't decide.

Rather than comment or question, she fed more sticks to the fire.

"Don't be using up all my wood. Unless you're going to carry in more."

She didn't look around, concentrating on stripping a splinter from a bigger log. "Where would I find more, if I were to carry it in?"

"Dirty your wizard-pure hands? I'll fetch it."

"My wizard-pure hands have carried wood for campfires as well as water from a stream. I've slept on the cold ground. I've nearly frozen when the rain put out my fire and soaked everything through."

"Next you'll tell me you walked all the way from Mont Nouris."

"No. Gobbers ate my horse."

He humphed, and she hoped that meant he was bending his stiff neck. If he didn't, it would break with pride. "Where did you meet Grim? Did you hire him away from the Citadel?"

"We met my second day in the Wilding. He saved me from a wyre." She didn't explain her misstep with the wyre, inviting the wolfen to *come and play*. She needed to score a point for her mission. "Grim wanted to send me back to the Lowlands. Then he realized we have common cause to come to the Haven, to enlist Rhoghieri in the battle—."

"The battle against Frost Clime," he finished with her. "I've got that pat. He wanted me to go with him two years ago."

"Why didn't you? The presence of Rho might have kept the sorcerers from enlisting more wyre from the north."

He was silent for so long that she thought she had stomped over more pride. A trick of the firelight cast shadows into his pale eyes, darkening the muddy brown. "I didn't want to," he finally admitted. "You can sleep in here. I'll show you where you can wash up, but don't go poking around back there." His thumb jerked at the tacked-up quilt.

"I have no wish to invade your privacy."

He didn't answer, just rested his head against the wall and shut his eyes. After seconds passed, Orielle returned to stripping another wick from a log.

A knock fell on the outer door. His eyes flashed open. He hadn't fallen asleep. He'd wanted to avoid her. "That's supper." He headed for the door.

Supper came in a basket. The young boy who delivered it followed Brok over to the table, waiting for the basket to be emptied. When Brok lifted the cloth, the aromas of fresh bread and spiced meat invaded the room. Orielle clambered to her feet. She disguised her eagerness by shifting her pack to the front of the chest. The boy snuck glances at her, but he ignored her smile and her greeting. Brok returned the basket. She heard a bright chink of coins. The boy's hand dove into his breeches pocket, then he snatched up the basket and hared out the door, shutting it behind him with a thunk.

"You want some of this or not?"

"I need to pay for my share."

"Grim will do it. You're Grim's concern, not mine."

More words designed to stop any conversation.

Her share was a bun that filled her hand, three slices of pork, still hot and dripping grease, and an apple. Brok placed his meat in his bun and began eating. She supposed the bread would swallow the grease. A stoppered flagon and two cups completed the fare.

He used a foot to shove back a chair. "Sit." He uncorked the flagon and poured a cup. The yeasty smell of ale entered the room. He lifted the flagon and drank from it before returning to the meat.

Orielle sipped the ale. Her tongue told her it was strong enough to cut the grease and mute the spices. She slid onto the chair and concentrated on the food.

Brok finished his bread and meat quickly. He ignored the apple. After another swig from the flagon, he dropped his head against the wall again. His eyelids dropped to a thin slit. He watched the shadows that flickered around the room, as if they were real and Orielle was the phantasm.

She needed to learn about the Haven. Grim would have answered her. Brok would have to. She dared a first question about the past. "Are you and Grim friends from childhood?"

"Six of us. Me, Grim, Waren, Ridger, Axe, and Fortis."

"Fortis? The one who is an elder? Not an elder. You called them mentors."

"That's him."

"And the others? Did they go with Grim?" If the Haven had lost four good fighters, Grim and three of his friends, then their departure had certainly weakened the Haven's defense. What had Tobit said? The wyre pack attacking them defeated but everything hadn't settled afterwards.

"No. They didn't go with Grim."

"They're still here in the Haven? Perhaps they will speak for him."

He made that frustrated sound from mouth and nose. "No. Waren's here. And Fortis. Axe and Ridger died. Years ago. That good enough? Or do you want to know how they died? What me and Grim and Fortis were doing when they died? What we thought and felt when they died?"

"No. I just—." Platitudes dug holes. "My regrets for the loss of your friends. I didn't intend—. I need to know more about this Haven, about your elder and the mentors. Fortis and the one with the living staff of wood. Surrect," she dredged up. "And the other."

"Lillias," he supplied. He drank from the flagon. "I ain't the person to ask."

"Simple information." She tried to keep the plea out of her voice. "Tobit is clearly hostile."

"I wouldn't say that." He thunked the flagon on the table, slid it a bit to tap against his apple. "Look." Then he stopped.

She gave him her full attention, eyes wide open, hands in her lap, back straight, best student in the class.

He caught her intention and snorted, a break in his rudeness. "Look, it's less your mission than your arrival with Grim."

"He hates Grim that much?" As he shook his head, she agreed, "No, hate is the wrong word. Was what Grim did so wrong? He said he left after the battle with the wyre was over. He said he had permission."

"He did have permission. Fortis, too. From Grim's father. But his father was days dead, killed in the first wyre attack. Tobit was new to elder. Grim insulted him by leaving without his permission. Fortis didn't leave. He got named mentor."

Politics, Orielle judged. Unseen rules and social markers riddled the Enclave. This small Haven, a pocket-sized corner of the Enclave, seemed to have an equal amount of rules and markers.

A braw man, Tobit, but he would want both feet steady before he followed any rules laid down by the one who came before him. He wouldn't like shifting sand. Fluid circumstances would rile him.

Earth power. She'd never encountered someone who wielded the pure element. That single quake clap—it opened a fissure under her feet, but the spell depended on an opponent standing still. What other spells did Tobit bring to battle?

She was used to Air and Water, riding one wave until expediency or necessity required plunging in to seek out the next wave.

"Who is the man who wears the eye patch?"

Brok sputtered into the flagon. He wiped his mouth then the side of the flagon. "You counting your enemies? That's the first bit of wisdom you've had."

~ 3 ~

A knock pounded on the door, rattling the weathered planks.

Brok dropped his half-devoured bun on the scuffed table and took the flagon with him to the door.

Orielle swivelled in her chair to watch. Had Brok expected this visitor? Was it the man in leathers? Would it be about Grim?

He opened the door wide, but his stocky body blocked her view. The person was definitely smaller. She couldn't hear their conversation. Brok must have dropped a Shield to prevent any eavesdropping.

Then he stepped aside.

The woman leader stood there. The mentor. What was her name? *And why am I having trouble remembering? I remember Tobit and Fortis and Surrect easily enough.*

"Fang's blood, you keep it dark, Brok," the woman scolded as she came deeper into the room. "Hello there, Orielle of the Wizard Enclave."

She set aside her nibbled supper. "Hello. Lillias," she remembered. She sparked another light sphere and sent it to hover between them.

The light revealed the state of the room. Brok's discarded clothes on the chair—leathers, like his friend in the lane and the sentinels who guarded the Haven's perimeter. A pile of wood dropped against the hearth wall. A bucket on the other side of the wood, with an empty flagon on top. The tacked-up quilt was stained from countless touches to sweep it aside. The shutter over the window had a broken hasp. Not filth, just a lack of care and attention.

"I thought you kept a neater home, Brok." Hands on hips, the mentor gave critical eyes to the room. "This is a retreat. This is not moving forward."

"Leave it, Lillias." He grabbed up the remainder of his supper. "You'll talk easier without me." He brushed past the quilt.

They listened to his stomping feet.

"I think a little Shield?" The woman framed it as a question even as she dropped the spell over them.

Orielle folded her hands in her lap, resuming the guise of eager student. The pretense had broken Brok's resentment against her. *More politics.* "Have we secret matters to discuss?"

Grey eyes narrowed. They looked like ice chips. The woman's aura also equally chilled. "Who knows into what paths our conversation will wander?"

Orielle indicated Brok's abandoned chair with a sweep of her hand.

Snow-white hair and fine lines around eyes and mouth revealed Lillias' age. Large boned hands grabbed the chair to angle it toward Orielle. Her frame was slender, but her posture conveyed strength. The depths of her elemental power? Or a physical toughness? Both?

"Brok is Grim's friend, but if you have complaints of him—."

"I do not foresee any complaints. Grim trusted him. Besides, I can defend myself."

The mentor's thin lips curved in the faintest smile. "You did say that you fought and killed wyre."

Orielle sipped her ale. "Do you have questions of me?"

"Nothing that I would ask outside the hearing."

"Then why—?" She waved a hand to indicate the Shield.

"Precaution. A lesson I learned early which has stood for years. As you should learn it. I came, truly, to answer any questions that you have. I know Brok can be … cross for no seeming reason. He has a short leash. His wife's disappearance preys upon him."

"His wife's disappearance?"

"The strangest thing." Lillias leaned back, as if she settled in for a long tale. "She disappeared while he was on sentinel duty. She was known for her little departures. She didn't like the Haven. No one noticed, not until he returned. We searched, but we found no sign of her. She took very few things with her. Their arguments were the talk of the lanes, usually caused by her flirtations. When she did not return, Brok refused to believe that she had left him and the Haven."

"Would she do that? Leave the Haven? The nearest Lowland farm is days away."

"She wasn't a Rho, and she's from those Lowland farms. Her friends here say she talked about going home."

She tore at the bun and worried the bite. "Did anyone check?"

"How could we? Why would we? She was unhappy. She said she would leave. She has. Either she will come back, or she will not. Brok cannot dwell on what is lost."

To Orielle, the woman's departure didn't sound like a simple departure. Lillias had called it the *strangest thing*, but it didn't sound like that either. It sounded … worse. "That's the reason you said Brok was retreating and not moving forward."

"We in the Havens are used to Lowlanders not sticking to our lives here. It can be difficult for them. A valley filled with fields which means work is all you see, that and the forest surrounding us. Nothing but work inside the walls as well. And her family was days and days away from here. Once the excitement of coming to the Haven wears off, and the fine shine of lust leaves the relationship, it's difficult for the mundane who come here. Even Rho can be tempted to resume hiding in the mundane world."

"I thought a Rho's element would burst out if it were not used."

"So it is, unless it is a small wielding of the element, simple and easily controlled. Poor Brok. Zairantze had few incentives to remain here. Her departure has devastated him. His friends attempt to fill the gap, and Tobit assigned him extra sentinel duties to keep him occupied. He will leave again tomorrow night. But see, we stray far from the path I intended. I know you have questions. I doubt the Enclave kept adequate records of Rhoghieri lives, and in the decades since the alliance collapsed, they would not have cared to improve their knowledge of us."

"That man in the crowd. He said *enslaved to the Enclave*."

"The past is the past."

"Until the past comes to your Haven, begging a renewed alliance."

"Clever. I see the reason your ArchClan chose you as emissary."

Clever. Grim would have a better word. And Orielle wasn't chosen. Her more talented sister had been. Yet Adorée had backed out of the mission, and Orielle jumped to volunteer. *Stupid*.

"From the little I have gathered, from Grim and from your fellows today, I believe that the Rho will not want a return to the old alliance, Mentor Lillias. I have limited authority to negotiate new terms, Mentor Lillias. Iscleft Citadel needs Rho to fight the increasing forces of wyre that Frost Clime throws into battle."

"Does Chanerro Pass not need Rho fighters?"

"I believe Commander Camisse did negotiate with a Rho Haven on that border. Their agreement can be the model for the Iscleft alliance."

"Yet again we wander into intriguing paths that I did not intend. These are words for the Council. Ask me something more immediate,

Orielle, wizard of the Enclave. Ask me about our Haven."

She winced inwardly at that *wizard of the Enclave*, her lie of omission biting her again. Here, though, was her opportunity to discover information valuable to her mission. Grim had never shared any specifics. He hadn't had time, with the Kyrgy menacing them and wyres and gobbers and the Ice Huldra attacking them.

"Tell me about Tobit and your fellow mentors. He is Earth element."

Lillias smiled and let the words flow as easily as the Air of her element. Surrect controlled Water. His staff with its growing branches marked him as a healer, as Orielle had guessed. The newest mentor, Fortis, wielded Fire.

"Not a community gathered for a single element then?"

Lillias laughed before she launched into the founding of the Havens with their mix of elemental wielders. Iscleft Haven had held this ground in the Wilding for centuries, before the last dragon disappeared into the Wastes beyond the Wilding. Although nearly self-sufficient, the village still traded with the Lowland farms and towns.

As the woman described how everyone relied on each other, Orielle felt a growing shadow. That very dependence on each other would be part of Tobit's accusation against Grim.

Lillias didn't lessen Orielle's worry. "Tobit will have other charges against him, including Grim's alliance with you." One white eyebrow lifted slightly. "The man has a long-standing grudge against all things wizardry. Brok is a brave man to commit to your protection."

"Because Grim asked him to do so. How much danger is Grim in?"

"Do not fear, wizard. We Rho are too few in number to execute one of our best fighters with both element and sword. A punishment is necessary, but Grim can withstand it. After all, we cannot have our young ones deciding they can come and go at will, slipping away from their responsibilities to our community."

"May I see Grim? Before his hearing?"

"You look as if you think he is in chains and Tobit wields a whip against him. That is not our way, wizard. Did he fight when he was led to the lock-up? No. He knew he would remain unharmed. Just as you have nothing to fear from us after your hearing. We live in the Wilding, elbow to elbow with the frontier, but we are not uncivilized." She clapped her hands to her knees and stood.

And the pop in Orielle's ears said the Shield was dropped, their conversation definitely over.

The woman paused at the door. "I hope I have answered enough of your questions to allay your worries, for yourself and for Grim. You do not need to fear our hearings. They are nothing like those in the Enclave."

"Thank you, Lillias. Is this correct? Or do I say Mentor Lillias?"

She gave that rich chuckle so at odds with her ice-cold eyes and snow-hard appearance. "Mentor and Elder are necessary only in the hearing. Have you anything you need? I thought Brok would rejoin us. Tomorrow night he returns to his tri-night duty as sentinel. He's likely asleep. The sentinels always run short of sleep. Do not wake him," she cautioned.

"I will not."

"Latch the door behind me."

Orielle remembered how Brok had jiggled the latch to unlock it then kicked the door when it stuck but said nothing.

Yet as she latched the door, she wondered who had latched it behind Brok when he left.

Door shut, she stared around the room. The disappearance of Brok's woman, Zairantze, explained the untidiness. Yet something felt wrong. Odd. Off.

Brok hadn't offered a private chamber with a bed. A pallet before the fire would do. Here in the Haven, inside a dwelling, she would not worry about gobbers invading her campsite.

Or the Kyrgy.

She unstrapped her blanket from the pack and unrolled it before the fire. Then she unwove her braid, ran her fingers through it to loosen her hair. She scratched her scalp before she re-braided her hair for the night. Her boots went to the foot of the blanket. She wiggled her toes then decided to remove her stockings as well.

Brok had mentioned a place to wash. The idea of sleeping in all the dirt of her journey repulsed her. Surely she could find the scullery or washroom without disturbing him? She called the still-hovering light sphere, dimmed its glow, then sent it before her, past the hanging quilt.

The corridor was short and narrow, night-dark except for the pale moonglow of her sphere. She saw three doors, the second one so close upon the first that she thought it must be storage—or a staircase to the upper floor.

The first door gave off the sense of emptiness. The second one reeked of Brok's essence. She could hear nothing behind the two planks that formed the door. Her hand hovered at the latch, and she sent an arrow of magic to the iron.

Her magic rebounded. It prickled through her hand, a thousand pin jabs, like returning circulation. She shook her hand to cast off the rebound. Brok must have spelled his door to keep her from blundering in.

Then she heard soft hissing, so muffled by the door she was shocked she heard it at all. And a groan. She snatched back.

The missing Zairantze. The door latched behind Brok. Maybe a stairway to the upper floor.

She headed to the end of the hall with its third door.

It opened easily, without a tingling spell to warn her away.

Her glowing sphere skittered around the room, showing another shuttered window and a barred door. She had found the scullery. On the outer wall ran a long bench with a dry sink beneath the window and beside it a basin and pitcher. Stacked beside the basin were folded cloths. Pegs on the inner and outer walls were joined by stretches of twine for hanging washing. Tucked beneath the bench were baskets with sprouting mounds, potatoes and onions and other root vegetables. She spied a bucket. The room felt dank, cold, and smelled of wet leather and lanolin.

The basin was empty, but the pitcher was full. Behind the basin was a small bowl with soap. Orielle splashed water in the basin, worked the soap into lather, then scrubbed her face. Then she rinsed away the soap and considered what more she could quickly do.

She shivered. Her hands prickled again. Her face prickled. Her back crawled. Ice shivered over her. Ice that felt like slime. Ice that felt weighty as stones. Skin crawling, she turned then took the two steps to see down the hall.

Light streamed under Brok's door.

She hadn't seen it earlier. Her own light sphere, dimmed though it was, had overwhelmed this faint light.

A faint greeny light, eerie and eldritch. Sorcery.

~ **4** ~

Brok worked sorcery?

She rejected that immediately. A Rhoghieri, he wielded the elements. He was Earth, like the elder Tobit. Grim wielded Air, as Orielle did.

Whoever was in that room with him, that person worked foul sorcery.

To enthrall him?

Zairantze? But she was missing, no one knew where she'd gone—or when, since she'd left while Brok served as sentinel.

Brok hadn't wanted Orielle here. He hadn't said the words. He hadn't hesitated to bring her to his dwelling. Yet he clearly begrudged her presence. Grief at Zairantze's departure? Or another cause? Did he begrudge Grim calling on their former friendship? Whatever the cause, he'd retreated to his room. He had retreated, not chosen to give Lillias and Orielle privacy. The Shield spell ensured their privacy. No, he'd retreated because his eagerness was to return to the person in his room.

For sex. That groan was deep pleasure.

And the sibilant hiss?

Orielle would have sworn that no one was in the house when they'd first entered. Where had the person been? Hiding upstairs? Or had Brok admitted them through the barred door in the scullery? Even with the Shield, though, she and Lillias would have heard that heavy bar lift.

Orielle called the light sphere close to her hand. She wasn't a wizard, no matter how many people in this Wilding believed it, Rho and Kyrgy included. She even doubted that she would pass the Wizard Trials to earn the rank.

She would have to be clever and smart.

She increased the sphere's brightness. She gave the light a special twist, to find and stick to sorcery. Then she called up the vortex spell that she'd used with Tobit. Air. Spiraling wind. She keened the outer rim with sharp magic. Sphere bobbing at her shoulder, she headed for Brok's room.

The spell on the latch should have alerted her. An Earth spell would have seated the iron against the wood, making the latch immobile. That prickling porcupine spell wasn't Rho.

Nor was it strong. It dissipated as soon as she lifted the latch. Whoever was with Brok hadn't wasted power on the latch. Their concentration worked the spell to enthrall him.

And he was enthralled, Orielle saw as soon as the door swung back.

He lay flat on his back on the narrow bed. A woman straddled him, riding his body.

Even expecting sorcery, Orielle still stepped back to give them privacy.

The woman tossed her hair, black and long and wavy. Her skin shimmered ghostly pale in the sphere's light. And her mouth was full of fangs.

A wraith.

Feeding on Brok's essence, for it had corporeal form.

"Zairantze," he groaned. "Close. Gods, my love. Close."

Orielle stared even as she tried to remember the little that she knew about wraiths. When had it attached to Brok? How? How had the wraith passed the wards that protected the Haven? Had it found him on sentinel duty, long hours standing alone, watching nothingness?

When the wraith took his semen, she—it might escape whatever tied it to Brok. It would be loose then, eager to feed on more of the Haveners, especially the elemental-wielding Rhoghieri.

It had taken his blood. Thin lines of red marred his shoulders. Claw marks. New lines and healed ones, older ones on his torso.

A wraith had ridden Orielle's shoulders. Grim had swept it away. By mistake, she'd used the name of her recently dead cousin, Raigeis, a wizard killed by a sorcerer.

This wraith would not be easily cast away, not with Brok's blood and semen feeding it.

"Raigeis," she whispered.

The wraith stopped moving. Eerie green light flashed out, leaving only the golden glow of her light sphere. The ghostly face turned to her.

Its eyes were mist, but the mouth had fangs sharper than a gobber's.

"Zairantze. Don't stop." Brok moved under the wraith. "Please. I need you."

Dangerous words said to a wraith.

It looked down at him. It dragged a claw down his chest. Blood beaded—.

And Orielle realized she stood there like a stupefied clod. She focused on the vortex, adding more energy to the sharply-bladed rim.

The wraith lifted blood-tipped claws and licked them. Then she—it blurred, became indistinct, and moved.

No. Part of it moved. A separate part. Whole of itself.

Two wraiths fed on Brok.

One remained with him, working its woman body to steal life-essence from him.

The other flowed off the bed. The misty vapor solidified as it swarmed across the floor. Lifted off the floor, formed shoulders and head. Arms separated from the central mass and shaped a man. The face formed. A lifted chin, flared nostrils, high brow and swept-back grey hair. Of her dead cousin Raigeis.

A newly dead man. Former magister of the Wizard Enclave. Killed by a sorcerer. Raigeis.

"Cousin," the wraith hissed. "We meet again."

Gods, it *knew* her.

"Come, cousin." It reached then recoiled, as if she'd stung it. Her active power?

She remembered the Kyrgy knight that had leashed the wraith. "I see you escaped Lady Bone."

It grinned, revealing its own fangs. Then its mouth opened wide, wider, becoming a sharp-toothed maw. The wraith's height grew. It loomed over her.

She flung the vortex into its gaping mouth.

Its jaws snapped shut. It looked shocked. Then it reached for her.

Vaporous hands with solidifying claws, red-tipped claws, lengthening as its hands neared.

Tatters appeared in the vapor. Ripped lines, tearing the wraith apart as her sharp-rimmed spell spun and spun inside it.

The wraith howled. The roar blasted her. She fell against the door jamb. The wraith reached for her again, but its arms lost shape. Bits of vapor drifted away. Then it shrank, snatching the vapor trails to it, whirling with her vortex, collapsing smaller and smaller until the wraith dissipated into nothing.

The other wraith sprang through the last wisp.

Orielle staggered into the hall then onto the floor. The wraith's weight smothered her. She tried to beat it away, but her hands went through nothing. It froze her, drawing heat from her body, deadening her senses, dulling her mind.

She panicked, tearing at the corporeal weight, writhing under it. The other wraith had lacked substance. Weaker, less fed with human essence, it had had only a tenuous hold. This one had fed on blood more than once. Had Brok spilled his semen into its assumed body? Had he given this soul-sucking creature another powerful life essence?

The talons tore, but they didn't penetrate her heavy tunic and skirt. Then it reached for her face.

She threw up her arms.

The wraith laughed and seized her hands. Then that fanged mouth fastened on her fingers, piercing her tender flesh. It sucked. Those milky grey eyes grew brighter, shimmered like silver. Her essence trickled away, a string pulling from the deep coil inside her.

It released her fingers with a pop. "So good. So soft. So powerful." Zairantze's black hair melted away into flyaway blonde. The silvery eyes became blue. Orielle was fighting herself.

The wraith licked the fingers of her other hand. "Give me a name," it sighed. "Give me your name." Then its mouth opened to bite her other fingers.

Desperate, Orielle shoved the light sphere into its mouth.

The wraith leaped away. It whirled, swirled—then realized it hadn't swallowed the spell that had dissipated its partner. "Trick," it hissed. The light sphere glowed within it, casting a golden halo around the monster.

"Yes." She levered to her knees. Her mind crawled like a snail. Stones weighted her limbs. But during the wraith's panic, she had remembered Grim sweeping the wraith off her back. "This isn't," and she shoved a wall of Air.

The spell pinned the wraith against the wall. She heard weeping. She felt tears on her face, the pain of her bloody fingers, the throb of her steady heartbeat. Warmth. Lightness. Life. The wraith no longer burdened her.

It writhed, caught between spell and wall, but it couldn't escape the blockading Air.

The wraith Orielle melted into Zairantze. It wept. It reached. "So alone," it cried. The golden light inside it paled. The wraith reached for more energy.

Orielle twisted her bloody hands. The wall of Air became a cage, shrinking, shrinking, even as the wraith thinned into a vaporous fog, caught inside a transparent box. The light sphere faded.

Then the fog burst outward, escaping the cage. The wraith howled as it swirled. It ripped at Orielle's hair then whooshed away.

The first door in the hall rattled on its hinges.

And it was gone, leaving Orielle, the light sphere, and Brok, weeping.

It had fed on her blood. That would give it a connection to her as long as it retained a pathway into this world.

The disturbed grave on the mountaintop had opened the door for the other wraith. It had slipped its bonds before she and Grim had re-sealed the grave.

Whatever scourging ordered by Lady Bone, the Kyrgy queen, the punishment hadn't cast the wraith back to Neothera.

The first wraith knew her dead cousin's name. This one had drank her blood. Both wraiths had a connection to Brok, through his blood and his semen.

Both would return. For him. For her. And any other unwary soul encountered when it had corporeal form.

Orielle climbed to her feet. The pangs from her fall clamored for attention. She picked up Brok's discarded breeches and flung them at him. They slapped into his face, stopping his weeping more effectively than sympathy. "Get dressed. We have work to do."

He stared at her then at his breeches. His mind started working, for he covered himself. Then he looked up with the ravaged face of a man who had touched happiness only to have it ripped away.

As it had been when Zairantze died. For the woman had to be dead, or the wraith could not take her form.

It took my form. I'm not dead.

Like a fetch.

Was it a fetch? Not a wraith?

That eerie green glow of sorcery in use. A foul spell.

Had it twisted the wraith? Had the spell given the wraith the capabilities of a fetch? Could it assume the guise of the living as well as the dead?

"Get up," she snapped.

Brok didn't move. "Zairantze—she was here. She was with me."

"No. You had two wraiths on you, feeding off you, taking your essence. They'll continue to haunt you if we don't find their path to you."

"I saw her," he insisted, and she remembered her own bleary mind when the wraith rode her back.

"That wasn't your Zairantze."

"She was *with* me." Pain twisted his face, and she remembered the fog lifting from her own wits, but she dared not give him more valuable seconds.

"No. Where is she now, Brok? If that was Zairantze, she would still be here."

He blinked then looked around.

When he stared owlishly at the light sphere, Orielle lost patience. "Move, Brok. Look, I understand what you want to believe. Wraiths prey on us by making us think our beloved ones are restored to us." Raigeis wasn't her beloved cousin, though. She had feared him. Magister for the ArchClan, he had rank and status that he wielded like a mace and a blade. Fear was just as powerful as love. "The wraiths scratched you. Look at the claw marks on your chest. They're still bleeding."

He looked. Obedient as a drugged man. He touched the marks, flinched at the raw flesh. Doubt began. "Not Zairantze?"

"Not her. One of them took your seed. Since they also have your blood, they can easily return to you. We have to block its path to you. Did you encounter her while on sentinel duty?"

"No. She never came to me there."

"Get dressed," she reminded since he listened to her now. She turned her back to give him privacy, although fear crawled up her spine that a wraith would leap out of a shadow. "When did Zairantze go, when she left?"

"I don't know." Rustling said he obeyed her order. "When I came off duty, she was gone."

"Sentinel duty is three nights? You came back, she was gone. You looked for her and couldn't find her. That's what Lillias said."

"Aye." He stomped into his boots.

Orielle turned away. He hadn't pulled on a shirt, and the claw marks on his chest looked like black streaks even in the golden glow of the sphere.

She saw a shirt near the door. She scooped it up and tossed it over. The wraiths must have been on him as soon as he shut the door.

Who had spelled the latch?

Brok couldn't have. Rho couldn't work sorcery.

No one else had entered the house except for Lillias. She hadn't left the common room.

Had someone else been here? "Did the wraith come here before your next sentinel duty? Or did it come to you while you were on duty?"

"Zairantze would never interfere with my post."

"That wasn't Zairantze."

"She was. She is."

"No. I'm not going to argue this, Brok. I know what creatures I just fought. Two wraiths, one more powerful than the other because your semen and blood gave it life-essence. You came back here after a sentinel duty. You saw a ghostly figure. You hoped it was Zairantze, and you gave the wraith her name. Once you did that, that ghostly figure took on her shape. It came out of the shadows looking like her. Am I correct?"

He scowled.

Good. Let him hate her for destroying his dream. Better that than he continue to look for his dead wife, giving power to any wraith he encountered.

"You fought two wraiths?"

She displayed her fingers that the wraith had bitten.

"You gave them life-essence, too, Orielle. Magickal essence. They'll crave more of you."

"Semen is more powerful than blood," she said flatly. "Both of us connected to them. That's the reason we have to find their entry point. Where is Zairantze? Did you kill her?"

"Gods, no!"

"Where is her body?"

"She's not dead. She can't be dead."

"She is. Or the wraiths would not have taken her appearance."

"No one would want her dead."

"Lillias said she was a Lowlander. That she had no family here, only you. Would someone have wanted her gone?"

He didn't answer. He brushed past her and headed for the scullery.

"Not there," she called. He turned on his heel. His scowl hadn't changed. She pointed at the first door in the hall.

His brows lifted. "I'm not going up there."

"Why not?"

"I can't."

"Can't or won't?"

"Can't. I couldn't. Not even when I realized Zairantze was missing."

"You didn't look for her up there?"

When he shook his head, cold hollowed her gut.

~ 5 ~

Orielle opened the door to the stairs.

Brok tried to block her. "Don't."

"I will," she said stubbornly. "The wraith came up here."

"You must not."

"Must not? Why?" When he only shook his head and repeated himself, Orielle pushed aside his arm. "Let us examine this rationally." Her old tutors would be proud of her. "Have you ever been upstairs? When was the last time? When Zairantze still lived?"

"She thought a shutter was flapping. I came up to fix it, but I found no shutter."

"How long was this before she went missing?"

"A few days."

"Have you not gone up since? Help me understand this, Brok. When Zairantze was missing, you searched the house, but you didn't search upstairs. How does that make sense?"

"I knew she wasn't upstairs."

"How did you know?"

"I ju-just d-did."

"Did other people search the house?"

"Not up there."

"Why not?"

"It wouldn't come unlatched."

She remembered the sorcery on the latch of his chamber door. It dissipated once she lifted the latch. This door hadn't had a repellent spell. Was that a spell to misdirect a Rhoghieri? It hadn't affected her magick. "Did no one question that they could not search upstairs? They merely accepted it? How many were involved in the search?"

As he named them, she knew the spell misdirected the Rho.

"Do you sense the spell now? I mean, are you repelled from going upstairs? Then up we go." She grabbed his forearm and tugged him after her.

Brok stumbled the first steps, then he groaned and followed.

The light sphere bobbed ahead of them, twisting around the landing as the stairs bent back to climb higher. No door barred the top of the steps, which opened upon a long hall. The layout mimicked the floor below, with a front room, then two doors further along the hall—but no scullery.

Orielle stepped back to use Brok's aversion as a guide. When he turned to go along the hall, she propelled him to the front room. When he dragged his feet, she shoved him forward.

The room's latch repeated the prickly porcupine aversion. That dissipated when she lifted it and shoved the door open. She sent the light sphere ahead and grew it brighter.

The added brightness wasn't needed.

A simple bed, plain boards at the head and foot, centered the room. Zairantze lay upon the coverlet, like a queen lying in state for a royal funeral.

Brok moaned. He broke free of Orielle and rushed to the bed. He reached for his wife—but stopped, hanging over the mattress as if he didn't dare touch the woman's body.

Hands crossed over her chest, Zairantze had not decayed in the days and days of death. Her eyes and mouth were closed, her long black hair trailing over the coverlet and falling off the side, a silken curtain. Her skin was a pale milky white. She was fine-boned and petite, a stark contrast to the rough-hewn Brok. And she looked ready to open her eyes and smile.

Except for the silver dagger thrust to its hilt in her breast. Her hands were crossed beneath it.

Brok grabbed the headboard. The whole bed shook as he grieved. "How—? Why—?"

The knife hilt had a deeply carved relief. Orielle couldn't decipher the pattern. She desperately wanted to see the design. That might reveal a clue about the powerful pathway it had opened for the wraiths. Had Zairantze been chosen? Or was she a victim of circumstance, a woman alone while Brok served as a sentinel? No one had noticed when she went missing.

The woman wore day clothes, a bib apron over her chambray blouse and brown skirt. Her shoes looked worn on the soles, but they were well-tended.

Standing beside Brok, looking closely at Zairantze, Orielle spotted something glistening on her lashes. Tears. Icy tears. One had tracked a rimey trail before the spell froze her.

Brok growled. He seized the knife. A shudder wracked him, then he jerked out the knife. "No!" Orielle cried, too late. As soon as the knife left Zairantze's body, it dissolved, melting in his hand, the water evaporating into a mist.

And the icy tears melted and evaporated.

Zairantze's body collapsed, shrinking on itself. Her body folded into creases, lost shape and form as if it voided. The flesh darkened, peeling away in flecks, dessicating and shifting into a fine powder the color of ash.

Air gusted up from the bed, lifting the coverlet, gusting up the skirt and apron. It sucked up the ash and whirled it around. Orielle caught a flashing glint and heard a ping as it whipped past her cheek. The remains swirled into a mimicry of a vortex, then it gusted to the fireplace and whooshed up the narrow chimney. Dislodged soot fell to the cold hearth, joining the piled ashes.

The wrongness in the house left with the ashy remains.

And only Zairantze's clothes remained on the coverlet.

Brok stared at the flattened clothes. Then he stared at the hand that had grabbed the dagger, as if expecting water to have remained. "She's gone." His voice was hoarse. "Nothing even to bury."

Orielle remembered the glinting flash and the ping. A shining object lay behind her, against the baseboard. She picked it up. A necklace with a pendant. It felt like an intrusion to examine it. She returned to the emptied bed and handed it to him.

He saw the glinting gold. He snatched it from her palm, stared at it, then lifted the pendant to his lips. Then he slipped the chain over his head. The pendant, a colored swirl of polished stone, glistened on his chest, just below a bloody claw mark. "I have to report this to Tobit."

"What will you report?"

He gave a questioning look. "The wraiths. Zairantze's death."

"Tonight? Shall I come with you?" She would need to fill in the gaps.

He nodded once. "You fought the wraiths. We are two witnesses."

"We have no evidence of battle. Just those marks on your chest. Will he believe us?"

"We have to tell him. What if the wraiths have enthralled more people, the way they did me?"

At his admission, she breathed more easily. He didn't know the worst of it, not yet. He thought the worst was Zairantze's death. Orielle knew the worst lay before them. Brok had strengthened the wraiths, both of them with his blood, one of them with his semen. The only gain they could count was the destruction of the pathway into the Haven.

She gestured to the window. "I must seal this room and all openings into this dwelling before we leave. Get whatever you will need for the next few days. You should not return until the whole house is cleansed."

Brok didn't argue, just turned and left. She heard him clump down the stairs. He hadn't argued since she'd confronted him about not searching for Zairantze abovestairs.

Bare toes curling against the flooring, Orielle built the spell wards to seal the room. She started on the opening side of the door then followed the cardinal points until she returned. She closed off the circle as she stepped into the hall and drew the chamber door shut. The spell she placed on the latch was stronger than the aversion spell of sorcery.

She sealed the windows in the two other rooms. Once below, she sealed the scullery door and window with the same repellent spell. It wouldn't harm any who touched it, but they would be revoltingly sick within seconds.

All the while she wondered how a sorceress had entered the Haven to work spells and wield a knife formed not of metal but of twisted energy. Three spells: the one on Brok's door, the aversion that kept him from exploring upstairs, and the one that enabled the wraiths to use Zairantze's body as their gate.

And fool that she was, Orielle hadn't sensed the miasma of sorcery that filled the house, not until it vanished.

Clever, smart, foolish. How would Grim judge this night's work?

Brok waited in the front room. He'd donned the discarded leathers. A sword dragged at his hip, a quiver from a strap over his shoulder. He carried a pack. He watched her seal the window then waited as she crammed her feet into her boots and stuffed her wadded-up stockings into the pack. Then he led her from the house and waited again as she sealed the door.

"Why her? Why Zairantze?"

Orielle didn't answer that question. She didn't know if he would ever have an answer.

.~.~.~.

Tobit looked at them as if they were mad.

They repeated the events a second time, elaborating when he butted in with questions. When Orielle repeated how she had sealed the house, the elder just stared.

Did he not realize that no thunderclap quake would defeat this enemy?

A man stepped into the front room. He lit the hearth fire. When he straightened and turned, she saw the dark patch over his eye. "I will wake Surrect. Our healer," he directed at Orielle.

"Yes. I saw his staff. Tell Surrect that the spells … ," she paused to amend her words to a less callous description for the strange decomposition, "the spells that dispersed Zairantze's body used Water, Fire, and Air."

"Not Earth?" Hackett's single eye didn't blink as he watched Tobit. The elder straightened his shoulders although his hands still clutched the carved back of his chair.

"I did not see Earth, but I do not wield that element. Although my grandfather allied to Galfrons, an Earth clan, my line is like the ArchClan

Letheina. We focus Air and Water. I may have missed the use of Earth."

"Go," Tobit said, and the patched man strode out. "Why not Earth?" Tobit asked.

Orielle shrugged. "I am not an expect on sorcery. Sorcery built the spell that opened Brok's house to the wraiths."

He didn't retort that as a wizard she'd failed to destroy the wraiths. He crossed to Brok. Big hands gripped the younger man's shoulders. He leaned close until their foreheads touched. "I did not know. I did not sense. Your grief is mine. Whatever you need, I will provide."

Brok inhaled deeply. "My only need is lost to me. You cannot provide it."

"I can stand beside you. I will stand beside you."

A shudder wracked his lean frame. He grasped Tobit's forearms then nodded.

The big man clapped his hands on Brok's shoulders. He studied the younger man's down-turned gaze before his eyes flicked to Orielle. "Rooms for you both until the house is cleansed."

"I sealed the openings," she repeated.

"Surrect will break the seal. He may wish you there."

Having expected that, she nodded.

"I won't return," Brok ground. "I'll see her everywhere—." He broke off, biting his lips.

"Then we will house you until another dwelling opens."

"No. Though I thank you. Waren will give us house room. We won't inconvenience you and Hackett."

Tobit's still-black brows drew together. His chin jutted, bottom lip protruding like a mastiff keeping its fangs hidden. "As you wish. Surrect should examine you. He will examine you both."

"I am not ill."

"Do not refuse your healer," Orielle said softly. "The wraiths stole your essence. Look at him, elder. He is hollowed. You can see it easily, now that we know to look for it. Look at his cheeks, caved with wasting. The darkness under his eyes. Surrect must examine him."

Tobit lifted a hand. Brok evaded. The bigger man's eyes narrowed, then he reached more deliberately.

Brok held still, but his gusted breath filled the audience room. That big hand covered his cheek, the sausage fingers sliding over his ear and into his hair. His thumb rubbed the tender skin under an eye. Then his touch drifted down to the sharp edge of his jaw. When he removed his hand, Brok's mouth twisted.

"How long, wizard?" the headman asked.

"I could not say, not without examining the spell or whatever triggered the spell. Perhaps not even then."

"A week?"

"He would not have survived a week, but he may need that long to recover."

"I am not weak!" Brok protested.

"Your life essence is damaged. Your healer will know best."

Tobit grimaced. "You need not stand sentinel, Brok, until Surrect says you can. Nor should you have any obligation to this Enclave wizard."

Brok crossed his arms. "Grim asked me to guard her. He is my friend. Until you release him, I will do as he asked. And I owe her a life debt."

"No, you do not!" Orielle snapped. "Not a life debt. Wizards fight sorcery where we find it. And you are Grim's friend, as you said. I would help you for that reason alone."

Brok's muddy gaze leveled on her. "A life debt," he insisted. He touched his chest, the spot over Zairantze's pendant. "Now I can grieve Zairantze. She didn't leave me. She was taken from me. Murdered by twisted sorcery. I will kill the one responsible. No matter who it is," he vowed. His fist struck his chest over his heart. "Sorcery has entered our Haven and killed one of us."

Tobit scratched fingers over his beard. "What Rho would work sorcery? Tell me that. Can you, wizard?"

She wished for an easy answer. Any help for this Haven against sorcery would win their alliance for the Enclave. Her mission would be complete. Simple—and not.

The sorceress who created the foul spell did not have to be the one who used that eldritch dagger that had melted when Brok removed it.

Those spells on the latches—could they have been prepared outside the Haven? Carried in and placed, just as the dagger was? But how had Brok repeatedly used the door to his room? That spell had to be renewed.

Whoever came in to renew it, that was the person allied to the sorceress. That was the person who must have plunged the dagger into Zairantze's heart, killing her and opening the pathway for the wraiths.

And that person had to be a Rho of this Haven.

Anger reddened Tobit's eyes. "A Rho is an ally to a sorceress? Working evil for a sorceress? For Frost Clime?" He had leapt to Orielle's conclusion. "That's not possible." The force of his conviction hardened. "It has to be someone else. Someone not Rho. Someone who has never fought sorcery or the wyre."

"And who would that be?" Orielle asked quietly. "Or should we consider a Rho who wants power and doesn't care who is harmed or how they get it?"

Tobit didn't like that question.

~ 6 ~

Tobit held them at the elder's house until Hackett returned with Mentor Surrect. Brok demanded that Orielle assist the healer with his examination, but Elder and Mentor overruled him.

When the two took Brok to another room, Hackett waved her to the planked floor before the hearth. He crouched before the fire as he dragged a pipe from an inner pocket of his leather jerkin along with a pouch of herbs. He tamped the herbs into the pipe well. After lighting his pipe, he shook out the wick while he puffed until the greeny herbs charred. Only then did he sit back, bracing his boots on a corner of the stone fireplace. "Let's hear it, then. How you and Grim killed a half-dozen wyre as you came through the Wilding."

"Seven wyre," she corrected. "Where is Grim? What did Tobit do with him? I want to see him."

"Now you sound like his friend. Don't worry. Tobit won't make any decision until after the hearing. Tell me about tonight."

She glared dissatisfaction, but he was Tobit's and said nothing more about Grim, no matter how she pressed. Grumbling, she settled more comfortably. Then she recited the events, stripping them to the bones rather than fleshing them with details and her emotions. The pipe glowed and died and glowed during her telling.

Hackett shrugged at her account of the gobbers. He had no interest in the Kyrgy until she mentioned the wraith's punishment. Then he dropped his feet and leaned elbows on his knees. "What kind of punishment did the Kyrgy give it?"

"I did not ask. I did not think it wise to question Lady Bone." Her throat had dried. "Do you think it relevant? Whatever happened to Zairantze was days ago, long before I entered the Wilding and met Grim."

"There's that, then. Tell us about the wraiths here."

"Didn't you hear—?"

"Humor a one-eyed man."

She scowled at his description of himself then told of the sorcery, of the two wraiths on Brok, and of the attack on her. As she reached Brok's removal of the dagger in Zairantze's breast, a commotion from the back silenced her.

Tobit emerged with the healer but not Brok. Both Orielle and Hackett clambered to their feet. "Where's Brok?" she asked.

Mentor Surrect braced his staff before him. "He sleeps a brief while. The healing was difficult." He scowled at her, as if she were responsible for Brok's condition. "He will wake in a few minutes. Is that acceptable, wizard?"

Tobit clicked his tongue. "She's not responsible, Surrect."

"So you say." Eyes narrowed like a snake, he didn't look away from her. "Tobit, the dwelling must be sealed."

"I did that," she shot out, "before we left. All openings, doors and windows. A greater spell on the room where we found Zairantze."

"Brok said nothing of a sealing."

"I sent him away. He was grieving. He didn't need to see—." She stopped, for the healer turned away.

He lowered his lanky frame onto a chair beside the elder's massive carved chair. He leaned the staff against his shoulder then leaned his head against it. With his eyes closed, shielding his fierce mind, she saw the stress lines and hollowed cheeks that marked a great expenditure of power.

Tobit dropped into his chair. "Surrect, she may be wizard and young with it, but she is not a fool."

She started to protest his reading, but Hackett spoke before she'd found the first word. "She has a tale of her travels through the Wilding that the Council will want to hear. Maybe more should hear it."

Tobit scratched his bearded jaw again. "Can it wait until the evening?"

"It can. What happens when Brok wakes?"

The big elder sighed and leaned against the back of his chair. "Before he wakes, we need to hear what happened from her. Brok only spoke of the dagger in Zairantze. He barely mentioned the wraiths, but I know, from what the wizard said, that they were feeding on him."

The healer sighed. His eyes opened. "You could let a man have a spare minute." Bracing his hands on his staff, he straightened. He shifted the staff to lean against his left shoulder. His bright eyes fixed Orielle. "Tell us the whole, wizard."

Her voice cracked when she finished this repetition of her battle against the wraiths. The healer quizzed her closely, especially about the spell that had held Zairantze in stasis.

A noise from the back stopped Surrect in mid-question. He rose and disappeared into the hallway. Tobit followed.

Hackett stretched then lowered his arms. "That's a fine scout report. That your pack?"

"Brok's."

He hoisted it, and Orielle divined that they would soon leave. She fetched her pack.

Brok looked less hollowed, still weary and eyes reddened. Hackett shrugged off Brok's offer to carry his own pack. "Let's move, then." He jabbed a thumb at Orielle. "That one's swaying on her feet."

Orielle trudged behind the two men, stopping only when Hackett pounded on a door. It opened and revealed Waren, scrubbing at his eyes—although the knife he held warned of a keen defense. The older man shouldered his way inside.

The dwelling was small, a front room with a door leading to a long hallway, darkened for the night. Peeking from the hallway was a young woman with sleep-tousled hair.

Hackett explained the night's battle. Waren snapped awake, grateful his friend wasn't wounded and offering to stand sentinel. "You're needed here," the patched-eye man growled. Then he said "Noon" to Orielle and walked out.

That woke her, but sleepiness returned when Waren's wife, Malva, opened the door to a room and Orielle saw the bed. She barely splashed her face and hands before she tugged off her boots. Sighing gratitude, she crawled between the bed coverings.

Only to crawl out and cast a cleansing spell. Nothing in the room reeked with viscid sorcery. Then she set her wards.

When she snuggled under the quilt, she remembered gobbers had crossed her wards without any pain and without a signal to her.

.~.~.~.

The sun blazed when Orielle woke. Since she hadn't opened the shutter in last night's darkness, she guessed Malva had ventured in, confirmed when she saw the water in the ewer was refreshed and the basin emptied.

She thrust her head out the window to a clear sky and crisp air.

Like Brok's dwelling, Waren's home backed into a narrow twisty lane. The buildings opposite matched this one, with a door below and a single window beside it. Several doors down, two women talked, one with a basket, the other with a broom. Neither saw Orielle watching. One door from the end, a man tended a boiling pot while children chased in circles in the opening behind him.

Grim's hearing would occur late afternoon, with hers to follow. With that in mind, Orielle scrubbed away the sweat and grime of her journey and last night's battle. She shook out clean clothes, crushed by long days rolled in her pack. Then she poured the water back into the ewer and carried it down.

Waren's wife came to the stairs. Malva greeted Orielle with a smile then led her to the scullery. She stayed to talk as Orielle scrubbed her clothes. She had an endless stream of words, asking about Orielle's sleep, exclaiming over bits of the battle against the wraiths, grieving over Zairantze's death, and marveling that a spell had held the body undecayed for days.

They hadn't shared that last detail. Orielle swished her clothes in the bucket, working out the soap. "Brok shared more this morning?"

"Not he, poor man. My neighbor heard the gossip. Poor Brok. He won't know what to do without Zairantze. He was breathing fire that Tobit hadn't called out the off-duty sentinels to search for the wights—wraiths, you call them—in the Haven. Could there be more wights? I pray not. We've had no recent deaths and no other person missing."

No one had considered Zairantze missing or dead. They'd claimed she had left the Haven.

Orielle wrung her garments and shook them out.

"We can hang them outside. Anyway, Brok wanted to hunt for more wights. My Waren told him that duty rightfully belongs to Surrect. He's our healer and mentor to the Water wielders. Surrect has already knocked on our door, wanting to see everyone in the house. Lillias was with him. Hackett's coming back 'round in a little while, so Waren said he said. He was here earlier, talking with Waren and Brok. He wanted to see you, but I told him you needed your sleep."

"Is it past noon? He said he would take me to see Grim."

"*Far* past noon. Don't you fret now. He'll come back. Waren took him off, he and Brok together. They wanted to help Surrect. Let's hang those up, then I'll do a quick egg for you, and you can be off to see your Grim."

What would Grim say about the wraiths? Had anyone told him?

Was he in danger from them? In his search for more wraiths feasting on Rho, had Surrect checked Grim?

She climbed the stair with a refilled pitcher then stood for a long moment in the chilly breeze through the window. A dullness fogged her mind, as if part of it still slept. She turned the other items in her pack onto the quilt and aired her blanket over the footboard. Then she gathered up her cloak and a good knife before heading downstairs.

Malva had fried eggs, toasted bread, and a honey jar ready when Orielle reached the front room. She poured tea and set it beside the plate. "There, a good fast-break."

Orielle had barely finished the first cup of tea when knocking came on the house door. She took a last bite of toast as Hackett dragged a knitted cap off his shaven skull.

"Some tea, if you please, Malva." He smiled, and the young woman hurried to comply, filling Orielle's empty cup as well.

Hackett bristled with weapons, as he had yesterday and last night. "Expecting trouble?" she asked.

One shoulder hunched. He blew across the cup. "Surrect wants a word before I escort you to the lock-up."

"I am under arrest?"

His crooked grin winked out. "To see Grim. Let him know about Brok's woman. Let him know you're safe here with Waren and his woman."

"And tell him about the wraiths?"

Again that hitch of his shoulder. "And that."

"Lillias is working with Surrect?" At his nod, she pursued more. "Will Tobit help? Or the other mentor? Fortis?"

"Mebbe Tobit. Fortis won't be there."

"Fortis is Fire and Lillias is Air." When he didn't respond, just sipped the tea, Orielle tried another track. "Is Tobit more inclined to believe us about the wyre after the wraiths?"

"I'll let him tell you that. I don't step into his elder business. I shouldn't. I'm not Rho."

Not Rho. She started to ask then heard Malva bustling back.

Not Rho. No wonder Hackett wore a short sword and several knives, even here in the Haven. Would weapons be a defense in a community of wielders of the elements? Grim's push of Air had flung a wyre over a dozen feet into a tree. Tobit's clap had opened the ground under her feet.

Perhaps not all Rho were as powerful as Grim and Tobit.

The Wizard Enclave had mundane guards, Naughts from the clans or soldiers with no trace of magic in their families. Clan leaders had their *comeis*, Fae guards bound to serve them. Yet *comeis* still had power, some as strong as wizards.

Was Hackett bound to serve Tobit? Or was his loyalty from love?

"Finished with that? Let's go on then."

Orielle held her questions until the dwelling's door shut. Children dashed past, last night's events not affecting them. The women talking with neighbors at doorsteps, though, had frowns and crossed arms and didn't even nod a greeting as Orielle and Hackett passed.

"Since you have no power, Hackett, how are you here in the Haven?" His resigned look said that he wouldn't explain what she wasn't smart enough to figure out. She hastily changed the question. "I mean, where did you meet Tobit?"

"Iscleft."

"The Citadel?"

"Aye. Heart of the battle on this frontier. Me a green recruit and him all Earth, astride the ramparts, like one of the great statues of the

Ancients. You ever see those?"

"Only as an illustration in a book. Are they truly ten times the height of a man?"

"Taller, though most are half-buried. I've climbed over one of those, fallen over, with sand drifted around it. A southern king's statue, whatever sword he once held long vanished and his crown covered by woodbine." He snorted. "Woodbine in bloom, at that."

"You must be from one of the Bois countries."

"Bois Argent," he confirmed. "With the Teeth Mountains to the south and the Sayidi desert trying to waste lowlands of the West. That's where the statue was, on the Argent border with the desert. But I left that to come here and fight sorcerers. Wanted to see me some power, fight me some wyre." The look he tossed held deprecating laughter. "Like I said, green recruit. Signed up in Gramina Aurus. Saw Tobit on the ramparts. Met him in battle. He kept a wyre from ripping my head off. Got this there." He motioned to the scars slashing across one side of his face.

The wyre's attack had likely infected his eye. Hackett was lucky that he hadn't lost both of his eyes. A whole story backed his brief words, but it was the contradiction Orielle pursued. "But Tobit opposed Grim joining the fight at Iscleft. He has Grim locked away for fighting there."

"No. Grim's locked up for leaving without permission—."

"His father—."

"And for leaving before we confirmed the wyre lair was destroyed."

"You both served at Iscleft Citadel. You know the danger from Frost Clime. How can you not support his enlistment? Why is he locked up?"

He gave that resigned look again.

"What am I missing?"

"Mebbe we might ally to the Enclave since they're turning out wizards who can admit they don't know all there is to know."

Orielle's shoulders hunched at yet another reminder that she lied by omission in letting them think her a wizard. *Would a wizard who has passed the trials admit to a weakness or a flaw, even a lack of information?* She thought of the arrogance of her elders and several of her friends. Even her sister gave pronouncements, as if wizard status were the only authority she needed.

"Look, me and Tobit served at Iscleft for ten years and more. Then that Ferro came in as commander. The asswipe 'bout killed the whole alliance. Even the Fae would have left, but they don't want their border open to Frost Clime."

She'd heard others rail against Commander Ferro, as many as railed against the Enclave's alliance with the Fae. Would the latter group rail against the Rhoghieri's renewed alliance?

"Look you, then. We're here."

Orielle recognized the lane of Brok's dwelling.

Then she saw the open door, darkness inside, her seal broken.

~ 7 ~

Hackett shot his arm out to block her advance. "Wait." He stuck his head through the doorway. "Surrect?" A woman's voice answered, but he dropped his arm. "Go on then."

Orielle didn't budge. "I wanted to see Grim."

"I ain't leaving. Surrect's got some questions about your spells. I didn't ask; power ain't my business. Go on."

She scowled, but when she crossed the threshold, she pasted on a smile and a pretense of willing help.

The dimness briefly blinded her, but her sight quickly adjusted.

Surrect stood at the hearth. His staff leaned against the stones. At the table before the shuttered window was Lillias. Neither mentor returned Orielle's smile.

If they intended to be difficult, she would—. No, she needed their support for her mission and for Grim.

She only hoped Lillias had heard of the battle from Surrect.

The two mentors barely acknowledged her entry. Lillias frowned at her fellow. "Surrect, Fortis should be here. We need him."

The healer shook his head, his unbound hair shifting along his shoulders and down his back. A sole braid, from behind his left ear, held colored beads with strips of leather woven in. He leaned on the healer's staff, the knotty wood casting off a cedary scent although the growth from the gnarled knot at the top was leafy rather than a sticky frond. "Fortis will attend the hearing. Time enough then. Or do you intend to influence his decision before we even meet? He is a young mentor."

"And a friend of Grim," the woman pointed out. "A childhood friend."

"He will not be influenced by that when he decides."

"So you say now. What will you say if his decision goes against what you want?"

Surrect shrugged. "We use the weapons at hand."

Orielle couldn't decipher that comment. How would Lillias' influence of Fortis ahead of the hearing be a weapon? Unless the woman expected him to decide for the alliance, which she must oppose. But why would Lillias oppose an alliance with the Enclave?

Hackett's brief judgment of Commander Ferro rang in her ears. She remembered the man from the crowd, who had asked if the wizards would once again enslave the Rhoghieri?

Orielle had thought the mission would be simple. She'd thought the weeks-long journey would be the difficulty. She hadn't anticipated the foul creatures of the Wilding or the Kyrgy. Now she must contend with an undocumented past between wizard and Rho?

She broke into their continued conversation with its obscure comments. "Why do you wish to see me before the hearing? Do you wish to hear again about the wraiths?"

The older woman hooked her hands in her belt. "I haven't heard about last night."

"I told you, Lillias," Surrect snapped. "*I* called for you, wizard. We intend to break your other seals. We will examine this dwelling before I cleanse it."

"Good. I did only the minimum last night. I sealed all the windows and doors. Nor did I do the grave ceremony for Zairantze, although nothing remains of her body. The sorcery sapped all of her. You may have intended to seal this dwelling against wraiths, but the grave seal is also needed."

Lillias snorted. "Surrect will oversee that. Women have volunteered to assist him. I want to know of last night's events. You battled wights at night, when they are strongest. You defeated two of them quite easily."

Again? Her spine sagged. "I would not say easily, Mentor Lillias. I was lucky."

"*Lucky?* An Enclave wizard claiming her victory is luck?"

"You defeated them," Surrect said, his hand running up and down his healing staff. "That is all that matters."

"I destroyed one, yes, but neither Brok nor I saw the other one take the pathway. We came upon Zairantze's body minutes later. And he destroyed the pathway when he removed the eldritch knife. I could not determine if the wraith took that pathway or if it hid somewhere."

"Which is our reason for cleansing the dwelling."

"Hackett," Lillias said, and the man stepped over the threshold. "We will be some time. You need not wait." She smiled as if her suggestion was amenable.

But Orielle didn't want him to leave. These two mentors should cleanse and seal the dwelling. That was Haven business that should be done by Haveners. Last night, she only intended her sealing to be temporary. Now she wanted to see Grim, to check how he endured their lock-up.

Hackett shoved a shoulder against the jamb and leaned, crossing his booted feet at the ankles. "My thanks, Mentor Lillias, but my orders are to see our lady wizard to Grim after you finish here."

His stubborn answer pleased Orielle, but both mentors grimaced.

Lillias turned away from him and concentrated on her fellow. "We should start. We have sorcery to ward against and wights to cleanse."

"We must discover first if the wights used another pathway."

"How can there be another pathway?" Lillias argued. "No sorcerer can enter the Haven."

"Then how did this strange knife come in? Brok and this wizard claim it melted when it was withdrawn, and her body collapsed then disappeared. That is power, and only foul sorcery kills. Were it her word alone, I would not believe it, but Brok described the same thing, to me and Tobit. He said it dissolved when he removed it. Someone killed Brok's woman with it and opened that pathway for the wights. And they were feeding off him to get enough energy to terrorize the whole Haven."

"Everyone will be on guard—."

"No, Lillias, you do not comprehend the danger. The wights came because that sorcered knife opened a path to Neothera."

"You keep saying sorcery. This *wizard* keeps saying sorcery."

"Because it is sorcery."

Gods, why did they argue this? They might not believe my word, but surely Brok's—.

"Wizards are forbidden from necromancy," the healer intoned, as if he taught someone new to magic. "Sorcerers are not forbidden from it. Sorcerers bind wights to them and loose them to wreck evil. Have you forgotten?"

"We have only this wizard's word—."

"And Brok's. Do you question Brok? His woman died. The wights came through her. They fed on him. He did not seek that evil, someone else did. Two evils. Murders and wights."

Lillias bowed her head. Her hair shone silver in the shadowed room. "I do not argue with you, Surrect. Perhaps I have forgotten the old lessons. I did not hear an account of the events, only what you reported. I will be interested to see what Grim says."

"You cannot blame Grim." Hackett straightened away from the door jamb and inserted himself into the conversation. "She were dead days before he arrived with this lady wizard."

Lillias studied Orielle. She didn't refute Hackett's words, however much she might want to. She finally turned to Surrect. "I agreed to help you. What do you need?"

He bent his fierce attention on Orielle. "I have questions about the seals and the spells you used. How did you know to go upstairs?"

She described the prickly spell that had tried to ward her away from the door latches as well as the wraith's retreat to the stairway.

Surrect led the way to the door. "That spell is now gone."

Orielle crowded to his elbow. "It dissipated when I touched the latch. After the wraith ripped through it, no ward was going to dissuade me. Brok said that he never went upstairs to search for Zairantze. That didn't make sense. Since the wraith went through the door, the ward spell was doubly suspicious. Even you would have thought suspicious that neglect to look upstairs for Zairantze."

"I don't understand the reason you entered his room down here. Which one? This?" Surrect swung open the door to the room. "Was the door not shut for privacy?"

"Why would you open this door?" Lillias asked. "Why would you enter without permission? What were you seeking?"

The questions raised a flush on Orielle's face. "I sensed sorcery."

"Really?"

"I do not understand what you are suggesting." She did not dare raise a stronger protest, for then Lillias would crow that her suspicions were founded. Did she not understand that Orielle was attracted to Grim? *How could she? He and I barely entered the Haven before they locked him away.*

"She ain't suggesting nothing good." Hackett had followed them into the hall. "The lady wizard said she sensed sorcery. That's enough of an answer."

"I did sense sorcery." Orielle expanded those brief words. "I saw a strange light come from under the door."

"Enough," Surrect said. "We waste time, and I have much to do. Tell me about the wights. What was their appearance?"

With her every answer, he asked more questions, about the sealing spell, about the pathway, about the knife and Zairantze's corpse. He carefully didn't use her name, and Orielle realized that he hadn't, not in the house. When he mentioned the cleansing and the grave-seal again, she said, "I didn't consider the hearth."

He stiffened. "Nor did I."

"I did," Lillias declared. "We will be certain to seal *all* openings. Your assistance, Wizard Orielle, has been invaluable. Now, I think Hackett is eager to escort you to the lock-up. You will be present at the hearing. Fair you well."

On the street, with the door shut behind them, Orielle gave Hackett the glare that she had hidden from the two mentors. "Are all of them so—?" She couldn't find a polite word.

He laughed, a rusty sound, cracked and gruff. "They're not usually confronted with a pretty wizard, younger and stronger. That's set both of 'em back on their heels. Don't know 'bout you, but my belly's grumbling. Let's have a pasty." Then he insisted she share a flagon of cider, "best of the Lowlands."

Afternoon was well advanced when Orielle finally saw what they called the lock-up. The shed stood apart, near the stables, with a corral and several animal pens between its back and the Haven's surrounding palisade wall. It looked little more than a converted shed, intended for storage, with a patched roof and a single door. The planks looked sturdy, though, and the door was stout and braced with iron. The sentry standing beside the door proved that little shed was the lock-up.

"You stay outside," Hackett ordered. "The doorway's sealed. Don't break the wards. You can stay till it's time for the hearing. Your hearing will be after his."

"When will the hearings be?"

"Sunset."

"Will Grim be released?"

"Now, Lady Wizard, how could I know that? Visitor," he told the guard.

The man looked her over. "She know he's sealed?"

"She does. Open up."

"On your head then." The guard took a heavy ring from a bent nail by the door. One thick key dangled from it. It didn't jangle as he inserted it in the lock. He stepped back as the door swung inward.

Orielle eagerly stepped forward, then she saw the iron gate, six bars held together by three horizontal crosspieces. Another stout lock kept the gate closed. The lockplate was larger than the one on the wooden door.

And beyond the iron gate was deep shadow, deeper than Brok's dwelling.

The gate's iron bars were thick, black and unrusted. No Fae would touch the iron, but the metal wouldn't hold a wizard. Would it hold a Rho? One push of Air from Grim would send the gate flying. Tobit's Earth could grip it and crush it. Fire could burn the jamb that supported it. How did they think the lock-up would hold anyone? A single sentry couldn't prevent an escape.

Or would any prisoner be bound by his word more than the gate's strength, as Grim would be bound?

She closed the distance, wanting to touch the gate but unsure which part was sealed. The gate? The threshold? Around the whole room? She didn't touch the iron, but she sensed a vibration in the metal, a simple warding spell.

Orielle peered through the thick bars, trying to see someone in the deep shadows. "Grim? Grim?"

"Here."

~ 8 ~

Grim came from the left. He looked rumpled, unshaved and tired. The gaol had no windows, but he'd only suffered it a night and a half-day. If he were wise, he'd slept rather than confront the boredom of darkness and no interaction.

He braced a hand on the wood inside the doorframe. Narrowed eyes looked her up and down. "You hurt? Then tell me all. I heard Brok was enjoying two wraiths." He lifted a quizzical eyebrow. "And you interrupted them."

Orielle flushed, the same intensity as at Lillias' insinuation. Grim's information would come from gossip. She could imagine how the story had spiralled. "I sensed sorcery. And I think it's more properly said that two wraiths were sucking the life from him."

"Two wraiths? One wasn't enough for Brok?"

His sarcasm kept her from taking offense. The sly tone also assured her that Grim hadn't changed. Nothing had stolen him away. The day's old beard looked scruffy, but his eyes were bright between the slits of his eyelids.

"I didn't choose to battle these wraiths. I didn't expect them, especially when they were ... well. They attacked when I tracked the sorcery. I destroyed one. The other escaped. We tracked it upstairs ... and found Brok's wife."

He grimaced. So, the stories carried that news as well. She didn't have to repeat the worst of it. When she closed her eyes, she still saw Zairantze, hands crossed on her breast, the tear frozen in her lashes.

"I heard the healer tended both you and Brok."

"Only him. The wraiths stole his life essence. Two of them."

"He might have enjoyed that death."

"Enjoy or not, he would still be dead," she retorted.

The sentry reacted, his head knocking against the wall. Rubbing the back of his head, he shifted over a few steps, giving them a semblance of privacy.

"If you heard all that," Orielle grimaced at the idea of gossip, "other people did as well. Or were you privileged to hear the gossip first?"

Grinning, he eyed the gate top to bottom. "I wouldn't say *privileged*. One of the earliest to hear."

"And you thought I was wounded in the battle?" She snorted, as much for Grim as for the sentry and those who would hear the gossip of their meeting. "Have you not learned that I'm a better fighter than that?"

"You have a tendency to jump into trouble."

Orielle accepted that. Grim had saved her from the wyre's prime when she was foolish enough to offer *Come out and play*. "If you thought I was wounded, other people would as well. Will they think my power is also weak?"

He shrugged. He surveyed her the way he had the gate. "The wraiths didn't hurt you? That's good."

She leaned close to the gate. She surveyed the iron bars and cross-pieces but could see no weakness. The sentry could hear their every word; she and Grim weren't whispering. Yet touching the gate would trigger the wards, and Orielle didn't wish to discover the repercussions. "How *are* you?"

He lifted his scruffy face to the brilliant sun. "Enjoying the daylight."

The room behind him was night-dark. The walls were fitted tightly, admitting no light. If the shed had a window, it was shuttered. She wanted to grip his hand, touch his arm … but she dared not break the wards that sealed the lock-up. The gaol. That was what it was, no matter what the Haveners called it. "Do they not leave the door open during the day? You could enjoy the sunlight then."

"They opened up to give me water and supper. This morning they opened the door for more water and a hard roll and boiled egg then stew at mid-day."

"Is that all?" This gaol was no better than a dungeon. Worse, for a dungeon used torchlight. The Haveners left him in absolute darkness.

"And to allow your visit. I amused myself this morning by inspecting my cell. Four walls. A pallet in the center. I tripped over that last night. A covered bucket to relieve myself. Nothing else. It is a lock-up." He sat cross-legged on the dirt-packed floor.

She mimicked him. Then she leaned over her knees and splayed her fingers on the ground, a bare inch from the gate's bottom cross-piece. The iron had its own ward, a repellent power that buzzed her fingertips. Not the prickly pain of sorcery. It felt like a reduced version of her own ward spell.

Grim imitated her, pleasing her. They smiled, comrades re-connecting, and something more firing the heat of their gazes.

Orielle hadn't dared investigate her feelings for Grim on the journey. She had hoped to explore their connection when they reached the Haven. Her disappointment when he'd gone to the gaol had concerned her more than the wraiths' attack.

"No touching," the sentry snapped. "Mind the wards."

She didn't move. "We aren't disturbing them." She considered a Shield spell. That use of power would only be necessary if they discussed something secret, not just private. Alerting the sentry with the Shield wouldn't help their causes, his of release, hers of alliance. She scooted an inch closer and lowered her voice. "No one has told me any specifics about this hearing."

"None to know. Ah, you're remembering Enclave hearings or a royal audience. We aren't that formal. Rho don't abide ceremony. This won't even be like a report to a Citadel officer. The elder cites the charge—."

"Charge?" That sounded criminal, with penance planned. A criminal hearing would be much more formal than he suggested, with dire consequences.

"What they say I've done wrong. Leaving the Haven without the elder's permission, which would be minor if not for Tobit's second charge, that I left before we cleared the wyres' lair."

"And this happened two years ago?"

"The time doesn't matter. Abandoning the Haven when the community needed a fighter against attack, that's serious. I had thought we cleared the lair. We'd killed all 13 wyre, ten males and 3 females. That's the usual size of a lair outside its territory. My father died in the last attack. His pyre kept me here extra days. Then I left. It was past time for me to leave. I didn't mention my leaving to Tobit. He was Earth mentor when my father gave me permission, during a hearing, before the first wyre attack. We hadn't voted on my father's replacement for Air mentor or on the new elder. I have reasons I'll tell at the hearing. We'll see if they care, or if Tobit's after trouble."

Orielle winced. She glanced at the sentry and wondered how sharply he could hear. Was the man allied to Tobit? Or was he simply of the community?

Last night, when Tobit grieved with Brok, she thought Grim's friend was also Tobit's man. Yet something Lillias said contradicted that. She tried to recall the words, but they had flown. Perhaps Orielle had only received an impression rather than heard something.

She wanted to know if the Haveners allied themselves based on a mentor's power or if they followed bloodlines or used some other arcane method. That question needed to come later. Grim had ended his explanation with a more concerning detail. "Why would Tobit want trouble?"

He shrugged. His gaze flashed to the sentry even though the man was down the exterior wall, out of sight. If the sentry reported to Tobit, Grim had a reason to say nothing.

"Tobit fought at Iscleft Citadel against Frost Clime. Did you know?"

"I knew he was village-born and raised and that he'd been away for a long time. Years. I knew he came back with a warrior in tow. Comrades, he said, and that they'd saved each other's lives."

"A bit more than comrades."

Grim lifted a shoulder. "Don't know much else."

"How did he become elder? For that matter, how did he become Earth mentor? If he were recently returned after years away, why did they elevate him?"

"He'd been back a few months, a season or two, I think, long enough that everyone knew he was the best wielder of Earth."

"His friend Hackett has no power."

"Doesn't matter. Choice of the individual, voted by those who wield that element."

Similar to the clan alliances, although Enclave clans also had ties through bloodlines and friendship. Clan Letheina was Air and Water, but her grandfather had chosen an Earth clan rather than ally to his sister the ArchClan. Galfrons had wizards of all elements, but Drakon Clan was pure Fire.

Orielle tossed her hair back. She could puzzle that out later. "Seems odd to me. Tobit is back only a few months then becomes not just a mentor but the Haven's elder."

"You think something else is involved?" he murmured, too soft for the sentry to hear.

She shrugged. "Just odd. I thought he was horrible to you and then to me, but he grieved with Brok. And Hackett has been friendly and helpful. I thought Lillias was friendly, but she's become—hostile is too strong a word."

"When was she hostile?"

"Not hostile. It's not that strong. She wasn't … friendly, just now, when she and Surrect questioned me about the wraiths and sealing Brok's dwelling." Orielle felt her tension ease as she shared that concern with Grim. She had known him only a handful of days, but last night and this morning she'd missed talking over her troubles, over details that concerned them both. She didn't need a solution, just someone to listen and ask questions and prod her at the right moment. "Surrect wasn't hostile either. He treated me as if I were an irritation. Lillias implied that I had brought the wraiths into the Haven. I discovered them. I didn't ally with them!"

"And you defeated them."

"One escaped."

"Enough of a victory that the mentors had to admit that one of the sentinels was under attack. The Haven's under their leadership. They are to keep a watch on the community. Yet they didn't know a woman had been killed by sorcery to form a portal that admitted wraiths who were preying upon a sentinel."

Grim had boiled down the events to their salient worries. What more could she say? Her mission should drive what she said and thought and did. Since their arrival, all too often she wanted to forget she had a reason to come to the Wilding and to this Haven and attempt to sway the leadership. Her mission had enabled her to meet Grim. She could not start any dissent. She would lose long before she won any forward steps.

Waiting for her reply, Grim tilted his head. He likely guessed everything that flew through her mind. His mouth quirked. "Nothing to add?"

"You are well informed."

"The whole village is talking. Everyone will want to attend your hearing. You're no longer just a wizard seeking an alliance, escorted by a Rho who once lived here and abandoned the Haven. You saved Brok and fought evil for us. That should win your bid for an alliance."

"It should, shouldn't it? If the mentors don't accuse me of bringing the wraiths. Lillias—." Remembering the sentry, she stopped.

"You didn't. You couldn't have. Brok's woman was the portal, and everything I've heard says that she disappeared days and days ago. She must have been murdered when she disappeared. You hadn't crossed the border into the Wilding then."

"Grim … Brok was heart-broken."

He didn't respond.

Orielle shifted her hands back from the gate. He withdrew more slowly. "At your hearing, Grim, will you bring up the wyre that we fought? No one wanted to discuss the wyre with me, even though I told them that we had killed seven of the lair."

"Two sentries left this morning to investigate the bend of the river where we fought. They'll confirm that during the hearing."

"Unless the remaining wyre attack them. Six remain. They will want vengeance."

"There's that. You ready for your hearing?"

"I've rehearsed the reasons for the alliance every day since I left Mont Nouris. After the past days, I can add the wyre and the gobbers and the wraiths, how no one in the Haven is safe and secure as long as Frost Clime is a growing force. The Haven cannot wait to remove the threat of the remaining wyre and the sorceress before they commit to the alliance."

"Or send anyone to Iscleft Citadel to battle Frost Clime."

"Tobit will oppose that. Hackett told me that Commander Ferro is a fool, and Tobit no doubt thinks the same. I'm beginning to agree with that opinion. Do you think the Kyrgy would fight against Frost Clime?"

That idea startled Grim. He frowned as he gave it serious

consideration. "I think a Kyrgy would not want to fight any element of Frost Clime."

Orielle remembered Lady Bone's reluctance to fight the sorceress who had come with the lair of wyre. Sorcery gave the wyre power to shift out of the moontime. She'd seen the eldritch green energy limning their claws, hovering in their eyes.

"You're not considering an alliance of wizards with Kyrgy, are you? The Fae might rebel."

"The Kyrgy were once part of the Fae."

"Dark Fae. An alliance would be like welcoming a dangerous enemy to your hearth, all to defend against a lesser enemy. The Kyrgy will devour you."

"Do you think the Kyrgy are more powerful than the sorcerers and wyre of Frost Clime? Why, then, was Lady Bone reluctant to go against the sorceress?"

"Wrong question, Orielle. You don't understand how dangerous the Kyrgy are." He refused to say more. He turned their conversation to an explanation of mentors and the other Haveners, even describing the sentinels to her.

And the afternoon advanced toward evening and the hearings.

~ 9 ~

Hackett returned as the sun touched the western mountain range. "Thought you'd be hungry. A woman's coming with Grim's meal."

Orielle accepted the warrior's hand to rise. "My thanks. I will be allowed to attend Grim's hearing?"

"You will. You won't get to speak."

"Not even should I have something relevant to say?"

He gave her a hard look. The wyre scars twisted one eyebrow that tried to pull in for a frown. His affability faded. "You cannot broach your proposed alliance at his hearing. Save it for your own."

"I do understand that. I would not have discussed it then. I believe I have something to say in Grim's support."

"Stand and wait to be recognized." The friendliness had vanished completely. "As Grim will stand and wait during your hearing."

"Hackett's right." Grim braced an arm on the interior jamb. "Better to say nothing. Tobit and the mentors will hear your mission with your every word, whether you speak of it or not."

"Look you. Your meal's here. Best we head back to Tobit's."

Orielle didn't want to leave. She yearned toward Grim. He shook his head, as if he knew how she felt. His gaze flashed to Hackett then the sentry, both men limiting their conversation. What more could be said? She'd heard enough of the hearing's protocol to know her presence wasn't begrudged … although a statement by her would be. *I'm an outsider, and outsiders shouldn't expect everything to flip toward them.* Grim's hearing would reveal anything more she needed to learn about the protocol.

He didn't appear apprehensive. The villagers had already expressed their support, yesterday when Grim and she entered the Haven. They supported Grim; they weren't agog to see her. He was well liked, for all that he'd left seasons ago. Whatever punishment was decided, the Rho leaders would be fools to harm him.

And she had no reading of foolishness from Tobit, Surrect, or Lillias.

She didn't know about Fortis. Grim had named him a friend. Would Fortis rescue Grim? Or swing whatever vote to aid him?

As for herself—that battle with the wraiths should have screamed in her favor.

To stay even with Hackett's long stride, she had to stretch her legs. He'd strolled earlier. Now he seemed hurried.

"Have you heard anymore of what Lillias and Surrect found at Brok's dwelling?"

"The mentors didn't make me privy to that conversation. You happy now that you've talked to Grim?"

"I won't be happy until he's no longer in lock-up."

Twilight deepened quickly in this broad valley that sheltered the Haven. When they reached Tobit's Elder House, night's darkness cast its shadows in alcoves and small alleys, under sheds and porch roofs.

Hackett took her through the large front room with its massive carved chair to a hearth room at the back. The window was shuttered for the evening. The cook greeted them and continued washing her knives and spoons, smaller pots and bowls, and a long bread bowl.

By the time they sat down, she had bowls of venison stew and hunks of quick bread for them. Hackett washed his meal down with cider while she received watered wine. The wine had the sour tang that verged on vinegar, but Orielle drank it. The acidic wine braced her for what she feared would be hours of talking and argument. No one spoke, the woman quicky disappearing and Hackett having concerns he didn't share.

"Hurry it," he warned when she slowly tore through the last of her bread.

When he led her back to the front room, she understood his wish for speed.

People had packed into the greatroom, squeezing onto the benches two-deep along the wall. Those who hadn't gotten a seat sat cross-legged on the floor or stood inside the door, edging out of the way whenever someone entered. The hearth slab was packed, with men leaning against the mantel. The fire hadn't been lighted; the press of bodies would keep the room warm.

Hackett cleared a space on the end of the bench beside the hearth room door then motioned to Orielle. He leaned against the jamb, arms folded.

Three chairs with high backs flanked the carved chair. The three mentors had taken those chairs. Surrect and Lillias sat together. Fortis had the sole chair on the left side of the elder's chair. Fortis—Fire, she remembered—talked with someone off to his right and seated on the floor, out of Orielle's view.

She studied Grim's old friend. He was big, like Tobit, broad of shoulder and with muscled arms, a barrel chest. Clean-shaven chin but a thick mustache topped thin lips. She remembered friends who had wielded Fire. They were clean-shaven, too, and wore tight-fitting sleeves, just as Fortis did. His size filled the chair, but he didn't look uncomfortable. He grinned at whatever the person said to him. His laugh was a deep chuckle that reverberated through the room. At his laugh, Lillias gave a level look, neither condemning nor supportive.

Maybe she was always hard to read.

The lanterns on the mantel burned steadily. Fire leapt in the braziers on tall poles at the corners of the room.

Orielle spied Waren and Malva. Of Brok there was no sign. Would he not attend this hearing for his friend Grim?

Lillias and Surrect talked, low murmurs that excluded those nearby. Sentries stood behind the chairs. Would they speak of the wraiths during her hearing? That battle would be a major point in her favor.

How had that eldritch knife, clearly sorcery, found its way into the Haven? Why was Zairantze targeted? Brok's wife had few friends in the Haven. How many people had spoken of that? Was she targeted because no one would note her absence, not until Brok returned from sentry duty and missed her?

Orielle puzzled over that—and wondered if she should open that query before or after her mission was approved … or not. *If the Haven doesn't approve my mission, should I care what they decide about the wraiths and sorcery? Will they rescind my welcome if they decide to punish Grim?*

Or am I worrying needlessly?

She didn't have enough of a grasp of Haven politics to decide.

The outer door opened. The people there stirred then crowded against their fellows, parting a way. She saw Tobit, towering over everyone he walked past. Behind him, equally tall, came Grim. A sentinel followed with two more after him. One closed the door then stood guard there.

Hackett closed the door to the back then stood before it, no longer leaning, his sinewy arms crossed over his chest.

She caught Tobit's flickering glance at Hackett and then her. The two men exchanged some signal. Then Tobit worked his way to the carved chair while Grim, flanked by the two sentinels, stood before the chairs.

Lillias murmured, and Surrect laughed. Tobit leaned forward and cleared his throat, and she fell silent.

"We meet this evening for three purposes. First to hear Grim, who departed from us to fight at Iscleft Citadel against Frost Clime. We have charges against him for his departure, not for his decision. Second, we hear from the wizard Orielle, who comes to renew our Haven's alliance to the Wizard Enclave. You all heard her request and have had time to consider."

A man seated on the floor spoke, a jumble of words. Hackett changed his stance, hooking his thumbs in his swordbelt. The people close to the man murmured.

Tobit heard the man out then shook his grizzled head. "We will follow the order. Raise your question at the appropriate time." Beady dark eyes swept the room. "All of you, speak at the appropriate time, not before, not after. The order keeps this meeting from chaos. As for our third trouble, most of you heard about the wraiths in Brok's dwelling and about the death of his woman Zairantze. I promise to separate fact from truth. Surrect, are you prepared to share what you learned?" When he received a nod from Surrect, Tobit lifted his voice then turned his gaze on Orielle. "Wizard, you must report what you saw and heard."

She stood. "I will." She sat back down, knocking elbows with the man beside her and asking forgiveness with a small smile and shrug. He grinned and shrugged in his turn.

"Where's Brok?"

"He waits," Lillias said. "I deemed he need not enter until we call for him. I know you all." Her benevolent smile encompassed the room. "You would press Brok for answers. You will whisper and gossip if he were with us now. He waits, as we all will wait, until we hear of the wraiths."

"Seems like," a white-haired man stepped forward from leaning against the mantel. Aged, he still dressed like the sentries. He scowled as he planted his feet wide on the hearth slab. "Seems like we should hear of the wraiths first. A greater danger. Deciding if we want that alliance or if we need to hold a grudge about Grim's departure, those aren't as important."

People nodded. Some agreed loudly. A few protested.

Tobit shook his head. Fortis and Surrect, flanking him, also shook their heads 'no'. "One leads to another then another. This we will see."

What does he mean? How does Grim's return or even my coming have anything to do with the wraiths and their pathway into the Haven?

"Before we begin, does anyone have other concerns to hear?"

"Zairantze" was the only word she heard clearly.

"We will deal with her later," Lillias said. "Grim and the wizard come first."

"Anyone else?" Tobit asked.

Another jumble of words, from a different corner of the room. 'Tinker' and 'supplies' and 'snow' were the only clear words.

"That doesn't need a hearing," and several nodded at Tobit's decision. "I can deal with that myself, on the morrow. If no one else—? Good. Grim, son of Holt, you are Haven-raised. You know our laws. Two years ago you left us to journey to Iscleft Citadel and fight against Frost Clime. Is that what you have done?"

A strange way to begin.

"I have."

"Why did you choose Iscleft Citadel?"

"I knew fighters there. I know Frost Clime had allied with wyre, and the wizards and Faeron would need the Rho to fight them."

"At the time you left—." Tobit stopped and raised his voice over the whispers. "At the time you left, the alliance of sorcerers with wyre was not new. For over a decade they have harried the border at the citadel. You know this. They fought there when I left the Citadel, years ago. Is this not true?"

Grim shifted. He clasped his hands behind him. "It is true."

"Then why did you wait to leave until the day you did? You waited almost a year."

His crossed hands fisted. Orielle wished she could see his face.

"I hoped to convince others to go with me. Brok. Waren. Fortis. A few others."

"Truth," Fortis said. He leaned his huge frame on the chair arm. He grinned at his childhood friend. "Grim asked. I wanted to wait. And Waren had recently married Malva. Then the wyre attacked, and we concentrated on them."

"Waren. Brok. Fortis. And yourself." Lillias ticked the names off on her fingers. "Our best fighters. You intended to remove the Haven's best fighters when we most needed them."

"I asked before the first wyre attack, not while the wyre attacked. I worked, like everyone, to defend the Haven. I fought the wyre. I went with the party to hunt the lair and kill the wyre."

"But you would have robbed us of our best fighters."

"Leave it, Lillias," Tobit snapped. "We had other fighters, and he didn't know the wyre were in the Wilding when he asked. No one knew."

"We have other dangers besides the wyre," she agreed. "The gobbers are a constant worry, and the Kyrgy think they rule the whole Wilding."

"Kyrgy have not disturbed us for many years, and the gobbers are no trouble unless someone crosses a nest of them."

The outer door opened.

The sentinel turned to bar entrance. Then he stepped back into the room. Everyone looked to see the latecomer.

A white-haired swordsman stood there, his face like white marble, a cloak of storm-purple covering his broad chest. Volk, the Kyrgy knight closest to Skuld, the leader of the Kyrgy, to be called Lady Bone rather than her name.

Ice covered Orielle.

Volk stepped inside, and people scrambled to open a broad path to the elder and mentors. Yet he stopped three steps from the door.

The sentinels had drawn their swords, as had Hackett. The sentinels crossed the blades before Tobit and the mentors, protecting them. Hackett's honed steel flashed in the corner of her eye.

Volk looked around the room, then he found Orielle. He lifted a white-skinned hand to her. "Aiwaz Solsken, wizard of the Enclave, Lady Bone requests your presence." His sharpened teeth flashed. "The Kyrgy ride the Hunt tonight, and you swore to ride with us."

~ 10 ~

The room fell so silent that the rustle of her clothes were loud as Orielle stood.

Grim turned. "You can't go with them."

She focused on Volk. "Tonight is not the moon. Tomorrow is the first round moon, Old Crone. I thought the Kyrgy only ride at the moon."

"Tonight is the time chosen by the Lady. Do you break your vow?"

"I do not." She dared not. A broken vow to any Fae was anathema, and the Kyrgy were Dark Fae. Nor did she dare risk a broken vow in front of a roomful of people who would decide about an alliance with the Enclave.

"Orielle, you can't go," Grim insisted.

Her gaze shifted from Volk to him. "I do not believe I have a choice. I vowed."

Tobit recovered. "Sir Knight, we're to hear the wizard this evening."

Volk's eyes, full black with no whites, didn't shift from Orielle. "Lady Bone waits for you." His outstretched hand didn't waver.

"You can't, Orielle. Not alone."

"I vowed," she repeated, "so Lady Bone would save your life."

"Do you refuse the Lady?"

She stepped forward. She wished the knight Sangrior had come for her. Sangrior had restored their horses and helped them against the gobbers. Following mysterious rules known only to her, Lady Bone deemed his actions too far away from sole loyalty to her. Those mysterious rules had led to one defection from the Lady's riders, the dame Saircuista. Sangrior had accepted punishment rather than defect.

Hackett interposed his body between her and the knight. "Tobit? What do you say?"

"Dangers," Lillias said. "The Kyrgy disturb us tonight."

Orielle scowled at the Air mentor.

"They do not threaten us," Tobit retorted.

The elder waved a hand, and Hackett stepped out of her way. Yet before she took the knight's hand, the older man caught her wrist. "You'll be safe?"

"She won't be safe," Grim growled.

She glared at Grim. "I have learned to be careful of words with the Kyrgy."

"She rides with Lady Bone," Volk intoned, his words emotionless. "No harm will come to the Aiwaz Solsken. Lady Bone swears."

"Then I am safe from harm," and she placed her hand in Volk's icy one.

His grip was strong and sure as he drew her against the coolness of his enscrolled breastplate. "You please the Lady." He turned to Grim. "You did not vow to ride with the Lady, but you may attend her."

"He cannot leave," Tobit declared loudly, stopping Grim's long step toward Orielle and the knight. "Her vow may precede the hearing, but as you say, he has no vow with Lady Bone. His hearing will go forward."

"What about Orielle's hearing?" Grim demanded. "She came into the Wilding on a mission for the Wizard Enclave. That precedes her vow to Lady Bone. The hearing will decide on a renewed alliance."

"Lady Bone requests. The ride is tonight."

"She need not be here," Lillias said. "Her mission is known to us. She shouldn't be present to hear our discussion."

"Wait—."

"No, Grim." Fortis stood. "My friend, let the wizard go. That is best, isn't it, Tobit?"

With a grin, the elder leaned back. "That should be part of our decision. Will we ally with the Wizard Enclave? Will we accept the request of this Aiwaz Solsken, so named by the Kyrgy of this Wilding? Those are strong arguments."

"Dammit," Grim protested. "Lady Bone wants a wizard to join her riders. You can't let her go alone."

"I will guard her." Volk's hand slid to her wrist and closed firmly around it. "The lady wizard vowed to ride three times, no more, no less. Come now. Lady Bone tarries only for you."

As his grip tightened, threatening pain, Orielle's bravery vanished. "I am in your keeping, Volk."

Light gleamed in his full-black eyes, not the yellow flame of the torches but a silver streak that crossed the orb. "As I said." Then he turned.

A bright blinding light flashed. Her ears popped. Then she heard a distant owl's hoot.

Orielle opened her eyes to a darkened clearing. Marble-white horses encircled her. Knights and dames stared at her.

One horse rode forward. She blinked, fighting the lingering blindness of that flash of light. Volk dropped his grip.

"Welcome, Not-Wizard."

She looked up and up, to the sharp-features of Lady Bone, her silken gown covered by an intricately chased breastplate. Her silver hair cascaded to her thighs. Her black eyes drew Orielle into an abyss. Kyrgy, Dark Fae, mysterious and dangerous, willful and capricious, long-lived and long of memory.

The Kyrgy smiled, revealing her sharp-pointed teeth. "You join us. I almost believed you would not."

What should I reply? To say she had looked forward to the Hunt would be a lie. *I keep my word* sounded defiant, and Orielle knew it wouldn't be wise to defy Skuld, known in this Wilding as Lady Bone. She settled for a curtsey.

Lady Bone laughed, a tinkling of ice crystals that shivered Orielle's bones. "Her horse," she called. One rider came forward, leading another marble-white horse. The other riders remained silent watchers.

As Orielle mounted, she looked for Sangrior, the sole Kyrgy knight that she could call friend. Was it only yesterday that he'd proved his loyalty to the Lady? With his sharpened teeth in that statue-white face, his eyes fully black, and his nails sharpened to claws, he no longer looked human, no longer looked like the man who had given her the Kyrgy name of Aiwaz Solsken or restored their horses or fought beside her and Grim against the gobbers. He looked like Volk.

Volk's loyalty to Lady Bone was unwavering.

She remembered the wraith's terror when Lady Bone declared he would pay a tithe for his lies and his attack on Orielle.

Sangrior must have also accepted a tithe, a punishment—all for the Lady. What hold did she have on the riders? They obeyed without question—although Saircuista had defected. What tithe would Saircuista owe to the Lady?

If Sangrior still proved his loyalty, Volk might be the better escort for a wizard who had vowed to ride three times with the Lady.

Settled into the richly-bossed saddle, Orielle leaned forward to pat the horse's neck and rub the flesh beneath the snow-white mane. Saddle and harness were pearly white with touches of ice blue in the embossing. The metals bits gleamed silvery, even without the not-risen moon to cast its light.

Then she felt the shivers beneath her hand. The horse seemed terrified. Did Lady Bone terrify all her creatures? No white had shown in the horse's black eyes. It hadn't shied away when she mounted.

"What is his name?"

The rider ignored her, returning to his own mount.

She patted the horse's shoulder. The shivers continued, but the horse was calming. Not fear, then. Excitement? Eagerness? Eager to be on the Hunt, before the rise of the guiding moon, not quite rounded to full.

Volk drew up beside her. She waited for him to speak, but he didn't look her way. He sat erect in the saddle, not stiff but straight, and his focus was on his Lady.

Orielle glanced at the other riders. All awaited the Lady's word. She, though, seemed sunk into thought. What idea consumed her? Saircuista's betrayal?

Five riders encircled them. The Lady and Volk made seven. Sangrior, wherever he was, made eight. Before Saircuista left, their number for the Hunt would have been nine, three and three and three. Orielle made them nine again—if Sangrior joined them.

The Lady's horse leaped forward, a slowed leap, then Volk flanked her. Orielle followed him, the other riders trailed.

As if he galloped, the horse's muscles gathered and stretched beneath her, yet they seemed to glide over the ground. Movement seemed fluid, elegant, without the thud of hoofbeats. She believed they rode slowly until she saw the trees flashing past.

Silvery shadows ran away from the riders. Red eyes glowed from the underbrush. Rabbits. Foxes. The small animals that ventured out with night's safety. She wondered at their silver-lit bodies and their red eyes. *Is that how the Kyrgy and the riders see anything mundane, moon-colored shadows and the fire of life ... while they were cold marble and black eyes?*

Have they lost the fire of life?

Is that what the Lady wants from me? Does wizardry make my life energies burn brighter?

They broke from the trees and sped along the shoreline, the water like a flat grey ribbon that should have sparkled with star shine and the light of waxing gibbous moon. Orielle saw the river bend to the right, and she recognized the shoreline. There, there was the mud slide and boulders and trees that had spilled into the river. Here was where she and Grim had fought the wyre. This place was where she'd bargained with Lady Bone to keep Grim from dying after a wyre bite.

She shivered and shivered again as Lady Bone halted. The other riders spread along the shore, only Volk staying with the Kyrgy and with Orielle. At her third body-wracking shiver, Orielle recognized her fear.

She tried to relax her grip on the reins. Her fingers cramped.

"You ride well," Volk murmured.

She acknowledged the compliment with a nod, not wanting to attract the Lady's attention. Her attempt failed, for Lady Bone wheeled her horse around to face Orielle.

The Lady's smile had a predator's look. "You seek an alliance between the wizards and the Rhoghieri."

Orielle dipped her head, not wishing to offend by correcting with 'a *renewed* alliance.' "To where do we ride, Lady?"

"Nowhere and everywhere."

"You speak in riddles, Lady."

"You speak in truths, Aiwaz Solsken. Do wizards need Rhoghieri that much?"

"Should the Rho join the alliance at Iscleft Citadel, that border crossing may repeat the success of Chanerro Pass." She made bold to add, "Kyrgy should join us as well."

"Kyrgy have no care for the mundane."

"Your riders began their lives as mundane."

"And will end them as Kyrgy-bound. Is this truth, Volk?"

"Truth, my lady."

"Not if they defect. Like Saircuista," she added, being clear.

"Ah. Prescient of you, to determine our destination. Saircuista." Her dark tongue ran over her colorless lips. "The traitor leagues herself with Frost Clime, the Frost Clime who fights at the Citadel. She returns to the mundane although my mantle remains over her until the three-Lady

Moon."

"When we find Saircuista, what will you do with her?"

The Lady laughed, that ice-cold twinkling sound that shattered through Orielle. "Do you fear I will kill her?"

"Will you?"

"She knows that she may no longer be my rider. She will anticipate that I will remove my mantle. *You* will kill that sorceress."

"Where is Saircuista?"

"Found already," Volk said when the Lady merely watched the rising moon. "The Lady knows the heartbeat of every one of her riders. Did you think she had escaped?"

Orielle shook her head. The horse shifted under her then tossed its head, the white mane rising and falling as if the motion had been violent. "I don't know why she chose a sorceress and her wyre. Does she believe the sorceress will protect her? She doesn't know sorcerers very well. They lie."

"As all mundane lie, even you, Solsken."

"I do not lie to you, Lady Bone."

"Because you dare not. You would lie if you dared, if it gave you any advantage. As you lie to the Rhoghieri."

"I have not lied to them."

"To omit the truth is still a lie."

"I have not lied to them. I explained my mission clearly."

"Then you were lied to," Those black eyes dropped from the moon and focused on Orielle. "The Wizard Enclave will never bow to an alliance with those they consider lesser. Come, we travel further."

As her horse leaped beside Volk's, after Lady Bone's, Orielle realized her mission would fail.

For the Lady spoke the truth.

~ 11 ~

Volk waved a hand forward. Lady Bone spurred her horse, and Orielle and the other riders, knight and dame, followed the Kyrgy into the campsite. The number of riders seemed less than when she'd first encountered the Lady. Had more than Saircuista defected? Or had the Kyrgy's sudden appearance overwhelmed her and she saw more than were there?

A man stood beside the cold ashes of an old campfire. He leaned on an ice blue sword, the tip buried in the ashes.

Orielle recognized Sangrior, the knight that had named her, helped her and Grim … and paid a penance for acting without the Lady's approval.

As Lady Bone and Volk dismounted, Sangrior flicked a glance her way. His gaze rapidly returned to the Lady. He bowed deeply then stirred the ashes with the sword's tip. "She camped here. She used a sorcered wick to light the fire."

"We are far west," Volk judged. He had looked around the enclosing trees then positioned himself between Lady Bone and the north edge of the campsite. "Did the gobbers not assail her?"

"I see no signs of it."

Lady Bone laughed. "A sorcered wick. Not-Wizard, give us your opinion."

Orielle slid down and approached the cold fire-ring. She sensed neither sorcery nor wizardry.

Sangrior lifted the glacial sword and extended the tip to her. "Taste," he offered.

She touched the ash-covered tip. She didn't have to taste to sense its origins. "Sorcery."

He wiped the ashes on leaves before he sheathed the sword. "The camp has no wards."

"With a sorcered fire, no one needs the wards. Most creatures avoid eldritch work."

Volk grimaced. He thrust his sword-hilt forward, as if eager to draw the blade. "Whereas they will attack wizard-born fires."

She didn't argue that. The gobbers had twice crossed her wards, first a single gobber attempting to steal her foodbag, then a pack of them intent on capturing or killing her and Grim. She examined the small camp but didn't sense any other power. City-born, she didn't know if there was aught else this campsite would reveal.

"The Lady's mantle still guards her. How does she use sorcery?" Sangrior's frown was puzzlement. He didn't look to the Lady to answer.

An eldritch knife had killed Zairantze and created a portal for the wraiths. No sorcerer had entered the Haven; their wards prevented that. A Rhoghieri, though, had used that knife and murdered a fellow Rho to open the pathway. Now Saircuista also used sorcery when her binding to a Kyrgy should make it impossible.

"The sorceress could have given Saircuista the fire-starting wick. As she gave an eldritch knife to a Rho."

Lady Bone whirled to face her. "What is this? An eldritch knife given to a Rhoghieri?"

Once more, Orielle explained the events of the previous night.

"That is the reason for your hearing before the elder and mentors?" Volk asked.

"We were to discuss the sorcered knife and the wraiths after they judged my mission."

"My need *is* greater." The Lady turned her horse.

Sangrior helped Orielle to re-mount. "We ride into danger," he whispered.

The riders waited again for Lady Bone to set the direction, and she waited for Sangrior.

As they rode, Volk flanked her. "What did he say?"

"He?"

"My fellow knight."

Orielle thought of continuing her mock confusion. Volk had already shown his low tolerance of it. "Sangrior merely warned me. Do we hunt Saircuista? She fled to the sorceress, the one who must have given her the fire-wick and likely the one who gave a Rho that eldritch knife. She will be with that sorceress."

"Does he think you are a fool, Not-Wizard?"

She looked at the Lady who rode ahead of them, Sangrior a little ahead of her. One of the silent knights that she didn't know had outpaced Orielle and Volk and rode just behind the Lady. The remainder trailed behind.

No hoofbeats sounded to guard any words. She didn't think it wise to drop a Shield for any conversation with Volk. Lady Bone would only become more suspicious. Eyes on the statue-erect Lady, she risked words that she dared not ask the Kyrgy. "I would have believed no rider would betray the Lady. Saircuista did, *and* she managed to escape. She allied with a sorceress. What turned her against the Lady?"

"You *are* a fool."

By that, she knew he wouldn't answer. One thing came clear. Whatever terms bound the riders to Lady Skuld, whatever punishment if they defected, Saircuista depended on the sorceress' protection.

The Lady had doubted Sangrior's loyalty for his bare friendship to a wizard. Now he rode with his Lady, his loyalty deepened to equal Volk's, with inky eyes that had lost the white sclera around the iris. His fingernails had grown dark talons.

Yet he still warned her.

The rider who had crowded to the vanguard slowed. The Lady and Sangrior drew up, and Orielle, Volk, and the others also halted, the riders spreading out through the trees. The Lady lifted a hand. Volk grabbed the bridle of Orielle's horse and led her forward.

"Aiwaz Solsken, what do you know of the sorceress and the wyre?"

"We killed seven. Six remain. With sorcery, they can shift out of moon-time."

"Saircuista makes eight we face. One more than us, my lady. This wizard equals the odds."

"Unless the wyre have recruited more, Volk," Orielle warned.

"They could not. The wyre need the Dragon Moons or the Lady Moons for the turn."

"We will test your mettle, Aiwaz Solsken." The Lady laughed. "Come, the night speeds away." She set her horse to a walk, through the last trees, onto a shoreline, different from where Orielle and Grim had fought the wyre.

The fire near the water's edge snared all eyes. Four people crouched beside it, with two clawing into whatever cooked on a spit above the flames. As the riders cleared the treeline, the men tossed aside the meat and stood. The other two also stood, angling toward the center where the Lady rode with her two knights and Orielle while her lesser knights and dames held the flanks. One drew a sword—Saircuista. She wore a jacket of plates and leather breeches, and the flames painted her sword amber. The fourth must be the sorceress.

"Give me mine," the Kyrgy lady called, her voice hollow yet clear.

The skirted woman crossed her arms. "None here belong to you."

"That one is mine."

Orielle saw movement in the corner of her eye. Lady Bone sent a shining candle of light to the fire-ring. It arrowed for Saircuista.

The sorceress stepped before the former rider. She waved a hand, and darkness enveloped the Lady's light.

"I do not choose to be yours," Saircuista called.

"You gave yourself to me. Now you take back that gift? No one does so to a Kyrgy."

"I asked you once to ally with me. Our alliance, sorcery and Kyrgy, could rule this Wilding."

Saircuista grabbed the woman's arm. "Do not give me to her. You don't know what she will do to me."

The sorceress laughed. "You are mine, Saircuista. I will not return you to a Fae, even a Dark Fae." Although her words to the former rider had carried, the sorceress lifted her voice again. "Dark Fae should ally with Frost Clime."

Volk drove his horse a length forward. "Your mistake, sorceress. Saircuista is the Lady's. She must return."

"No!" The armed woman stomped her foot on the soggy sand. "I will not return. Do you hear me, Skuld? The burden is onerous. Release me. Take the wizard in my place."

What?

"The wizard does not swear loyalty to me. She will not as long as her heart remains in the Haven and her mind remains Enclave. You attacked that Haven, sorceress."

"Did I?" The woman's smile was as predatory as a wolf's, as Lady Bone's could be. "What will you do? Your rider refuses to return to you."

"I keep what is mine."

The sorceress clapped her hands. A blast of energy cracked toward them.

Orielle threw up a shining barrier. The shield flared golden light then thinned to a veil, weaker yet still gleaming with wizardry.

Shouts and growls broke from her left. A scream and shriek of claws on steel came from the right. Orielle dared not look. Her battle was before her. With the barrier in place, she slid off the horse and planted herself solidly on the shore above the damp sand. Only then did she risk a glance to her flanks.

Two riders were down. Volk fought, swinging his sword against two attacking swordsmen. From the right came more clashes of swords and claws, more fighting of riders against wyre and rider against swordsman.

Crackling sorcery hit her barrier, weakening it to a translucent shimmer. The two wyre at the camp plunged into the fighting on her right.

A shining orb surrounded the Lady and enveloped the rider fighting from his mount. Blood stained his ice-blue sword, black against the shining steel. Beyond him another rider was down, fighting the ambush that no one had expected.

Another greeny spell blasted over her barrier. It held and held then flickered and winked out.

Orielle threw her prepared spell.

Saircuista's sword flashed up, intercepting the darting spell. The energy exploded over the steel. She laughed and strode to the water's edge, stopping only to brace herself for more exploding energy. The sorceress kept behind her. She gathered gleaming sorcery, shaping it into an orb.

Orielle divided her power, a gust of Air flung at Saircuista, a golden dart for the sorceress' heart. The former rider staggered then fell backwards. The dart of energy pierced the orb in the sorceress' hands. Light flared, blinding, crackling like static. Then it died, the energies sucking away the campfire, leaving them night-blind.

She jerked up another piercing dart, and the snatched power lit up everything around her.

The sorceress stepped over Saircuista, into the verge of water. The former rider lay on the sand, her sword out of reach. The woman laughed. "Little wizard, what are you doing so deep in the Wilding? A dragon will incinerate you with one breath."

"Have dragons dared to leave the Wastes?"

The woman scowled. She glanced right and left. Then her hands flung forward. Greeny power flashed. Orielle threw up a hasty barrier. It dissolved when the sorcery struck it. The spell flew on, weakened by the barrier. Orielle funneled Air to catch the spell, deflecting it upward.

Silvery light flared to her right. A spell powered toward the sorceress … and sped past her, to overwhelm Saircuista, who crawled toward her sword. The light poured over her, like liquid silver. And Saircuista screamed.

More light came from the right, expanding to encompass Orielle. It swept past her, gathered up Volk—who sagged on a bent knee.

Then the light flared, blinding Orielle. She tried to shield her eyes. Too late, for silver washed into her sight, filled her brain, filled her body, until she *was* the light, one *with* the light. The energy poured through her. She felt as strong as an Ancient, as insubstantial as drifting vapor, as powerful as the greatest wizard, as weak as a newborn. New and old, clear and solid, light and dark.

The light blinked out, leaving her in darkness, with a voice calling "Volk! Volk! My Volk."

~ 12 ~

"You will live," Lady Bone commanded. "Volk, you will live."

Blood trickled from a gash on his temple, masking half his face with the red-black gore. More blood streamed from gashes on his arms. It poured through the mail protecting his torso.

He sagged to the leaf-covered ground.

Lady Bone bent over him. "Volk, my Volk. You may not leave me. My Volk, you must stay with me." Silvery light blazed from her skin. It spread to him. The healing light outshone the moon and stars. Her silver hair spilled around them like a cloak, swirling with energy.

He spasmed. The Lady covered him, energy from her invading him.

"Gods," breathed Sangrior to her right.

Lady Bone had transported them elsewhere. The sandy shoreline and rushing river had vanished. They stood under trees, a wide leaf-littered ground, the underbrush thick around them. The moon and stars peered through the canopy, a tracery of branches that had lost their leaves, the other leaves aflutter in the wind gusting through. Without the silver gleaming from Lady Bone and her wounded knight, all was night-black.

One rider held a handful of horses that had no riders. Their muzzles brushed the ground, black stains scarring their sides. Besides Sangrior and herself, Lady Bone and Volk, and the knight holding the horses, no other rider remained, eight reduced to five in bare minutes. Three killed in the ambush. The sorceress had lured them in by revealing only three others at the campsite.

"Four more wyre," Orielle counted, "and at least three other fighters." Those had attacked from ambush.

"Lady Bone was fated not to lose all her riders."

Sangrior wasn't watching the Lady heal her fallen consort knight. No, he looked away from them to a long object on the ground several feet away. An object that had a human shape, swaddled in shimmery silk that encased the twisting and contorting body.

"Is that—?"

"Aye," he breathed. "The Lady keeps those who are hers."

When Lady Bone lifted away from Volk, the sky had lightened. Above the tracery canopy, distant clouds tinged to pink and cerise. The Lady moved like her bones creaked and her muscles were unsteady, her balance off and her strength gone.

Volk knelt before her. He bent forward and kissed the hem of the Lady's white gown, darkly stained with his blood. Her long-fingered hand touched the white crown of his head. He looked up. His face shone, retaining that strange glow that had healed him. When he stood, the Lady's hand slipped to his shoulder then down his arm to grasp his hand, intertwining their fingers.

"My knight." The Lady's words had the strength of a vow, and both Sangrior and the remaining rider inhaled sharply. She didn't look away from Volk as she called, "Sangrior!"

"My lady."

"Escort the Aiwaz Solsken to the Haven."

"As you wish."

"Wait." Orielle couldn't believe she protested her return. "Is Volk healed? What will you do for riders? What are you going to do with Saircuista?"

"Hist, the Lady commands and you obey."

"No. The sorceress will attack the Haven. I know it. I had hoped Lady Bone would assist us. Another ride, Lady. I vowed three rides."

Keeping her grip on Volk's arm, the Lady faced her. "You are sworn to two more rides."

"That is my vow, in return for Grim's healing. Can you hunt when you have only three knights?"

She laughed, that musical tinkling with the sharp edge. "I will ride if my only escort is an Enclave wizard. Never fear that, Aiwaz Solsken. The sorceress lost as well, two wyre and two of her mundane swordsmen." She looked smugly at the silk-shrouded body. "And Saircuista."

A muffled scream came from the shrouded body.

"I fear you do not really need my power, Lady. Where will you recruit more riders?"

"Hist," Sangrior warned again.

Yet Lady Bone laughed. "Perchance I will recruit from the Haven." She turned to the east, the direction of the Haven and the pinkened clouds. A somber expression dimmed the lingering Fae glow. "Some of the Haven will look for what I can offer. Not Rhoghieri but instead the mundane who live with them."

"And Saircuista?"

Sangrior gripped her upper arm, his fingers biting into her soft flesh, punishment and warning. "You should not ask what does not concern you, Solsken."

"My knight speaks truly. Saircuista will know my judgment for her defection. Then, tomorrow, as the first Lady's Moon shines on us, I will remove my mantle, and she will know what has been long delayed. Perchance you should ride with us that night, to see justice done. Justice, not punishment, for you should know I am not a monstrous ruler of my riders."

"I didn't—I never said—."

The Lady laughed. "I have someone you will meet."

As Sangrior cried, "No, Lady!" the other rider jolted, and the horses jerked at the reins he held. The consort knight recovered himself and bowed, but when he straightened, he implored, "No, my Lady, not him."

"You will not speak of him to Aiwaz Solsken, Sangrior."

He bowed again, obedient to her will. "No, my lady."

"So it is decided. We will ride tomorrow, first night of the round moon, the old Crone Moon. We shall see if any of these Haveners wish to ride with me. And then we will ride to this sorceress and her eldritch wyre. She will not catch us so unprepared again. Will she, Not-Wizard?"

"No, my Lady," although Orielle wasn't quite sure what she had agreed to.

"We will have deeds on the morrow, Not-Wizard. Sangrior, escort her to Iscleft Haven."

The knight tugged her close. Then came that blinding light of the transition, through a blazing golden veil.

Sangrior steadied her while she blinked and stumbled and blinked and wavered, until the central square of the Haven came into focus.

Torches were lit at eight points around the square. People milled about. They sounded angry, scared, hurt. When Sangrior appeared with her, their shouts of shock and fear scared her.

"It's the wizard and that Kyrgy knight!"

"Tell Lillias."

"Tell Grim!"

"Get Fortis."

"Call the sentries!"

Sangrior kept his painful grip on her arm. He looked around at the people, all turned toward them but not yet pressing close. "Aiwaz Solsken, do you wish me to stay?"

"Lady Bone didn't say that you should linger. Will you come for me tonight?"

He grimaced. "The Lady herself will come. Where she goes, we all go."

Orielle nodded, not quite comprehending the whole and more concerned by the Haveners who filled the square at this early hour.

"Then tonight," she told Sangrior, "after twilight," for she'd learned that much about the Kyrgy: their realm was the night's darkness.

No wonder they called her *Solsken,* sun's kin. She was indeed sister to the sun, for the day was her realm, as strange to them as the night-dark was strange to her.

Although she expected Sangrior to leave in another blinding transition, he did not release her arm. He looked around at the gathering people, now silent and solemn. "What happened here?"

No one answered immediately, then a young woman with a babe snugged against her stepped forward. "Tobit is dead."

Orielle felt her jaw drop. She struggled against the words. "Dead? Tobit? No! How could that happen?"

The young woman muttered something, then the lanky man with her stepped out of the fringe, into the empty space encircling them that no one had dared enter. "He was murdered. Killed with one of those melting knives."

While she grappled with Tobit's death, Sangrior released her. Hand clapped to his sword-hilt, he glared at the surrounding people. "What do you mean 'melting knives'?"

"Wizard-work," the man claimed. "When Hackett pulled the blade from Tobit's body, it melted."

Orielle skipped over that damning *wizard-work*. "Where's Grim?"

"No," Sangrior interrupted. "Who is in charge?"

The young man grimaced. He looked to either side then around the crowd, then his face twisted. "I guess I can answer both of those questions. Grim's back in lock-up. Lillias ordered him there. She accused him of involvement."

"That's not possible," Orielle immediately defended. "Grim wasn't here when Zairantze was killed with just such a knife. Nor was I." Where were these Haveners' minds? Why hadn't someone spoken up? Why hadn't they protested with the facts? "And that knife is sorcery, not wizardry. Sorcerers deal in blood-work, not wizards. Tell anyone you speak to, that knife is sorcery. Sorcery is the evil attacking you. Not wizardry. Not myself. Certainly not Grim."

"What about that Kyrgy? He came into our Haven."

"Not him. He's a friend to wizardry and an ally to you." She didn't mention that Volk, not Sangrior, had come for her last evening. Best to keep events simple. Sangrior was her friend, and she was more than a friend to Grim. Grim was of this Haven, and she wanted to ally with it. That connection linked Sangrior as an ally to the Haven as well. "So, Lillias is in charge?"

"Her and Fortis," an old man said. "Surrect's in the lock-up with Grim." He leaned on a staff much like the healer's, only the knotty wood of his staff had no greeny growth.

"Why is Surrect in lock-up?"

"The knife turned to water. Surrect controls Water."

She could see that connection, but she didn't think Surrect, a healer, would ever ally with the sorceress or even kill. "Take us to Lillias, No, wait. Take us to Hackett."

"He's mourning Tobit," someone said, behind others, hidden.

Orielle turned to the voice. "Take us to him anyway." She hoped Sangrior wouldn't protest that he must return to Lady Bone.

The knight remained as the old man and the lanky one led them out of the square, where the Elder's House was located, and into the warren of streets. She stayed close to Sangrior's shield side. She didn't know these streets, except that they did not lead to the lock-up.

The villagers stopped to watch their passage. More Rho fell into the group. Orielle hoped that meant they, too, were not accepting of Lillias' decision to lock up Surrect and Grim. Was Grim included in their dissatisfaction? Why had Lillias ordered him locked up after Tobit's murder? At least, he walked free before that; the earlier hearing had cleared him of the elder's charges. A worse one, though, had now sent him back to that shed.

They twisted along side lanes until they reached a narrow byway. It was more crowded than the square. The people's silence weighed heavy, like an ominous blow expected and braced against.

The old man murmured to people at the edge of the crowd. They moved, then more people moved and more, splitting apart to open a passage to a dwelling's doorway. The younger man kept back, but the old man continued to lead them. At the door, he advanced his knotted staff, and the man there stepped aside so they could enter.

Like Brok's, the door opened directly into a front room, just as crowded as the byway. The people here were also strangely silent. Orielle heard two people talking softly.

As a way cleared, she pressed forward. Sangrior remained beside her although he no longer gripped his swordhilt.

And here was Hackett, seated at the table under the unshuttered window, the growing light of sunrise revealing the haggard lines that marred his face as much as the scar did.

~ 13 ~

Hackett stopped talking when he saw Orielle with the Kyrgy knight. The gravid woman who talked with him turned in her seat.

"Lady Wizard."

"Hackett. I grieve for Tobit."

His face altered, hollowed and shadowed although the first daylight struck it. "You bring the Kyrgy knight here?"

"We battled the sorceress as Tobit must have battled her representative. We heard an eldritch knife dealt the fatal blow."

"Tobit had no chance to fight. The coward struck him from behind. He knocked him on the head then turned him over and struck with the knife."

"When?"

"I set the sentries to their second watch. When I returned, there he was, still warm."

"Like Zairantze? Hands crossed over his breast?"

The woman inhaled sharply. Orielle didn't look at her.

The shadowed hollows gave way to Hackett's twisted anger. He stood. "Just like that, Lady Wizard. You know something."

Whispers started behind her. Sangrior surveyed the press of people around them.

"No, Hackett, I do not know. I think, that's all. A man said Grim and Surrect are in your gaol."

"Aye, that's—Shut your traps. I can't hear myself talk."

"She's the wizard. She knows about Tobit's death."

Orielle looked then, for the man who accused with those words.

"She ain't involved," Hackett snarled.

"Sorcery." Orielle tried to make eye contact with several people. Some looked away, some stared back belligerently, some waited judgment. "Sorcery. Eldritch and twisted, as sorcery is. The knife came from the sorceress in this valley. A sorceress who travels with a lair of wyre." She didn't actually know that the sorceress and the wyre were in the Haven's valley, but Frost Clime had definitely come closer than these Rho realized. "You need to act before you're over-run. That's two eldritch knives. Were you attacked by wraiths, Hackett?"

"He were still warm when I found him. And the lady's right. It's sorcery, not wizard-work."

"Lillias said—."

"Stop repeating what Lillias said and think, you fools. Zairantze was murdered with a sorcered knife. Tobit was. Zairantze died before Grim and this wizard got close to our Haven. They don't have nothing to do with these murders."

"Where was the wizard then? Lillias said—."

Hackett growled, and the speaker didn't finish. "Time we found out who actually wielded those knives and is allied with sorcery, don't you think?" Hackett crossed his arms and glared at the crowd.

"I rode with the Kyrgy." Orielle didn't think it wise to leave questions. "This is the Kyrgy knight Sangrior, who rides with Lady Bone. We fought the sorceress and her wyre. They ambushed us, and we barely escaped."

Then someone said, "You aren't Rho, Hackett."

"I live here, don't I?" he retorted. "I've lived here for five years, going on six. I'll live here until I die—or until you run me out. 'Course, you run me out, you'll need to run out anyone else who ain't Rho. You married the mundane, and you brought 'em here. You going to say they ain't got a bone in this fight? I lost Tobit. I want whoever killed him to pay. It ain't Grim. Sure as blood it ain't Surrect. He's a healer. He ain't no murderer allied with a sorceress. You can track sorcery, can you, Lady Wizard?"

She dared not lie on this point. "Only if it's active. With the knife gone—."

"We'll track it." He turned to the gravid woman, still seated, the rising sun turning her silver hair to gold. "You'll help us, Trebetha."

She stood. Her body showed short and sturdy, made rounder by the scarf doubled around her neck and the colorful shawl draped over the shoulders of her knitted sweater. Yet her face was clear, unlined, unworried. Nor did she have Hackett's anger, just his shadowed hollows of weariness, not the age revealed by her silvered hair. "I am with you, Hackett. And with you, Lady Wizard, and you, Sir Knight. We all are.

All Earth." She raised her voice. "All Earth."

And the gathered people lifted their voices to echo "All Earth."

The room began to clear. The people held purpose, some angry determination, others with sturdy resolve.

Orielle watched them leave then turned to Hackett. "We should free Grim and Surrect first."

"Lillias accused them—."

Hackett turned on the man, one of the few who remained, stubbornly refusing to leave and still ready to argue. "Ain't you learned yet not to listen to what Lillias claims? Or do you think Surrect wielded that knife? Your chief healer?"

"You will soon know." Sangrior's deep boom surprised those who hadn't left. The words were his first since entering the house. He looked around then returned to Hackett, flicking a glance at the woman then at Orielle. "Sorcery will stain the hand that wielded the eldritch blade."

They poured out of the dwelling into the now-packed byway. The crowd channeled through the side lanes before reaching a main street and then turning to the square. More people had gathered, not attempting to work, and the noise of talk increased as the Earth Rho explained to whoever would listen about their plans.

Hackett and the woman with Orielle and Sangrior crossed the square to the street that led to the lock-up, and the number of those following swelled as other Haveners joined in.

"Will they try to stop us from reaching the lock-up?"

"I wish," Hackett gritted. "Doubt it, though. Just Lillias and Fortis stood for that. He sided with her."

"Against Grim? I thought Fortis was Grim's friend."

"He said he had to stay objective," the woman said, and Hackett spit his view of that comment. "He and Lillias are to decide at tonight's hearing. However, whatever is decided will be now and in the street."

"Tobit's way," the veteran soldier said. Then grief dragged down his face.

Seeing his fellow villagers' approach, the sentry on the lock-up opened the outer door. As he unlocked the iron gate, Grim and Surrect appeared. The mentor looked startled by the crowd, growing in number every minute as word spread through the village.

Grim ignored the people. As the gate opened, he thrust past the sentry and crossed the yard to reach Orielle. He grabbed her upper arms, held her away for a few seconds, then hauled her close.

As his arms wrapped around her, she buried her face in his neck. A tug on her arm brought her head up. He kissed her, drinking from her like a man who had crossed the desert. She sank all her hopes and attractions into that kiss. At her intense response, he growled. His arms tightened.

When the kiss ended, Orielle tugged at his shoulders. "I should have stayed."

"No. You could not deny the Kyrgy. Besides, you would have been only one voice in the clamor to lock up someone for Tobit's death."

"Why was Surrect locked up?"

"He's Water. The knife turned to water. On that little, they decided."

Surrect was speaking with the gravid woman. Staff leaning on his shoulder, he described something with wide sweeps of his hands. Sangrior stood to one side, no expression on his marble face. He'd returned a hand to his swordhilt. Orielle recalled last night's shoreline, swords flashing as he countered claws and blades. Did he expect the Haveners to attack?

Hackett scowled as he listened to the sentry. "She's duly elected," he retorted, "just not before the Council."

"The wizard?"

"Trebetha, you arse. And we've two mentors now, her and Surrect. What more do you need?"

The sentry stammered.

Trebetha, the gravid woman, planted her stocky frame before the sentry. "Albit, you had no authority to put anyone in lock-up. With Tobit's death, the Council can make no decisions. No one can be locked up on the order of one or two mentors."

"Fortis was right there beside Lillias. He agreed."

"You're not casting off the burden for not thinking, Albit. Lillias and Fortis are still only two votes. Lock-up requires three votes from the Council of the Four Elements."

"Lillias will have my job."

"Lillias may not be a mentor herself for much longer."

Surrect touched the woman's shoulder. "We need to move."

The crowd worked back to the square.

"Will Lillias stand against us?" she whispered to Grim.

"We're having a battle in the Haven!" a boy shouted.

"Surely not?" someone countered.

"We ain't barbarians," a man's voice declared. "We got a rule of law."

"Maybe we should first consult Fortis?"

The argument worked through the crowd, echoing Orielle's thoughts. Grim kept their hands clasped. He didn't have his short sword or a knife or any weapon, just his element. Sangrior paced beside her.

Orielle guiltily realized that she had involved a Kyrgy knight in Rhoghieri matters. Lady Bone would not be pleased. "You need not stay with us, Sangrior."

"The Haven has yet to deal with the wraiths. I stay until then. Lady Bone would require it."

She remembering the Kyrgy lady, so cold, so mysterious, covering Volk's wounded body. *My Volk! You may not leave me. My Volk, you must stay with me.* Would the lady have reacted that way if Sangrior had been severely wounded? Or did she only care for Volk?

That opened a maze of questions that might never be answered.

The other riders must have died, falling to the ambush.

How many of the sorceress' group survive?

That blinding transition interrupted Orielle's battle with the sorceress. Even with the surprise of ambush, the wyre couldn't have killed the riders without losing their own.

"How many wyre did we kill, before Lady Bone took us away?"

"I took one. Volk took one. The three mundane swordsmen are dead."

"What will Lady Bone do with Saircuista?"

He met her eyes. Those full-black eyes briefly flickered to Grim, then Sangrior looked away. His gaze fastened on Surrect and the woman Trebetha, leading the way to Fortis' dwelling. "Your concerns are here, with the Haven. Kyrgy do not concern you."

"But Saircuista—."

"What Lady Bone does with the traitor does not concern you."

That flat tone chilled her, as emotionless as when she'd first encountered him. No, less, for he'd had a banked fire when he'd raised his sword to the velvet dark sky and named her Aiwaz Solsken. Did her obvious relationship with Grim kill whatever alliance he'd had with her?

Orielle didn't understand the riders' devotion to Skuld. What benefit did they receive from riding with the Lady? She had healed Volk; she cried that he would not leave her. Did she lengthen their lives?

Was that the mantle she would remove from Saircuista on the first night of Lady's Moon?

Lady's Moon.

Mere designations of that moon, that's what the tutors had claimed. None ever explored how people counted time. The three-night Lady's Moon was Crone, Lady, then Maiden. Knight's Moon. Knave's moon. Dragon Moon, with its three unlit nights of Wyvern, Dragon, and Lindworm. Worm Moon. Womb Moon.

Was it mere coincidence that the Kyrgy rode their Hunt on the moons for the three-part Lady and for the three-part Dragon? They'd fought the sorceress and her minions in the night before the first of Lady Moon.

And they'd lost.

Did the Kyrgy and their riders have increased power on the Lady-Moon nights? Was it called Lady's Moon and Knight's Moon and Knave for these riders? Lady Bone and her knights Volk and Sangrior, and the other knights and dames.

An abyss of new knowledge gaped before her.

And Dragon Moon? The alliance fought Frost Clime, who claimed to prepare for the dragons. The Fae vowed Dragon Rising would return them to the decades of Dragon Dark, so long ago. Was Dragon Moon named during Dragon Dark?

Surrect and Trebetha stopped. She stepped forward and knocked on the door of a dwelling.

"Whose?" Orielle whispered.

"Fortis," Grim said, equally soft.

Trebetha knocked again. Then again and a third time before the door opened.

And an orb of fire shot through the door. Flames exploded over the woman. She screamed then crumbled … and writhed on the ground as the fire consumed her. People screamed. The crowd behind them thinned.

Then water doused the flames.

Head bowed, Surrect knelt. He touched the steaming char that had been Trebetha. Then he straightened and walked into the dwelling.

Orielle rushed after him, Grim and Sangrior with her.

~ **14** ~

Surrect had continued through the front room to the hallway. Flames not doused by his Water power lit the hall and room in alternate flashes. A lantern centered the table, and its steady sphere of light showed the front room not empty. A body huddled on the floor before the unlit hearth.

Orielle rushed to the body, a woman by the head scarf and long skirts. She rolled her to her back.

A knife was embedded to the hilt in her breast. No blood had seeped around it. And a wraith lifted its head out of the hilt.

It poured up, striking at Orielle with hooked claws. She fell back then scrambled away, impeded by her long skirts.

The wraith formed over her, separating from the eldritch knife.

She recognized her dead great-uncle's face. Raigeis bared his teeth, a grimace that the cold magister had never had in life. This was the wraith that had attacked her off the mountaintop. It heard her speak Raigeis' name. It suffered Lady Bone's punishment.

She felt the weight of a corporeal body on her legs as it flowed up. "Wizard," it hissed.

Then Sangrior's sword scythed the air.

The wraith darted back with the speed of a gusty wind. A second wraith had followed it out of the knife. Glacial steel snicked through the wispy vapor, dissipating it with the sword's magic.

A third wraith started through the knife.

Sangrior swung for it, but the first wraith assaulted him. It seized his face and kissed his mouth … and began sucking life from him.

Grim leaped past her, going for the eldritch knife. The third wraith grabbed at him for a life-sucking kiss. Orielle hit it with a gusty burst of energy. It screamed as the wizardry blasted over it.

Grim fell back, eldritch knife in his hand, melting in his grasp.

As Orielle scrambled up, she glanced at the woman. Like Tobit, her body hadn't vanished, flesh and bones not yet used up before the eldritch knife was removed. She must be the age of Zairantze, of Malva. Fortis' woman? She had no time for more, for she focused on tracking the third wraith, still intent on Grim.

Enclave tutoring hadn't prepared her for fighting wraiths or gobbers or wyre or Kyrgy. The ones that had fed from Brok had only drawn from him, not sucked away his life. She had killed the first by sending wizardry into it, a vortex spell that it had sucked down. The other, though, had escaped.

The second wraith reached for Grim. She stepped in the way. When it grabbed her, she funneled power into a glass-sharded orb and shoved it into that opening mouth. She stuffed it down with a gust of Air.

The wraith screeched and writhed away.

She stayed long enough to see that her power ripped the vaporous form. Then she turned to the other, the corporeal one, the one sucking the life out of Sangrior.

The knight had fallen to one knee. The wraith clung, kissing, destroying his life. Veins like black roots spread over his marbled face and neck. He still clutched his sword, but the tip rested on the ground.

Grim had climbed to his feet.

Fiery flames lit the doorway.

"Help Surrect," she ordered and drew more wizardry as he headed for the hall.

She needed to distract the wraith from Sangrior's life-essence. She tried pushing it away. It moved a little, but her hands went deep into its form, as if it only had the beginning of a real body. A sphere of energy didn't tempt it. She dug her hands back into its solidifying form, but the crackling energy she poured out sank into Sangrior, convulsing through him. His marble skin looked cloud-grey.

More fire streamed through the doorway. A yell came, but she dared not abandon Sangrior.

As he struggled with the wraith, Orielle gathered the few fragments she knew about wraiths. The wraith had come from an eldritch knife that melted to water. Zairantze's tears had turned to ice. Was that merely the iciness of sorcery? It formed as a wispy vapor then slowly took on flesh. The Kyrgy had leashed it with the strange magic of the Fae. Grim had whisked away the wraith that had clung to her. Only ingested wizardry affected it.

It drank life.

Another orb crackled with energy. It wouldn't tempt the wraith that wanted life essence.

She knelt beside Sangrior. With each suck by the wraith, grunts jerked from him. Its tip on the floor, the ice-blue sword flashed amber in the fiery light pouring from the hallway.

Orielle grasped the sword, double-edged and sharp. She tightened her grip—and the sharp steel bit into her fingers and palm. Orielle edged her blood with bright energy, with sharp wizardry, alluring power.

She waved her bloody hand beside the wraith's head. It turned away from the kiss. Sangrior collapsed, and the wraith dropped him to the floor. Snake-quick, it struck.

She'd expected the speed. She wanted it. She hadn't expected the life-sucking intensity with which the wraith latched onto her bloody palm. It felt like teeth digging into her skin.

But she had it now. She poured the golden energy of her spell into her blood, and the wraith drank it down.

Then it recoiled, fangs bloody—and she shoved more wizardry into its reddened mouth.

Power began to rip it apart, throat, chest, belly. It wailed, then its head shredded apart.

Orielle scrambled to Sangrior as the wisps drifted apart. He looked lifeless-but his chest rose slowly, so slowly she wouldn't have seen it if her hand on his chest hadn't risen with his inhalation. He looked ghastly grey, with blackened veins branching across his skin—but he was alive, and alive meant she didn't owe Lady Bone another rider.

Then Grim staggered into the room. Fortis appeared in the doorway.

With one glance, the Fire mentor saw the wraiths were defeated. His gaze fastened on Orielle. She threw up a barrier in a second, and in the next second, fire hit it. The flames bent around her shied.

And Orielle remembered that she wasn't a wizard. She hadn't gone through the Wizard Trials. Lady Bone called her Not-Wizard. *What am*

I doing?

That first gush of flames ceased. Fortis leaned against the jamb. Under his bracing hand, the wood smoked then charred.

Like Trebetha's body.

Had Surrect met the same end?

Orielle swayed when she climbed to her feet. The wraith must have sucked more of her life essence than she realized.

"Wizard."

She saw flames tip Fortis' fingers. "I thought you were Grim's friend."

He gave Grim the barest glance. "No longer."

Grim straightened from the wall as if it pained him.

Fortis drew a dagger from his belt.

Orielle thought the handle looked twisted. *More sorcery?* "Is that for me or Grim?"

The Fire mentor grinned. His eyes had a weird light. "Either one."

"Why are you working with the sorceress?"

"Why not?"

"Do you think to rule the Haven?"

Grim held up his hand. It blurred, and Orielle knew he created his own barrier, a barrier that must have saved him from Fortis' earlier attack. Surrect must be dead. Like Trebetha.

Fortis had killed Tobit. Only Hackett's timely arrival had prevented wraiths from pouring through the knife-opened pathway.

"Did you kill Zairantze? And you killed your own wife!"

He still grinned. "Look at you, joining all the pieces together into a cabinet. Six drawers, Four shelves. Four doors to hide things away."

Is he insane?

He laughed. "What color should I paint your cabinet?" The flames tipping his fingers burned red then purple then yellow and green.

"How did you meet the sorceress?" Orielle wanted to keep him talking. She had to figure out how to stop him.

"Ask her yourself. You'll be dead when she rides in tomorrow. She does like communing with wraiths, and that's what you'll be."

Grim gaped. "She's coming here? Into the Haven? That's forbidden."

"Not if I say so, and no one can deny me, not now. No one will stand against me. I rule this Haven, and she's my friend."

"Only until the sorceress cows you to her will," Orielle pointed out.

She earned his scowl. "That will never be." Fortis turned back to his childhood friend. "Work with me, Grim. We'll rule the Haven."

"This is my home, Fortis."

"Exactly. And they gaoled you. Ally with me."

"I didn't fight against Frost Clime to welcome it into my home now."

Fortis shrugged his sloped shoulders. "When you change your mind as I kill you, it will be too late." He flung out his hand.

And the dagger cut straight through Grim's defense.

Fortis, though, had misjudged its weight. Not meant for throwing, the handle overbalanced it. With a thunk, the weighty end struck Grim in the chest.

Before it struck, though, Fortis flung a flame at Orielle. The fire struck her barrier and exploded. Little tongues of flames and bright orange sparks blinked over her barrier.

Grim had staggered a step but recovered as the dagger clattered to the floor.

Fortis threw a flaming orb. Before it struck her barrier, Grim pushed—and the orb ricocheted back into Fortis' face. He hadn't anticipated the rebound. The orb burst over him. Flames singed his hair, set fire to his clothes, fried his flesh. He screamed … and flung another orb. Then he beat out the fire in his clothes.

Grim had snatched up the dagger. As the orb struck Orielle's barrier, he dashed forward. Fortis tried to fend him off, but Air whipped the flames out, whisking away any fuel. He plunged the eldritch dagger into Fortis' chest.

The big man goggled. His hands clutched Grim's shoulders. Then he sagged. "What did—why did—?"

Grim jerked the dagger out. As it melted, Fortis sank to his knees. Then he toppled forward.

EPILOGUE

Day's end found Orielle, Grim, and Sangrior settled in the last rays of sunshine, on a bench outside the Elder's House.

A large flock of birds crossed, chittering and twittering as they sought shelter for the coming night. Crone's Moon would rise late, so the birds and smaller prey searched for their night's shelter.

In the early afternoon they had reported the morning's events for the entire village, gathered into the square, much as they had gathered when Orielle and Grim first entered the Haven. The Haven swirled with the chaos of losing two mentors plus Trebetha, voted mentor but never accepted onto the Council. Fortis' betrayal staggered everyone. His fellow Fire Rho had argued until Hackett and the Earth Rho recounted the battle they had glimpsed. Then they had mourned Surrect, Trebetha, and Fortis' woman, named Ellisia. Grim was praised, Orielle admired, yet the villagers still gaped at Sangrior.

The Kyrgy knight had not yet spoken of his return to Lady Bone. Orielle dared not ask. As the Haven milled in disarray, flailing about without orders from their lost mentors, Sangrior posted himself at Orielle's left and refused to budge.

Grim was as determined to stick to her right hand.

Hackett took charge of the sentinels and sentries, calling them away to maintain Iscleft's protection, for the sorceress and her wyre remained a threat.

Orielle did not think Hackett would remain in the Haven, not without Tobit. She hoped for a quiet word. He would be both friend and guard if he accompanied her to the Citadel. He'd fought Frost Clime when the Citadel had no hope of gaining ground. If the Rho renewed the alliance, the Citadel allies of Fae, wizards, Rho, and mundane could force Frost Clime back into the Wilding and then the frontier and on to the Wastes.

As the sun disappeared behind the mountains, the sole mentor Lillias wearied of the lingering crowd. Anger warred with grief, neither winning and both likely to shred the woman, but she ordered the Rho to select new mentors. "No decisions can be made until mentors are chosen for Earth, Water, and Fire. Those must be voted upon before we scatter ashes for those we lost. Gather as Elements and begin your conference. Air will meet here, in the Elder's House."

The Rho had left the well square first, then the unmagicked of them returned to their dwellings. A few children played at lane's end.

Hands on hips, Lillias had watched them disperse. When only a few lingerers remained, she turned to Grim. "You're not going inside? You're Air. Your vote is needed."

He didn't stir a finger. "Tobit didn't welcome me back to the community. And what vote does Air need to have? You're the mentor."

Planning to be stubborn, Lillias crossed her arms and canted a lean hip. "I will act as elder until the new mentors are chosen, but I'll not accept elder rank. Others are better suited. Others are better suited as mentor for Air. Grim, you would be a better mentor."

"I'm not looking for the rank."

"All the more reason to take it. The best leaders never want rank. Surrect didn't. Tobit didn't. Fortis was eager for it."

"I remember you claimed not to want Air mentor, and now you claim not to want elder."

Lillias scowled. "If Tobit had welcomed you, I could drive you inside and let Air decide. The clan can welcome you. No elder needed.

You don't want mentor rank, then serve as my second. You know as well as I what the rank needs. What this Haven needs."

"I return to the Citadel." He moved then, unfolding his arms, dropping a hand to Orielle's thigh. "I go with Orielle, as soon as her mission is complete, as soon as we deal with this sorceress and her wyre."

The mentor didn't like his answer, but she dropped the argument. "Tell me we have no more wraiths in the Haven."

"None that escaped in our presence." Orielle shuddered as she remembered the drain on her life essence. "Hackett was in time to prevent any after Tobit's death, and Mentor Surrect confirmed none in the village." The mentor's expression shadowed with grief when Orielle mentioned the healer. She'd known Lillias and Surrect were close. They must have been much closer than she'd reckoned.

Yet she'd only had two days since she'd met the both of them.

"No wraiths," she added, to assure her answer was clear, "but the sorceress and her wyre are still out there, waiting to attack again. Fortis planned for them to come into the Haven, after he became elder."

Lillias swore. "One good thing. That didn't happen, so they can't come."

Orielle didn't want to look back on that battle with Fortis and the wraiths. She needed to focus on the battle with the sorceress and the remaining wyre.

"Will the sorceress know that Fortis is dead?"

Orielle winced. *How can I know?* "Only if he bound himself to her," she guessed. "She will know his daggers have been used."

"You found no other strange knives in Fortis' dwelling?"

Grim had that answer. "None."

"And no other signs of sorcery?"

"None." Sangrior ground the single word. He sat statue-still beside Orielle. He'd recovered his marble-white skin. The black veins that had starkly marked his face had receded. Those black eyes were hooded. Death no longer courted him.

Lady Bone was danger enough. The Kyrgy lady had only attacked the sorceress to retrieve Saircuista. Would she ally with Orielle against the sorceress again?

Lillias looked away from them to the second flock of birds arrowing overhead. She watched sentries head to their posts at the gate and the towers that overlooked the walls. Following them were sentinels going to their posts in the valley. Then she saluted them—Grim, more likely— and headed into the Elder's House.

Twilight deepened. A sentry came through at twilight. He carried a flaming brand and lit the torches around the square before he headed on.

The Kyrgy knight inhaled sharply.

"Sangrior?"

He ignored Orielle. He stood and stepped several paces away from the Elder's House.

Grim nudged her. "We need to hunt up a bed for the night."

Brok had likely abandoned his dwelling and still bunked with Waren and Malva. Grim would not want to stay in rooms that had seen battles with wraiths or recent deaths. "You've spent two nights in gaol. I battled wraiths and fought a sorceress. Sleep is welcome. Do you have a suggestion?"

"Another friend, although the first one didn't work out."

"We can take a chance on another friend. I don't mind."

"Nor do I. Only thing I care about is that we're together." He touched her chin and turned her face to him.

Yet as their lips met, light flashed bright and blinding.

Orielle and Grim jerked away from each other.

Sangrior stood before them. Beside him, newly arrived in the transition, was Volk.

Lady Bone's consort knight looked fully healed. He and Sangrior looked like twins, with a cascade of white hair and depthless black eyes, their white faces glowing in the darkness, the one clad in a storm-blue cloak, the other in ice-blue.

Volk extended a hand to Orielle, just as he had the prior evening. "Come. Lady Bone awaits."

Orielle stood, but she didn't take the knight's hand. "The Lady lost so many riders. I did not think she would lead a Hunt tonight."

"The Lady always rides the nights of Full Moon and No Moon."

Grim placed his body before hers. "Do you hunt the sorceress and the wyre?"

"If we find them, they will suffer for attacking the Kyrgy in their Wilding."

"The Aiwaz Solsken must come," Sangrior said. "She vowed three rides."

"I'm not refusing," Orielle started, but Grim still blocked her.

"I will go with Aiwaz Solsken. I am her guard."

"You are Rhoghieri. No Rhoghieri has ever ridden the Hunt."

"I will. Guard to Aiwaz Solsken."

"Then come," Volk said. "Give me your hand. Solsken, take Sangrior's hand. The Lady waits."

The transition was just as blinding as before, just as disorienting. Sangrior released her before she was steady. She heard the Lady's twinkling laugh and then another laugh, deeper, mellifluous ... darkly dangerous.

Orielle blinked rapidly.

Sangrior and Volk had joined the Lady, a blur that sharpened as Orielle grounded herself in the transition.

"You came," the Lady said.

"As I vowed."

"The mundane and the wizards always seek a way to break their vows. The Rhoghieri do not, but this is not your ride, Rho."

"I am the Solsken's guard," Grim insisted, as if the transition had not disoriented him.

Orielle curtsied. "I did not expect to ride tonight, Lady Bone."

"We are not so weakened, for we join with my brother. Lord Skull leads tonight's Hunt."

The Kyrgy lord came out of the shadows. He wore his silver hair cropped close to his skull. His face looked narrower than the Lady, with bones as sharp as blades. More riders appeared behind him, looming out of the shadows. Mostly knights, a few women, the riders were twice the number that had ridden with Lady Bone.

The lord was taller than his sister, broader of build. He wore steel armor worked with Fae scrolling. He had no gauntlets, and his marble-white hand thrust forward the hilt of a moon-bright dark sword.

Then he smiled, all black eyes and sharpened teeth, and he looked very like Lady Bone. He laughed at Orielle. "Surprised, Not-Wizard?"

She felt like a weak opponent before a mad king looking for blood. She curtsied again, more deeply than before, and Grim bowed stiffly. "You read us well, Lord ... Lord Skull."

"You shall ride beside me, Not-Wizard. Your guard is behind us." He extended a hand.

When she grasped his hand, the chill of his icy skin shot into her, straight to her bones, straight into her blood.

"To the Hunt!" he shouted.

Riders flooded past them, heading for horses as black as the sky behind the stars.

"We will enjoy our Hunt, Solsken, and then we will feast."

. ~ . ~ . ~ .

With the help of Lord Skull and Lady Bone, Orielle and Grim will continue the fight against the sorceress and her wyre in **To Curse the Wyre** *~~ Coming Soon!*

To Curse the Wyre

Orielle vowed to the Kyrgy Lord Skull and Lady Bone that she would kill the sorceress in the Wilding. Yet the sorceress sends her shape-shifting wyre to kill Orielle.

Who's the hunted now?

~ 1 ~

The midnight-black horses thundered along the forest road. To Orielle's eye, they moved slowly, muscles bunching and stretching gently, manes drifting in the cold night air, their speed a deceptive glide over the ground. Yet moon-silvered trees passed in a blur. The road sped by beneath the enchanted horses' hoofs.

The Lady's Moon rose quickly in the velvet-dark sky.

She rode on Lord Skull's left. Mounted on his snow-white steed, the knight Sangrior rode to the Kyrgy Lord's right, the place of honor. Ever wary, Grim followed. Lord Skull's knights and dames came after.

A russet hart with a weighty rack of antlers leapt across the road. As it fled into the trees, Lord Skull reined in his horse. He flung up a hand to stop the following riders. Then he stared into the trees, tracking the hart's long run until it vanished in the deeper forest. "Magnificent."

"Worthy of a Hunt," Sangrior commented.

"Not this Hunt. We seek foul sorcery. Not-Wizard, you ride well."

Orielle patted her night-black mount. They had ridden for miles, but the horse wasn't blown. "Thank you, my Lord, but I prefer the name Solsken."

The Kyrgy Lord chuckled, which Lady Bone would never have done. "Not-Wizard is *what* you are. Solsken is *when* you are." He fixed her with his black-on-black eyes. His horse stood calm while hers shifted, as if the Lord's gaze burdened it. "I do not know *who* you are. I am not certain you know yourself."

"I am no more and no less than Orielle of Galfrons Clan of the Enclave, a Not-Wizard named Aiwaz Solsken by a Kyrgy knight."

Sangrior smiled at her use of the name he'd given her. That smile revealed his recently sharpened teeth in that marble-white skin, a statue who lived and acted and reacted.

She shifted in her saddle to look behind, meeting Grim's cautious gaze. "More than friend," she added, "to Grim Holtson, a Rhoghieri."

"More than friend?" Lord Skull glanced at the Rho. When he again faced forward, the rising moon glinted on his Fae-scrolled armor. "Grim Holtson is only more than a friend? You have not shared your true names?"

"We look forward to becoming more." Grim sounded firm, and he returned her smile. "We have had little time, my lord. Wyre and gobbers—."

"And wraiths," she added.

"Have prevented the more."

"Kyrgy know" was Lord Skull's only comment. "Come. We ride on. Wyre and sorcery are at the end of our Hunt." Yet he didn't set the thundering pace of before.

Orielle dared not ask questions. Lady Bone could be capricious. Both the Lady and her brother were dangerous Dark Fae. She hadn't found the limits of their tolerance, and she didn't wish to.

At this cantering pace, she glimpsed more than passing trees. A twinkling nest of sprites flickered in the distant forest. With wizard-sight, she spotted mundane creatures scurrying away from the road, fleeing the Hunt's passage. Dark bulks with silver glints and the occasional flash of red eyes helped her see them as they dove into tangled undergrowth or they scurried up tree trunks. The little animals were safe, too small to tempt the riders into pursuit.

After they crossed a ridge, Lord Skull slowed the ride, walking the horses down. A knight rode forward, jostling Sangrior to the road's verge. Skull didn't acknowledge him. The knight took the lead. He paused at a distant bend of the road and drew his sword. The dark steel winked in the silvery light of Lady's Moon.

When the Hunt reached the bend, Orielle heard rushing water, but the trees blocked any view of the river. She didn't know if the shore they neared was where they had battled the wyre and the sorceress. Was it where she and Grim alone had defeated wyre? Or was it yet another rushing stream that emptied into the main tributary that poured into the Lowlands?

The knight waited by a dense tangle of withy undergrowth that spilled down the steep-climbing mountainside. Farther along, the road descended between banks of trees, an old wagon trace. The knight pointed to the tangle with his sword. "Here. The entrance is here."

Lord Skull rode closer, and Orielle remained at his side. Sangrior came as well and drew his sword, the steel glinting ice-blue. He was Lady Bone's knight, lent to her brother while the consort knight Volk and Sir Kristofin remained at the Lady's side, not on this ride.

Grim drew up on her left. His sword was drawn, ready, Fae bright where the riders' weapons were dark steel.

Hands crossed on his saddle pommel, Lord Skull waited. The lead knight dismounted. He threw his reins to Sangrior. Sword leading the way, he ducked into the writhe of woodbine and disappeared into the thicket against the mountainside.

"What is it?" she asked Sangrior.

"Old lair. Lord Skull thought the wyre would have returned to it."

"Did they not camp on the shore?"

"This lair is older, from years ago."

Grim inhaled sharply. "Aye, I thought I recognized it. Three years old."

"The wyre who attacked the Haven? Before you left for the Citadel?"

"Aye. Nothing should be here except bones. The bones of the last wyre we killed."

"Unless the other wyre did use it for shelter."

"How would they find it?" Grim countered the kyrgy knight. "None survived. Any scent is old, weathered to nothing."

Orielle didn't care about their argument. "Would the wyre with the sorceress have created a lair? Or found a cave for shelter? Or did they just camp on the shore?"

"They left their dead on the shore," Sangrior said with a dogmatic assurance. "They left their dead for gobbers and scavengers to feed on."

"Lady Bone's knights and dames, those who were killed? Were they also left on the shore?"

"The Lady scattered their ashes, giving them back to the sun at its zenith."

How did Sangrior know? He'd been with her in the Haven throughout the day. Did he have some connection to the Lady, so that he knew what she wanted him to know? Orielle remembered that blinding transition from place to place, which shifted her and Sangrior from the glade where the Lady had healed Volk and to the Haven. They had also shifted back to another glade where they'd met her and Lord Skull … and begun this ride.

The fight against the sorceress and her wyre had decimated Lady Bone's riders—although Sangrior showed no grief for his fellow knights and dames. Only the two consort knights and one other had survived, Volk gravely wounded. If he had not been wounded, would the Lady have continued the fight? When Volk had staggered under the attack of two shifted wyre, the Lady gathered him and her two remaining knights, the betraying Saircuista, and Orielle ... then they fled, transitioning from the shore to that starlit meadow surrounded by old-growth trees.

From there, Sangrior returned with her to the Haven. Then he fought at her side against wraiths and a Fire mentor allied to the sorceress. *Since he remained with me, how does he know what Lady Bone did with the dead riders? How does he know the sorceress abandoned her dead wyre and the three mundane swordsmen?*

Skull's knight reappeared, his sword advancing first through the tangle. He bowed. "No one, my Lord. Cold fire. Days old. No taint of sorcery."

"Used, though?" Skull leaned over his pommel. "The wyre did choose to return here. Where have they gone?" He contemplated the forest surrounding them, ahead where the land steeply rose on both sides of the forest road and the tangle of undergrowth that grew round the old-growth trees. His eyes narrowed as he tracked deeper into the forest.

What does he see with his Fae eyes? Wizard-sight painted the nocturnal world in silver of varying hues, from ghostly pale rocks to the black trunks of virgin trees, glimmering creatures that cowered in the undergrowth and charcoal masses of bushes heaped over with woodbine. Orielle saw nothing more than what any mundane would see in sunlight. Did Kyrgy eyes see the lingering traces of life essence? Did Skull distinguish mundane from magical, wizardry from sorcery, powered from weirded?

He saw something, for he spurred his horse forward on the road. Sangrior followed him. Orielle wanted to drop back with Grim. The Kyrgy lord drew his horse up short. It snorted and tossed its head, the white mane lifting then falling over the black hide. "Stay with me, Solsken."

Pleased that he used her preferred name, she urged her horse to his shield side. She prayed Skull did not think she was his shield against the sorceress.

The road descended between the rising land. It worked through a cleft that funneled them two abreast. Orielle dropped back, as did Sangrior. The Kyrgy's knight took shield-side to his lord. Like an old wagon trace, beat down by the passage of heavy cargo, the road descended, a foot, three feet, five feet, the height of the horses and riders, and more. The trees towered on both sides, joining their branches to block out the Crone Moon.

The passage squeezed tighter and muddied from a seeping spring.

Ice rimed the edge of the puddle. A wagon would barely scrape through. The deepness of the road, the denseness of the trees, both muffled the hoot of an owl winging by. The horses' hoofs clicked over exposed rocks. The bridles jingled like silver chimes.

An animal leaped down to the descending road. Wolf. No, wyre, for the eldritch green transformation gleamed in its eyes. The wyre bared his fangs and snarled. Ruffled pale blonde fur increased its size.

Skull halted. Then he laughed. "Is that all, little wyre?"

A flash to the left, then a dark shape leaped upon the knight riding beside Skull. It growled as it struck, knocking the knight out of the saddle and to the muddy ground. The wyre followed the knight down, landing between the horses. Then it latched onto the rider's neck and choked off his shout.

The close confines of the narrowed road crowded the horses together. Man and wyre grappled beneath the horses.

Skull whipped out his sword when the wyre struck, but he couldn't strike down to help, not without seriously wounding his man. He used the flattened blade to drive the man's horse forward. It leaped ahead, straight for the snarling wyre athwart the road. That wyre jumped away then raced after the running horse.

With the horse fled, the Lord struck. Skull's blade flashed downward. The wyre yelped but didn't open his jaws. The man lay limp beneath him. Skull struck again. The wyre flattened onto the man. He whimpered. Skull struck a third time, and the whimpering stopped.

Sangrior and Grim had drawn their swords. Orielle quickly scanned the banks on either side, watching for another ambush.

Sword black with blood, the Kyrgy looked around. "Trap."

Sangrior scanned around them, alert for ambush. Grim and the riders behind him were equally alert. Their party was stuffed into the cleft, unable to move forward unless Skull did, able to retreat only one at a time after they turned their horses.

"I can follow the escaped wyre," Sangrior offered. "What would you, my Lord?"

"Do not follow. Ride ahead and guard. You, Rhoghieri, stand with him. We will hold this space." He rode a few paces forward, opening a way past his downed rider and the dead wyre that had killed him.

Orielle had to follow Sangrior past the rider and wyre so Grim could also pass. Skull leaned out and caught her reins as she edged by. With Sangrior and Grim going on, he pulled her horse around to fetch up against him, so close their legs butted against each other. He tossed her his reins then dismounted.

Two of his knights had ridden forward and also dismounted. The others remained mounted, alert, swords drawn. The last two riders had faced about, guarding the rear.

The Kyrgy prodded the wyre with the blood-black point of his sword. Then he wedged the blade underneath the inert furred body and flipped it off his man and to the side of the road, against the wall of earth. He knelt beside his rider. Blood covered the man's face and clenched hands, locked into a futile defense by death. The wyre had torn out his throat.

Skull closed the man's staring eyes. He didn't wipe the blood from his fingers. Resting his hand on the rider's chest, he bowed his head and murmured.

Orielle couldn't hear, but she sensed the energy drawn by the Kyrgy lord. It rushed past her, a drawing on all the elements. Crackling with Fire, weighty with Earth, dampening her chilled cheeks with more than tears, ruffling her hair and skirts and her horse's mane as the Air swirled. Even dark Chaos whorled around Lord Skull, stiffening, coalescing, until it obscured him and the dead knight.

Then the elements faded. The Fire winked out. The Earth trembled then quieted. The Water dried. Air drifted away. And Chaos vanished. All the elements dissipating as if never evoked for use.

Skull alone remained on the road, still kneeling with bowed head beside where his rider lay covered by a black cloak. The wyre lay lifeless at the base of the ascending earth.

He straightened. Face blank of expression, he looked past her to his riders then to Sangrior and Grim. With an equal lack of expression, he scanned the elevated ground. Then he flicked his hefty sword, an easy gesture, as if the weapon was weightless. The blood that blackened the blade flicked off.

Sword aloft, he met Orielle's gaze. "We fight wyre, Not-Wizard. Do you still Hunt with us?"

*Does he think I am appalled at battle? I **am** appalled, but killing the sorceress and her wyre **must** happen.* "As I vowed to do, Lord Skull."

"The Hunt continues." He didn't have to lift his voice. A spell carried the words, sparkling with energy, past her and to his riders, back to Grim and Sangrior, guarding the road ahead. "They hunted the hunters. Time to hunt them down."

His knights lifted an ululating cry, throat and tongues giving cry. Orielle shivered as the eerie sound lasted and lasted before it faded as echoes.

Skull vaulted into the saddle. The mud hadn't clung to his leathers or armor. He lifted a hand. Two riders broke past her. They saluted their Lord then passed Grim and Sangrior, breaking into a trot when they reached clear road.

With his still-bloody hand, the Kyrgy lord grabbed energy out of the air. He shaped it into an orb then flung it ahead. The orb lit the road like a weak, unnatural sun. It raced past Grim and Sangrior, past his riders, and on ahead, guiding the way.

"Solsken, stay with me."

Orielle spurred her horse to remain close to Skull.

For the Hunt was on, tracking the wyre that had escaped.

~ 2 ~

They sped along the road, following the faded sun orb.

The road gradually ascended, rising to meet the ground on either side. Then the land itself rose, angling toward the mountaintop. The black horse under Orielle didn't flag as the road steepened. It galloped like a fresh mount. The trees once more flashed past them.

A wolf howled, distant, lone.

Skull drew the pace to a canter as another wolf howled, also distant.

Grim and Sangrior rode behind the knights leading the way. At their lord's signal, they had slowed. They had re-sheathed their swords but kept alert to attacks.

Another howl, sending chills up her spine. "Are those wyre?"

"Wolves. Mundane."

"Not wyre." *Why, then, did I feel that chill?*

"Still dangerous. A pack runs the Wilding."

"The wyre didn't drive them out?"

"Not yet. They belong. I will not allow them to leave." He smiled grimly. "Predators are needed. My sister said you and your Rhoghieri had killed wyre."

"By my count, four remain."

His grin turned wolfish. "Three now." He looked away, across the mountain's flank. His nostrils flared. He growled. His silvered brows arrowed down his angular face. "She makes more."

"The sorceress? She makes more wyre? How can—?"

"Hiya!" His shout stopped the leading knights. They returned down the steep incline. Grim and Sangrior fell in behind them. The other knights crowded up, until they were bunched on the road.

The orb remained ahead, hovering.

"The sorceress guides a moon-change," Skull announced.

The knights muttered. She heard curses. "This trail is a distraction, my Lord."

"How many undergo the change?" Sangrior asked.

"Two." His nostrils flared. "No. Three."

Can he smell the wyrding at work?

"Where?" was Grim's only question.

Skull raised a hand.

The orb streaked to him. When it struck his hand, it flared, sun-radiant and blinding. Orielle shut her eyes too late, and the negative image remained stark in her mind. She heard the knights behind her muttering. When light flared again, she opened her eyes to see a new orb hovering above Skull's opened hand. Its light looked more golden than white, giving it human warmth.

Skull's eyes looked flat black in his gilded face.

The orb bobbed then rose above their heads. It spun, taking on color, the blue of Water, the green of Earth, the grey of Air, all swirling into the gold energy. Then it left the road and floated into the trees, in the direction Skull had looked when he sensed the moon-change.

And the Hunt followed.

The advance riders picked a way among the trees and the undergrowth. Off the road the ground was rockier, stony outcroppings, hidden gouges, fallen trees. Boulder-fall from the granite heights had to be worked around. Tangled laurel had to be bypassed. The orb remained ahead, advancing only as Skull advanced.

They rode quiet, no thunder of horses' hoofs, the metal bridle bits barely clinking, the leather not creaking. Only the snorting breaths of horses, the occasional murmur of a rider who spied a hint of trouble—a nest of sprites in a passing glade, the green-silver of a gobber winking from a tangle of cover, tendrils of fog drifting over ground.

They veered around the foggy ground. Ice chilled Orielle as they avoided the mist trails. The wraith had risen like vaporous mist, head and shoulders forming, arms and hands separating from the central mass.

The knights and dames didn't speak until they were well past the foggy drifts.

"Old death," Skull murmured. "Bones scattered over the ground."

"A Hunt?"

"A battle. Mundanes, though one set of bones tolled with magic."

She didn't understand the reason he explained—unless he wanted her to realize the dangers of wraiths. *He doesn't know what happened in the Haven.* Wraiths. "The Rhoghieri call them *wights*."

"Never sealed to Neothera? They are dangerous. Without the orb—." He didn't finish, for the advance riders had stopped. He rode ahead to consult.

Without the guiding orb, she realized, the Hunt would have stumbled into the old killing ground. The wraiths would have attacked them or, more invidious, would have attached themselves to the riders and gradually sapped their life essence. A mundane man would gradually die, as Brok would soon have died if the wraiths continued unstopped. Would the knights and dames bound to a Kyrgy lord or lady die? Could the wraith draw on Fae essence through those bound to the Kyrgy?

She let her horse pick its way forward until she reached Grim and Sangrior. Lady Bone's knight studied her then looked ahead, to where Lord Skull listened to his knights' report. The orb hovered not far ahead of them. Behind the fallen boulders, the road had worked over the mountain's flank and began another descent.

Grim's lightened expression welcomed her. "How are you doing?"

"Everyone keeps asking that."

"Kyrgy knights don't feel weariness. They're nearly unstoppable in battle. Fae strength gives them energy."

She glanced at Sangrior. Lady Bone's strength would bolster him. *Did he feel energy fade when the Lady poured healing into Volk?* "What's ahead? What did they see—or sense?"

Sangrior shrugged. Grim stiffened then stood in his stirrups. He stared at Lord Skull.

No. Beyond Skull. To the next boulder-fall. Something moved among the smaller rocks then sprang onto a larger boulder. It scrabbled for purchase then leaped onto the highest stone. Pale-skinned, it looked as marble-white as the Kyrgy and their riders. Then the thing straightened, no longer a crouching animal but—a woman. Moonlight glinted on her naked skin. Pale hair haloed around her head. She lifted her arms. Eldritch green glowed around her hands, her fingertips, her claws.

She snatched at the orb above her, leaped for it and missed but landed with agility on the curved top of the boulder. She leaped again, but the orb was out of reach.

The riders shouted at their lord. Orielle knew the moment Skull spotted the woman with sorcery lengthening her claws. He stiffened. Then he flung out his hand.

The orb exploded above the female wyre. She ducked away from the shower of sparks. Then she straightened. "Catch me if you can find me!"

She jumped off the boulder, ignoring the lower rocks. She shifted mid-leap, transforming into the pale-furred wolf, the one that had taunted them on the forest road, before her fellow leaped upon the rider and killed him. She landed. Leaves scattered out. She yipped then scurried away, around the smaller rocks of the boulder-fall.

Skull and the two scouts sprang after her, their horses leaping to full speed from a shocked standstill.

And the largest, round-backed boulder moved, twisting, writhing, then straightening from a humped crouch. It stretched up, up and up, reached overhead and snagged tree limbs in its meaty hands. The rock-troll flung them down with a snarl.

Two horses spooked. As the troll stretched to its height, the black horses reared and bucked. One knight lost his seat and thudded onto the ground.

Skull had curbed his horse, controlling its reaction. His sword flashed out. He drove for the troll. His uplifted sword ran dark along the keen edge. Along the fuller, the silvered moonlight coursed down the Fae scrollwork.

Sangrior shouted and spurred his horse forward, a second after the Kyrgy lord. He brandished his ice-blue sword. A breath behind him was Grim. Then the other knights streamed past, all heading for the troll. Three broke off and took up their bows, aiming for the troll's eyes and throat and chest.

The troll broke more tree limbs. He swiped them in wheeling arcs, one then the other, but his movements were slow, sluggish. Skull darted in and cut at his torso, opening a thin line of red on the mottled grey skin. Then he drove on past, avoiding the sweeping branches. Another knight followed, then Sangrior, distinct on his snow-white horse, and then Grim, brown shirt and steel grey mail where the Kyrgy armor was black and moon-threaded.

Her horse wanted to join the fight. Orielle fought to rein him back. He danced under her, then bucked, nearly unseating her.

Something flashed to her left. Unable to look, she fought the horse, willing him to calm with strength and energy. Another flash. The horse wheeled then struck out with its hind hooves. A yip—and a growl.

Cold certainty told Orielle to let the horse fight. She let the reins go slack. She grabbed the pommel and tightened her legs. A wyre darted in. The horse stomped and whirled and struck with its hind legs—and the wyre yelped as it darted away. The pale wyre rushed under the horse. She snarled and snapped. The horse kicked and whirled, stomped then lunged. The wyre scrambled away. The horse turned to face it, legs splayed, body trembling as much as Orielle's did.

The dark-furred wyre feinted side to side, pretended to rush in then leaped back as the horse struck out, half-rearing. It doubled around, and Orielle and the horse turned to face it.

The blow surprised her, coming from the left as the horse wheeled right. It struck her from the saddle. She tumbled and landed hard, discovering rocks hidden under the leaves. Air left her lungs. She panicked, trying to gasp breath back into her shocked lungs.

Then a pale shape struck her, flattening her anew. The wyre leaped.

Orielle rolled. The wyre missed, but a rock didn't, thudding into her chest. But she could breathe. She tried to scramble away, but the wyre came from behind this time. It landed on her back. She fell forward, face in the leaves, mouth full of them, breathing them. The wyre snarled. She felt a grab, but it missed her neck.

Magic, her mind screamed, then *No! Air*, and she yanked the element to her. Before she shaped it into a defense, the wyre yelped. Its weight vanished. She rolled, spitting out leaves and shaping the Air into a gust of wind—and saw Grim beside her, facing the battle. Beyond it were two shapes, pale and dark, hurtling over the ground to the forest road.

Many voices shouted, smothered by a guttural growl that caught in the middle.

Grim turned. His gaze swept her, then he reached down to help her stand. The ground shuddered, nearly knocking her off her regained feet. She staggered and clutched his arm. As one, they looked at the knights fighting the troll.

It was on its knees. Arrows peppered its chest and face. Blood streamed from scores of slices and punctures. Bare-handed, it swiped at a knight that cut into his leg, but it moved like it waded through mire. Another knight darted in and opened a long slash along its arm. It wailed.

Then an arrow found its mark in the troll's eye. The rock troll froze in mid-swing. It gurgled. Blood trickled from its mouth. Then it toppled to one side.

The ground shook again. The troll lay still. The knights rushed forward and jabbed and hacked until their enemy was a bloody mess—and not once did it moan or move.

Then Lord Skull spoke, one word. The knights fell back, retrieving their horses, cleaning their blades.

Orielle leaned against Grim. He was sturdy, sure, living, and he'd saved her life again. He wrapped an arm around her. "Hush. It's over."

"For now."

"Aye, for the nonce. He's coming."

She shuddered then drew a deep breath. She spat out the remnants of the leaves. Then she turned to face Lord Skull.

~ **3** ~

Troll blood spattered his face. His armor remained clean of the battle.

Skull ignored the blood on his skin but carefully wiped his sword as he approached. "An unexpected battle."

"Another ambush." Grim pointed to the forest road continuing along the mountain's flank. "The wyre ran off."

"Aye. Back to the old lair? Or to a new one, wherever it is. We must locate it. Close, I think."

"Whichever, we'll need to be wary. That's twice they've ambushed us."

"What think you, Not-Wizard?"

Orielle stopped worrying about the leaves she might have swallowed. She coughed then said, "The wyre intended to lead us away from their new camp, on orders of the sorceress."

Sangrior had neared. Blood streaked his sword and his armor. Like the Kyrgy lord, he tended to his weapon rather than the troll's blood. "What reason do they lead us away?"

"This is Crone Moon. As Lord Skull said, the sorceress had three people to moon-change into new wyres. Will they be able to fight us on the night of their transformation?"

Grim frowned. "Wyre can fight immediately. Why wait? Why not send every fighter into battle? Three veteran wyre, three new, and the sorceress. Even odds."

Orielle turned to him. "What do you mean, *even*? Lord Skull has twelve riders and himself, plus you and Sangrior, and me. We outnumber them."

"I've seen his riders fight. Your pardon, my lord, but unless it's you or Sangrior, no single rider can take a wyre. It would need two or three of them."

"You took on three."

"And nearly died," he reminded Orielle. "I can barely defend myself if three attack at once. And not for long. Even odds, like I said."

"Sorcerer or wizard," Lord Skull gave a slight bow to Orielle, "they will want overwhelming odds when they go into battle. Has the sorceress other fighters?"

"She had three mundane swordsmen when we fought on the shoreline. Two died in that fight."

"And she moon-changes three tonight. She has other mundane then. Perhaps a troop from Frost Clime. She would need the Prime wyre for the moon-change, if they are to obey him. We killed one at the old lair. We saw two here. She has changed others before tonight."

"When?" Orielle felt hollow. "When could she have done so? We saw her whole force at the shoreline."

"Did you, Not-Wizard?"

"Where else would they have been?"

"How long?" Grim confronted Sangrior. "How long has the sorceress had a pact with Lady Bone?"

The consort knight grimaced. He directed his answer at Skull. "Since Dragon Moon the wyre pack has run the Wilding."

"Which night of Dragon Moon? Wyvern? Dragon? Or Lindworm?"

"Lindworm. She would not add to the lair, though. She had ten males then."

"And she has had days to achieve that number again. How many females were in the lair?"

Orielle remembered the woman standing naked on the boulder, the woman who transformed into the pale wolf. One female wyre. "None of the ones we fought earlier were female," she murmured. "Just the one tonight."

Sangrior looked abashed. "I do not know how many females."

Lord Skull chuckled. "We are remiss in your training. No Prime moves without his consort prime. No consort prime moves without two attendants. No lair moves without five consorts. A full lair has all ten consorts."

"I did not know that," Grim muttered. "That's good knowledge to have."

"Fifteen wyre," Orielle counted. "We must assume that number. Plus the sorceress and Saircuista. And swordsmen, one or two tent groups or *temes*. We were outnumbered from the beginning."

"We killed seven," Grim reminded, "plus one tonight. That leaves seven of the original fifteen."

"Plus the three she moon-changed, ten. And however many females and mundane swordsmen and the sorceress herself."

"Who is Saircuista?" Skull asked.

Sangrior didn't answer, nor did Grim. Still distracted by numbers, Orielle said, "One of Lady Bone's dames, one who betrayed her to ally with the sorceress. I knew the sorceress had been in the Wilding for days. Now we find that she has been here half-a-month. Time enough to recruit Fortis and convince him to use those eldritch blades to open a pathway for the wraiths."

"You go beyond me." The Kyrgy lord spoke without emotion, but his intense stare broke her distraction and warned her to focus. "My lady sister did not tell me that one of her riders had defected. Certainly not that a dame of the Hunt had allied to a sorceress."

Sangrior shifted uncomfortably. Lord Skull's knights and dames had gradually retrieved their mounts then walked over to encircle them, and Sangrior looked at each one, as if answering unspoken questions. "The Lady has dealt with the traitor. She did so yesterday. This night the traitor is no more."

"Skuld has removed her mantle on the dame?"

"She did, Lord Vrigsmal."

Orielle fastened on the Kyrgy lord's true name. Sangrior had slipped out the Lady's name days ago: Skuld. Now she knew Lord Skull's: Vrigsmal. Said three times, his true name would bring him to her aid, just as she had called upon the knights Sangrior and Volk, and upon the Lady herself, to save Grim.

Only in dire circumstances, though, would she ever call upon a Kyrgy. Their aid came with a required sacrifice. These three Hunts, that she had sworn to give Lady Bone, they were a minor sacrifice, not dire, dangerous but not soul-stealing.

Vrigsmal might choose the dire and soul-stealing in return for his aid.

The Kyrgy lord bent his head in acknowledgement of Sangrior's answer. Then he looked to Orielle and Grim. "Who is this Fortis that you mention has eldritch knives? A Rhoghieri? Why would a Rho bind himself to a sorceress? She is allied to wyre. All Frost Clime sorcerers have wyre leashed for their use. Rho and wyre are enemies."

That answer belonged to Grim. He cleared his throat. "Fortis was a mentor. He's dead."

"Yet this mentor made pact with a sorceress. He used her eldritch knives. How many?"

"I do not know, my lord."

"Three," Orielle supplied. "We did not find more. He killed people to create paths for the wraiths to enter the Haven, but—." She didn't think it wise to brag about her battles with the wraiths. "He was unsuccessful. We fought him yesterday."

"You killed him?"

"We did, my lord," Grim said firmly, with no hint that Fortis had been a childhood friend.

"And the wraiths?"

"Destroyed, my lord."

"Then we need not return to the Haven to purge any lingering corruption." He addressed that to Grim, no doubt considering him as the Rho's representative to the Kyrgy. "The corruption that infected my lady sister's riders is also removed. The Haven is no longer corrupted. That is *guot*. We have the sorceress and her wyre to remove, to restore the Wilding. The pact with this sorceress should never have occurred." His glinting gaze bore on Sangrior, who shrank under its weight.

The knight knelt. "My lord. Do you require that I return to my Lady?"

"You ride with me, a gift from my sister until we defeat the sorceress and her wyre and mundane, however many remain to her. As for Lady

Skuld, my sister will answer to me. Come, we have wyre to hunt and a sorceress to kill." He glanced at Orielle. "Your debt will clear with the death of the sorceress, Aiwaz Solsken. You need to be wizard now, no longer Not-Wizard."

She did hate that name. "As you say, my lord."

A rider handed over the reins to Vrigsmal's black steed. He vaulted into the saddle. They hastened to mount, Grim helping Orielle then leaping into his own saddle. The Lord ordered Orielle and Sangrior to flank him once more, then they rode from the boulderfall, back around the battle ground with its wisps of wraiths, and to the forest road.

.~.~.~.

The old lair looked as empty and smelled as musty as before. They found signs of recent wyre, three distinct tracks on the forest side of the lair. The wyre that had killed the knight had disappeared.

Lord Vrigsmal removed the cloak over the fallen knight. He knelt beside the stiffening body. Passing his hand over the stilled face, he bent his head.

A crackling of flames over new wood sounded, but no one had kindled a fire. No flickering light appeared; no smoke rose. The light, when it came, blazed suddenly, appearing on the knight's exposed skin. The fire lacked the orangey yellow of flames. It shone with gold, white gold and yellow gold, shimmering gold that flickered over the knight. The strange flame consumed flesh and bone and metal, for when it died, the knight's body had vanished, even his armor and leathers consumed.

Lady Bone hadn't tended her fallen riders this way. She burned them where they lay on the shore—after she healed Volk.

The Kyrgy lord straightened. He studied where the knight had lain, then he turned to his riders, some wounded in the battle against the rock troll. "Sir Kalleth will never be forgotten. His memory will be lifted when we feast. A smoke will lift to him from Maiden's Moon to Maiden's Moon. His name will be worked into the tapestry of my hall. To Kalleth!"

"To Kalleth!" returned his knights and dames.

As Vrigsmal mounted his horse, Orielle decided that the Kyrgy lord knew how to lead. Even when he lost a rider, he honored the rider's memory. Knights and dames would remember that. No matter the terms of their binding, the signs of his appreciation of their sacrifice increased their loyalty to him.

How had Lady Bone increased loyalty? Sir Volk gave her complete loyalty. She called him hers: "my Volk, you cannot leave me." Yet Sangrior looked beyond the Lady, still harking to the mundane world.

Saircuista had tried to defect and suffered before she was given death. The Lady hadn't said anything special about the riders lost on the shore. Yet who would have heard her? Volk, who she already held, and Sangrior and that third knight, whose name she didn't remember. Did the Lady do nothing to inspire loyalty?

Lady Bone was fearsome.

Yet she had two consort knights while her brother appeared to have no consorts. Was that because his consorts were at his hall—and where was that? What kind of place would be fitting for a Kyrgy lord? Vrigsmal ruled; his sister ruled because of him. Did that prevent him from choosing a consort? Was it his choice as leader? Would he pick no favorite to keep every knight and dame striving to win his approval?

Lord Vrigsmal was terrifying—for Orielle admitted that he could wring allegiance from her. She feared Lady Bone. Vrigsmal inspired Orielle with awe.

A knight shouted, and the Lord rode to consult with him. He reported another wyre track leading from the old lair, in the direction of the river. Orielle expected a hard ride as they tracked the wyre to the sorceress.

Yet Vrigsmal did not spur to follow. He stared at the sky. The round Crone's Moon had cast over to the inky western vault. "The night nears its end. I will not follow the trail only to confront this sorceress as the sun rises. She will expect us." He leaned toward Orielle, as if he spoke to her alone, yet his voice carried to all the riders. "You are Solsken. The hours of the sun are your blessing. Not so for the Kyrgy. The Moon gives us her blessing, and the Lady Moon doubles her blessing." He straightened and turned to meet every rider's gaze. "We have fought well tonight. We have killed enemies, expected and unexpected. We mark this Wilding as ours. In the sunlight hours, we will prepare for the Lady's Moon, when we shall hunt again, hunt a sorceress who fouls our Wilding, and hunt the wyre who serve her. We ride."

And they rode, the trees rushing past as the horses covered ground in their dream-like gallop. Orielle and Grim rode with them; Sangrior rode to the right. Would they not return to the Haven or to Lady Bone?

The transition started so gradually that she didn't notice until the horses' hoofs no longer thudded over bare ground but clanged on stone. The trees rising to surround them became buildings of pale amber stone and white marble. Underbrush transformed into half-walls. Twisted branches became carved ornamentation on the stone buildings.

As dawn lightened the sky, they rode along a wide street toward a many-storied building with ornate decoration on doors and windows and the roofline. Walls rose high, three stories, dwarfing them. The road appeared cobbled, but the horses' hoofs remained soundless.

She tried to see everything, but it passed in a blur, just as the sky brightened in a blur.

The building they approached had a single spire reaching for the blueing sky. Glass glittered amber along the three stories of the facade, the panes gilded by the rising sun. The palace looked as gracious as any in Tres Lucerna, capitol of Mont Nouris.

The massive entrance had silver-aged doors gilded with a coppery arabesque design. The doors opened as they drew up before the stairway. Soldiers marched out, each taking a step that mounted to the doors. Nine men on each side.

Vrigsmal sprang down. A rider caught the reins of his mount. The Kyrgy lord ran lightly up the steps. Then he turned. The sun glinted on his Fae-graved armor. He flung out his arms. "Welcome to Ifendrayl, my hall. Today, we prepare. Tonight, we hunt. Tomorrow, we feast." With that, he disappeared through the open door.

~ **4** ~

As they dismounted, two long-limbed women with gold-glinting hair came down the nine steps. Eyes moss green and skin of a burnished hue, they waited on the final step.

"Lucent Fae," Grim muttered as he helped Orielle dismount.

The Fae that had never left Faeron, unlike the Kyrgy whose silver hair, full-black eyes, and marble-white skin were imitated by their riders. When Orielle, Grim, and Sangrior approached, the expressionless women turned and led the way up the stair. The sentries in their Fae-scrolled steel armor didn't move. Their gazes remained distant, not returning Orielle's curiosity. When the riders entered the palace with its polished oak floors, the sentries filed in after. All but two dispersed.

The women had paused. When the sentries passed, they continued, gliding along the hall. Tall mirrors with golden frames lined the hall. Tapestries covered the walls between the mirrors. The staggered mirrors reflected the tapestries, not each other into infinity. The reflected images doubled the splashing fountains and fanciful beasts, flowering gardens and fruit-laden orchards. The last two tapestries depicted horses, rampant, one snow-white, the other inky black, the images doubled by the mirrors.

The Lucent Fae opened the smoke-glazed doors at the hall's end then stood expressionless beside the doors.

Sangrior passed without a pause. Grim and Orielle followed, Orielle sneaking glances at the women. She'd never been this close to a Fae. For years she hadn't even know that Dark Fae, Kyrgy, existed. To find Fae with Dark Fae amazed her.

Once they had entered the room, the women shut the doors, leaving them in the dining hall.

Facing them was a wall of clear glass. It looked upon the forest with its autumn canopy and the blue sky of sunrise. The wall at one end of the room had painted dancers, women in long white dresses, men in blue tunics and loose breeches. At the other end, people in stiff court attire milled about two carved thrones, both of silver with gold filigree on the backs and the arms and legs. Purple cushions with stylized silver embroidery covered the seats.

Orielle turned, trying to see everything. The palace-side wall had more gilt mirrors and tapestries. The intricate arras were of musicians. The tall mirrors should have reflected the long table with its dozens of chairs, but the glass was silvered and empty, glistening like water.

As she approached a mirror to investigate its lack of a reflection, the doors again opened. Three women entered, the two from before and one more. Each bore a tray. The first brought three crystal goblets with two carafes, one with a burgundy liquid while the other was a deep golden. The second carried in covered plates. The third tray held three bowls of fruit. The women placed the trays at the dancers' end of the table then retired, shutting the glazed doors again.

Sangrior poured burgundy wine then extended it to Orielle. "We're privileged guests. Do you wish wine?" He indicated the other carafe. "Or ale?"

"What is this?" Distracted from her inspection, she accepted a goblet and sipped. The wine tasted mulled and thinned, as if it were spiced and watered.

The knight removed a cover, revealing a plate with meat and bread and something golden. "Break your fast." He drew out the chair at the table's end and sat, uncovered a plate, and placed it before him.

Grim uncovered a similar plate. He poured himself ale then drew out the chair to Sangrior's left. "Orielle, here." He placed a small bowl of the compote beside her plate. By then she had seated herself, and he scooted her closer before taking the seat beside her and helping himself to the third plate.

Sangrior poured more wine into his glass. For minutes, the only sounds were the clinking silverware on crystal plates.

Hunger assuaged, Orielle sipped her wine as she studied the embossed floral carving of the silverware. "What is this place?"

"The palace of Vrigsmal. Is it not wondrous? Such a place this deep in the Wilding." Sangrior looked more relaxed than she'd ever seen him. He toasted her with his glass, drank, then poured more wine, leaving enough for her to have a second glass.

"It's not real. It's illusion." Grim motioned to the bread she hadn't finished. When she nodded, he quickly broke it into pieces and smeared each one with compote.

"Real enough," Sangrior disputed. "This food is real. The people are real, Kyrgy and Fae and mundane riders. The chairs and this table are real." His hand smoothed across the acorn-carved table edge.

"This room? This palace?"

"Illusion," Grim said firmly. "Mirrors. Paintings. Tapestry."

"If all this is illusion, it would take a tremendous amount of power to appear real. Lord Skull must be extremely powerful."

The knight shrugged. "He is Kyrgy. Their power is weirded, not like wizardry or sorcery, certainly not like elemental wielding. How did you know the palace is illusion?"

"Look at the edges. Not directly. Look for a shimmer. That's the sign of illusion."

Orielle didn't see the shimmer. She might not be looking the way Grim suggested; she also might not be able to see the shimmer. He was Rho, an enchanted being, not a mundane who worked spells. Few wizards retained enough of the enchanted blood inherited from a distant Fae ancestor.

"What are we to do now?"

"Rest. We hunt tonight. We will hunt until the sorceress and her wyre are destroyed."

"And Lord Skull? Will we see him today? Is Lady Bone here? Or does she have her own palace?" She glanced at the empty thrones. Were they for a king and queen? For a Fae Lord and the Lady? Or for Vrigsmal and Skuld?

"We will see them later. We will dine before we hunt. They will be there."

"Are we still in the Wilding?"

He snorted, as if she asked an inane question, but Grim stopped eating the last of her bread and looked at her as if he'd never considered that question. "Because Fae can transition from place to place?"

Other transitions had had a blinding light. "Did the Lord take us someplace else?"

"We would have that flashing light of a transition."

"Would we? If this place is illusion—? If he can command such vast power—?"

"Ask him." Sangrior drained his wine. "I care only for a place to lay my head."

The glazed doors opened. The women reappeared, as mute as before.

Sangrior pushed back his chair. "Come," but it was an order, not a request.

Orielle left her unfinished wine and followed Grim. He waited past the doors for her. Sangrior had paused just a few steps beyond.

The women closed the room, and the glazing seemed to darken. At an unhurried pace, they glided along the hall, stopping halfway back to the entrance. One of them drew back a tapestry, revealing a flight of stairs. The other started up, her footsteps soundless on the time-stained oak. Sangrior followed, his steps sounding. With a gesture, Grim cautioned her before they followed.

The stairway walls were painted with tree canopies and the sky. Birds in flight climbed with them. The woman pushed aside another tapestry then held it as they passed into another long hall.

This hall had doors rather than tapestries and mirrors. The walls were painted in forest scenes, trees and meadows, deer with a watching stag. On the opposite side, wolves ran in a hunt past several doorways.

The other Fae woman had followed them up the stairway. She held aside the sole tapestry, beside the vigilant stag, revealing another short passage and another hall beyond. "Sir Knight." Her voice was low harmonies, and Orielle heard the chords of a lute after she spoke.

Sangrior huffed. "I will see you at the feast." He bowed then obeyed the Fae's direction. She disappeared behind the tapestry with him.

The other Fae walked to a door flanked by two does. "Lady Wizard," she announced and opened the door.

Grim quickly said, "We stay together," and Orielle didn't refute his claim.

The woman remained at the door.

Orielle glanced at Grim then entered. He followed. The door shut behind him.

A curtained bed dominated the chamber. As she dropped her cloak on a low chest beside the door, Orielle turned in a circle. No window. No hearth. Two chairs beside a small round table. A stand held a basin and a flower-decorated ewer with a gilded lip and handle. The carpet looked like an old tapestry, a weaving of sprites dancing through a trickling waterfall.

Grim tossed back the bed curtains. Then he began tugging the mail shirt over his head. When he emerged from it and dropped it onto a chair, he asked, "Are you tired?"

"Not really. I shall probably drop to sleep with no trouble, but I feel strange." He crossed to her. He touched her cheek, and she leaned into the touch. "I have ever since we entered this—I don't know what to call it other than palace."

His storm-grey eyes narrowed as he scanned her. "How strange?"

"Sparkling with energy. Bubbles of it popping inside me, like expensive wine."

He smiled. "Fae power." His arms encircled her waist, drawing their bodies together.

"Is that what it feels like? I've known Fae. In the Enclave." She spread her fingers on his shoulders and tilted her face to him. "The bonded *comeis* and Fae wielders. I don't sparkle like this around them. Is it because this is all Kyrgy power?"

"No. It's the illusion of this place. Or wherever we actually are. We could be in Faeron itself. I don't know."

"I thought the Kyrgy abandoned Faeron when the dragons were defeated."

"Do we truly know what Fae and Kyrgy did then?" His other hand came to her cheek. His skin was rough, calloused by years of wielding swords. "Orielle, you're not complaining of my touch."

"No. I want you, Grim." She saw no reason to be coquettish.

He growled, like one of the wolves running the hunt. Then he kissed her, his mouth devouring her thoughts, and she could only feel.

Long, exploring kisses turned urgent. Grim tugged at her bodice, and they separated only to shed their clothes. She kicked out of her boots; he shed his brown shirt. He tugged off his breeches; she flung away her skirts. Then he lifted her to the bed and came down beside her, bracing himself on an arm. The kisses consumed them. Careful touches became harder, intense, his hand shaping her, her nails digging into his muscles. Sensation ramped up their driving emotions as desire surged past frustration, longing melted into need, and care deepened into a more powerful, enduring emotion.

And when they joined, Orielle knew a completion that she'd never glimpsed nor anticipated.

~ **5** ~

Orielle woke entwined with Grim. His breath tickled her neck; his body was a furnace keeping her warm. They'd neglected the bed curtains. The uncovered parts of her—toes, shins, an arm, her nose— were icy.

That was one thing Lord Skull's palace did not have: warmth in these bedrooms. The cold air frosted her breath.

She felt alert, awake, and that relief hadn't come from assuaging the need that had gradually deepened with every hour she knew Grim.

Two nights ago she had battled wraiths. Last night she fought a sorceress and her troop of wyre and mundane swordsmen. The next morning they had fought with Fortis. How long had they slept? The weariness of those two missed night's sleep no longer dogged her.

She wiggled a little, trying to get her toes to a warm spot. Nothing warmed the room. Had it been this cold when they'd entered? She'd only noticed the barest furniture. The bed dominated everything.

Grim grunted. He burrowed closer, and she threaded her fingers through his hair.

"You're awake," he complained.

"Reality intrudes."

He lifted his head, and cold air rushed to chill her neck. "What hour is it?"

"There speaks a man who's stood watches."

He levered up more and looked around. She shivered at the intruding air. "No windows. No fireplace." He touched her cheek. "How do you feel?"

"Awake. Energized."

He grinned, as if she complimented him. Then he rolled out of the bed. She tugged the coverlet from beneath her and covered up. At least their bodies had warmed the bedding.

Fastening his breeches, he opened the hall door and looked out. He shut it rapidly.

Orielle sat up. "What is it?"

"Frost."

"What?"

"Frost in the corridor." He searched for his second boot.

"That's not natural."

He stomped into his boots. He tossed her the white bodice he'd nearly torn. His brown shirt was beneath it. She slid out of bed and searched for her skirts.

The air seemed to freeze even more as they finished dressing The hair on her nape prickled with warning. When Grim opened the door again, he held a hand to hold her back. He looked both ways then stepped out, motioning her to follow.

Their breaths fogged in the frigid air. Looking like enlarged snowflakes, frost speckled the planking. The door knobs were rimed with frost. The frozen animals on the walls seemed to watch their progress.

At the vigilant stag, Grim swept aside the tapestry to the little corridor into which Sangrior had gone. The narrow space seemed warmer, but the hallway it opened upon was chilly. Doors only opened on the opposite side of the hall while cleverly painted water poured along the feet of quaking aspens on the walls.

He opened the door across from the little corridor. They saw armor on the floor and a curtained bed. The room was as chilled as theirs.

Grim threw back a bed curtain. Sangrior lay there, stilly marble, covered to his chin. He breathed, slow and deep.

Orielle stopped Grim from shaking the knight. An abrupt awakening could be dangerous. She squeezed Sangrior's shoulder then again and again until his eyes opened.

For the briefest second they were a blue as clear as the sky, then deep black flooded in, filling the sclera. He stayed marble-still, but his eyes cast over to see Grim. Then he sat up, entirely clothed beneath the bed coverings. "What is wrong?"

"The air—it's too cold."

"Frost in the hall," Grim added. "Is that usual?"

For answer, Sangrior slid off the bed and searched for his spurred boots. "How long?"

"We don't know. We just woke."

He buckled on his breastplate then reached for his swordbelt. He checked that the ice-blue sword slid easily in the scabbard, then strode to the door, impatient with the tapestry. When he saw the frost ruining the flooring, he grunted. "Have you seen anyone? Heard anything? No? Then be alert."

Sangrior led them to the stairway and down. He went slowly, carefully, for the steps were more iced than the hallway.

Ice covered the mirrors along the entrance hallway. Their breaths frosted, hanging heavy in the cold, cold air.

Sangrior turned to the dining room rather than the front door. He opened a glazed door. His sharp inhalation alerted them. Power tracked to Orielle's fingers, ready, warming.

The two Fae women stood on either side of the glazed doors. Their faces had turned as white as Sangrior's, the burnished glint of gold vanished from their skin. Their eyes were shut, their lips bluish. Their eyelashes looked rimed, reminding Orielle of the icy tear dripping from Zairantze's lashes. Yet they breathed, the faintest exhalation of frosty vapor. A pulse beat in one woman's temple.

Beyond the wall of windows, the colorful trees outside were prematurely ice-covered. Snow smothered the ground, limned the edges of the autumn leaves, created a tracery that patterned the bark on the tree limbs. The snow lay inches thick, a frozen wonderland.

And dangerous, for Sangrior swore and looked like he wanted to attack it.

"Not natural?" Grim asked.

"No. Not now, not so quickly."

"Frost Clime."

He growled. "The sorceress must be powerful."

"Or her spell unexpected," Orielle pointed out. *Not powerful. Please, not powerful.* "Should we wake them?"

"Can you?"

She took the hand of the nearest. It seemed lifeless—yet she sensed a throbbing life essence. She clasped one hand over it, the other cupping it. She did not know any strong healing spells, just the basic healing spells that every wizard knew. She flooded a warming spell in with a simple awakening spell and prayed that was enough.

It was. The blue left the woman's lips. Her skin warmed. Then her eyes flashed open, moss-green in her still pale face.

"What—?"

"The sorceress. Ice." She reached for the other Fae.

The snowy forest seemed to capture the woman's attention. When her companion woke, the scene also snared her.

"Where is the Lord and the Lady?"

They jerked at that question. Fae did not dramatize any emotion, yet they seemed guilty. "Come." They led the way into the hall.

"Is everyone frozen asleep?"

"You are the first we found," Sangrior assured them.

The green-eyed one turned to Orielle. "What spell did you work?"

"Awakening and warming."

"Simple spells. This ice seems a great magic."

At their looks of wonder, Orielle cringed. She had started with simple spells, not expecting them to work. *But why wouldn't simple spells work? I've faced the sorceress in battle. If she could have destroyed me, she would have. She did not.* Did their powers match? To ice over the whole palace would require a well-prepared spell, not great power. And it depended on the Kyrgy being caught unawares. The sorceress must have depended on catching the palace's inhabitants unprepared for defense.

Another ambush.

Grim held back a tapestry for her to follow the Fae women into a corridor similar to the stag and wolves above. These walls were painted with great trunks of oaks and a leafy green canopy that stretched across the ceiling.

"Another trick," she whispered to Grim, "one that depended on lowering our guard."

Sangrior had heard her. "The sentries—." Then he shook his head. "The power would have crept over them, wouldn't it?"

"Frost Clime will be coming. They expect us to be caught in sleep and ice."

"Easy prey," Grim growled.

They passed into another corridor, narrow this time and not as long. The walls were covered with mirrors in gilt frames and heavily worked tapestries. The arras depicted riders on a Hunt through a stylized forest.

The woman swept back a tapestry of three knights on black horses. Behind it was a carved door, a stag wreathed by evergreens decorated with nuts and berries on the central panel. Wide-eyed, she looked from Orielle to Sangrior and to Grim. "My lord Vrigsmal is here. He asked not to be disturbed."

Grim reached past her and turned the icy knob. He pushed the door open and revealed a huge bedchamber, thrice the size of their own, filled with silver-painted furniture. This room was not as cold as the others. Storm-purple curtains surrounded the bed. Grim tossed those back as well.

Lord Skull lay entwined with a Fae woman, her golden hair spilling across his marble-white skin. His eyes flashed open. "What do you here?"

Sangrior bent to one knee. "Lord Skull, the sorceress and her wyre will soon attack."

The Kyrgy sat up, dislodging the woman. Shifted to the mattress, she slept on, undisturbed. He stared at her, then his nostrils flared. "Sorcery." He sprang from the bed. "Who is affected?"

"It crept over the court. The Aiwaz Solsken awakened me before the spell killed me." Sangrior indicated the women. "These Fae were caught in it, though. The Solsken awakened them."

Uncaring of his nudity, Vrigsmal turned to Orielle. "You masquerade as a Not-Wizard?"

"Two simple spells dispersed the sorcery, my lord. Anyone who can work a light spell can disrupt it."

"Even so?" His head tilted. Then he reached for his leather breeches. "Simple spells that invade my palace? Ice sleep dissipated by my Solsken? Wake Ysafrona," he ordered a Fae woman who hastened to obey. "Wake the sentries," he ordered the other, and she hurried from the room. "Have you warned my sister?"

"Lady Skuld is here?"

"With her consort knight, aye. Show him," he tossed to the first Fae woman, for the one he had bedded was awake, blinking and stretching, not yet alert. "We shall see if this sorceress dares to attack."

Sangrior followed the Fae from the room. Vrigsmal buckled on his breastplate, and Grim moved to serve like a squire.

"How did you escape the spell, Solsken?"

"I do not know. I woke chilled. The room was not iced, not like the hallways and Sangrior's chamber, but it was becoming so."

"The spell invaded the passages first?" he mused. "That sounds logical." He grinned then, revealing his sharpened teeth, a predator's relish of the Hunt for his prey. "She does not understand my palace."

Does anyone? Orielle wondered, for Grim claimed it was illusion. Yet how did illusion have three stories and a spire as well as a lower level for the servants who kept the palace functioning with meals and practicalities? *Or perhaps the Fae, whether Lucent or Kyrgy, are beyond such mundanities?*

"Ysafrona, see my other servants are awake. Have them prepare a quick meal. Wine, bread, meat. We may not have time to dine before the sorceress and her wyre attack." He turned back to Orielle. "The spell came in, through the passages and thence to the chambers, climbing up, because she expected us to rest after our Hunt."

"As we did."

"Ah, but you were awake and dressed before the spell would have taken you. I would study this more."

One of the Fae women hurried in. Her Fae reserve had broken into horror. "My Lord. Oh, my Lord!" She dropped to her knees and bent forward, her brow touching the floor at his feet. "The sentries, my Lord. Those who were without—they are dead! Frozen!"

The skin around his full-black eyes tightened. "Frozen how?"

"They stand in their place, but frost covers them and their skin is blue with cold. They are like ice statues. Even their halberds are frozen. When I touched one, his hand broke and fell to the ground! Four sentries, my Lord."

"Wake the others. Wake my riders."

"My Lord." She scrambled up and rushed out.

"We may have lost others. My sword," the Kyrgy ordered. Grim hoisted the ornate sword sheathed in an embroidered scabbard, silver thread scrolled into Fae words. When Vrigsmal fastened the swordbelt around him, the sword hung nearly to the floor.

Sangrior waited in the corridor. He looked statue-still except for his eyes, flickering from tapestry to tapestry.

"My sister?"

"Awake and donning armor, my lord. Volk is with her. Her last rider bunks with your own." As he spoke, the tapestry behind him was swept aside. Volk emerged, and he held the heavy arras for the Lady to come through.

"Brother."

"Sister. Did the spell snare you?"

"Nay, I was untouched. I woke when Sangrior entered. Beside me, though, Volk was taken without my knowledge, yet he woke easily."

"So it has been. Riders and sentries and companions snared, we in a natural sleep."

"I sense no sorcery."

"Would we? The sorceress has used simple spells to slip inside our wards."

"How did you learn of it?"

"We are indebted to the Solsken," and he bowed to Orielle.

Expressionless, Lady Bone surveyed Orielle. "You surprise me yet again, Not-Wizard. I acknowledge the debt and release you from the vow."

Orielle curtsied. "My Lady, we have common cause against the sorceress and her followers. I do not seek to escape my vow. I would serve until we defeat her."

"An honorable wizard," Vrigsmal murmured while Skuld's brow contracted, a minute sign of displeasure.

Indebted to the Solsken. Vrigsmal claimed the debt, for himself and his sister. A Kyrgy in debt to a wizard. Accustomed to absolute command, the Lady would not relish that debt.

"Come." The Lord strode to the short passage and into the longer corridor.

A few riders had reached the longer corridor. Although armed, they did not seem alert or ready for battle. One bowed. "My Lord. We cannot wake three of our number. They are like ice."

Vrigsmal bowed his head. "I will mourn them later. After we have dealt with this foul sorceress of Frost Clime."

The three Fae companions waited before a tall mirror, their backs reflected. They sank into deep curtsies as Vrigsmal approached . He gently cupped the face of Ysafrona then briefly touched the cascading gilt hair of the other two. "You will return to Faeron."

"My Lord, no!"

"You will not be protected here, Ysafrona. Take the others with you and return to the Third Sister's court at Eiron. Give my thanks to her."

Vrigsmal's brief order scattered the bits of knowledge that she'd learned about the Fae, as if those few facts dropped into a deep chasm. *What did I never know?*

Orielle knew of the Third Sister. When the Enclave renewed its alliance with Faeron, her tutors had drilled all the wizardry students over the Fae septs. The Maorketh queen had three sisters and three brothers, each with a clan or sept. Were the Kyrgy part of a clan, an unknown part? The Third Sister was Veirnt Skuld.

Two Fae *comeis*, swordshields sent by the Veirnt Skuld, were bound to Pater d'Aulnois and Mater Rochein. Pater Galfrons, her clan, was protected by the *comeis* Dagorr Sigir of the First Sister's sept. Every wizard clan leader had a bound *comeis* from a sept. The ArchClan under protest had accepted a *comeis*. Fae warriors, immediate protection if Frost Clime attacked the Enclave—as they had two days before Orielle began her mission to Iscleft Haven. A handful of *comeis* and wizards and the ArchClan's magister Raigeis, her cousin, had died in the fight against two sorcerers and their bound wyre. *What did I never understand?*

Ysafrona had knelt. She looked up at Vrigsmal, her face a shining oval, gilded as the Kyrgy was marble-white. "My Lord, should we tell the Veirnt Skuld of the sorceress and the wyre?"

"I do not call upon her for aid. You may explain, you may not request, even without words. I ask only that she welcome you to her court."

Ysafrona reached for his hand, but she did not touch. "My Lord, I would not leave you."

"The wards will be dropped. The illusion will be shattered." At those stony sentences, the women cried in dismay. "Go," he ordered. "Return to Eiron."

The mirror rippled like water. When it cleared, the reflection was of a room filled with silver-gilt furniture and blue upholstery, a floor with white marble veined with grey, and a tapestry of a unicorn beside a blue-stone fountain. No one was in the room. The three Fae stepped through the mirror. As they turned to look back at Vrigsmal, the mirror rippled then it once more reflected the hall.

"Sentimental," Lady Bone judged. "They must learn to control that."

Her brother ignored her. He turned to his riders and sentries, whose ranks had filled as he dealt with the Lucent Fae. "We have an enemy who dares invade my court with her spells. She will not live to the dawn. Fill your bellies with food now. Fill them with blood on the Hunt."

The riders' shouts rang in the corridor.

~ **6** ~

Lord Vrigsmal maintained his palace until they had eaten. When riders and sentries flooded out to the waiting horses, he lifted both hands. With his eyes closed, his stilled face looked lifeless. Then he began shaping spells, signs glistening with gold power as he destroyed the illusion, fragment upon fragment, the stairs, the doors and windows.

Shards of the interior unveiled. The tapestries and mirrors and paintings sparkled as they faded.

Orielle recognized only three of the signs Vrigsmal used. An old tutor taught the signs, but she'd scarce heeded those lessons. How could substance be fashioned from nothing? She'd never realized—and no tutors never explained—that spell-working could build a palace from the thinniest Air.

The palace dissolved. It released glittering energy, a half-sensed essence that trickled along her power. Each bit vanished with a tinkling of chimes. The amber stone faded into a rustic timbered building, leaving fragments of the interior.

A gusty wind ripped through the surrounding oaks, tearing at the autumn colors. The snow-rimed leaves whipped and swirled, sweeping away into the forest. And the clouds overhead thickened. The temperature began to drop, descending deeper from the chill of autumn into the frigidity of winter.

Last to disappear into the two-storied timbered longhouse was the quarried foundation of amber stone. Then even that faded, and only the rustic buildings and outbuildings remained.

The magic that tingled through her also faded. Vrigsmal had released great energy.

No, not released. Drawn it back into himself.

They mounted and rode along the forest road, with the late afternoon sunlight deepening as the clouds overhead thickened and the wind increased. The road forked. Lady Bone, flanked by both of her consort knights, led them to the left fork. She seemed to have a destination. *Did the Lady know where to meet the sorceress?*

On the night before last, the Lady had led them straight to the sorceress' camp on the shoreline They crossed at that camp now, the river shallow and broad. Crows lifted from the shoreline. Orielle caught a glimpse of a brace of gobbers slinking into the covering undergrowth. Ash heaps dotted the sand and shingle. Fire-consumed bodies, the riders that Lady Bone had lost. The scavengers had been at the dead wyre and swordsmen that had followed the sorceress. Flesh devoured, bones scattered, with wispy fog trailing over a few of the bones.

The horses splashed across the river. The lead rider dismounted, and the Hunt waited as he strode past the ringed campfire. On the shore there had waited the sorceress and Saircuista and two wyre, tricking them so that no one expected an ambush.

The rider studied the ground. He walked several paces along the treeline. He seemed to sniff the air then ventured into the trees, deep enough that the forest closed around him.

"He has power?" Grim asked the rider nearest.

"A scant trace of it. Enough to sense sorcery." The rider sounded disgusted. "The sorceress is foul. Her fighters are fodder for the gobbers."

The rider emerged. He strode quickly to his horse which he wheeled around to give a report to Vrigsmal. "Fading scent, but a clear track away. Signs of them coming, a greater number than those who left. Moving slow as they came, rapidly as they left."

The Kyrgy lord's black horse tossed its head. "Flight or intent?"

"Intent. The trail is determined, not scattered. Found where a handful more waited well back."

"Ah. Reinforcements if my sister's attack overwhelmed them."

"We would have," Lady Bone interjected, "if Saircuista had fought for us, not against us."

Vrigsmal didn't look her way or acknowledge her words. "The trail away—were they returning to their true lair?"

"So it would seem, my Lord."

"Take another. Scout ahead. We will follow."

The rider whirled around and plunged his horse into the forest. A second rider came past and quickly followed. The rest of them came slowly behind. The Hunt worked up a ridge then descended. They came upon another forest road. One of the riders waited to turn them onto it, then he urged his horse forward again to resume scouting.

The road climbed the mountain slope through a series of gentle switchbacks. Over the crest it forked again, and the rider once more waited. When he spotted them, he spurred the horse on, rejoining the scout farther along where the road bent around the mountain's flank.

Orielle rode once more at Vrigsmal's side. She wondered if he would miss his court with its elaborate paintings and tapestries, carved doors and glazed windows. Beautiful—and spelled from nothing. Great power ....

But not a fighting power. Spells of illusion, spells that wrought the tangible from the intangible.

Fae were great swordsmen, flicking place to place. One could defeat his opponent simply by shifting so constantly that he surrounded him. Sangrior and Volk didn't have that power; their transitions from place to place were at Lady Bone's command—and her power. The Lady herself removed them from the shoreline before the sorceress and her fighters wiped them out.

The Fae women at Vrigsmal's palace had transitioned through a mirror to the Veirnt Skuld's court in Eiron. Had they themselves triggered that spell, or had the Lord worked the spell for the transition?

How much could a lesser Fae do? *Will I ever know that answer?*

Remembering the palace's beauty, Orielle wondered how much

more beautiful would be a court of a Lucent Fae. How much more beautiful would be the court of the Fae queen, the Maorketh Alaisa?

Were the courts of Faeron also illusion?

After years of ignoring her dry lessons, she dredged up her old tutor's droning voice as he described illusions that required much effort and puissance and time. *Is the difficulty only for wizards? Is it easier for Fae? When Vrigsmal rebuilds his palace, how long will he have to work the magic?*

If Vrigsmal survived the upcoming battle.

Fae could die, even Kyrgy.

"You are deep in thought, Solsken."

"My Lord, your court was beautiful."

"I will miss it."

That answer didn't approach her questions, and she dared ask nothing intrusive.

She heard Volk speak to Lady Bone, words hidden by the thunder of hoofbeats. Their passage along the forest road seemed slow, yet she knew that speed was deceptive.

"My Lord, you sent Ysafrona and the others into Faeron, to the court of the Veirnt Skuld."

He chuckled. "You hide a wealth of questions, do you not, Solsken? The Third Sister is an old friend, even with our exile after Dragon Dark. We find a common enemy in Frost Clime."

Mutely she recalled the Enclave's mission to Faeron, sending only carefully vetted wizards who stayed at the court of the Maorketh. Venturing to the other Fae septs—rocky Petrosse and its west-bordering Scree, Dagomer on the cold bays of the eastern sea, the great valley of Moutelle, forested Bermarck, green-growing Eiron, and the queen's Harrows of the North—that was not permitted. Those lands were mysteries to the Enclave. Yet surely wizards of the past had walked them, for the seven realms of Fae were described in the closely guarded documents of the archives.

She wished she had studied the Fae. *Vrigsmal said* **exile**. *Is it exile when Lucent Fae come as his companions? How much connection do the Kyrgy still have to Faeron?*

Is it only coincidence that Lady Bone, with her true name of Skuld, shares that name with the Third Sister Veirnt Skuld?

Am I looking for connections that aren't there?

Or had the Kyrgy gone into a self-exile, not a forced exile? Did the Kyrgy willingly take the frontier-bordering Wildings to rule? How many Wildings are there? How many Wildings guard against the rise of the dragons in the Wastes?

She shook her head. Too many questions she dared not ask, and no answers forthcoming. She settled for something related to her mission, something she would be expected to ask and have answered. "Will you and Lady Bone ride with us against Frost Clime?"

"Let us fight this battle before we speak of a different battlefield."

"As you wish, my Lord. The sorceress will know her spells did not wipe out her enemy. She will anticipate your numbers."

"She will be wrong, for I have more riders with me now. Have you battled sorcerers?"

"When I rode with the Lady, the night she reclaimed her traitorous rider."

"At great cost but necessary. Have you ever fought beside Fae?"

"Only with your sister, my Lord."

"My sister did not engage with the sorceress?"

"No, my Lord. That was my task."

"And still your task, Solsken. My sister calls you Not-Wizard. I think she does not understand you."

"I have not yet faced my Wizard Trials," she confessed.

He laughed. "Ah, Solsken, you have faced a greater trial, for you have fought wyre and not only survived but defeated them. Not a wizard, something more, something unexpected." He paused, glanced over his shoulder at the riders behind, then added, "And matched to a Rhoghieri. You are fated to defeat this sorceress, Solsken."

"Hopefully."

"Fae do not hope. They know or do not know. I look forward to this battle."

So he said. She was not so sure.

The road descended then renewed its steady climb to follow the crest of the next mountain. The wind along the top intensified the frigid air.

The Ice Huldra had controlled a mountaintop. Did they ride into another Huldra's territory?

Both of the scouting riders waited at another fork, and the whole troop stopped to rest their horses, working hard along the vagaries the mountain road.

Orielle peered at the rolling mountains beyond their own. "Where does this road go?"

"Caravan road," Sangrior said. "Used for centuries to avoid brigands lurking in the south Lowlands. North of here, at the Citadel, it turns back to the Lowlands. South goes to the great river that floods out of the Argent Vale." Then he turned away to listen to Lady Bone's conversation with her brother.

Orielle knew her role in the upcoming battle: defeat the sorceress, nameless to her, tricky with her ambushes. The sorceress had won the loyalty of a Kyrgy rider, away from Lady Bone and to herself. How many others beside Saircuista had defected to the sorceress? Surely she would have used them in the battle on the shoreline—or had they waited with the others in the forest? Lady Bone had only been concerned with Saircuista. Had no other riders defected?

Vrigsmal said the sorceress had moon-changed three mundane swordsmen last night.

She and Grim had reduced the lair to six males, yet a female had fought them last night. They hadn't reckoned on the females. One or three or a full compliment of ten.

What had Grim said? A wyre could take two or three mundane. All the riders were mundane, bound to the Kyrgy but still mundane. Grim had credited Volk and Sangrior with greater skill—and Volk had nearly died.

Did Vrigsmal have any skilled knights?

The Kyrgy rode toward battle as if numbers didn't matter, but only a fool or a reckless leader did not consider the size of his own force against the opposing one.

With one spell, the sorceress had reduced Vrigsmal's force by a third. The six sentries who rode with his eight knights and dames wouldn't have a rider's skill. She could count the sentries' number but not their skill. They might be merely another body to kill.

How many did the sorceress have? The Prime male. Perhaps two more veteran wyre. Three moon-changed. An unknown number of females. How many mundane? The sorceress could have a whole troop that she could transform into wyre.

As Orielle worried over numbers, she realized that one of the scouts cantered beyond the fork while the other took the trail, too narrow to ride three abreast or even two abreast.

The trail didn't follow the broad flank but ventured up the steep slope with its granite outcroppings and exposed boulders. The mountain rose higher than its surrounding brothers and sisters. At one point, the trail overlooked the frontiers and the Wastes to the east, then it worked around the mountain to look north.

Autumn had abandoned the highest slopes. Only the evergreens gave color to the crests. Reddish plum and vivid orange dominated the mid-slopes. Flashes of yellow brightened the deep hollows between the steep slopes.

Vrigsmal pointed to a far-away sparkle on a distant mountain crest, itself higher than its surroundings. "Iscleft Citadel."

Orielle stared at the tiny speck where wizards fought sorcerers, Rhoghieri fought wyre, and Fae fought both parts of Frost Clime. There her brother Saithe had died, all unknown to her. There she had determined to go, to join the battle, to fight rather than live blithely while others' blood spilled freely.

The Citadel defended a narrow passage between the steep mountains into the frontier. The fortress straddled a gap only wide enough for a wagon. In the centuries since Dragon Dark, only a token garrison had maintained it. After Saldoran's rebellion, mundane kings and the Enclave had enlarged the garrison. In the last half-century the incursions from Frost Clime began, and the Fae entered the alliance soon afterward.

As the forest trail worked behind concealing trees, she rose in her stirrups to have a longer look at the Citadel. Iscleft held the line between the fertile lowlands and the Wastes, the realms of mundane and wizardry and Faeron against the exiled sorcerers. Although the Fae warned of Dragon Rising, she knew of no dragon that had yet ventured beyond the Wastes.

The forest road bent back toward the west. Orielle settled in the saddle as her horse clopped over exposed rocks, hoofs slipping on the flatter stones. The mountain had exposed its rocky bones on this side, with fallen boulders on the steeply descending slopes. The trail switched back several times.

Vrigsmal drew up and studied the switchbacks below them, the plum-colored leaves thinned by the wind, and the bright cast of yellow far below. Lady Bone pushed her horse to join him. "You will re-build, brother."

"His palace was below," Sangrior whispered, and Orielle peered down, trying to see the cleared space with its rustic buildings that gave no hint of the beautiful palace.

"From here she worked her sorcery," the Kyrgy lord said.

They continued on. Occasionally the trail veered out, with no trees to bar the vista. Most often the vivid canopies, trailing vines, and thick trunks barred their view.

At a third switchback the trail forked, one side continuing its slow descent, the other veering off to drop steeply then follow the side of the mountain.

Lady Bone drew up. "We have a lair to Hunt, brother. My first consort and my sole knight will guard me. Sir Sangrior will continue with you."

"The lair will not be undefended, sister."

"I will destroy the lair and the crone with her escort who defend it. You, brother, will end the others."

"Joy in the Hunt."

"Joy," she echoed then set her snow-white horse at the other trail, Volk and Khristofin following.

The switchbacks ended, and the trail grew steeper as it descended. Her horse slid on rocks hidden by leaves, and Orielle considered dismounting. Then the descent eased. Her glimpses through the trees revealed a wide vista.

The trail curved around a steep edge of the mountain, an old rockfall opening the view. Boulders had scattered along the slope, and they had to pick their way around them and the rotted trees that the slide had taken with it.

Then, where a huge granite boulder had rolled to a stop, the trail bent steeply down.

The scouts waited there. They pointed first to a crossbow on the ground. Then to the body kneeling on the angled flat surface of the boulder's top.

~ 7 ~

The dead man knelt with head bowed, as if he prayed as he overlooked the valley. His arms, though, were limp at his sides.

Blood had trickled down and pooled beneath his knees on one of the sharded bits where the boulders had sheared off from the rocky escarp above. His blood had drained toward the road but hadn't reached where the stone formed part of the road. It was not long pooled, for it still had a reddish gleam.

Snowflakes drifted down, gently falling, swirling.

The man wore leathers that Orielle recognized. The sentinels of Iscleft Haven had that soft hide, tanned and smooth. Grim's friends Brok and Waren had both worn similar leathers. This man had pale hair, a shock of flax so white that the snow blended in.

She didn't recognize him.

A quiver full of arrows was slung over his back. An empty scabbard was fastened to his belt.

With a muffled curse, Grim slid off his horse and leaped across the planed side of the boulder.

Orielle screwed her eyes shut. Death. So many deaths—when she had expected none—and more to come. She opened her eyes and deliberately looked at the massed heavy clouds, deep slate with the snow that rapidly fell, more flakes now, big, slushy with ice. The snow fell onto the bared tree limbs, caught in the curve of dried leaves, clung to the colored leaves that clutched at life.

Grim straightened. "They cut his throat. From the blood, I'd say he just entered rigor."

"Bare hours ago. Not a battle, then, but—is that not a sword?" Vrigsmal pointed down the rock-tumble that the boulder had grounded itself on.

A sword stood upright from the rocks. The blade was driven into a crevice. Hilt up, it waited for a hand to wield it. Whoever had killed the sentry had taken him from behind, held him while a partner disposed of the sword, then killed him. The sentry hadn't struggled.

Grim looked as ashen as she'd ever seen, even after the fight with his former friend Fortis, who had intended to betray the whole Haven.

This was the day, she remembered, that Fortis had claimed the sorceress and her wyre would ride into Iscleft Haven and he would welcome her.

Wyre were the enchanted enemies of the elemental-wielding Rhoghieri. How had Fortis intended to convince the Rho to welcome Frost Clime?

Days ago, when she first met Grim, a wyre had come after them. He'd planted himself on a switchback. Grim had avoided the forest road she'd been following and angled up the mountainside. They'd come out above the wyre.

She missed Grim's first words. She heard "a residue of sorcery around him." Orielle jerked to the here, the now.

"Ah," Vrigsmal said, as if the sorcery explained everything.

And likely it did. Sentry frozen by sorcery then killed. Who or how didn't matter, just that death occurred.

They were on a road to the Haven, a backroad that came deeper in the valley, working south from Iscleft Citadel ... where Frost Clime attacked the fragile alliance. This sentinel had watched one of the approaches to the Haven. Grim hadn't used this road when they first entered the valley and reached the Haven.

"Where does this road lead?" she asked Sangrior.

"Forks up ahead. The upper trail works around the mountain then heads north. A back road to the Citadel. The lower trail drops to the valley. That's it working down the mountainside." He pointed to the switchback.

"The valley. With Iscleft Haven in the center of it."

The snow fell more rapidly, covering the flat surfaces and burying the crevices. The flakes were thicker, icy wet, clinging to whatever they landed on, sticking to each other before melting, thickening their coverage. They covered the sentinel's slumped shoulders, his bowed head, the boulder and dried leaves scattered by last night's frigid wind. The flakes fastened upon branches and evergreen boughs and the road ahead and behind. They dropped onto the black horse's mane and quickly melted while the snow that landed on her cloak didn't melt, just accumulated more and more, freezing her where she sat.

Grim left the sentinel as he was. The stiffened corpse would not release his death pose until rigor had passed.

He grabbed the silver-embossed bridle of Vrigsmal's horse. His low words didn't carry. Vrigsmal attended closely. Then the Kyrgy's gaze lifted from Grim. He didn't look at the dead sentinel or at any of his riders, the ones who had scouted ahead or the many who crowded behind Orielle and Sangrior. His gaze lifted to the slaty snow clouds and to the land of the horizon, the low foothills like waves surging before the steeper ridges and the massy bulk of mountain upon mountain, blockading the east, blockading the Wastes.

The last dragons lived in the Wastes.

Grim finished. Vrigsmal didn't respond. He took a deep breath and opened his mouth to say more, perhaps to convince the Lord.

Then Vrigsmal spoke. She didn't hear the words; she felt them, like a deep bell tolling, reverberating through her whole body and leaving a waiting silence. The Dark Fae lifted a hand. Even with the quickly falling snow, she saw silvery light, moon's light, swirling around his fingers. He stretched his hand to the dead man.

Moon-colored light streamed to the sentry. It poured over him like a cascading wave—his head, his snow-covered shoulders, down his torso and encompassing his arms, over his bent legs. It pooled around him, covering the thin skim of dried blood, making a silver-glinting puddle. The silver hardened, thickened. It lost the glossy sheen and looked like dark steel.

The snow still gathered on the man's head, his shoulders. It didn't melt.

Vrigsmal spoke, a normal voice that faintly carried. Grim dropped to one knee, and the Kyrgy lord looked pleased. Then his head cocked to one side. He exclaimed and stood in his stirrups.

Grim leapt up.

"Look," Vrigsmal pointed.

Grim bounded onto the boulder, passing the silver-encased sentry without a glance. He stopped at the very edge, where the boulder jutted out to overlook the downward slope and viewed the valley. He didn't look long. "They're attacking."

Vrigsmal cursed.

And Orielle was shocked, for she'd heard that Fae never gave vent to any emotions. She'd expected the same of the Kyrgy. Twice, today, she'd seen Fae express emotion, fear and now anger.

"Solsken," he snapped. "Come to me."

She pressed forward. Grim hurried back and caught the reins that

Sangrior tossed him.

"Time for you to be a wizard. The sorceress attacks the Haven."

She glanced at the valley, but she couldn't see the Haven. Did she imagine that clash of battle? "My Lord, what would you have of me?"

"The Rho will fight the wyre, but they have no defense against sorcery. I will shift a hand of us to the Haven, but I will have little power afterwards."

"My Lord—."

"The sorceress is yours."

Orielle winced, wishing she'd never let the lie of her wizardry stand. It would be fortune indeed if she survived to face her Wizard Trial. But what other answer could she give to a Dark Fae except "Aye, my Lord."

Vrigsmal turned to the knights behind. "You will ride to the Haven and meet us there. Sangrior. Grim Holtson. Rothven. With me."

Sangrior grabbed the reins of Orielle's horse. She didn't protest as he towed them closer to Vrigsmal.

Grim had scrambled onto his mount. They clustered around the Lord, they three and a scout. "Hold tight," Sangrior ordered. "You do not easily suffer the transition."

She had a half-breath to understand, then the transition took them.

The world blinded her. Her mind lost orientation.

Even with her eyes screwed tight, the light blazed, a brilliant radiance that cast negative images to blind her.

A rushing wind filled her ears. Ice, colder than ice, caught in her lungs and burned.

Her horse panicked.

Sangrior shouted. Eyes blind, she could only cling. Cursing filled her ears.

Hands grabbed her leg, her hip then jerked her down the wrong side of the horse. But the biting hands caught her, righted her. A voice soothed her with "Ssh, ssh. I've got you."

She dared to open her eyes.

The light hurt. Tears streamed from her cold-burning eyes. She blinked to adjust her sight. The world glistened and wavered, rippling with disorientation—but the edges of things formed.

Grim had her. She trusted to him. His voice. His grip. His warmth. The parts of her not pressed against him were icy numb, with more cold invading.

"We will leave the horses here. Ruthven, you guard."

The wind in her ears died. She heard Grim breathing, the sharp clear jangle of bridle bits, the creak of leather and snick of steel, two men murmuring—then came distant shouts, screams, breaking wood, a screech of metal.

Orielle dashed the tears from her eyes and dared to lift her head from Grim's shoulder. "What—? Where—?"

"You have her horse?" Vrigsmal asked. A murmur, then he said, "We will approach on foot. Our ambush, this time, not theirs. Solsken."

She removed her shielding hand.

Snow came down, a heavy rain of icy flakes. It covered the ground in pristine white. It dusted the knight holding the horses. It fell upon Grim and Sangrior and the trees and the tangled undergrowth behind them.

The snow didn't touch Lord Vrigsmal.

He smiled, that predator's smile that shivered through her. "I do not have many occasions to see a wizard's weakness. You do not easily endure the rigors of the transition."

"My Lord." She winced at the crack in her voice. "My Lord, it seems to worsen each time."

"And so it will be if you do not learn to endure it."

She bowed her head at that truth. "My Lord, what will you have of me?"

"The battle for Iscleft Haven has begun."

The wood hid the cause of the screams and clash of steel. "I would not think the wyre would fight with swords."

"They do not. Do not forget her troop. She has also her wyre, veteran females, maybe a handful of males. The other wyre will be those she moon-changed. Rhoghieri, how many of your fellows can battle?"

"Maybe a dozen good fighters. That many more able to fight, but their powers are weak. The majority in the Haven are children and mundane."

"Her mundane troop will take the weak and half the fighters. The wyre will take the rest." He grinned, pointed teeth flashing. "I have missed a fight that matters. Solsken, the sorceress must not continue to aid her wyre and mundane."

Orielle pulled away from Grim. "How long before the other knights arrive?"

"Two hours at speed," Grim answered, "even the speed of Fae horses."

"Why do we wait then?" she asked with more boldness than she felt. "Two hours' time can see the battle lost or won."

Vrigsmal laughed. "You gladden my heart, Solsken. Sangrior, you have guard of her. Grim Holtson, you have guard with me. My sister will regret she chose a different Hunt. Lady Winter blesses our battle. Come. It is a day to spill blood, rich and red."

~ 8 ~

The old growth forest ended long before they neared the Haven. They entered a wood of stumps and coppiced growth, thin and thick shoots, sprouting from the other rim of the trunks.

Vrigsmal hunched. "The trees cry." Then he shook off whatever affected him and stiffly straightened. He lifted his face to the snowing sky. The flakes graced his white skin, creating a glistening rime that neither melted nor drifted away. "Stay near to me."

Orielle sensed the sparkling magic of Fae power, like the energy released at Vrigsmal's forest palace—although she hadn't recognized that subtle energy until he removed the illusions and the palace of golden stone faded back to a timber-framed longhouse and planked outbuildings.

She didn't know what he did now, only that he worked with the power he'd retrieved from the illusion of his palace.

The icy wind on the heights hadn't descended to the valley. The withy coppices didn't stir. The snow fell straight down. It didn't swirl or dance, just steadily dropped to blanket everything in flaky ice. A trail of footprints revealed their passage toward the palisaded Haven.

The thick snow didn't muffle the screams. The clash of battle sounded louder as they worked through the coppice. Orielle wanted to urge "Hurry. Faster." All those children who had played along the lanes teared in her eyes. Until Hackett spoke of them, she hadn't realized the Haven had so many mundane, defenseless against power. They needed to hurry, but outpacing Vrigsmal's spell wouldn't help the innocent.

They reached the wood's verge. Stretching to the palisade were fields, the sod turned to lie fallow for winter. The clumps of sod were barely visible through the lacy veil of snow. The fields were open, with no places to hide their advance except for a few storage buildings that squatted at the corners of the fields.

Then a screech came, louder than the other screams. A flash gilded the falling snow. The sounds of battle ebbed ... then roared back with shrieking metal and crashing wood.

Grim inhaled sharply. "The towers are gone!"

Wooden watchtowers had vanished from the corners of the palisade. The wall remained, protecting the Haven from the Wilding's predators.

"Only the towers at the front." Vrigsmal pointed to a barely visible structure off to their left. He scowled. "No one mans them."

Orielle couldn't see the tower. The snow fell too quickly. "Hurry," she whispered. "The children."

"Any other entrance?" Vrigsmal asked.

"Only the main gate."

"A trap when you're betrayed."

"We never were. Almost, but yesterday we ended that problem."

"Not even when the wyre attacked a hand of years ago?"

"Not even then. The lair wasn't large enough to trap us inside. Tobit did argue for a deep tunnel, coming up in the forest. Only he with his Earth power could have dug it, and keeping up the shaft—."

"I sense no disruption of the ground."

How could the Kyrgy lord sense a tunnel that burrowed deep underground? Fae had an uncanny sense of the natural, but she hadn't realized it extended beneath the surface.

"Come. Near to me," and Vrigsmal strode out of the sheltering coppice and across the field, his long strides skimming the open area.

Impeded by her skirts, Orielle scrambled to stay abreast. Vrigsmal angled for the front corner of the palisade.

Out of breath, she pressed against the upright timbers that formed the wall as the Kyrgy lord looked around the corner. Then he strode out, not attempting to hide.

She knew the reason when she turned the corner. No one was without the wall. She hiked her skirts and ran to the gate, passing the lord.

There, inside the gate, was the destruction.

A spell had broken the gate. Splintered timbers lay scattered on the ground, digging into the cobbles, piled on each other. Snow dusted the jagged spars that reached up to the heavy clouds. Broken pieces had flown into buildings on both sides of the street, penetrating walls, breaking doors open, and shattering windows and shutters.

She saw legs trapped beneath a support beam. Snow collected on the breeches and boots, blanketing the dead. More bodies lay sprawled beneath the broken timbers. A woman's skirt. A man. A man in leather.

Nothing moved, just the steadily falling snow.

Then Vrigsmal passed her, Sangrior on her other side, and Grim came behind her and urged her forward.

Her numbness receded. She heard a whoosh of power ahead, the clash of steel, shouts, screams.

"Solsken!"

The word helped break her focus on the crushed bodies. The three men had half-turned to her. Their drawn swords glinted with a strange light. Eldritch green, as if the steel warned of the power that had destroyed the gate.

"The sorceress is there, Solsken." The Kyrgy lord pointed along the main lane. Buildings crowded in to block the view, but she knew the lane led to the main well square. "The Rhoghieri and I," Vrigsmal smiled, toothy and manic, "will hunt wyre." He pointed with the sword to a side lane.

High-pitched screams erupted from there. Children.

"Solsken!" he snapped.

"The sorceress——." She cleared the salty tears clogging her throat. "She will not see sunset," she vowed.

The insane glint in those depthless eyes seemed brighter. "To the Hunt!"

Vrigsmal and Grim ran toward the screaming children.

Sangrior turned when she reached him. "A good day to Hunt. Our prey is trapped. The only exit is behind us. We will soon rid the world of this sorceress."

Orielle nearly laughed at his optimism.

They found more dead Haveners at a shop front where flames burned merrily in the doorway. The fire melted the accumulated snow which froze into a puddle. She recognized one man. He had spoken at the hearing before Volk took her to ride with Lady Bone.

They had hunted the sorceress then. She had ambushed them and reduced the Lady's riders to three.

Now, again, they hunted the sorceress who would expect their arrival. *What trick will she have this time?*

The snow gave her ready access to Water. Orielle used it to douse the fire.

Rho fought with elements, Water and Air, Earth and Fire. Tobit had opened the ground under her feet. Fortis had thrown fireballs that incinerated whatever and whoever they struck. Air and Water she had wielded.

The sorceress worked with power, spells.

I need the elements for wyre. Sangrior can't take them, for Grim had warned that few mundane could fight the wolfen. *I need power against the sorceress.*

I'm not a named wizard, but I can fight like a wizard and like a Rho. Surely that gives me an edge.

Not far beyond the shop they came on a trail of blood over a threshold and into a darkened shop. She saw the after-image of pale flesh. She stopped Sangrior.

"The battle's ahead."

She shook her head. "I want no enemy at my back." She stepped through the open door and to one side. She thrust an orb of light into the room.

A growl. There, crawling for the passage, an unshifted wyre. Blood covered her naked back. She tore at the floor even as she looked at Orielle and snarled.

A knife flashed past. It hit the wyre's throat and stayed quivering. Sangrior took long strides to the female. He crouched to ensure the kill then wiped the blood on his sleeve.

Orielle returned to the quiet street before he finished.

And jumped back as a sword slashed down.

The man brought the sword back, a lethal back stroke. She fell away, into Sangrior.

The knight thrust her aside. He met the sword with his knife and deflected it with a screech of steel. Then he dove through the doorway and crashed into the swordsman.

Orielle righted herself. *Faster! I must get to the sorceress before she kills more people and destroys more of the Haven.*

The men grappled a few paces away. Sangrior had the shorter blade, better at close quarters. The swordsman realized it. He flung away his sword to grab the knight's knife arm. Sangrior bent the man's arm back. He laughed.

Trapped in the doorway, Orielle tore her gaze from the fight to the street, watching for trouble. Hoping no one would come on them, hoping she could use the power ready in her hand.

Sangrior and the man fell to the snow-covered cobbles. The knight grunted as he landed on bottom. The swordsman heaved, grunted, bending forward with all his strength.

Then everything quieted, bare seconds before explosions rocked the buildings a few streets over. Shouts, screams, more fighting urged her to hurry. Even more distant were the high-pitched screams of children, not so many now. She heard nothing in this street but her own panicked breathing and the hoarse rasp of a man's breath.

The swordsman rolled off Sangrior.

The knight sat up. He wiped the knife on the man's tabard. Then he levered to his feet. When he saw the crackling orb in her hand, he grinned with a manic edge like Vrigsmal. Then he bent and picked up the man's discarded sword. He drew his own. "Onward."

Orielle caught her rapid breath, held it deliberately, then let it out with a whoosh. She looked at the straining energy in the orb, fighting her hold, desperate for use.

She stepped over the dead swordsman and headed for the well square.

All streets and lanes bore straight to the Haven's heart.

When she and Grim had entered, the Haven had seemed crowded.

As she and Sangrior covered the last ground, she realized how small the community was. All of the leading adults must have filled the front room in the Elder House, wanting to hear how Grim and she would answer Tobit and the four mentors.

The dwellings near Brok's had seemed crammed together in a maze, but all the Haven's dwellings must have tracked along only a few lanes. Shops and work areas were massed on the Haven's other side, with storage and corrals and pens and the lock-up at the back.

For the Haven's defense, Grim had expected no more than a dozen fighters, with a few more who could only weakly wield the elements. *It's a community, not a garrison.*

They came on more dead as they reached the square. She saw the fighting. An older man in leathers fought one in a tabard—was that Hackett? Another burning shop. Four Rho ranged against someone she couldn't see. Three men stood behind a petite woman, shaping a Fire spell. One of the men threw an orb filled with flames, but the fire was pale yellow, barely maintaining it circle.

Then she saw power, green-limned and eldritch.

She had found the sorceress.

~ **9** ~

Sangrior tore into another swordsman, his ice-blue sword casting sparks as it met the other blade.

The sorceress flung a crackling orb of green energy. It sizzled as it arced through the icy snow pellets. The four Rho didn't try to avoid it, and the orb struck an unseen barrier. It exploded and dripped down the invisible shield … and one of the Rho men crumpled.

Orielle flung her own orb at the sorceress, hoping the woman's shield didn't extend around her.

And it struck, exploding on her back.

The sorceress stumbled forward. Her barrier flashed that weirded green then a greeny yellow before it firmed. As she straightened, she backed to her right, turning to add Orielle to her sight. With a quick glance, she flung a yellow bolt at the Rho.

One of the men had bent to help the fallen man. The other two crossed their elements, Water and Flame, and built a glimmering barrier. The yellow bolt struck it, pierced it, and arrowed into the Flame Rho.

The woman fell to her knees.

The sorceress flicked a similar bolt at Orielle. Even as she flung up a barrier, the strongest she'd learned, she pushed a gust of Air into the wyre. The three shifters stumbled, one propelled back several feet into a wall. He crumpled to the ground. The other two straightened, and she recognized the Prime wyre from so many days ago, the one who'd escaped, the one who hadn't been on the shoreline.

"Is this how you play, pretty lady?" he called.

For answer, she pushed another gust. The three wyre leaned into the Air. As the Air struck, the sorceress flung another bolt, then she poured power at the Rho, a sole man standing who had nothing but Water for defense.

Hackett lunged in with his sword. He caught an edge of the stream of shivering energy. It deflected from the Rho, into the building behind him. The wood wall splintered and collapsed inward.

A wyre lunged toward her. He'd go straight through her wizard-wrought barrier. Orielle yanked Air to her.

Sangrior leaped before her, a steely defense, and the wyre skidded to a stop.

Water deluged the wyre. He sputtered and went down, and Sangrior's blade finished him. The knight headed for the Prime standing beside the sorceress who flung greeny flames. Sangrior barred the sorcery with his sword but staggered.

Orielle stepped from behind him. Air in one hand, she flung her best orb at the sorceress. It hit the woman's barrier and dissipated into sparks. A bolt came through the sparks, straight for Orielle as she shaped another orb of energy. She dodged the bolt and concentrated on the orb, crackling and leaping in her hand. The sorceress worked just as hurriedly. Her attention centered on Orielle, a greater threat than the sole remaining Rho.

Only he was no longer alone. The woman had returned to his side. Sword at ready, Hackett stood before the two fallen Rho. He nearly straddled the fallen Rho . The first Rho was sitting up, both hands holding his head.

She had no time to see more. The sorceress had finished her orb, and she flung it at Orielle.

The barrier held again although the edge shimmered. *The sorceress works faster than me. That means more experience.* The woman's barrier didn't waver—more puissance. *Gods, how will I defeat her?*

Then Fire cascaded over the woman. Her shield flashed. The bare second after came a second deluge of Water, icing after it struck.

The sorceress spluttered. The orb she tried to shape sparked then winked out. She formed an eldritch green bolt, but it shivered and lost its true line.

That was how she could be defeated. Water, turning to ice.

Trusting Sangrior would keep the wyre off her, Orielle flung her own bolt of energy, blue with power, sparkling with silver and gold.

It struck the sorceress' barrier and burrowed in—but it lost energy as it penetrated. Only the tail survived. It struck the woman's hand as she shaped another bolt enveloped in yellow flames—and the remnant bolt vanished.

Orielle hadn't waited to see the bolt's success. She pushed Air into that fist-sized hole. The element hit the barrier. Some Air dissipated. A narrow force found the hole and funneled through, concentrating its energy into a punch. The element struck the sorceress in the shoulder.

She staggered and threw a horrified look. Orielle grinned, feeling as manic as Vrigsmal.

Then the woman's horror became a smile, mocking, sneering.

And Orielle dropped to the snow-trampled cobbles.

A wolf sailed over her head, so close she felt its passing.

The wolf landed. Blonde fur. It leaped again, striking Sangrior's arm a glancing blow. The knight mis-stepped. His blade missed the Prime entirely. The wolf reached the sorceress.

The Prime used Sangrior's stumble to retreat. He grabbed the bleeding man as he passed, jerking him along.

And the three wyre and the sorceress ran into a narrow byway before Orielle scrambled to her feet.

She headed after them, but Sangrior blocked her with his ice-blue sword. "Lady Wizard, are you hurt?"

He was. Wyre claws had opened his arm, his thigh. Snow pelted down, more ice than flakes. Her breath steamed the air. The temperature still dropped.

Hackett reached them, the two Rho behind him. "We should get after them. Let them escape, and we'll have more to fight tomorrow. The Prime can moon-change three on the Lady's Moon, and that sorceress can likely do the same."

"And the Prime's consort," the Rho man said. He looked weary, but he wasn't bleeding. Nor was the woman.

"Are you alone?" Hackett asked.

"Grim's with Lord—." She thought better of giving the Kyrgy lord's true name. "Lord Skull, brother to Lady Bone."

"Another Dark Fae?"

"Where's Lilias?"

"Protecting the children. They split their forces when they came into the Haven. We sent our best to defend the children."

Orielle nodded as she judged Sangrior not seriously wounded. Those open gashes weren't gushing blood. If Vrigsmal couldn't stop the bleeding, Lady Bone would.

"I thought that wyre would take you in the back," Hackett said. "How did you know it was coming behind you?"

"The sorceress looked too pleased." She pushed at Sangrior's sword arm, pushing away the ice-blue sword that blocked her advance. He'd fought two wyre and killed two swordsmen, but his arm didn't waver.

"Did that sorceress wound you?" His gaze swept her, looking for magical burns or cuts.

"No. We're not evenly matched, but the Rho made the difference." The two Rho looked pleased at Orielle's praise. "Are your fellows greatly wounded?"

"Greinn isn't." The woman's mouth twisted. She looked back at the fallen Rho. "Barro is dead."

Orielle pushed again at the ice-blue sword. "I don't want to fight that sorceress tomorrow, when she's fresh, Sangrior. I want her dead today." She looked up, but the dark slaty clouds of snow prevented any way to tell the passage of time. They'd left Vrigsmal's fading palace in the afternoon. They would have reached the Haven in late afternoon. *How long did I battle the sorceress?* "Before twilight."

"I cannot defend you from sorceress and wyre."

"The Rho will fight the wyre. Lady, sir, your powers are best for that, aye? Sangrior can defend me from any swordsmen. I'll take the sorceress, as Lord Skull commanded."

"Can you?"

She didn't blast Sangrior. He was right to question. Lady Bone, though, would not have accepted any question. "I am the Aiwaz Solsken," she said with bravado. "Of course I can take her."

At her fourth push against his sword, he let her pass.

They hurried down the byway. It led to a lane then a twisty allée, and Orielle was lost by the next turn. The Rho pushed forward. "We can sense the wyre," the Fire Rho explained, and she took the lead.

By another street, the sounds of fighting once again reached them, yet it lacked the crackle of power. Was the sorceress not there?

When they came out of the lane and saw swordsmen fighting Grim and Vrigsmal, with more clashing fighters with them, Orielle knew the sorceress was more intent on escape than on killing the defenseless.

She grabbed the Fire Rho's arm as she lifted it to throw a flaming sphere at a knot of swordsmen in tabards. "The sorceress isn't here. She's headed for the gate with her wyre."

The sphere winked out. "This way. Arendt! Stay with me. We go after the sorceress." She jogged to a side lane, and they followed the Rho between the buildings.

In two turns they were on the broad street that led to the well square. As the street worked around a burning building, they saw the destroyed gate—and the sorceress, a handful of wyre, and three swordsmen clambering over the broken timbers.

"Remember your targets," Orielle called then threw a crackling orb of power.

It flew straight and true, passing a lagging swordsman and a wyre then threading between the other wyre, two males and two females, including the Prime and the pale blonde. It struck the sorceress in the back, where Orielle's first attack had hit.

The energy flung the woman forward. She fell on the timbers.

The wyre turned as one. The Prime shifted, the blonde female seconds after. All five charged, the two shifted outpacing the others. The men came behind them, drawing their swords.

A wall of flames met the wyre. They halted. The shifted wolfen crouched.

The swordsmen set themselves between the wyre and the Fire— which died.

"I can't maintain it," the woman husked.

The man threw up a glittering wall of Water. Ice formed.

The swordsmen came through—and two unshifted wyre.

Behind them, barely seen, the three other wyre had retreated to the sorceress. The woman had crawled to her hands and knees. The unshifted female helped her stand. Leaning on her support, the woman hobbled to the gate.

Sangrior and Hackett had engaged the swordsmen, two on Hackett. The wyre arrowed to the Rho—and the wall of Water splashed down, freezing when it hit the ground. Between wyre and swordsmen, the path to the gate was blocked.

The sorceress would escape.

Orielle ran back to the first lane and plunged between the buildings. The snow covered the ground here, untrampled by anyone passing and barely dusted with snow. The lane was too narrow for the steadily falling snow flakes to have collected. She skidded a little when she took the first turn toward the palisade wall. She could see the timbered wall ahead, but there wasn't another turn to work back to the gate.

She flung power at a door. It bounced open. She plunged into the cold scullery, as cold as outside but without the falling snow. She slid through the doorway—aye, it led to a passage and the front room. She had to fumble with the door.

She exploded into the main street with its broken timbers and splintered stubs and two people and two wolfen crawling across the debris.

~ 10 ~

"Sorceress!"

The woman didn't pause. Only the unshifted wyre turned toward her. The others kept going, off the last fallen timber, through the gate, out of her sight.

One wyre.

She flung an orb and behind it a gust shaped into a wedge.

The wizardry struck the wyre and dissipated. She laughed. Then the wedge of Air hit. It flung her with its speed of travel. She landed hard on a splintered stub.

She didn't move.

Orielle ran.

They hadn't gone far. Supported by the Prime, the sorceress was still near the gate. The other—.

Orielle slipped on the snow, and a wyre missed its strike. *Her* strike, for the ambush was again sprung by the pale female.

The wyre didn't stay for another attack. She tore across the snow. She didn't slow as she came abreast of the sorceress. She leaped as she passed the Prime, landing on four paws and still running.

The Prime released the sorceress. With a bound he was air-borne, arcing through the icy pellets of snow. He raced after the other wyre.

The sorceress had stopped. She watched them fade into the snowy ice. Then she turned and faced Orielle, still scrambling over the last timber.

"Wizard. You have surprised me, more than once."

Orielle thought of the ambushes by the wyre and the ambush on the shoreline. She walked carefully beyond the gate debris. Behind her were the Rho and Sangrior and Hackett. She moved to place the palisade behind her. "I vowed to Lord Skull and Lady Bone to kill you."

"I have a pact with the Kyrgy, with Lady Bone."

"Not after Saircuista defected to you. Not with Lord Skull. Certainly not after you attacked his palace."

She laughed, soundless like a wolf. "*Saircuista* is the reason Lady Bone attacked?"

"Did you doubt the Lady would?"

She laughed again. Then she lifted her hands. Eldritch fire

surrounded them, as strong as when Orielle had first reached the well square. The sorceress didn't try to straighten her body, just confronted her with a hunched back and dropped shoulders. "Prepare." Her hands stretched toward the younger woman. A strangely weirded power streamed out, melting the icy pellets to a hissing steam.

It hit Orielle's barrier and kept pouring in, burning into the wizardry, burning it away.

Orielle threw an orb—but it dissipated when it struck the sorceress' barrier. She tried another burning bolt with a fist of Air. The bolt burned its hole, but the Air that poured in didn't affect the sorceress.

Did she have a second barrier, closer to her body?

The eldritch stream of flame kept burning away. The barrier flickered. It wouldn't hold long. She threw up her own second shield.

Her mind raced. A bolt with another behind it and a wedge of Air ... and she would deplete her energy. If this didn't work—. *I'm not a full wizard.*

So? A man's voice. The Kyrgy lord? *Have you given up?*

She threw the first bolt. Time it needed, and she counted out the seconds. Then she threw the second bolt on the same trajectory. It flew through the sorceress' first barrier and struck the second. *Could she have a third? Gods*, she prayed and doubled the Air that flew behind the second bolt.

Power drained from her. Never had she sensed that sink of wizardry. Tutors had warned of it, for draining power was part of the Wizard Trial, to see how deeply a wizard could draw. Like a well in summer, nearly dried up, slowed by heat and lack of rain. *The elements remain.*

She didn't wield Fire. Oh, how powerful if she did. Or Earth. Ice cold Water and Air were in abundance around her.

She threw a gush of Water, and she froze the Air around the sorceress.

The Water froze.

The sorceress staggered in that hardened deluge. The greeny flames striking Orielle's second barrier winked out. Time slowed the snowflakes, suspended in the Air. Then they began falling again, and the sorceress collapsed.

Orielle ran forward, crunching through the ice-crusted snow. She drew her beltknife. It tried to tangle in her cloak, but she had it free as she reached the woman.

She fell to her knees and rolled the crumped woman over.

"How—? How did you—? Your power ... deep."

Orielle didn't explain. She ended the woman with a single clean cut that released steaming red blood to stain the snow. She gagged as she did it. Then she fell back and tried to feel regret. Only guilt wasn't there, not when she counted the Rho that had died in the attack, those killed by eldritch knives, those that Fortis had killed, and those that the wyre had killed.

Frost Clime was the enemy.

Someone ran toward her. She struggled upright, more drained than tired.

Grim fell to his knees beside her. "Are you hurt? Where are you hurt?"

"Not hurt. She didn't touch me. I'm cold. Empty. We still have wyre to kill."

He didn't argue. "How many?"

"None in the Haven?"

"Not now."

"Two escaped. The Prime and his consort. How is Vrigsmal?"

"Talking to Lilias."

"Sangrior? Hackett?"

"Hackett's wounded. Sangrior ... wait."

"We must go. The wyre cannot be far ahead."

Grim helped her stand. When she started for the woods and the horses, he held her fast. "You're not waiting for Vrigsmal?"

"I have you. We've fought wyre before."

He grinned. "So we have."

A horse's high-pitched scream pierced the smothering snow. Not from the Haven but from the coppiced wood.

"Go," Orielle urged. "I'm coming."

Grim ran, crunching through the crusted snow. Orielle hurried, but she didn't have his speed even when she hadn't fought a sorceress and her skirts didn't hamper her progress.

Before she reached the coppice, a horse plunged out of the withy growth. Reins trailed it. It ran for the Haven. Another one followed then two more.

She followed Grim's footprints through the wood. Swords clashed. Wolves snarled. A man shouted for help.

The transition from coppice to forest was abrupt. The taller trees were easier to dash through, and the fighting grew louder as she neared.

She burst into the clearing to see Grim fending off a massive wolf while the blonde wolf worried at a downed rider's throat. Orielle snatched falling snow into an orb, grew it into a sphere, then threw it at the female. The snow exploded on her back, leaving white crystals and water that quickly refroze.

The female turned to her. She snarled. Then she jumped over the fallen rider, running away. She stopped beside an ancient oak, weighty limbs gnarled and leafless, hollowed at the roots. She barked.

The Prime dodged under Grim's sword. Orielle snatched more snow, but the wyre wasn't attacking. He dashed past. He veered as he ran, not toward the female but in a wide circuit that put trees between him and any thrown element.

The female ducked behind the oak.

When Orielle reached the oak, the wyre was nowhere to be seen. "We've lost them!"

"No, we haven't. We'll follow."

"Grim—how will we track them?"

"I can. We don't need them turning others. We'll need horses."

Twilight deepened as they plowed through thickening snow to the Haven. The gate debris had halted the horses' dash for safety. A boy and a girl had caught their reins. Both grinned proudly as Orielle and Grim crossed the fields. The pride vanished as Grim ordered the girl to tell Vrigsmal that his knight had died.

He took the reins of the two horses that the girl held. "Tell him we're going after the last two wyre."

She ran to the gate and scrambled over the snow-covered timbers.

"You're going by yourselves?" the boy asked. "Is that wizard any good with wyre?"

"As good as a Rho." He handed the reins of a black horse to Orielle. When she had settled into the saddle, he vaulted up.

Under the heavy snow clouds, twilight descended rapidly. The snow became fitful, falling rapidly then sputtering out only to drop steadily, slowly, before it repeated the pattern.

Beneath the trees the snow had covered the ground but not as deeply as on the fields. It had still frozen.

Wolves could run lightly over the ground, whether dry or snowy.

By the time they reached the gnarled oak, the daylight had faded entirely. Not believing she had more than the barest flicker of power remaining to her, Orielle cast a light sphere. It faltered then steadied. *Maybe I am a wizard.* She sent the sphere ahead of them. The light revealed the trampled ground, the fallen knight dusted with snowfall.

No birds flitted in the trees. The animals had burrowed into their shelters.

"Can you lower the sphere to a couple of feet off the ground?"

Orielle obeyed. She quickly saw the reason Grim had asked. The light cast ahead made shadows on the ice-crystal snow, and round shadows revealed the female wyre's tracks.

Chase was slower than flight. Orielle began to worry the wyre would reach the lair and begin a moon-change before she and Grim found them. Two wyre they could fight; three would be difficult; four—.

She didn't want Grim bitten again. Lady Bone might not bargain a second time. Vrigsmal might exact a greater sacrifice from her before he healed Grim.

I will bargain anything to keep Grim alive.

The trail followed the climbing forest road. That surprised her. She would have expected the wyre to plunge into the wild forest. Yet most of the wyre in Frost Clime were bound to sorcerers. They weren't forest-bred. Their minds were human, not wolf. They had their own villages on the edge of the Wastes. Only the recently-allied wyre from the far North were familiar with running forests.

The female led. Her paws were smaller than the Prime's. Their flight occasionally paused, with the smaller prints circling around the bigger male. The wyre had fled at a full-out run. As the road climbed, the sphere lighted on red droplets, aligning with the bigger paws. The tracks no longer raced far apart but looked like a walk. At the last stop, the red droplets pooled. The male was injured.

The road climbed higher. Orielle was surprised they hadn't encountered Vrigsmal's other knights. Where had they gone? They were supposed to follow the forest road to the Haven.

Had they run into another troop of Frost Clime? Another sorceress? More wyre?

The trail left the road.

A howl, long and eerie, sounded close. A second howl, higher, longer, like a wail. It didn't end, just broke then resumed. The sound hurt Orielle's heart. Both wyre joined together in the next howl, their breaking cries distinct, disparate.

Then the howls broke off and didn't continue.

The pale wyre stood before them, snarling, feet planted wide.

~ 11 ~

Orielle expanded the light sphere for more illumination.

The female wyre crouched low, as if prepared to leap. Behind her was a rocky outcropping. The boulders fallen from above had created side walls and a roof, like a portal tomb. There, just inside, lay the other wyre, the Prime. His tongue lolled out from the exertion of the climb. Droplets of red on the snow had become a steady stream in the last feet to the lair. Dark matted his fur on the side.

The iron tang of blood scented too strongly to be from his wound alone. And they had howled grief.

Grim drew his sword and slid from the black horse. He formed Air.

"Wait," she hastily told him.

He set himself, but he didn't attack. He didn't look away from the wyre.

She slipped down as well. She kept her grip on the bridle, keeping the horse's head down. The snow above the boulders was trampled. It looked like horses then men's feet had tromped down to the lair.

"Grim, we need—." She never finished the need, for a blinding light formed at the snow-trampled ground. It flashed then faded, and Lady Bone stood with them, Volk beside her, his sword at the ready. He came down the slope before the Lady.

The wyre turned to face them. The male struggled to his feet. The female backed away until her haunches nearly brushed the rock. She whined then started a howl, only to break off at the first upturn. She finished with a snarl. Then her fur rippled. She transformed. The male hunched, then he also shifted, and Orielle saw the wound over his ribs, the blood trickling and smeared but no longer freely bleeding, healed by the transforming shift. He looked shaky, pale.

"Why?" The female dashed a hand over her eyes. "They harmed no one."

Lady Bone gave that icicle-tinkling laugh that Orielle hated. "That toothless old crone can hurt no one ever again. Not so the whelp. He tried to defend her. But we did not kill them. The guard did."

"No!"

"Truth. We do not make war on children and the defenseless, not even wyre. Your mundane swordsman killed him and then her. Then he expected to bargain with me. You will find his body above, on the rock where he left the Rhoghieri sentry to die."

The female whimpered.

"Your whelp? I grieve with you." Lady Bone signed something. It flickered gold before dissipating.

The male pushed his consort behind him. "You have come to kill us now." When the Lady smiled, that curve of lips that gave no assurance, merely bared her sharpened teeth, the male hunched. "What do you want with us?"

"What should I want with you? I care that you do not ruin the Wilding. How best can I ensure that?"

"We will leave. We will go from here."

Orielle pressed forward, past Grim. "No. My Lady Bone, no, do not send them from here. They will rejoin Frost Clime. I will have to fight them again at Iscleft Citadel." She confronted the wyre. "I will not allow that. I do not condone your murder or those of your lair. Death in battle is honest, but murder, no. I do not want to fight you again."

Grim had growled throughout Orielle's objection. Now he added, "Can we trust them? They are wyre, tricky, devious. Is their word any good?"

"You hear them, Prime. How do you answer them?"

He knelt on one knee. "Please, great Lady, show us mercy. We fought, aye, but does that mean you hate us?"

"Foul sorcery I hate. Sorcerers care not who they hurt, what they destroy. They relish the blood magic. They seek to enslave. Their power is tainted. I hate them."

"We are not sorcerers." He held up his hands, a supplicant to a goddess. "My pack in the North allied with the sorcerers last spring. The decision to serve them was not my own. Jenniste was raised with sorcerers. She has only known slavery under them. She is my consort. She has heard me weep for freedom. She deserves to run free." The words poured out of him, as if he'd thought long before this hour about the life that he wanted. "Great Lady, if you do not hate us, then let us run free. We will go to the Lowlands, far from Iscleft Citadel, far south of Gramina Aurus."

"Can we trust them to keep their word?" Grim objected again. "Without the binding to a sorcerer of Frost Clime, we have no idea what they will do and no reason to trust anything they say."

Lady Bone's ravening smile widened. "They will keep their word, or I will see to their torture before they die." She stepped closer to the wyre. Volk stayed close, his sword a barrier between. "I have no reason to hate you or to distrust you. I hated the sorceress. She broke pact with me. She suaded my dame Saircuista to desert me. These two are here," she indicated Orielle and Grim, "thus I know the sorceress is dead. My Hunt for your mistress is over."

"The Lady Wizard killed her."

"Aye, that was my duty as a wizard," Orielle admitted, "to kill this sorceress of Frost Clime. She called up the dead as wraiths. Is it my duty to kill the last two wyre in this lair? Aye, as long as they are a danger. Prove to me you will not be a danger."

"Orielle!" Grim protested.

She spoke past him, wanting to find some ground that didn't require more deaths. "I do not wish to fight you again, but how can I know you will not return to Frost Clime, either at the Citadel or reinforcing the fighters at Chanerro Pass? How do I know you will not join a strike force when it gathers in the Wastes? You make promises to Lady Bone, but how do I know you will no longer be a threat?" For that was the crux, to extract teeth and claws so they never again fought Rho or Fae, wizard or mundane.

The female whined. The Prime struck his chest, over his heart. "The one we were bound to serve is dead. We are no longer slaves. We will run free."

"Run free in what place?" Lady Bone's head tilted, an inquisitive bird—a hawk looking at prey before she swooped on a hare. "You cannot return to the North. They allied to Frost Clime. They will know you broke your pact. And tell me—convince me—should you not serve penance for your attack on the Haven?"

"Great Lady, that attack was not our choice. The sorceress ordered it."

"Even so, you would have killed the innocent children of the Haven."

The female started up. "My Gherdin is dead."

The Prime grabbed her arm. "Not killed by them, Jenniste, but by that mundane swordsman, one of the troop from Frost Clime."

She snarled. "It matters not. He is dead. He was not of my body but my heart, a child I protected. Now he is dead."

"And the one who killed him is dead. Take your revenge elsewhere, not on these."

Her head bowed. "My Prime, I hear and obey. You decide. I cannot. I care not. I am … hollow."

He stared at her bent head then turned to Lady Bone. "You see, Great Lady. We no longer follow the purpose of Frost Clime. We did not attack the children of the Haven. Our role was to guard the sorceress. The children were well-defended. Our threat was as nothing to them. Have mercy, Great Lady. We will leave the Wilding. We will go to the Lowlands, to the land south of here, where sorcerers and wizards alike must stay hidden. Let us be free."

"Let you be free?" The Lady shook her head, her long white hair shifting to cascade over her shoulders. "What will you do when you reach the Lowlands, the lands solely of mundanes? Will you stay hidden? Or will you seize captives then Moon-change them? Will you create a lair and terrorize the mundane?"

"Please, Great Lady, one chance. We have never had a single chance."

"You seek a bargain with me? With a Kyrgy? Wyre, do you know what you ask?"

"We want to run free."

She huffed.

"Lady," Volk murmured.

"My consort knight adds his voice. I find it weightier than a wizard and a Rhoghieri."

"Lady Bone—."

Her sharp gesture silenced Orielle. Grim's steady growl of frustration grew. The male looked hopeful. Even the female perked up.

The Lady raised her arms.

Orielle's lighted orb flickered as Lady Bone drew energy from around them. It spun like a vortex, ripping dead leaves from the trees, picking up a dust of flurries, wringing icy drops from the fallen snow. She brought her hands together. The energy coalesced into two iridescent whirling spheres. Orielle's light orb flickered again then steadied. And Lady Bone shoved her spheres at the wyre.

The energy blasted over them. It poured over their skin, turning it iridescent, changing to a golden sheen. The female embraced herself. The male gaped at the gold on his chest, his outstretched arms. Gradually, the golden sheen faded. "What have you done?" the Prime wondered.

"You live. Be grateful for life."

"Great Lady, what have you done to us? What was this spell? I feel … strange."

"I am missing," the female cried. "What have you taken?"

"You cursed us, didn't you?" he accused. "Oh Great Lady, how could you?"

"You live," Lady Bone repeated. "Be grateful. You will live as mundane, not as wyre. Be grateful you are not bound to wolf-shape, human minds trapped in animal form."

"We cannot shift?"

Relief flooded Orielle. Grim's growled anger died.

"You may not shift. As long as I live, you are bound to one form. And to me." Her smile widened. Her teeth glinted wickedly. "Kyrgy are long-lived."

"You have doomed us."

"Curse you may call it, but I give you life—if you live it rather than fight it away. You wish to run free. Do so."

"We will live like mundanes," and he swore, a long stream of invective that damned Dark Fae and wizards and sorcerers alike.

"But you will live. Or do you wish to die, here, now? I can grant you that as well."

The wyre appeared to consider. The female grabbed his hand, linked their fingers. "We will be free? We choose how we live?"

"Aye, wyre."

"Then we will live." The female bowed at the waist. The Prime quickly imitated her. Then she straightened. "We will tend our dead then gather provisions. Tomorrow we will go down the mountains. We will leave your Wilding. We will not return. We will go south, away from Frost Clime."

"No matter where you go, you remain linked to me. I will know what you do," the Lady warned. "I will punish when you go astray."

"We will not," he vowed.

"We will live." The female tugged on his hand. They disappeared into the rocks.

Lady Bone and Volk came to Orielle and Grim. "Gather your horses. My brother does not leave the Haven. His knights should be there now. Sangrior and Kristofin are also there. 'Tis time we joined them. We have won this battle."

"Not in the way I expected," Orielle dared to say, "but we preserved life."

"A Fae decision," Grim remarked, as if he hadn't agreed with it.

"You would have no enemies at the end of any battle?" the Lady asked curiously, as if complete victory was not to be desired.

"I would have all battles over." He jerked his head at the rocks. "They can do mischief and harm, whether man-shape or wolf-shape."

"They will not dare," Lady Bone claimed. "Come. We return."

~ 12 ~

Lady Bone's transition dropped them in the well square, outside the Elder's House.

Haveners milled about. The torches at the square's corners revealed that most of the debris was cleared away. They hurried from one lane to the next, busy with purpose. The snow still fell, softer and slower, idly swirling in the barest breeze. Yet the smell of cooking filled the air. People brushed past, carrying pots to the Elder's. They called to each other. They stopped to talk. They laughed.

Once she'd recovered from the transition, Orielle gaped at them. A group of women chattered as they held covered pots. Two older men joked as they drew water from the well. A man and a woman practiced a song. Children darted about, as if the afternoon hadn't held terror.

Did they not remember that people had died? Did they not care?

Children had short memories. She couldn't believe the adults' good humor.

Perhaps those grieving were murred up with those they'd lost?

Two boys led away their horses, joking with each other while the black mounts acted as if they were used to young boys who jigged as they walked.

Lady Bone asked for the direction of her brother. A Havener indicated the Elder House. "He takes it as his," he added, merry at the prospect which earned him an odd mute query from the Lady. She drew Volk with her to the Elder's.

Before Orielle and Grim followed, a shout hailed him.

Waren jogged across the square to join them. "Ho, there, Grim. What have we yet to fight?" The prospect of another battle seemed to cheer the sentinel.

"We have none left. We … dispensed with the last wyre, and Lady Bone and her knight ended the last swordsman. You look like you're preparing for a feast."

"Lord Skull's orders. After a Hunt, a feast. He gave such great help, how can we deny him?"

"But the injured? The dead?" Grim asked Orielle's own questions.

"The Lord healed the worst injured. Our healers tended the ones with simple wounds. We've gathered the dead in the lock-up. Tomorrow we'll see to them. Sotted heads dealing with rotting heads. So it has been. So it will be." The sentinel held up his forearm. "Slashed to the bone this was. Lord Skull healed it. I owe him for that."

Orielle inhaled sharply. "Waren, the Kyrgy exact payment for healing."

"True enough. I'm bound to him now, and Malva agreed to serve him. Brok, too. He wasn't wounded. He wanted the bond. He said Lord Skull promised he would no longer grieve for Zairantze. Skull promises to be an easy taskmaster."

What the Kyrgy lord considered an easy task would likely not match Waren's view, but the vow was made. She wouldn't stir dissent. Crossing glances with her, Grim thought the same.

"We'll select new mentors the day after," Waren continued, eyes clear, brow unfurrowed, voice easy. "For now, Lilias works as go-between for the Haven with the Lord. Does she know you're back?"

"No. We should speak with her. Is she with Lord Skull?"

"Last I saw she was at the lock-up, but that's an hour or more ago. She'll sit beside the Lord at the feast. He requested it, and she agreed without a quibble. First for her, I reckon."

"You have no concerns about the Kyrgy lord?" Orielle couldn't dam the question. *What can I do if Waren does have a concern?*

He lifted his healed arm. "Little late to worry now. But no, I ain't worried. He's already proving a benefit. Didn't you see how he repaired the gate?"

"No. Lady Bone brought us here, through a transition."

"Oh. Well, you should see the gate. Wished you could have seen him work. He waved his hands, and those broken timbers lifted as one mass and went straight out to the road. We'll be using all that for firewood for a month, at least."

The palace's beautiful ornamentations had been an illusion that *seemed* tangible, solid as reality yet easily removed. "What does Vrigmal's gate look like?" she wondered.

"Fancy metalwork. Scrolling vines with leaves and berries and nuts. Stronger than iron, he said. He'll replace the towers soon, but we're protected tonight. No gobbers or wraiths can make their way inside. Any wyre still left?"

"No. I said. They're gone, unless more break off from Frost Clime and come down from the Citadel."

"The Lord's going to have wards against that. He's got his knights serving as sentries for now. First thing tomorrow, he said, he'll set the wards." Waren sobered. "While we tend our dead."

"Waren!" a woman called. Orielle saw Malva carrying a pot into the square. Her husband hurried to take it from her.

"Time we saw the benevolent lord." Grim linked hands with Orielle.

"Grim, I don't think they—."

"Don't say it aloud. Too many people will hear. We've got no Shield in place, and dropping one for cover over our talk is probably not wise."

He had as little trust in the Kyrgy lord as she. The Haveners seemed delighted to accept Vrigsmal's rule. What would they do when he tightened his fist?

Or when he decided to end the illusion and leave?

Yet a contrary wish was *I would love to see how he transforms Iscleft Haven.*

They entered the Elder's House. The brightness struck first. Although night had fallen, the room was bright as if daylight flooded through every window. The few torches and the hearthfire did not supply that radiance. The busyness in the room also overwhelmed. In a far corner, a musician played a harp. Met set up the last long boards for tables and brought benches forward from the walls. Women placed dishes on the table: bread, apples, covered pots, platters with sliced meat, bowls and flagons. Children skipped behind them, snatching bites only to be scolded. A couple of men brought in chopped wood for the great fire. The Haveners had managed a quick preparation for Vrigsmal's required feast.

They passed several knights and dames, still armored. Orielle recognized them as well as Sir Kristofin, mingling as they sat at board. She didn't see Sangrior. She supposed someone had to serve as sentry; perhaps he was there.

The Kyrgy lord sat in the elder's chair at the table's end, formed by turning a short board perpendicular to the long one. He drank from a flagon as he listened to his sister, in a mentor's chair on his left, with Volk seated beside her. The mentor's chair on his right remained empty.

As Orielle and Grim approached, Vrigsmal broke off his conversation with Lady Bone. He saluted them. "Our Solsken arrives, she who defeated the sorceress. We can no longer call you Not-Wizard, for today you have proved yourself. Sit. Drink. A toast to our Solsken. Another to the Rhoghieri Grim Holtson, a worthy fighter to have at my side."

"My lord," a woman said and placed a pewter ewer near his hand. She awkwardly bowed then scurried away.

Lady Bone gave the woman a jaundiced look. "They must learn the ways of court."

"They show great capacity for learning." He grasped the curved handle of the ewer. Energy gleamed from his hand. Then it flowed into the metal, transforming it to cut crystal. "Already they brew a tasty ale which needs no touch from me."

"It is not wine."

"It need not be." He gave a closed-mouth smile then turned back to Orielle and Grim. "Iscleft Haven owes you both a great debt."

A man carrying the gnarled staff of a healer came to Vrigsmal's shoulder. He bent and spoke softly in his ear. The Lord leaned to listen.

What concerned the healer? Waren said those hurt had been healed, by Vrigsmal or Rho healers.

Lady Bone leaned forward. "Solsken, I have told my brother everything he needs to know about the wyre who were at the lair."

"That ... is good." *How much had the Lady told her brother?* When Saircuista had defected, the Lady hadn't told her brother anything. *But who am I to argue with a Kyrgy?*

The healer handed Vrigsmal a scroll. He unrolled it. After a brief study, he dismissed the man with a nod. He turned the scroll so they could see. "He is a weaver. Aye, as well as healer. He tells me he can weave a visual record of our battles, and he can work the names of Ruthven and Kalleth into the tapestry. I find myself eager to have my fallen knights' names in permanence. All my knights, the veteran and the new. Grim Holtson, I still need riders, as does Lady Skuld. What say you to a bond with me or with my sister?"

"My Lord, you distinguish me with this request, but I have a prior commitment at Iscleft Citadel."

"Ah. The battle with Frost Clime. I would be willing to send a hand of my knights and another hand of Rhoghieri to the Citadel, with more to come after we have recovered here. I ask that you command them."

"My Lord, I would be honored."

"And in this, you are bound a little to me, aye?" His smile had that worrisome edge that hinted at unanticipated plans. "Solsken, your service would greatly please me. I would keep a wizard with my riders."

Her prior bond to the Enclave had kept Lady Bone from claiming her. Would it work with the Lord? "I grieve that I must disappoint my lord Vrigsmal, but I am bound to my mission for the Wizard Enclave."

He continued to smile, but it looked stiff, artificial. *Had he expected us to accept service to him?*

Grim stood. "My Lord, I see someone that we must speak with. Please excuse us." Orielle hurriedly climbed off her bench, less worried about the abrupt departure than about walking into a verbal trap if they lingered.

Vrigsmal touched a finger to his brow, a dismissing salute. Grim bowed. Orielle sank into a deep curtsey, courtesy reserved for a king. Not even the Enclave's ArchClan received that honor. As she and Grim escaped, Lady Bone said in a carrying voice, "I would she remained if only to teach these Haveners how to show proper respect for the Fae, Kyrgy and Lucent alike."

They slid onto the bench opposite Hackett. He stopped spooning stew. "There you are. Couldn't find either of you after the fight was over."

"We still had wyre to fight," Grim told him.

"And?"

"The wyre won't be bothering the Haven anymore. Lady Bone— well, she cursed them then exiled them."

"Did she, now? A curse and exile? Death might be easier. As for you two, what next?"

"The Citadel."

"Back there again?"

"With a double hand of men, sent by Lord Vrigsmal. Knights and Rho."

Hackett leaned back, studied Grim, then nodded and returned to his stew. "I'll join that, I think."

"I thought you said you wouldn't fight under Commander Ferro?"

He grimaced at Orielle's question. "Happen I need to rethink what I will and won't do. For sure, I'm not staying here, not with Tobit dead and," he lowered his voice, "the change in leadership."

"I think it will be very interesting to see what the Lord does with the Haven." She wished she could have captured images of his palace in the forest, especially the paintings and tapestries.

"I think," he retorted, "it will be very uncomfortable to serve a couple of Dark Fae."

"There's that," Grim agreed.

"When do you plan to leave?"

"It would be rude to leave tomorrow," Orielle said quickly. "We should mourn with everyone."

"The day after?" Hackett asked.

"The day after what?" Lilias swung a leg over the bench and sat beside Orielle. She picked up a flagon and drank deeply. "Talking's thirsty work, and that's all I'll be doing for the next few days."

"I think," Orielle said cautiously, "that the chair beside Lord Skull is for you, Lilias. Waren said you were consulting with the Lord on leading the Haven."

"*Consulting?*" The woman sputtered. She wiped the froth of ale from her mouth. "Waren would call it that. So would his mighty lordship. He gives an order and expects me to see it done. Then I have to tell him what everyone expects will happen. I haven't walked on eggshells before. Every conversation with him—."

"You're not bound to him, yet," Hackett said. "But one unwary word—."

"I know. I *know*. I suppose you're escaping to the Citadel."

"I wouldn't call it escaping," Grim said around Orielle. "There's fierce fighting there."

"What I wouldn't give to go with you."

"You should," Orielle urged, then she thought of all the duties a mentor had and would have, especially to draw a line between the Haveners and the Kyrgy.

"Stay until the vote the day after tomorrow, and I will," Lilias claimed. "Time I got off my arse and fought Frost Clime. That would protect the Haven better than waiting for them to come here. Besides, with that Lord and Lady here, I don't think a sorcerer will stick his nose in to get it bloodied. Aye," she mused, "that's an answer."

"If Lord Skull lets you go."

"If I don't say something crosswise, he can't hold me here. Can he? I have to give him power over me. That I won't do. Not even Surrect—." The older woman stopped. The hand she rested on the table formed a tight fist. "No one's had that power over me since I left my parents' house."

. ~ . ~ . ~ .

Grim lifted the covers when Orielle reached the bed. "What did you report to the Enclave?" he asked as she settled beside him.

"I didn't report to the Enclave." Orielle expected a pang of guilt, but only peace greeted her review of her scryed contact with her grandfather Malboys. "Grandfather will report my mission's success to the ArchClan

Letheina. Rho will fight at the Citadel with more to come."

"You think those who don't bind themselves to the Lord or Lady will come to the Citadel?"

"I do indeed." She snuggled her head on his shoulder and traced her fingers through the whorls of hair on his chest. "The Rho are fighting as part of the alliance. Not the renewed alliance I was sent to secure but still an increase in fighters."

"It's a better alliance for the Rho."

"Aye. I told him about the Kyrgy sending knights as well. He was ... surprised."

"Shocked. You can say he was shocked."

She snorted. "Well, aye, that is the word. Not what he expected, at all. I also told him that I wouldn't return to the Enclave. I would be traveling to the Citadel with you."

"No traveling to it. You *are* with me."

That deserved a kiss. She stretched up and landed one on his chin. As she settled back, Grim asked, "Did you tell him your new name is Aiwaz Solsken?"

"No. That will need a letter, not a hurried scrying. And Solsken is *when* I am, like Lady Bone calling me Not-Wizard is *what* I am."

"After today, I don't think anyone will ever call you that."

"They had better not," she said direly, and he laughed.

Then his arm tightened around her. "Orielle, you've never asked my true name."

"*True name*? I surprised you when I called you *Grim*. Did I guess part of it?"

"Part, aye. The whole of it is Vuzgrim Holtson."

"Truly? I only called you Grim because you were so grim, especially since I'd asked that wyre to—."

"Don't say it," he warned.

She giggled. "Wizards don't have true names. You can't say my name three times then I appear, like Sangrior and Volk and the Lady did. I suppose they could appear because they took on a portion of her enchanting power when she bound them. Does saying a name three times work with Rhoghieri?"

"I don't know. My heart has never called my true name before."

"Oh!" She gave him a kiss for those lovely words.

That kiss led to touches and more important words. She decided to use *Vuzgrim*, and that set him on fire. Touches and words became tangled bodies and hearts racing. It was long until they were pleased and drowsy and sated.

Orielle pressed against Grim's side and listened to his rapid heartbeat. This mission had had so many unexpected events, terrifying ones. Tonight and yesterday, though, balanced all the terror. Overwhelmed it, with happiness. "My parents called me *Chardonneret*," she whispered, sharing a closely guarded secret, for her sister used to laugh about it. "It was years before I knew it meant *Goldspark*, the yellow bird with black bars on its wings."

His fingers threaded through her blonde hair. "Goldspark? For the energy you call?"

She hadn't looked at her power that way, but "Aye. Just like that."

"Goldspark," he repeated then nuzzled her hair.

How strange. I volunteered for this mission that no one wanted, and I have more than I ever expected. Wielder of Air. Aiwaz Solsken. Fighter against wyre and sorceress. Wizard. And love. Grim slept while Orielle basked in *what* she was, *how* and *when* she was … and *who* she was.

THANK YOU!

Thank you for reading *Spells of Air,* all part of the **Fae Mark'd World**. This story of Orielle and Grim was great fun to write. I look forward to the next novella trilogy in **Fae Mark'd World**—but I cannot decide which magical element to have as a focus.

Join our newsletter by popping an email to winkbooks@aol.com.

Use that email if you have questions, comments, and speculations. All of my stories can be found on Writers Ink Books (www.writersinkbooks.com). W.Ink won't bombard you with emails, only announcements when something special occurs, such as new book releases. Look for my Facebook page, as well.

WRITE A REVIEW!

Indie writers thrive on reviews. For any story that you enjoy, please share a review with other readers looking for escape from the stresses of life.

DREAM IT. BELIEVE IT. DO IT.
~~ REMI BLACK

CALENDAR AND TIMES

Year 635
11-Month Year
The months are 32 days, with each week having eight days.

- Deep Winter
- Winter's End
- First Growth > Vernal Equinox on the 24th, which is Knight's Night (day 88 of the year)
- Spring
- Blooming
- Best Summer > Summer Solstice on the 16th, which is Lady's Night (the so-called Lady's Day) (day 176 of the year)
- High Summer
- Harvest
- Leaf-Turn > Brumal Equinox on the 8th, which is Knave's Night (day 264 of the year)
- Leaf Gone
- First Winter > Winter Solstice on the 32nd (day 352 of the year, last day of the year)

8 Days in a Week / 8 Moon Phases through a Single Month

Sunnes (sun)	Sturmen (storm)	Boltkan (kobolt)	Orthen (earth)	Luftein (air)	Vattein (water)	Brandt (fire)	Moones (moon)
1 Lindworm Moon	2	3	4 Worm Moon	5	6	7	8 Knave Moon (1st qtr.)
9	10	11	12 Horn Moon	13	14	15 Maiden's Night	16 Lady's Moon (full moon)
17 Crone's Night	18	19	20 Womb Moon	21	22	23	24 Knight's Moon (last qtr.)
25	26	27	28 Saber Moon	29	30	31 Wyvern Moon	32 Dragon Moon (new moon)

22 Hours in each Day

- Daggy (dawn) is the 5th Bell
- Sunring (sunrise) is the 6th Bell
- Middag (midday) is the 11th Bell
- Fyraften (sunset, end of day) is the 15th Bell
- Kvaeld is evening (16th Bell)
- Mulm is full dark (17th Bell)
- Tus-morke (after full dark, "lights out" for most) (18th Bell)
- Sidste is the last bell (22nd Bell), equivalent to midnight
- 1st Bell that coincides to 1 a.m. is Forst

THE FAE MARK'D SERIES
complete novels with no cliff-hangers
Available on Amazon

FAE MARK'D WIZARD 1, 2 & 3

Watch for TANGLED SPELLS, the bundle.

Weave a Wizardry Web
Two wizards travel sharp-bladed roads in *Weave a Wizardry Web*. When a wyre pack begins hunting one of the wizards, and the other practices a sharing linkage one time too many, will they survive the sharp blades on their chosen roads?

Dream a Deadly Dream
Assassination. A fugitive comtesse. A lethal sleep-spell. Wyre and wraiths. Wizardry against sorcery. And regicide.

In *Dream a Deadly Dream*, a sorcerous plot to kill the king weaves together past and present, dream and reality, to create a nightmare that can kill.

Can Alstera stop the dreams before the Comtesse is killed?

Sing a Graveyard Song
Can Alstera defeat Death Walking before it takes yet another life? Or will wielding blood-magic against a blood-spelled creature force Alstera across the tenuous barrier that separates wizardry from foul sorcery?

FAE MARK'D WORLD: SPELLS OF AIR

Novella 1 ~ To Wield the Wind
On a mission for the Wizard Enclave, Orielle ventures into the Wilding, a strange frontier filled with magical creatures. There she discovers sprites and wraiths, gobbers and wyre. All view her as prey.

Novella 2 ~ To Charm the Air
When Orielle and Grim reach the Haven, the elder arrests him. The Haveners aren't interested in a renewed alliance with the Wizard Enclave.

Is her mission for the Enclave in vain? Will she ever escape the Wilding?

And what of her vow to the Kyrgy Lady Bone?

Novella 3 ~ *To Curse the Wyre*

Hunter. Hunted. Who is who?

The sorceress and her servants, the shifter wyre, seek to destroy Orielle's allies in the Wilding. Orielle has gathered Dark Fae and Rhoghieri to defeat them.

She rides with the Dark Fae Lord Skull and Lady Bone—but can she trust them?

www.ingramcontent.com/pod-product-compliance
Lightning Source LLC
Chambersburg PA
CBHW051238250626
47155CB00009B/3081